Everlastin'
Mickee Madden

PINNACLE BOOKS
WINDSOR PUBLISHING CORP.

PINNACLE BOOKS are published by

Windsor Publishing Corp.
850 Third Avenue
New York, NY 10022

First Printing: February, 1995

Printed in the United States of America

To my husband, Steve, for all the years of unselfish love and support; and to my children, Gwen, Buddy, and Brehan.

Special thanks to my brothers and sisters; nieces and nephews; and friends who are very much my family.

To Cindy Stapleton. What can I say, kiddo? I'd be lost without you.

Eugenia. Thanks for hanging in there!

And last but never never least, Denise.

GLOSSARY

'afore/before
a'/at
abou'/about
ain/own
an'/and
aneuch/enough
aught/anything
auld/old
brither/brother
cauld/cold
deil/devil
didna/didn't
dinna/don't
e'er/ever
e'ery/every
efter/after
faither/father
gae/go
guid/good
haud/hold
het/hot

hoor/hour
i'/it
ither/other
ma/my
mair/more
mairrit/married
maist/most
mak/make
mither/mother
mon/man
na/no
no'/not
nocht/nothing
o'/of
o'er/over
oop/up
oor/our
ou'/out
sa/so
sarry/sorry
shartly/shortly

sud/should
ta/to
tae/too
tak/take
teuk/took
tha'/that
thegither/
   together
thin'/thing
tis/it's
verra/verry
wad/would
wadna/wouldn't
wark/work
warld/world
weel/well
whan/when
wi'/with
winna/won't
yer/your

One

Scotland
Summer, 1994

The pale hand trembled as it drew back the last of the heavy, ruby-red drapes on the tall windows. Sunlight burst into the parlor, lending bright beams for the dust motes to dance within. A mistlike ambiance surrounded the young woman standing there, caused a shiver to pass through her slender body.

Carlene Cambridge was half-tempted to close the drapes, but she knew Lachlan would not take kindly to her denying his favorite room its daily kiss of light. Besides, enshrouding herself in darkness would not alter the fact that the day of reckoning was upon her.

Tears filled her blue eyes, then spilled down her cheeks. Her life had been so much simpler before she'd come to Scotland. More than ever she missed David— needed him beside her. But he had gone on, refusing to be a part of the laird's scheme.

Why hadn't she listened to her husband?

Because Lachlan had convinced her to aid him, that was why, damn his persuasive hide!

Something touched upon her awareness.

Although she could not see across the room for the brightness of the sunlight flooding it, she knew *he* was there, staring at the portrait with a look of unyielding determination in his fathomless dark eyes. Shuddering, she rubbed her upper arms for warmth. It was a futile gesture, for she would never feel warm again.

There was no simple resolution for the predicament she'd unwittingly stumbled into. Damn Lachlan's black heart, and his control on her proliferating conscience!

If only he hadn't manipulated her into plunging headlong into initiating the deception!

Tears spilled faster down her ashen face. Her shoulders sagging, she crossed the room, her despondent gaze trained to where she knew she would find *him*. And he was there, seeming a giant amidst the solar radiance enveloping him. She stopped a few feet away when he slowly turned his head to give her an assessing look. Unnerved by the suspicion creeping into his face, she shifted her gaze to one side.

"Pull yerself thegither."

Carlene closed her eyes momentarily as a fresh shiver of self-disgust coursed through her. The deep resonance of his Scottish burr still held the ability to strike some primitive chord within her sexual awareness. And she resented him for that as well. She loved David. But since her first meeting with this devil of a laird before her, she'd betrayed her husband a hundred times within the deepest, darkest recesses of her mind.

Thank God she had never tried to test her curiosities, for she never would have stood a chance against a man like him. One kiss from his seductive mouth . . .

In a quiet tone, she said finally, "If we told her the truth—"

"Tis no' oor place. Besides, tis tae late ta warn her."

Carlene looked up at the portrait hanging above the white marble fireplace. In some macabre way, she was sure Lachlan *had* indeed fallen in love with the woman in the portrait. She had never known him to be more attentive or subdued than when she spoke of her high school and brief college days with Beth.

"Carlene, lass."

The deep, reproachful tone of Lachlan's voice drew her gaze to his face.

Those damn, piercing eyes, so dark the irises couldn't be seen. Black expressive pools in a rugged, light-toned face.

"I allowed you yer time o' whingin' yestreen. Now be off wi' you."

Turning on her heel, she headed toward one of the doors. Yes, the night before he had permitted her to complain and fret to her heart's desire, but none of it had made the slightest impression on him. At the threshold to the main hall, she stopped and turned, then considered the laird's indomitable stubbornness.

"How do you think she's going to react when she learns that I betrayed her— that *you* planned this whole sham of a vacation to get her here?"

"I'll worry abou' i' when the time comes."

"You're one arrogant bastard, Lachlan!"

Unruffled by her remark, he looked up at the portrait and sighed with deep longing. "We agreed this was best for her." His gaze shifted to Carlene. "Right?"

"It's different now!"

"How?"

Carlene moved her shoulders in a gesture of helplessness. "After you told me, I went into shock. I wasn't thinking clearly when you came up with this idea."

A tense stretch of silence passed between them before Lachlan lowered his head and gave it a shake.

"I-I could make up some story and send her right back to the States."

"Na."

"How can you hold me to a promise that is tearing me up inside?"

The laird's head slowly lifted. His stormy gaze searched Carlene's tear-streaked face. "I'm no' heartless."

"The hell you aren't!" she wailed. "You have no right to play God! Dammit, Lachlan, what we're doing is *wrong!*"

His nostrils flared. "Next, you'll be tellin' me the link is a gift o' the deil, eh?"

"I don't know anymore. Please—"

"Dinna you understand? I can *feel* her stirrin' in ma blood. E'ery second tha' passes, e'ery mile tha' closes between us, I can feel her e'er stronger!

"Carlene," he went on, with such intensity behind his words they vibrated in the air, "I can offer her e'erlastin' sunsets an' dawns. I can fulfill her e'ery dream, her e'ery fantasy! For wha'e'er reason, God *gave* me this gift! An' he's given me a second chance a' happiness!"

"At Beth's expense?" Carlene flung bitterly. "How *bloody* convenient!"

A moment of silence passed before Lachlan spoke in a low, guttural tone. "Mind yer words, girl."

"Is that a threat?"

"Tak i' as you please."

Carlene held out her hands in a gesture of supplication. "I know Beth. She's going to feel betrayed and trapped. She's going to hate you for—"

"Na!" he shouted, slicing the air with a hand. "You gave me yer word, an' yer word I'll haud you ta." He straightened his shoulders with an air of determination, his chest rose on a slow, controlled breath. "I understand yer doubts, but tis *ma* instincts I trust in this matter. Do you fancy a notion yer conscience wad be less troublesome— knowin' wha' you do— if you left her alone like she is?"

"I don't know!"

"Gae wash yer face. I dinna want her seein' you in such a state."

"All right, Lachlan, you win. I'll carry out my part," she promised, her tone as chilly as a Scottish winter's night. "Then I'll gladly wash my *hands* of *you!*"

When the parlor door to the main hall slammed after her, Lachlan threw back his head and laughed. The resounding sound echoed within the mansion's walls, clear up into the tower that stretched skyward past the third story. As his laughter wound down, his gaze settled on the arresting features of the woman in the portrait. Peacefulness washed over him, softening the sharp angles of his face.

His chin, bisected by a cleft, lifted fractionally. The grooves in his cheeks deepened with his solemn smile.

"Wash yer hands o' me, Carlene. I've waited tae long for a new bride ta care abou' wha' you think o' me."

With the gentleness of a lover, he reached up and touched his finger tips to the portrait's breasts. "An' ma bride you shall be, Beth Staples."

For some time, he stood with his hands clasped at the small of his back, his softened gaze studying every stroke of the painting. He could easily have stood there until Beth's arrival, lost in the impressions of her filling him, lost in his dreams of the days to come. But another image invaded his reverie like a well-aimed knife.

His face a contorted mask of rage, he ran from the room, up the stairs to the third floor, and burst into one of the bedrooms. Carlene guiltily bolted up from her bent position over an antique desk.

Her eyes wide with fear, she peered at him as though expecting some horrible consequence for her attempted betrayal of his trust. She stood frozen as he stormed across the room and snatched up the pink parchment paper she'd been writing on. Her gaze never left his face, his livid countenance, as he scanned the hastily written message. Only when he looked at her with raw accusation did she avert her gaze.

Crumpling the note in a white-knuckled fist, Lachlan drew in a fortifying breath. "Do I deserve this . . . this disloyalty?" he grated out, shaking the fist in front of her face.

Anger doused Carlene's fear, and she glared at him defiantly. "This isn't about *you*. But if you must know, my first loyalty lies with Beth!"

Lowering his fist to the desk, he leaned to, placing his face inches from hers. The sheer curtains covering the open windows began to flap with the advent of a strong breeze.

Thunder rumbled above Baird House.

The sky darkened.

Lightning lowered from the heavens, seeming like massive white fingers about to pluck the mansion into its grasp.

"You'll no' rest a day if you betray me, girl. Do yer part, then be off. *Do you understand me?*"

"Perfectly," Carlene croaked.

Lachlan straightened up, a storm of emotions building again within his dark eyes.

Then an ecstatic sigh passed his lips.

"She's arrived," he murmured.

All color drained from Carlene's face. The dam of her tears burst as she fled the room, her sobs lingering behind. Lachlan stood as still as a statue. Eyes closed amid an oddly rapt expression, he homed in on Beth's image.

"Sweet Jesus, she's lovely," he moaned. "Ah, Beth, ma darlin'. A' long last, we meet."

Beth landed at Prestwick Airport after a grueling nine-and-a-half hour flight in coach. Exhausted to the bone, her feet and ankles swollen, her loafers tucked into her shoulder purse, she deplaned with less zeal than most of the other passengers. Although she had to admit the invite from Carlene to visit for a couple of weeks couldn't have come at a better time, she wished she was feeling up to par. A mild headache left her in apprehension of a larger one to come.

Indifferent to her barefoot status, she kept up with the hectic pace of the others traveling the concourse. Thoughts of her best friend, and all they had to catch up on after eight long years, helped her to ignore the ache in her back and legs.

After retrieving her luggage and going through customs, she anxiously traversed the terminal looking for Carlene. What she found instead was a portly little man holding up a placard bearing her name. Walking up to him, she hesitantly said, "I'm Beth Staples."

A flash of white teeth beamed at her from between ruddy cheeks. Tucking the placard beneath an arm, he pushed back a navy-plaid cap from his brow. "From Washington, Miss?"

Running the back of a hand across her moist brow, Beth made an absent attempt to brush the riotous curls of her light brown hair back from her heart-shaped face. "Yes."

"Miss Cooke paid me ta fetch you, Miss."

"I don't know anyone by the name of Cooke."

"Are you here ta visit Kist House?"

Beth smiled patiently. "Kist House . . . ?"

The old man grinned, his eyes youthful, full of sparkle. Two curly locks of snow-white hair rested on his creased brow. "Does the name Carlene mean anythin' ta you?"

Perplexed, Beth gave a single nod of her head.

"Ah." Without haste, the old man pried the two suitcases from Beth's hands and started to turn toward one set of the exit doors. "Then yer're the right Beth Staples. Miss Cooke said ta mention the name o' Carlene if you seemed wary o' me. Come along. We've a fair drive ahead o' us."

Humid heat greeted Beth as she passed beyond the doors of the terminal. Yesterday, she'd left behind a heat wave in the Tri-Cities, Washington, expecting the drizzle of Great Britain's rainy season. Carlene had described the weather to her the previous week.

"Calum's ma name," the old man offered while loading Beth's luggage into the trunk of a blue Volvo with a taxi sign on the roof. He opened the left front door for her. When she was seated, he closed it and sprightly went around to the driver's side. "Buckle up, Miss."

A film of perspiration coated Beth's lightly tanned skin. Her white jersey and pale-blue slacks clung to her. With the seatbelt secured, she laid her blue jacket across her lap and placed her purse atop that. As the vehicle left the multi-leveled parking lot, she removed her shoes from the purse and snugged them back onto her feet.

"Comfortable, Miss?"

"Yes, thank you. How far is Crossmichael?"

"Abou' an hoor's drive. Dinna mind ma silence for a bit, Miss. The traffic here needs ma full attention. You Yanks get frantic wi' oor motorways an' roundabou's. Dinna want ta risk takin' the wrong exit."

By the time they had reached Ayr on the A79 and were heading southeast on the A713, Beth's heart was in her throat. The two-laned highway was narrow, winding, and somewhat of a rollercoaster in places, but fellow travelers were brazen and swift in passing at every opportunity. To give respite to her nerves, she smiled wanly at the driver, and asked, "You do this for a living?"

"I've been a cabbie near twenty years. An' I plan ta drive till I've got one foot in the grave."

"You must have nerves of steel. I thought Seattle was bad."

Chuckling, Calum adjusted the visor of his cap to just above his bushy eyebrows. "I dinna usually go as far as all this, but Miss Cooke paid me handsomely ta fetch you."

"She must be a friend of Carlene's. Do you live in Crossmichael?"

"Castle Douglas."

"You live in a castle?"

Calum's laugh was smooth and cheery. "Tis a burgh, Miss. But' we do have a castle ta boast o'. Castle Threave—"

Calum winced as a small car whizzed past his taxi, just missing the oncoming traffic by a narrow margin.

"Where was I? Oh, Threave. It's the remains o' a keep . . . a war castle tha' sits on a grassy island in the River Dee.

"Whan the House o' Stewart decided ta overthrow the Black Douglases in 1450, Threave was the last stronghaud ta fall. King James II went wi' his army ta overthrow i', an' brought wi' him a huge cannon called Mons Meg. Threave wi'stood a two-month siege in the summer o' 1455, then the garrison surrendered. The Black Douglases were destroyed, an' their estates were forfeited."

Winking at Beth, he added, "Memorized the tour speech, I did. Oh, Threave's no' fancy like Culzean or Edinburgh, but i' has a strong feelin' o' history abou' i'. Perhaps you'll get the chance ta visit i' durin' yer stay."

"I hope so. That sign back there? What does 'Give Way' mean?"

"Yield. Is this yer first visit ta Scotland?"

Beth sighed and dreamily gazed out the window to her left. "Yes. It's certainly a beautiful country."

Green rolling landscape stretched out in every

direction. Now and then, Calum pointed out three-foot-high stone walls separating the properties, walls, he explained, that had stood for centuries without benefit of mortar. Sheep and cattle grazed in some sections. Tiny clusters of towns dotted the land, more perfect than anything an artist could depict in a painting. Wildflowers of every imaginable color grew in sections along the roadsides. Occasionally, Beth saw a building with a thatched roof.

"We're nearin' Crossmichael."

The cabbie's declaration snapped Beth from her reverie and she cast the driver a look of apology. "I'm afraid I wasn't much company, was I? Your scenery bewitched me."

"Ahh, yer words warm ma heart, Miss. You know, the estate yer're goin' ta has quite a history i'self. Know any o' i'?"

"All Carlene told me was that it was a Victorian mansion built in the early eighteen forties."

"Aye, a grand place i' is. I've been inside twice. Once whan I was a young lad, an' again some years back whan there were tours through the place. 'Tis mentioned in all the books on Scottish ghosts."

"It's reputed to be haunted?"

"Aye. The story goes, Lannie Baird built i' in 1843, then returned oop north ta search for a wife ta fill i' wi' children.

"He wed a seventeen-year-auld Highland girl named Tessa Aitkin. One month later, Lannie vanished. Tessa was made ta wait two years 'fore Lannie was decreed dead. Right efter, she caught herself a young mon, Robert Ingliss, from her home village, an' they got married and resided in Baird House till their deaths.

"Efter that, in 1904, her eldest son took o'er the house. Robbie Ingliss was renovatin' a portion o' the tower whan the body o' Lannie Baird was discovered. It seems someone drove a knife through the poor mon's heart 'fore wallin' him oop."

"How gruesome."

"Aye, an' since the discovery, Baird House has been called Kist House. Kist in Scottish means a chest or box or . . . *coffin*."

With a low, skeptical laugh, Beth asked, "And does Lannie walk the halls at night?"

To her dismay, there was no laughter in Calum's eyes when they turned her way. "The local folk believe sa. Kist House has had a string o' renters o'er the years. Some say auld Lannie will ne'er leave the place."

Beth fell silent. She wanted to laugh at the old man's attempt to shake her up, but a voice within her mind whispered that something in his words rang true. But if the house was haunted, wouldn't Carlene have mentioned it during their telephone conversations during the past few months?

Unless Carlene didn't want her to feel spooked—

Beth grinned at her musings.

Jet lag.

She was exhausted and wired at the same time. The idea of staying at a haunted house wasn't all that unappealing.

The past eight years had been trying ones for Beth, but she looked back on them without regret or a sense of loss for the youthful times that had waned so quickly. In a few days, she would be thirty years old. At the moment, she felt much older.

But this vacation would soon take care of that.

She and Carlene had shared wonderful times together during high school and two-and-a-half years at Washington State University. It was then that her adoptive mother had taken ill, her weak heart rendering her an invalid. There was nothing Beth could do but drop out of college and care for the woman who had raised her. Jonathan Staples had died unexpectedly of a stroke when Beth was nine, five years after the loving couple had taken her in. Rita Staples had poured all of her love into Beth's every waking day, striving to be both parents.

It had been hard for Beth to watch her mother languish away over the years, but she had never allowed Rita to see her fears, or the premature grief which had companioned her every night when she lay her head upon her bed pillows. Rita Staples had passed away in her sleep two months prior. Now it was time for Beth to apply the same determination to getting her business degree and beginning her adult life.

"Here we go. This is the private road ta the house."

Beth silently took in her surroundings. The road was narrow, bordered on each side in segments by large rhododendron bushes, and tall blue bellflowers. Evergreens and various bushes dotted the plump slopes of the hillside to her left. Barely seen above these was a crenelated structure.

To her right, beyond a thicker foliage of trees and shrubs, she glimpsed a cluster of homes situated along a splendid blue loch.

As the cab climbed a slightly steeper incline, Beth was awed by groupings of rosebushes and white lilies, and of ivy draping several scattered, lattice-work structures.

Then the house came into full view.

Regarding the magnificent building looming up a short distance away, her pulse quickened. Awe lent a flattering tint to her cheeks. The cabbie pulled onto a graveled area to the right of the house. As soon as the vehicle had come to a full stop, she was out the door and staring up at the brown stone structure, sheer wonder lighting up her features. To add to the magic of the building and its plush greenery, peacocks were scattered everywhere. Some were as still as statues and watching her, others strutted their feather finery around the building and parking area.

Several looked down from the high peaks of the mansion's multiple roofs.

"Here you go, Miss." Calum placed Beth's luggage by her left foot. "I'm off, now. Was tauld no' ta hang aroond."

Getting into his cab, he tooted his horn twice. "Enjoy yer stay!" he called out the window, then backed the car up, made a turn, and was driving away before Beth raised her hand to wave goodbye.

"Beth?"

Round blue eyes swung around to light upon a familiar face. Beth's features glowed and she smiled as she looked over her dearest friend, who was still slim and stunning in a lightweight suit, her short, dark hair as chic as ever.

But Beth's smile wavered as she noted something in Carlene's eyes that belied the welcoming grin on her face. Beth couldn't define what was trying to surface at the periphery of her mind, nor could she understand why finally seeing Carlene after all these years would cause a chill to worm up her spine.

Jet lag.

"Come here, you," Beth laughed, opening her arms.

The embrace was brief. Guarding her disappointment as Carlene pulled away and took the largest suitcase in hand, Beth absently massaged the back of her stiff neck.

"Scat," Carlene shooed impatiently, flagging a hand at a peacock strutting her way.

"Are they yours?"

"They're wild. They never seem to wander from the grounds, though."

Watching the bird head off in the direction of the rhododendrons, Beth lifted the last suitcase. As she followed Carlene across the graveled ground leading to the front of the house, she noticed a beautiful carriage house to her right, set back from the main structure. Then her gaze swung up to the left side of the mansion, where a square tower extended above the highest roof line.

"This place is absolutely incredible," Beth said breathlessly.

"Wait until you see the inside."

Carlene walked to a set of dark wood double doors that fronted a glass greenhouse. "All the furnishings are original. Everything remains as the builder left it in the mid-eighteen-hundreds."

"I think I'm in love," Beth sighed, then felt a breath lodge in her throat as she caught Carlene pass her a furtive, brooding look. Beth was speared by a feeling that something was wrong, that she was intruding, and about to venture into something almost . . . sinister.

She gave herself a shake and mutely scolded herself for letting her fatigue fire up her imagination.

Jet lag.

She was finally reunited with her best friend. And she was in Scotland. *Scotland,* of all places!

Yes, she was in love. In love with life.

Beth followed Carlene through the small greenhouse of various houseplants, to another double door of bird's eye maple. A breath spilled past her lips as they entered an elongated hall.

A setting from out of the past stretched before her. The wall to her left was occupied by a tiled fireplace and a display of artifacts made of animal bones and wood and copper from days long gone by. An antique settee of polished cherry wood, combined with a hat rack, umbrella stand, and a tall mirror, stood against the wall nearest the doors. Sliding mahogany doors were closed to her right. At the end of this wall was a wide staircase. An Oriental runner carpet, identical in pattern to that on the floor, was held in place by a series of metal rods at the back of each step.

Filled with elation at the beauty of this place, Beth dropped her suitcase to the floor at the foot of the stairs. Carlene placed the larger suitcase alongside its mate, then gestured for Beth to follow her to a closed door perpendicular to the fireplace wall.

"This is the parlor." She opened the door and crossed the threshold.

Beth followed, trying to take everything in at one time. The far end of the room, to her left, ended with enormously tall windows set in a bay with mahogany window seats. Three pink and gold sofas were carefully arranged on an enormous Persian rug. The wall across from her was wainscoted to a height of five feet, then tinted rose up to the twenty-foot-high vaulted ceiling. Built within the center of the wall was an immense, intricately carved wall unit with countless shelves and cubbyholes displaying souvenirs and mementos of a time long passed. To each side of the unit, ancient swords, their points meeting in a tight center, formed circular patterns.

"I've made some tea," Carlene said, directing Beth to one of the sofas. For the moment, Beth curbed her inspection of the room and focused on the steaming brew her friend was pouring from a silver pot into two dainty cups on the coffee table.

"Thank you." Accepting one of the cups, Beth took a sip. "This is good."

"There's cream and sugar—"

"Oh, no, I prefer mine plain, thank you."

Beth watched Carlene sit alongside her. Her friend's petite frame and delicate features were as beautiful as ever. "You look terrific."

"So do you. I must say, I was expecting you to look rather . . . ragged."

"Ragged?" Beth grinned, showing the deep dimples in her cheeks to their best advantage. "Thanks."

Smiling apologetically, Carlene returned her cup to its saucer on the table. "It's so good to see you again."

"You, too. For almost eight years, you've been a voice on the phone, and an occasional scribble on paper."

Beth didn't mean the words unkindly, but Carlene received them with a look of despondency. "I really have missed you, kiddo. It amazes me how fast time has gone by. Well . . . probably not so fast for you."

"It wasn't so bad."

"It couldn't have been easy watching your mother waste away like that."

"No, it wasn't. Ma really hated feeling helpless."

How well I know that feeling, Carlene thought, tears springing to her eyes.

"Carlene?"

"Oh, I'm all right." Carlene swiped a finger across her moist cheeks. "She really was a sweet woman," she went on, her voice quavering despite her efforts to control her emotions. "I never heard her say a harsh word. I wish I could have made it to the funeral."

Beth laid a hand on Carlene's shoulder and gave it a gentle squeeze. "We're not going to dwell on anything sad or depressing, do you hear me? I want to feel like I did in high school. Carefree and full of hell."

"God, we were full of ourselves back then, weren't we?" Carlene looked down at her lap, as if to look into Beth's eyes was too painful. "I should have stayed around to help you with your mother, Beth, but I was too sel— "

"Listen to you," Beth cut off kindly. "I never expected you to hang around and wait for me. Look at all you would have missed."

Missed?

Carlene was close to bursting into tears. She wanted desperately to warn Beth, to hug her and try to explain what had really brought them together again.

Why had she painted that damn portrait?

What had drawn her and David to Kist House?

"Carlene, are you okay?"

Clamping down on her emotions, Carlene made an airy gesture with a hand. "I'm fine." She smiled with all the earnestness she could muster, but it was not enough to shield the shadow of shame in her blue eyes. Her worst fear at this moment was that her foreknowledge would brand itself on her brow for Beth to see.

Allowing a few seconds to pass while she sipped her tea, Beth wondered if perhaps Carlene and David were having marital problems. Beth had hoped to finally meet the Englishman who had swept Carlene off her feet just over a year ago. Perhaps David wasn't thrilled with the idea of Beth coming for a two-week stay.

This thought brought a frown to her face. Now that she thought about it, David hadn't talked to her on the phone for some time. "Does David mind me visiting?"

"Of course not. Why do you ask?"

Beth shrugged. "You seem a little preoccupied. Are *you* sure about this visit?"

Carlene's laugh didn't strike Beth as being genuine. "Don't be silly. I'm dying to show off . . . my house. So is David. It's this humidity, Beth. I never have gotten used to it. If it doesn't rain soon— But I'm feeling much better now that you're here. I've missed you terribly."

"Oh, sure," Beth teased, refusing to dwell on the niggling doubts in her mind. "Who was the one who decided after college to roam Europe before settling down to a career? Leave it to you to land an Englishman and wind up the mistress of a Scottish mansion."

That's a curse, not a blessing, Carlene thought ruefully. In a light tone, she crooned, "Who knows? Maybe you'll find yourself a strapping Scotsman to whisk you off your feet."

Beth groaned inwardly. "You're not planning to fix me up with someone, are you?"

"Me? No, I wouldn't do that to you." A sly grin brightened Carlene's features. "But if you happen to see one who strikes your fancy . . ."

"My fancy is focused on college this fall."

Carlene grimaced. "Sounds absolutely boring." Careful not to sound too eager, she cast her bait. "Are you still having the migraines?"

"Now and then."

"Have you, umm, seen a doctor about them?"

"Not yet."

Carlene clicked her tongue reprovingly. "You should, you know. They began after a fall, you said?"

"I'm still the same old klutz," Beth chuckled. "I'd just given Ma a bath and put her to bed, when the doorbell rang. I literally went flying down the steps." She shrugged. "I've still got a lump on the back of my head."

"How soon after the fall did the headaches begin?"

Beth was thoughtful for a moment. "A couple of days, I think. That was a week before Ma died. She'd been ill for so long, her death actually came as a shock."

"Did she suffer? Dying, I mean."

"No. She went to sleep and never . . . never woke up."

"I'm so sorry, Beth. I wish . . ."

"I know. I miss her so much. Sometimes, Carlene, I forget she's gone, and I start to ask her something— The house seems so empty now. So quiet."

"Must be lonely for you."

Beth gave an absent nod, her eyes staring off into space. "I was seriously thinking about selling the house before you called and asked me to visit." The dullness in her eyes faded to a genuine smile. "I can't believe I'm here."

"There are a few things I need to tell you about this house— "

"The cabbie told me its history."

A smile strained at Carlene's mouth. "No doubt. There's no electricity— oh, but don't worry. There's plumbing, and there are plenty of loos on every floor— not to mention the private one in your room."

"Loos?"

"Bathrooms. We don't have servants, but we do have a woman who comes in to cook breakfast every day. You know how I am in the morning, and David loves a big breakfast."

Carlene was amazed at how easily the lies were passing her lips. "And we have a groundskeeper. Lachlan's a bit gruff when he does talk, but he really loves the place."

"That's an unusual name."

"Yes. He's an unusual man. Why don't I show you to your room? We'll have plenty of time to talk later."

Placing her cup and saucer on the coffee table, Beth rose to her feet. "The cabbie said your house was haunted."

"Oh?" Carlene turned away. "The locals are teeming with superstitions. Don't pay them any attention."

Carlene walked toward the door they'd come through. Again, it struck Beth there was something deeply disturbing her friend. She followed Carlene nearly to the door, but stopped to look over a magnificent fireplace to her left.

The facing was of Victorian marble, the lining and hearth of glazed red tiles, and the back of iron. The mantel bore wax flowers and fruits under glass domes, several carved pipes on brass stands, and two fan-tailed brass peacocks.

Beth stopped for a look back. Her first impression of the room had been that it was exquisitely feminine, but now she realized that, amidst the vibrant dashes of colors, it was the most masculine room she'd ever been in. She was about to voice her admiration of the decor when she happened to look up at a painting hanging above the mantelpiece. Her jaw went slack. Her blood seemed to plummet to her feet.

Carlene gripped the brass knob of the door, her knuckles whitening under the strain as she looked up at the portrait.

She knew she should despise it, want to haul it down and destroy it in recompense for the grief it had brought her during the past months. But it was impossible for her heart not to fill with pride at her ability to have captured the real Beth on canvas, that free spirit within her friend that was most of the time hidden behind the woman's shyness.

"I don't believe this," Beth murmured. In their twelfth year at Kennewick High, Carlene had talked her into letting her paint her portrait. And there Beth sat in the painting, amidst a field of wildflowers, her riotous, light brown curls dancing on a breeze. The lace, shoulderless dress Carlene had loaned her was flapping about a bent knee that her forearms were casually resting upon. In the background, shafts of sunlight gleamed on the Columbia River.

"Now you see why I wanted to keep it," Carlene said softly. "I think I must have known there would one day be a place like this to display it."

Although Beth was embarrassed by the blatantly carefree pose of herself depicted in the painting, she couldn't have been more pleased with it having a place in such a house.

"It looks pretty good up there," she admitted, then looked at the shorter woman. "When am I going to meet this dashing husband of yours?"

Masking her hesitation, Carlene turned toward the door. "He's in Edinburgh on business. This is lousy timing, kiddo, but I'm going to have to take off in a little while to get him."

Carlene reached for the heaviest of the two suitcases in the hall, but Beth was quick to take it in hand. Lifting the smaller one, Carlene started up the stairs. "It's a long drive, so we'll probably stay at a B & B for the night— " Speaking as she turned her head to look at Beth, another sight caused her to gasp.

Beth was on the second step when she glanced over her shoulder. The instant she looked into the face of the man standing at the bottom of the steps, she felt icy fingers of fear clutch at her heart. She didn't know exactly what caused this reaction in her, but when she looked up again, Carlene was frozen on the sixth step.

"You're just in time to carry Miss Staples' bags

to her room," Carlene said, her authoritative tone strained.

"Beth, this is the groundskeeper I told you about."

Beth looked again at the man and detected a glint of expectancy in his nearly-black eyes. It took her aback. He had a remarkable face— angles and ruggedness, a face which possessed a powerful magnetism to the female eye, hers being no exception. But when he tried to take the suitcase from her hand, she stubbornly, instinctively, tightened her grip.

"I can manage, thank you," Beth said self-consciously.

"Swallow yer pride, lass," he chided, his eyes staring deeply into her own with uncanny boldness.

A vague sense of familiarity touched Beth, planting the notion in her mind that she had known this man in another life— which was absurd, since she didn't believe in reincarnation, or anything remotely like it. But when he reached out again for her suitcase, his hand brushed against her fingers, causing a sensation of electricity to slither up her arm. She somehow knew the contact had been deliberate, his way of heightening her awareness of him. With a slow grin, he tugged the suitcase from her grasp.

Beth looked down at her empty hand, then glanced up to see him crossing the second floor landing to another set of stairs.

"You did say he was gruff. Is he always so pushy?"

Carlene continued to look up the stairs after the

man. "At times he can be infuriating, but he'll take good care of you after I leave."

Beth's curiosity was resigned to a lesser plane of importance by the time she reached the third floor and followed Carlene through a set of French doors, down another hall, and into one of the rooms. Just beyond the threshold, Beth stopped.

There was no sign of the groundskeeper. Her suitcase was set atop a canopy bed of cherry wood carved with leaves and cherubs. Heavy, dark green velvet draperies were tied at the posts. Through the matching drapes hanging on two large windows, a colorful male peacock, perched atop an adjoining roof, craned its neck to peer at the occupants through the French panes.

"This is *my* room?"

"Yep. Unless you don't care for it."

Entering the room, Beth laughed and dropped her purse atop one of the Oriental throw rugs scattered on the highly polished wooden floor. "I love it!"

Which was an understatement. Beth's face glowed as she took in her surroundings. Two dressers and a wardrobe were also made of cherry wood and stained a burnished red. Leaves and cherubs were lavishly carved on each piece, as well as on an elaborate vanity by another door leading to a private bathroom. All of the pieces had marble tops. The wainscoting matched the furniture, the wallpaper a rich cream tone with raised dark green velvet print. On the wall across from the bed was a fieldstone fireplace with a Victorian marble mantel. Set by the hearth was a picture frame embroidery stand— a fire screen— bearing an unfinished cloth of a country scene.

"It's so . . . beautiful," Beth beamed.

Carlene abruptly swept past Beth and went to the door. "Explore the house. Help yourself to anything you want." Turning at the threshold, she offered Beth a tremulous smile. "There's plenty of food in the ice box and larder."

Then she reached up to indicate a light fixture on the wall. "All the light fixtures operate on gas. There are matches on the mantel. Light one, then just turn this key. When you want the light out, turn the key counter-clockwise and the gas shuts off."

"Do you have to leave right away?"

"Yes. Lachlan will see to the fires until David and I get back. Pull the cord by the bed and he'll come right away."

Beth felt a moment's panic but smiled nonetheless. "What time do you think you'll get back tomorrow?"

"I'm not sure."

As Carlene began to close the door, Beth asked, "Would you like company on the drive?"

"N-no. You're tired, and British cars are cramped."

Beth opened her mouth to tell Carlene she didn't mind the cramped quarters, or another drive, but the door closed, cutting her off from her friend.

Although unnerved, she stopped herself from running after Carlene. There was definitely something wrong, but she couldn't put her finger on what it was.

Unless David and Carlene had had a squabble. Then perhaps Carlene was hoping the drive home would give her the opportunity to smooth out matters before Beth became aware of any problems between them.

It was a logical enough possibility. But Beth could not shake a burgeoning sense of foreboding.

Two

The hours faded by unnoticed. Before Beth realized it, dusk was settling about Kist House. She had explored nearly every room on the top two floors, with two exceptions. The door to the room directly across from her bedroom was locked. And fatigue stopped her from looking beyond the stone newel staircase to the tower.

Descending the main staircase in slow, easy strides, she thought about making herself a hot cup of tea, and enjoying it while soaking in a hot bath—in her private, Victorian, clawfoot tub. This brought a smile to her face until she stepped down from the last stair and the absolute stillness of the house closed in around her. A thin sheen of perspiration broke out on her brow. An all too familiar tightness settled in the back of her neck.

Not a migraine now, she groaned mutely, gingerly massaging the ache.

A shrill cry, unlike anything Beth had ever heard, razored the air. A squeal of surprise erupted from her, and in the silence that followed, she could feel the wild thrumming of her heart rise in her throat. The front doors at the end of the hall seemed to zoom in on her vision, then as quickly, fall back into the far distance.

Pain drummed at her temples. Once again she became overly conscious of the stifling stillness within the walls. Air weighed heavily in her lungs. Her body temperature rose. Breathing in hoarse spurts, she walked toward the doors. Her passage through the greenhouse lessened the fever in her. Passing through the last outer door, she stepped into the cooling air of dusk, and slowly filled her lungs with it. Surprisingly, there was a mist of rain, and she raised her face to welcome its reviving chill.

The cry rang out again.

She was about to dash back into the house when a hand settled on her shoulder. Another squeal was wrenched from her throat before she could stop it, and on reflex, she slapped the broad chest coming around to her left. The groundskeeper's face finally came into focus through the haze of her vision, and she backhanded him in the midriff out of sheer irritability.

"Don't ever do that again!" she shrilled, shucking off the man's hand and stepping back two paces.

Lachlan chuckled low as he raked his fingers through his thick shoulder-length hair. "Didna mean ta frighten the wits ou' o' you, lass. I saw you give a start a' the call o' the bird."

"That horrible sound came from a bird?"

"Auld Braussaw." Lachlan pointed to a tall hedge. "There he is. See him?"

Beth strained to discern something within the

shadows of the closing daylight, but couldn't. "I thought someone had run over a cat."

"He's a paughty one, he is," he chuckled. "Peacocks truly have a terrible cry. You'll get used ta i'."

"How can anything so beautiful sound so awful?" she asked breathlessly, still trying to locate the bird.

Lachlan gave an airy shrug of his shoulders. "They're maist vocal in the wee hoors o' the morn."

"Wonderful. My blood feels like ice."

With a slow, utterly charming smile, he tilted his head to one side and unabashedly studied Beth's features. "Tis no' sa bad when you've been aroond them awhile."

Beth tried to smile through her taut facial muscles, but found she couldn't. The man's perusal of her made her uncomfortable. When she had met him earlier, standing two steps above him on the staircase, she hadn't noticed how tall he was. She did now. He was well over six foot, a full head taller than she was.

"Feelin' the walls close in on you?"

"No . . . well, a little." Beth tried to relax the tension in her body. "It's a bit spooky being alone in such a large place."

Lachlan nodded understandingly, then, to her disbelief, he clasped one of her hands with one of his and gave her a gentle tug. "Tha' tae will pass, in time. Come, lass. Tis a full moon this night. I've a place ta show you as i' rises."

"Well I . . ."

Beth's legs began to move of their own volition,

keeping in stride with the man's long gait. As he led her away from the house, along a pathway to the east that was thickly canopied by tree branches, she couldn't help but dwell on his warm grasp. He had large, powerful hands. She'd noticed that earlier when he'd taken her suitcase from her. His hold was gentle, not the least threatening, but nonetheless, she felt intimidated by the masculinity of him— and the ease with which he had stepped into her life. He responded to her as if they had known one another for some time.

The way through the hedges and brush was growing ever darker, but he walked with a confidence that bespoke his familiarity with the property. He kept her close to his side, like a protective lover. Traversing the path, she couldn't help but ruminate the anomaly of walking at night with a man she didn't know. It made her realize how sheltered a life she'd led. The years had simply passed by. She was almost thirty, and hadn't dated since college.

"We're here," Lachlan said softly, in an almost reverent whisper. He came to a stop by a white, four-foot corral-style fence, and drew Beth closer to his side. "The moonlight blesses this field."

Beth felt a fluttering sensation within the pit of her stomach. The field, a farmhouse in the far distance, and the hills beyond, were bathed in ethereal silver light.

"Tis a sight ta soothe the soul, eh?"

"It's beautiful."

"Aye. Tis ne'er had competition, till you came." Noting with wry amusement Beth's quick glance of disapproval, he went on, "The Lauders live in the farmhouse you see across the way. Eleven or mair generations have lived on an' warked this land."

"Did they once own this property, too?"

"Aye. Baird's offer ta purchase these forty-five acres came a' a time whan the Lauders were in dire need o' money."

Lachlan smiled as he dipped his head and his gaze caressed her features. "They liked the auld boy, appreciated his love an' plans for this piece o' their history."

The chill of the evening's drizzle caused a shiver to pass through her. She was prepared to ignore it when Lachlan stepped behind her and draped his arms about her upper torso.

Instinctually, she stiffened.

"Haud yer indignancies," he chuckled by her ear. "I'm only tryin' ta keep the chill ou' o' you."

"I'm f-fine."

"Aye, an' the chatterin' o' yer teeth is really fairies dancin' on the rocks yonder? Relax."

"I'd relax a lot better if you weren't wrapped around me," she bristled.

Lachlan sighed, then rested his chin atop the crown of her head. She thought to shove him away, but his closeness did award her much-needed warmth.

"Wha' do you see whan you look across tha' field?"

She took a few seconds to regulate her breathing. "Moonlight."

"An'?"

"Space. Openness." Now she sighed, and unknowingly she leaned into the man. "Incredible beauty and . . . serenity."

"Aye, tis all tha' an' mair.

> — *The herrin' loves the merry moonlight,*
> *The mackerel loves the wind,*
> *But the oyster loves the dredgin' sang,*
> *For they come o' a gentle kind.—* "

Beth pondered the words for some time before asking, "What does it mean?"

"I'm hungry, an' thinkin' o' fish, I suppose."

The laughter in his tone brought a smile to her face.

Despite his unnerving proximity, the tension in her body began to ebb. Something she couldn't define tingled along her skin. With it came a sense of loftiness, as if she were absorbing his ease and contentment, his confidence.

"Wha' do you think o' Scotland?"

She shrugged within the band of muscular arms embracing her. "What I've seen is wonderful, but I really haven't had a chance to see much."

"You'll come ta love i' here. Maybe almaist as much as me."

Mindless of what her next move might provoke, Beth innocently turned in Lachlan's arms and looked up into his eyes. "I can't understand everything you're saying. Your accent is very thick."

Lachlan's smoldering dark gaze dipped unsettlingly on Beth's full, shapely mouth. He wanted to tell her what her dulcet tone did to him, what her physical presence meant to him. Keeping a tight rein on his desire to possess her on this very spot, he grinned crookedly. "I'm speakin' as slow as I can. Beth . . . I'm glad yer're here."

"Are you?"

"Aye. I've waited a long time ta meet you."

Beth felt a sudden compulsion to laugh. She didn't know why, but she could feel a giggle working itself up within her The idea of succumbing to this also struck her as funny at this peculiar moment—peculiar because every nerve in her body was sensitized by the man's mere presence. A quirky smile was playing on his lips, as if he were able to read her mind, or understand that part of her which was at the outer reaches of her comprehension.

She was almost thirty. Not a schoolgirl.

So why did her heart rise into her throat when his hands came to light on her upper arms?

Why was she unable to move or speak when, while staring deeply into her eyes, he began to lower his head?

Cool, chiseled lips covered her own in a teasing, almost experimental kiss. She stood immobile, while her insides were pumping, swelling, twisting and bursting. She experienced a spiritual soaring and swooping, then soaring again as the kiss deepened. Sinewy arms enveloped her, molding her against the length of his incredibly hard body. She became lost within a sense of rightness, of belonging as she'd never known—

Stranger.

The word detonated within the confines of her skull and she reacted like a startled kitten. Wrenching out of Lachlan's arms, she braced herself against the fence. Mortification scorched her skin. A streak of moonlight passing through the branches above ran aslant across Lachlan's face, illuminating his mesmerizing eyes.

Beth tried to speak, to say something— *anything*— to break the suffocating silence between them. When she found her vocal cords wouldn't respond, she pushed off the fence and broke into a run along the path.

Low branches and brush scraped and clawed at her. Blindly, desperately hoping she was going in the right direction, she continued on. The stillness was all around her once again. If not for the chill of the drizzle—

She ran into something solid and would have fallen backward if not for steadying hands on her shoulders.

"Have a heart, girl!"

Beth's vision cleared.

"A simple *na* wad have sufficed!"

Her temper erupted. "Hold it!"

"Yer hand, you say?" A roguish gleam lit up his rugged features as he reached out, but Beth was quick to slap his hand away.

"Stop manhandling me, Mr.— "

"Lachlan. I think tis a wee late ta be formal now, dinna you?"

Blood rushed up into Beth's face. "I'm sorry if I've given you the wrong impression."

"Fegs, lass!" he laughed. "You've a fine temper."

"I'm tired and cold. Now, if you'll excuse me—"

"No' so fast." Lachlan gave a sober shake of his head. "Tis for me ta say I'm sorry. I got a wee lost in yer beautiful eyes back there. An' I'm afraid I'm an incorrigible tease. I've never been able ta resist makin' a beautiful womon blush."

Although every nerve in her body was as tight as a spring, she managed to stare into the man's eyes without wavering. "You've had your fun."

"Aye, an' I felt yer ain appreciation ta ma verra soul, sweet darlin'. But I'm modest enough ta know i' was the moonlight an' no' ma kissin' skills tha' put tha' sparkle in yer eyes. Alas—" He sighed deeply. "— I'll have ta practice wi' you in the cauld light o' day ta know whan tis *me* stirrin' yer blood."

Straightening her shoulders, Beth glared at the silent laughter in the man's handsome face. "I didn't come all this way just to entertain you, you twerp."

Lachlan's dark brows peaked. "Twerp, you say? Wad tha' be a guid twerp, or a bad twerp?"

"Personally, I don't care how you translate it."

"Wad help if I knew wha' a twerp was," he said absently, then offered, "Let me make you a cup o' tea."

"I'll fix my own, thank you."

Passing Lachlan, Beth trained her gaze on the front of the house some fifty feet away. She was nearly to the outer doors, believing the puzzling man had given up, when he dashed in front of her and opened the entry for her. Bowing at the waist, he motioned her into the house.

He was again at the second set of doors before her.

"Lachlan," she sighed, a foot up on the bottom of the three stone steps. "I'm too tired to play cat-and-mouse."

"Cat-an'-mouse, you say? Darlin', I gave Carlene ma word I'd watch efter you. Besides, i' wadna be right ta let you suffer a moment's boredom here now, wad i'?"

A smile strained to appear on Beth's lips. "Is this what I have to look forward to until Carlene and David return?"

With a mock wounded look, Lachlan reached down, clasped her hand, then drew her into the house. Beth closed the door behind her. She was beginning to wonder if the man understood the word 'no', or had ever been denied a thing in his life. He was the most carefree person she'd ever met.

He pulled her down a narrower, secondary hall that ended at the kitchen. As if thoroughly enjoying himself, he urged Beth to sit at a two-chair table in the corner of the spacious room, then swaggered to the antique stove and flamboyantly swung a kettle up into his hand.

Beth watched him. A smile strained at her lips, resisted her efforts to subdue it. He had somehow made her experience more emotions in one day than she had felt in years. Resting her elbow on the table, she lowered her chin onto her upturned palm and watched him.

He certainly was a character, someone who could have easily just returned home from pirating on the high seas.

Pirate.

Yes. His shoulder-length, dark auburn hair. The powerful breadth of his shoulders and back, accentuated by the white shirt he wore— a shirt very much in the style the pirate-types had worn in centuries past. Black, tight-fitting pants covered his slim hips, rounded backside, and muscular thighs, and tapered into shiny black, knee-high boots. But he was minus an earring. Although if she woke in the morning and found him wearing one, she doubted she would be surprised.

"How do you tak yer tea?"

Beth reluctantly withdrew from her reverie. "Excuse me?"

"Yer tea, lass."

"Straight's fine."

Lachlan cocked a brow in her direction and started pouring. After a few seconds, he walked to the table and set down two steaming cups, one in front of Beth, one where he was lowering himself onto a chair across from her. "I knew we had somethin' in common, lass. Straight tea an' kissin in the moonlight."

"Just what do you do around here?" Beth asked, forcing a lightness into her tone to camouflage her nervousness.

He shrugged. "A bit o' this, a bit o' tha'."

"Have you worked here long?"

"Depends."

Beth stopped in the process of taking a sip of tea, and lowered her cup. "Depends on what?"

"Some say I dinna wark a' all." He shrugged again. "Are you hungry?"

"No, thank you."

"So tell me then, wha' do you think o' Baird House?"

Beth took several leisurely sips of her tea before answering. "It's magnificent."

"Aye, tis tha', but I've a feelin' you've mair ta say abou' the place than wha' yer eyes tell you."

Beth frowned and smiled at the same time. Whether it was the man's presence, or his cryptic statements, he possessed the uncanny ability to raise the hairs on the back of her neck and arms. "What a curious thing to say."

"No' really."

Setting down her cup, Beth folded her arms atop the table. "What do *your* other senses tell you about this place?"

A secretive grin touched upon his mouth. "Weel, there's a guid feelin' wi'in these walls. If you close yer eyes an' keep yer fears a' bay, you can hear the heartbeat o' this house."

"Oh, pl—ease!"

"Dinna laugh, Beth," he said with a sad smile. "Some say this house is alive. It has a soul, as e'er-lastin' as tha' o' a mon or a womon."

"That's eerie," Beth said quietly, staring down into her cup.

"Na. Tis the thinkin' o' a mon who loves this place."

She looked up, her gaze instantly drawn to his eyes. Again she had the feeling that he was reading her mind, somehow looking inside her. It was disconcerting, and yet, comforting in some odd way.

"Have you ever been to the United States?"

"Na." He sipped his tea, then lowered his cup. "I've ne'er had a mind ta leave Great Britain."

"That's a shame. There are a lot of places in the States I think you would enjoy."

The mischievous laughter returned to his eyes. "Especially on moonlit nights wi' the right womon, eh?"

"You have a one-track mind."

"A wha'?"

Standing, Beth lifted her cup. "Never mind. Look, I-umm, I hate to be a party pooper, but I really am tired."

"O' course. Forgive me." He rose to his feet, leaving his cup on the table. "I'll walk you ta yer room."

"I can find my way, thank you."

"In the dark?"

Beth experienced a chill of a start. She'd just realized the gas lamps in the kitchen and main hall had been lit. She wasn't sure why this bothered her, but a suspicion was nibbling at her outer consciousness, trying to push something to the fore of her brain. "Did you light the lamps?"

"Aye."

"When?"

"A while ago. Why do you ask?"

Beth released a nervous chuckle. "Don't mind me. Jet lag."

"Jet lag, you say?"

"You know . . . crossing the ocean? The time difference?"

A frown puckered Lachlan's broad brow. "I'll have ta tak yer word for i'. Let me get a candle ta light oor way."

Beth didn't feel the nervous twitching within her stomach again until the ascent of the stairs. By the first landing, it was all she could do to keep her hand steady enough to keep her tea from sloshing over the gold-rimmed lip of her cup. The golden glow of candlelight gave the staircase a completely different look. With Lachlan by her side, she watched the surrounding shadows through troubled eyes. She'd always hated the dark, but she had discovered the soft, dancing glow of the candle did more to feed her imagination than any inky night.

Things moved.

Shadows stretched eerily, creeping up the walls.

As if sensing her unease, Lachlan's strong fingers closed over her free hand and gave it a squeeze. She didn't look at him. Without relaying how comforting she found his gesture, she steeled herself not to give in to the jitters.

Lachlan opened the door to her bedroom and walked in ahead of her. Placing the candle on the mantel of the fireplace, he turned to face her. His features cast in shadow, she found herself straining to discern his expression as she walked up to him.

"Thank you. I can manage now."

Lachlan looked down, then quickly entwined his fingers through Beth's. Before she could gather her wits about her, he lifted one of her hands and pressed the back of her knuckles to his mouth. A sensual shiver moved through her.

"You have long fingers. Beautiful hands," he said in a low, amorous tone.

"You're certainly not shy about flirting," she said nervously, withdrawing her hands and crossing her arms against her chest to give her a place to tuck them away.

A solemn smile touched his mouth. "I admire beauty in all forms, darlin'. Inner beauty as weel. Wad you like a fire ta warm the room?"

"No. No, I'm sure I'll be warm enough."

"A warm body ta snuggle oop ta?" He grinned.

"G-goodnight, Lachlan."

He sighed. "Guid night, Beth." He started toward the door, then turned and searched her face for a long moment. "Dinna e'er be afraid in this house. There's nocht here tha' wad harm you."

"I'd like that in writing, please," she said with a nervous little laugh. "Oh, is there a portrait of Lannie Baird in the house?"

For a moment, Beth thought he would not answer her. He was staring at her with something akin to impatience.

"Hangin' above the mantel in the room across the hall."

"The locked room?"

Lachlan smiled, and a flurry of excitement swirled about her heart. Whatever she expected next, it was not for the man to close the distance between them and plant a gentle, yet lingering, kiss on her lips.

"Pull tha' cord if you need aught," he said, straightening up and pointing toward the bed. *"I'm across the hall, tae."*

Beth gave a visible start. Why did that piece of information thrill her, and yet cause a sinking feeling deep within her? Lost to self-consciousness, she asked inanely, "You sleep *in* this house?"

"Aye. In a big . . . *looonely* bed. Does tha' distress you?"

"N-no. Why should I care if you sleep lonely— in a lonely— never mind."

In an absent gesture, Lachlan brushed aside a curl at Beth's temple. "I can sleep in the carriage house. There's a cot— "

"N-no, of course not. I don't mind you sleeping in the same *house* with me. It's just that I didn't know groundskeepers slept in their employers' houses," she added lamely, heat rushing through her body at the mere idea of him sleeping so close to her.

"Depends on the importance o' the mon."

"Are you always so . . . ?" Beth frowned for a moment until the right word came to her. "Outgoing?"

Tucking his thumbs into the waistband of his trousers, Lachlan gave a shake of his head. "Only when I'm verra comfortable aroond someone. This can be a lonely house a' times. Yer bein' here is like a fresh ray o' sunlight."

He smiled inwardly when Beth shyly looked off

to one side. "There's extra blankets in the cedar chest a' the foot o' the bed. Oor nights can get a wee chilly."

Beth stiltedly nodded her head in acknowledgement, and Lachlan sighed deeply.

"Girl?"

His trilling of the 'r' in the word caused Beth's heart to skip a beat. She looked into the disquieting depths of his eyes and experienced a fluttering sensation low in her abdomen.

"Sometimes I can be a blusterin' fool. Some say I have no' a single social grace abou' me, an' tis true for the maist part. But I am a mon who knows wha' he wants."

"What *is* it you want?" Beth asked in a whisper of a tone.

Lachlan gave a slow roll of his eyes before answering. "The e'er elusive happiness. For the mon who hesitates, i' slips through his grasp, an' becomes nigh impossible ta reclaim. Do you understand?"

"I don't believe it's ever too late to go after a dream."

"Spoken from yer heart," he murmured. He bent to kiss her again, but she placed her palms to his chest and gave him a nudge.

"Goodnight."

An impish gleam lit up his eyes. "It cad have been. Sweet dreams, Beth."

When the door closed behind him, Beth went to the bed and stretched out on her stomach atop it, propping up her chin on upturned palms.

It was too incredible to believe a man like Lachlan was truly interested in her. He was handsome, charming, and witty. And surprisingly tender and profound at the most peculiar moments. She hadn't given a thought to a man in her future— let alone her near future— until she'd met him.

Rolling onto her back, she stared unseeingly up at the ceiling. She knew she was vulnerable, especially to a man like him. It just seemed too incredible his attentiveness could stem from anything more than his flirtatious nature.

It disturbed her to realize her heart was primed to fall in love, but at least her mind was prepared to wage resistance.

She understood only too well what isolation and loneliness could do to the psyche.

"One day at a time," she whispered.

Drawing herself up into a sitting position, she gazed absently about her surroundings. She couldn't help but wonder how she was going to feel in the morning. Waking up in such a magnificent house. In Scotland.

Alone.

She frowned at the latter and rose from the bed. A chill moved along the skin of her arms. Hugging herself, she sighed deeply.

Never would she have imagined being lonelier than in the first few weeks following her mother's death. But she felt it now; an isolation so intense, it almost possessed substance.

Her throat tightened.

She wasn't particularly fond of the shadows accompanying her. Candlelight did not cast the renowned romantic ambiance when one was alone, in a manor, in a strange country.

"Or abundant in imagination," she murmured. Massaging the back of her neck, she cast a look of despair in the direction of the door.

"I wonder if he plays cards . . . Knock, knock. Oh, Lachlan, would you care for a game of Gin Rummy? Oh. Okay. How about Fish?"

She grimaced.

"I'd settle for a deck to play a game of solitaire— not that I could see much in this lighting."

Something intruded upon her awareness.

Turning her head sharply to look at the windows, she tried to swallow down the feeling of her heart rising into her throat. Impressions bombarded her. A strong sense of not being alone filled her completely. Straining to see in the dim, flickering light, she reflexively held her breath.

The air about her stirred. Goose flesh broke out all over her skin.

"Lachlan," she called, but the sound was little more than a hoarse whisper.

He had told her he was across the hall. She could cry out— and hope he didn't believe she was a hopeless weakling who was spooked by a mere draft. Or . . . she could go to his door—

Shivering, she gave her head an adamant shake.

Scratch that. If she approached him now, he would construe it as her wanting more than a *little* company to temper her jitters.

Old houses were infamously drafty. Baird House was no exception.

But it did no good for her to repeatedly tell herself this.

Hastily changing into her nightgown, she left her day clothing on the floor and scrambled beneath the bed covers, cowering beneath them. Pain throbbed at her temples. Tears pressed behind her eyes.

"Dammit, get a grip on yourself," she whimpered as something air-light moved against her exposed cheek. She yanked the covers over her head, her deathlike hold cramping her fingers. After several long minutes, the ridiculousness of scaring herself like this elicited a dry chuckle from her.

A cry rang out.

For a horrible moment, she feared *she* had released the unearthly wail. Then . . .

Those damn birds! she realized.

Unclenching her hands, she turned onto her side and folded her arms against her chest. Although the covers remained over her head, she found herself laughing.

"Beth Staples, it's pretty bad when you cringe at the cry of a bird."

She continued to laugh, flexing her legs between the warmth of the bed and the covers.

"Mary had a little lamb, its fleece as white as snow; and when Mary lost her little lamb— it came back to haunt Baird house. Ha."

She drew in a deep breath. This was no way to spend her first night in Scotland. Determined to prove to herself that she was alone in the room, she bolted up, tossing back the covers. For the first second, relief washed through her, then she spied movement at the foot of the bed. She watched as a greenish mist shifted, as if in response to her unexpected action. The flame atop the candle flickered, almost extinguished, then righted once again. Her gaze cut briefly to it, then back— only to find the mist was now positioned to the left of the bed. Its soft glow dimmed, seemed to fade before brightening and moving closer.

"Lannie?" she choked. "No. . . . No, go away. I don't believe in ghosts. *Go away.*"

The mist inched closer. Jumping from the bed, Beth ran for the door. She turned and yanked on the knob, but the door would not budge.

"Lachlan!" she cried, pounding her fists against the recessed wood panel. "Lachlan, please!"

At the same instant she looked over her shoulder, the mist was upon her. Utter coldness seized every part of her. A wheezed gasp of breath rushed from her lungs. Turning her back to the door, her mouth agape, she fought against the panic swelling within her. The mist had completely enveloped her. Green. Sparkling with an intensity that increased with every passing second. Despite her terror, she sensed a presence within the anomaly. Sensed something trying to communicate.

A scream ejected from her throat.

In the next second, the mist evaporated. A weeping Beth sagged against the door and sank to a sit-

ting position on the floor. Another cry escaped her when a loud rap on the door startled her.

"Beth! Girl— " The door opened minutely, ramming her back and shoulders. "Beth, get away from the door. Beth, *do you hear me?*"

The concern in Lachlan's tone snapped her from her shock. Getting unsteadily to her feet, she stepped back several paces as Lachlan pushed wide the door and crossed the threshold. Although she wanted to fling herself into his arms, she stood as still as a statue, her eyes seeming too large for her face.

Lachlan went to her, his arms readily drawing her stiff body into them. "Wha's wrong, lass?"

"Something . . . *touched* me."

Framing one side of her face with a hand, he peered deeply into her glazed eyes. "Touched you?"

She nodded stiltedly. "Lachlan . . . is this place haunted?"

Lachlan's attempt to laugh the matter off fell short. "Some believe sa."

"Do you?"

"Aye."

"Lannie? Is it Lannie Baird?"

Placing a hand at the back of her head, Lachlan urged her to rest a cheek against his chest. For a time, he stared off into the shadows of the room, his gaze troubled. "He wadna hurt you."

Beth shivered before winding her arms about Lachlan's middle. "I . . . I really didn't think he would. It just . . . took me by surprise."

A sad smile moved along his mouth. "First time

Carlene encountered him, she nearly screamed the walls doon."

"Carlene?" Beth looked up into his eyes. "She's seen him?"

"Aye."

"David?"

"He was a bit mair steady abou' Lannie." He sighed, his smile deepening, drawing Beth's gaze to the seductive fullness of his mouth. "Once Carlene got used ta the idea, she teuk a likin' ta the auld boy."

"But . . . When I told her the cabbie had said this place was haunted, she denied it."

Lachlan's broad shoulders moved in a shrug. "She probably didna want ta spook you."

Spook.

A laugh gurgled in Beth's throat as she pressed her brow to his chest. "I feel like such an idiot."

"'Tis a shock a' first. He was probably lookin' in on you."

Beth searched Lachlan's face with a question in her eyes.

"Wha' is i', love?"

"Why would he . . . *look in* on me?"

With a low laugh, he kissed the tip of her nose. "Yer're new here. He was probably curious. No' much else for a ghost ta do, you know." He gestured with his right arm as he went on, "Besides roamin' the halls, moanin' an' groanin'."

"He moans and groans?"

"Na, no' really. Though he's reputed ta have a fine temper."

Suddenly overly conscious of Lachlan's proximity, Beth withdrew her arms from about him and walked to the bed, where she kept her back to him. Nervously running a hand through her hair, she said as lightly as she could, "I'm all right, now. Thank you."

"Tis a cool night," he said, coming up behind her and placing his hands on her shoulders. "We cad snuggle by a fire—"

"I'm really tired."

"Wary," he countered evenly. "Canna blame you. Me. Then Lannie. Tis a lot ta adjust ta."

Smiling, Beth turned and met his teasing gaze. *"You* probably more than Lannie."

"Ooch" he chuckled, a hand over his heart. "An' here, darlin', I was offerin' ta haud you through the night."

"I know exactly what you were offering," Beth said, the heat of a blush rushing up her face. "Thank you, again. I'm glad you're just across the hall."

"Small comfort, eh?"

Taking her hand, Lachlan was about to kiss the palm when she jerked it away.

"Beth?"

"Oh God, I'm sorry! Your hand was so cold, it startled me. I'm sorry."

Lachlan's gaze lowered to his hands. He flexed them, an unreadable expression shielding his thoughts from her. Beth reached out and touched his arm. When he looked up, she lowered the hand to her side.

"I'm not usually this jittery."

A half smile tugged at one corner of his mouth. "Strange land. Strange house. Strange mon. An' strange occurrences. I'd say you were owed a bit o' the jitters. An' I *am* cauld."

Whatever Beth expected, it was not to find herself being drawn into his arms, drawn into a kiss that easily melted her fears. Even his lips were cold, but the kiss was warm, heating with every passing second, lulling her into a state of blissful security. It felt natural to be in his embrace, mastered by his kisses, as if somewhere deep in her subconscious, she'd fantasized about just such a man.

When he ended the kiss, she looked up at him with disappointment in her expressive eyes.

"I may no' be here whan you wake in the morn. I'll get back ta you as soon as possible."

"You're not going away!"

He smiled disarmingly and brushed the back of a hand beneath her chin. "Na, darlin'. I've things ta do abou' the place. I wadna leave yer side for a moment unless need be."

Beth gave a nod of her head. "Hopefully, Carlene and David will return early."

"Hard ta say. Sleep, lass. Tis been a long day for you."

"Certainly one I'll never forget."

"One guid thin' abou' Lannie's visit," he said, a teasing lilt in his tone, his eyes sparkling. "Now I know tis no' the moonlight tha' maks you glow."

Again Beth blushed, and she gave a light shove to his chest. "Goodnight, Lachlan."

"You *sure* this time?"

Beth nodded, a gleam of mischief in her own eyes. "I think you've chased away the boogie man."

"Might be, lass, I cad call him back."

"Goodnight."

With a low laugh, he planted a quick kiss on her cheek. "Dream o' me, darlin'."

After the door closed behind him, Beth got beneath the covers and lowered her head to the pillows. Wrapped in a dreamy state, she stared unseeingly up at the ceiling, unaware the candle on the mantel was nearly burned out. Beyond the windows, she could hear a breeze swaying the tree tops, branches scratching against the side of the house and against the single-glassed panes.

Her lips tingled in memory of his kiss. The blood flowing through her veins was very warm.

Thick eyelashes lowered on her flushed cheeks.

"No . . . it wasn't the moonlight," she murmured, a faint smile on her mouth. Then, "Thank you, Lannie. But next time, give me some warning."

Rolling onto her side, she nested a cheek into one of the plump pillows. Sleep fell upon her quickly.

Unbeknown to her, the mist returned, hovering by her bedside, watching, ever vigilant.

It had never been Lannie's intention to frighten her.

Quite the opposite.

Three

A restless night's sleep had Beth up before the crack of dawn. She took a hot, leisurely soak in the tub, dressed, and opted for a cup of tea for breakfast. After fidgeting about the kitchen for some time, she took an apple from a basket on one of the counters, then left the house.

Bright sunlight greeted her, as did several cries from the peacocks. The air was cooler than it had been upon her arrival yesterday, a slight breeze frolicking amid the manicured grounds. Everywhere she looked, the birds perched, watching her, eyeing her as if wary of her presence. It would always amaze her how such extraordinarily beautiful creatures could be so gratingly vocal, especially in the wee hours of the morning.

It was late morning by the time she tired of meandering the grounds and inspecting the gardens to the south. She was on her way back to the house when the smaller structure captured her notice.

The carriage house proved to be delightful, furnished with a cot, a small dresser, and a two-seater carriage— the design of which told her it was definitely from the previous century, although looking at it, she could not find a scratch or worn spot.

The whitewashed walls of the opened room sported all sorts of harnesses, whips, and reins. She took down one of the whips and gingerly tested it. She couldn't imagine anyone actually using such a thing on a horse. It felt heavy in her hand. Almost sinister. But as she flexed her fingers on the leather-bound handle, she felt a thrill of power. Daringly, she gave a firm snap of her wrist. The tip of the lash cracked ominously close to her chin. Replacing it on its hook, she chose instead to run her finger tips over the other items.

The musky smell of leather filled her nostrils. Inhaling deeply, she made a slow appraisal of the room, then headed out the double doors.

She looked up at the cry of a peacock. Perched on the highest peak, it looked down at her and ruffled its feathers. A smile turned up the corners of her mouth. Then she sighed as she glanced at the front door of the main house. There was so little to do to pass away the time more quickly. Certainly there was no housework; everything in the place was spotless. The gardens were weed-free. Perfection. She wasn't used to being idle, not after eight years of catering to her mother's every need. Then, there had hardly been time to curl up and read a book. Always so much to do.

A pensive frown creasing her brow, Beth strolled to the east side of the property, where the largest of the rose gardens created a low-walled maze. Bees zipped from flower to flower, their seemingly overzealous buzzing giving her pause about getting too close. Until one particular section of the garden zoomed into her awareness.

Pale purple roses.

Folding her legs beneath her, Beth settled comfortably on the ground.

Memories surfaced.

Shortly before her mother's death, Beth had planted a row of similar bushes along the fenceline across from her mother's bedroom window. The roses, Rita's favorite flower, had been intended for her to enjoy. But she had died before the first blossom had opened.

"Life never goes as we expect it to," Beth said sadly, running a finger along the edge of one of the soft petals. "I wish . . ." Tears welled up in her eyes, but she fought them back. "You didn't deserve to suffer, Ma. I did everything I could. But it wasn't enough, was it?"

Her chin quivered.

"As many times as I wanted to end your pain, I couldn't bring myself. . . . The anger and frustration I read in your eyes will always haunt me. Forgive me. Please . . . forgive—"

In place of her heart, an enormous ache thrummed and, despite the control she'd mastered over the years, a sob escaped her.

A movement close by gave her a start.

She looked up. The heaviness which had been building within her chest waned at the sight of Lachlan sitting down beside her.

"Good morning," she managed with a half-hearted smile.

"Tis a heart-wrenchin' sound you make, Beth. Wha's wrong?"

"Nothing."

"I've a broad shoulder ta cry on."

A strained laugh escaped her. "Why would anyone wish to cry on such a beautiful morning?"

"Hmmm. Somethin' tells me you've held in yer feelin's tae long."

Choosing not to respond to his uncanny ability to delve into her psyche, she gazed absently at the purple roses.

"Did you manage ta sleep?"

"Yes." Drawing in a fortifying breath, she added, "The bed is very comfortable."

"Hmm. An' here I thought I'd detected shadows beneath yer eyes."

Reflexively, Beth swiped the side of a hand above her cheeks. "It's probably a residue of mascara."

"Tha' black goop women plaster on their eyes?" He chuckled deep in his throat, then crooked a thumb beneath her chin and turned her face to his scrutiny. "Yer're a melancholy lass. Tell me wha's troublin' you."

An attempt to smile failed. "It's nothing. Really."

"No' this 'jet lag' thin', eh?"

"It could be," she defended evenly, a twinkle of amusement coming to life in her eyes. But then a cloud of unease passed over her features, and she shivered as she scanned the roses surrounding her. "Wha' is i'?"

"The bees."

"Wha' abou' them?"

"There were hundreds of them . . . They're gone."

Lachlan glanced about him. "Yer sobbin' sent them off in a fit o' despair," he quipped.

Lowering her head, Beth chuckled. "It wasn't *that* bad."

"Teuk the heart ou' o' me."

Beth found herself looking into his eyes. Even out here in the bright sunlight, she could not discern his irises. His fair skin made his eyes appear darker, fathomless. Then he smiled crookedly, drawing her attention to his mouth. The right groove in his cheek deepened. Before she could suppress it, a sigh escaped her.

"I understand yer mither died no' long ago," he said casually, although the intensity in his eyes warned Beth that he knew what had brought on her tears. "You teuk care o' her for a long time. Eight years, I understand."

"Yes." She pointedly focused on the roses in front of her. "It began with heart problems, Later, she suffered with cancer."

"Cadna the doctors— "

"No." Beth spared him a quick glance. "She would have suffered as much in the hospital. She wanted to die— be at home."

"Was tha' fair ta you?"

Beth stiffened, the fire in her eyes warning him the subject was taboo. "What has *fair* got to do with anything?"

"Yer're bitter, lass."

Jumping to her feet, Beth irritably smoothed her calf-length skirt. She stared down at his upturned face, resentment lending her a strained, gaunt look. "I'm not bitter. I took care of her because I wanted to." When Lachlan rose to his feet, she continued to glare at him. "I may not have had your . . . your care-free life, Lachlan, but I certainly don't regret— "

"Haud i'! I said you cad cry on ma shoulder, no' tak ou' yer frustration on me."

Beth clenched her hands by her sides. "Then mind your own damn business in the future," she flung the words at him, turned, and walked away.

Thorny hedges blocked her escape, slowing her, fueling her raw emotions. Although she could see the exit of the maze, her every attempt to walk there failed. Thorns snagged her cotton skirt. The fragrance of the roses became overwhelming. Blinded by her frustration, she stopped and clenched her hands once again.

Labored breaths roared in her ears.

Panic lodged behind her breasts.

"Yer're one stubborn woman," Lachlan bit out as he snatched up one of her hands in a steely hold. He expected her to protest as he led her out of the maze, but she only followed him, occasionally tugging defiantly at his hand. Crossing the graveled front of the house and a section of lawn, he stepped up into the largest gazebo and directed her to one of the white, wooden chairs. Beth sat, then planted her elbows atop the table and buried her face in her hands to hide the heat of indignation in her face. Lachlan seated himself across from her, impatience imprinted on his face.

"Yer're no' one ta accept help graciously, are you?"

"You don't know anything about me."

"Mair than you know." When Beth lowered her hands and looked at him, he smugly arched a brow. "Yer're pretty easy ta read. Strong-willed. Independent."

"How very observant of you."

Lachlan fell silent for a time, watching her attempt to brush back her riotous curls with her hands. "Watchin' yer mither languish—"

"Why do you keep harping on her?"

"—as you did, I can weel imagine you no' wantin' to e'er be dependent on anyone."

"What are you . . . a closet psychiatrist?"

"I've a reliable sixth sense."

"How nice for you," she grumbled.

"You must have resented her—"

"Give it a rest!"

"—haud on you."

Bolting to her feet, Beth turned to escape the gazebo. But Lachlan swiftly went to her, the fingers of a hand cinching one of her wrists in a viselike hold. He jerked her around to face him.

"She teuk away yer life for—"

"Let me go!"

"—eight years!"

"Stop it, *please!*"

Lachlan steeled himself against the tears misting her eyes. "You wanted ta free yerself o' those emotional shackles." Beth's struggle to escape him intensified. "But i' was impossible. Right, girl?"

Gripping her upper arms, he gave her a shake. "Who tauld you that you cadna demand a life o' yer ain, eh? Guid God, Beth, na one expected you ta sacrifice yer all for the womon!"

"She sacrificed for me!"

"Adopted you, I understand."

"You don't understand anything!"

"I do. An' tis a weighty burden ta bear."

Trembling violently, Beth stared at him in bewilderment. She didn't want him or anyone else prying into her business.

Lachlan sighed as a semblance of calm befell him. "Guilt is a wicked tool, love. The hangmon's hands." He smiled sadly. "Tis a means we use ta keep ithers in toll."

"I don't understand."

"I know you dinna." He drew her into his arms and kissed the crown of her head. "You've always been beholden ta the couple who *chose* you. They were guid people, Beth. Kind. Lovin'. They gave you the emotional an' financial security you needed."

"Yes."

"You were there ta help yer mither efter yer faither died, an' there for her whan she was befallen wi' illness." Framing one side of her face with a hand, he prompted her to look up at him. "But she had na right ta take away those precious years. Na right a' all."

"She was terrified."

"Aye. Tis understandable. But how cad she look a' you an' no' see wha' the isolation was doin' ta you?"

"I was all she had," Beth murmured, staring unseeingly at his chest.

"Na."

"Yes. Within a few months after she was bedridden, her friends stopped calling and coming over. What little family was left, simply ignored us."

"Leavin' you ta believe i' was all upon yer shoulders?"

Beth's dull gaze lifted. "I don't regret taking care of her."

For a long moment, Lachlan became lost in her eyes. When she started to look away, he brushed the back of his fingers along her cheek. "Wha' else did she ask o' you?"

A gasp escaped her. She tried to step from his hold, but his hands again anchored her upper arms.

"Beth?"

"I need to lie down for a while."

"Wha' did yer mither ask tha' still troubles you?"

"Why are you doing this?"

"Some gentle persuasion, perhaps," he murmured.

Anger fueled Beth's struggles to escape his hold. He was asking the impossible of her, to reveal something so painful she could hardly think of it, let alone confide in someone else.

She freed her right arm. Planting the palm to his chest, she gave a forceful shove, which didn't move him at all. One of his hands went to the back of her head, drawing her closer.

"No, dammit!"

But Lachlan wasn't listening. His heated gaze was riveted on her shapely mouth. The more she struggled, the tighter he drew her against him, until he was vitally aware of her breasts flattening against his chest. He dipped his head and brushed his mouth across hers. Then, sensing a protest rising up in her, he captured her lips in a masterful kiss.

Warmth suffused Beth. Experiencing a soaring headiness, she unwittingly clutched the sides of his dark shirt. The musky scent of him, the feel of his masculinity surrounding her, and the manner in which his mouth moved slowly over hers, promised to abolish the warring emotions she'd carried for so long.

"You feel sa guid. Sa guid," he rasped against her lips, one of his hands freeing the back of her blouse from the waistline of her skirt. His palm smoothed along the contours of her back, over heated, soft skin. It took him several seconds to comprehend and release the two hooks securing her bra. When he at last succeeded, he caressed the length of her spine, then slowly, seductively, inched the hand over one side of her small waist. Deepening the kiss, he moved his fingers upward to the underpart of her left breast. Her moan encouraged him to go on. The firm swell of the breast became lost within his large hand, the rigid nipple tautly pressed into his palm. His fingers kneaded, caressed, eliciting a deeper moan from her.

Breathing in spurts, he trailed his lips across her cheek to a gentle depression below her ear. Lost in the maddening sensations building rapidly within her, she tilted back her head and exposed the sensitive skin of her graceful neck. His teeth nipped, his lips probed. His hands gripped her hips and flattened her abdomen against the rigid implement of his manhood.

Quivers of desire racked him. Fevered by a need to possess her, he kissed her passionately, one hand at the back of her head, the other at her buttocks, grinding her against him in a futile attempt to relieve the tormenting fires in his groin.

On the verge of losing control, he began to lift her skirt. His palms pressed to the rounded contours of her hips. His thumbs hooked into the waistband of her panties, began to lower the intrusive barrier . . .

Then reality slammed home. Beth's fingers were prying free the buttons of his shirt. Gripping her arms, he hastily jerked her back a step.

Large blue eyes stared dazedly up at him from a flushed face. The lips he'd kissed only moments before were slightly swollen and more inviting than ever.

"Fegs, lass," he breathed unsteadily. "You damn near lost me ma purpose."

"What?"

Running a hand down the front of his shirt, he took two steps back. "How can you trust me ta mak love ta you?"

Confused, and fighting back a whirling sensation

in her head, Beth made a feeble gesture with her hand. "I-I don't understand what's g-going on."

"We damn near made love!"

"I was here, remember?"

"'Tis burned in ma mind."

"Is this a question of morals?"

A mirthless laugh burst from his throat. "Morals, ma eye!"

"Then what the hell is wrong with you? What kind of game are you playing?"

"Temper, lass," he chided, his chest still rising and falling with desire. "My purpose was ta persuade you ta unburden yer woes, no' have ma way wi' you 'fore the proper time an' place."

The cobwebs filling Beth's mind multiplied.

"Proper time and place?"

"I asked you a question 'fore we got lip-locked."

Beth tried to remember what it was. Frustrated, she reached up under the back of her blouse and secured the hooks of her bra, then haphazardly tucked the blouse into the skirt's waistband. She'd known this man for less than twenty-four hours, and yet she'd nearly given in to an impulse to be taken by him, virtually out in the open.

"You're the most maddening . . ." She glared at him through a pained expression. "I'm going back to the house. I'd appreciate it if you'd leave me alone until Carlene returns."

"No' so fast," he said huskily, taking her arm as she tried to pass him to reach the steps of the gazebo. "We were talkin' abou' yer mither."

"That conversation is over."

Lachlan's expressive eyebrows drew down in a frown. "Whan you learn ta trust me, we'll mak love."

A mask of utter incredulity slid over Beth's features. "Is that a promise . . . or a threat?"

Lachlan grimaced. "I'll no' let yer snide tone rattle me."

"I hope you and your ego have a nice day," she clipped, wrenching her arm from his hold. Undaunted this time, she lit across the lawn in a half-run, leaving Lachlan to stare forlornly after her.

"Ah, Beth, yer're no' an easy womon ta know. If no' for ma gift, we'd be strangers always. Tae much you hide in yer heart."

Folding his arms over his chest, he leaned against one of the decorative moldings of the archway. "Tae independent, these modern women." He clicked his tongue in disapproval. "Aye, me an' ma ego. Come along, then. We've a wee visit ta pay auld Aggie."

It was humid and hot within the cottage, but Agnes Ingliss paid it no mind. The repeated clacking of her knitting needles kept her mind preoccupied. As she rocked back and forth in a rocker three generations old, her thin fingers deftly worked the red yarn. A length of scarf lay upon her lap. Come Christmas it would be a gift for her son, Borgie. There was a time when she could have whipped up a scarf in a matter of days, but the stiffness in her hands forced her to plan her projects months in advance now.

A sense of intrusion lifted her head. Her pale blue eyes sharpened, her ears keened. The leathery, wrinkled skin on her arms seemed to twitch.

Compressing her pale lips in a tight line, she cut her gaze to the left. The sight of Lachlan standing by the parlor door, his arms crossed over his chest, his expression guarded, caused a sharp tightening in her chest. Without taking her eyes off him, she dumped the yarn and needles to the floor beside the rocker.

Resentment flared in her eyes as she cranked herself up onto her feet. Her chin lifted defiantly. "How dare you come ta ma home," she charged. "Get ou', you black-hearted beast!"

After a moment of tense silence, Lachlan sauntered farther into the room. He stopped within arm's reach of the old woman, his brooding gaze riveted on her face. "Spare me the endearments," he drawled, lowering his arms to his sides. "I thought perhaps you'd be ill, auld womon. Itherwise, why else wad you fail ta prepare breakfast for Miss Staples, eh?"

"She's *yer* guest. *You* serve her."

A slow, sardonic grin manifested on Lachlan's generous mouth. His eyebrow arched, signaling Agnes he was short on patience. "I mistakenly thought this business settled."

"I've changed ma mind."

Lachlan's expression made light of her defiance,

but a storm brewed within his eyes. "Be a' the house in the morn."

"Or wha'?" she sniffed with disdain. "I'm tae auld ta give a damn, anymair, yer *lordship*. Sa stick yer paughty threats in yer—"

The front door of the house slammed shut. A flicker of uncertainty moved across Agnes' face, then she grew pale. Lifting a trembling hand to rest over her heart, her watery gaze observed the glint of malice in Lachlan's eyes.

She looked beyond him to the living room. "Begone wi' you," she whispered in a plea. "I'll be there ta serve Miss Staples."

"Will you now?" Lachlan crooned.

"Get ou'! I dinna want ma son layin' eyes on you!"

"Mum, where's ma lunch?" boomed a voice. Shortly, a tall man in his early thirties came bounding into the room. "Kelly an' the boys are goin' ta meet me—"

The sight of a stranger standing in the parlor gave the man pause, and a cocky grin quirked on his mouth. "Sarry, Mum. Didna know we had company . . ."

His voice trailed off as he became aware of the stranger's attire. He looked into the man's eyes. How he knew, he didn't understand, but the truth lanced him with unmerciful accuracy. His dark blue eyes appeared enormous in his ashen face as he fell back a step.

"Borgie," Lachlan said, giving the man a mocking nod of greeting. "We meet a' last."

After several attempts to speak, Borgie managed, "Wha' do you want?"

Lachlan searched Agnes' taut expression. "Checkin' in on yer mither." Looking at Borgie, he asked, "Have you a job, mon, or are you still a worthless lump o' flesh?"

"Get ou'!" Agnes shrilled, blue veins mapping her brow and temples. "You canna come inta ma home an' insult ma boy!"

With a smug smile, Lachlan walked up to Borgie and placed a heavy hand on his shoulder. "Yer bastard's a mon, no' a boy, Aggie." Placing his face inches from the terrified man's nose, he grinned off to one side. "Yer're lookin' a wee pale, lad. A pint— " he clipped Borgie in the gut with the back of a hand "— will stiffen yer spine, eh?"

Befuddled, Borgie shook his head, then nodded.

Straightening back, Lachlan cast Agnes a pitying look. "In the morn. It'll do you guid ta wait on someone worth their spit."

The sudsy hot water served to ease the tension in Beth's aching body. Only the throbbing knot at the back of her head remained. Submerged to her chin, her knees poking above the iridescent bubbles, she closed her eyes and tried to ignore the thoughts which had been plaguing her since she'd left the gazebo two hours earlier.

At any time, Carlene and David should return. Then she would have plenty to occupy her mind.

She could shut out Lachlan and the pain his inquisition had prompted.

— *Please.* —

The softly spoken voice in her head caused her to squeeze her eyes shut.

— *Do it for me.* —

"Don't ask me, Ma."

— *The pain, Beth. It never stops.* —

Beth blinked hard, refusing to give in to a threat of tears.

— *How can you ignore my suffering? Damn you!* —

— *Damn you.* —

A burning sensation swelled within her chest. "I c-can't. Don't ask me again."

"Ask wha', lass?"

The deep voice crashed down on her. She nearly sprang up out of the bath, stopping herself when she spied Lachlan leaning against the doorjamb across from her. He held a plate laden with fruits and cheese. Ignoring the crimson in her face, he casually seated himself on the closed lid of the toilet next to her.

"Have you eaten today?"

She blinked at him as if disbelieving he was in the bathroom with her. He popped one of the purple grapes into his mouth and took his time chewing it, his gaze studying her. When he proffered the plate, she shrank back into the bubbles.

"Get out!"

In response to her shrill tone, he placed an isolated finger in his ear and jiggled it. "Ma day for bein' tauld where ta gae," he sighed.

"You can't come in here!"

He looked about him in mock bewilderment. "But I am in here. Have I embarrassed you?" He chuckled when she glared at him. "Guess I have."

"I asked you to stay away from me."

"I must have forgotten," he grinned, and proffered the plate once again. A smile of satisfaction played on his mouth when she churlishly plucked a wedge of sharp cheddar from the plate. "Wha' wad you like for . . ." He frowned. "You Yanks call i' supper, na?"

"If I'm hungry, I'll fix myself something."

"I thought perhaps we cad picnic in one o' the south gardens."

"No thank you."

He released a dry chuckle and placed the plate behind him on the tank. "You plan ta waste the day sulkin', do you?"

"Leave me alone."

"Ah." He pensively scratched the back of his neck. "I wad have thought you'd had yer fill o' bein' alone. Silly me, eh?"

Swallowing the last of the wedge, Beth sliced a hand along the surface of the water. A wave jumped the edge of the tub and landed on Lachlan's lap.

"Nice," he said with a grimace.

"I prefer to bathe in private, thank you!"

"Tell me, Beth," he began, resting his elbows just above his bent knees, "wad you have gone all the way? In the gazebo, I mean."

Beth glared at him, her face dark purple.

"You see, I have a wee problem understandin'

women. Wha' they say, an' wha' they do, is often contradictory."

"Men are simply black and white?"

"Aye."

"You'd better get a shovel."

Her words perplexed him. "Wha' for?"

"To start unloading the shit piling up in here."

Lachlan's jaw dropped. "'Tis na way for a lady— "

"Which you obviously don't consider me, or you wouldn't be sitting there gawking at me!"

For the first time, Beth was awarded the pleasure of seeing Lachlan brought down a notch. Obviously ruffled, he rose to his feet and exited the room. From beyond the door, he called, "I'll be in the kitchen whan yer're done. Kindly bring doon the plate."

Beth sprang up out of the tub. Grabbing a towel from the wooden rack to her left, she carelessly held it against her and took the plate in hand. She ran into the bedroom in time to see him approaching the door to the hall. Before he made it across the threshold, she flung the plate. Fruit and cheese scattered in all directions, but the plate itself caught him between the shoulder blades. With a cry of surprise, he turned and glowered at her.

Her anger plummeted to a feeling of utter vulnerability. Suddenly aware that she was naked but for a towel, in a house alone with a man she knew very little about, she took a hesitant step back.

Lachlan crossed the room, his chest rising and falling with each breath. Never had Beth seen anyone's eyes betray such intensity, seem to possess the ability to see into her soul.

"Feelin' better?" he asked huskily, coming to stand directly in front of her.

"S-somewhat."

"Hmmm. 'Fore you set foot in this house, I was o' the impression you were o' a gentle nature."

Beth lifted her chin in defiance. "I'm a little . . . out of sorts."

"Bitchy, you mean."

"Bitchy. Yes."

"Jet lag."

She nervously moistened her lips with the tip of her tongue. "Possibly."

"Perhaps you sud gae by sea next time."

"There will never *be* a next time."

A shadow fell across Lachlan's face before he sharply turned away and began to gather up the fruit and cheese. Beth watched him warily, her arms tightly folded across the towel section covering her breasts. She remained silent until he had returned everything to the plate, and had placed it on the nightstand beside her bed. This time when he looked at her, there was a disquieting air about him that elicited a chilly feeling along her spine.

"I regret yer're sa unhappy. I'll leave you be."

Beth stood very still for some time after the door had closed behind him. He'd been right about one thing; she'd never known she possessed a temper until she'd arrived in this house.

By the time she dressed in a pair of jeans and a baggy cotton top, she felt drained. Incapable of self-examining her uncharacteristic behavior, she brushed her hair into a ponytail, then stood at the window and peered out across the gardens. After a time, she spied movement down by the nearest trellis display of ivy.

A breath gushed from her nostrils.

So her reunion with Carlene hadn't gone as she'd planned, but it was no excuse for taking out her disappointment on Lachlan. He'd tried his best to entertain her. Anyone else would have turned his back on her.

She exited the front of the house and walked directly to where she'd seen him from the window. But to her dismay, he was nowhere in sight. Which served her right. She had a tendency to fall into his arms at the first signal he was going to kiss her. And yet, whenever he reached out to offer her emotional comfort, she lashed out at him. She'd always considered herself a level-headed woman. Now she was beginning to wonder if she knew herself at all.

A cool breeze swept around her, and she crossed her arms and drew in her shoulders. After inspecting her surroundings for a sign of Lachlan, she sat on the ground and curled her legs close to her.

The ache thrumming at the back of her head reminded her she'd forgotten to take some aspirin. She considered going back inside the house for the pills, but couldn't bring herself to move from this spot.

Not a sound stirred. Above her, white, fluffy clouds were shredding across the azure sky.

Bringing up a knee, she folded her arms atop it

to pillow her head. Deep, fortifying breaths moved in and out of her lungs. Although she could feel the sun on her back, her skin felt unnaturally cold, as did her insides.

Lulled by the serenity of the outdoors, and the fragrances of flowers and evergreens, she closed her eyes. She was almost in sleep's embrace when something lit upon her back. As she lifted her head, a half-smile played along her lips. She drowsily watched Lachlan sit across from her, his legs bent to each side of her, his hands gripping the corners of the blanket he'd placed over her shoulders.

"I was thinkin', girl," he sighed. "I've been tae impatient wi' you."

"I shouldn't have thrown the dish at you."

His smile made her suddenly aware of her own heartbeat.

"I've had worse done ta me."

"Never by me . . . I hope."

A somber mood fell upon Lachlan. "Yer're lookin' pale again."

"I can't help worrying about Carlene and David. You don't think something has happened to them, do you?"

"Na."

"Shouldn't they have been back by now?"

He gave a negligent shrug. "Hard ta say. They're young an' in love."

Drawing up her other knee, she linked her arms about both. "I guess I really don't know her anymore. Eight years is a long time."

"I dinna think she's changed much o'er the years."

"How long have you known her and David?"

"Little mair than a year."

"You've worked for them that long?"

He nodded. "I come wi' the house."

"You do, huh," she chuckled, then sobered. "Why aren't you married?"

Lachlan's eyebrows quirked upward. "I was once."

"What happened?"

"She died."

"I'm sorry."

"It wasna a guid mairriage."

"Why?"

"I was a rash young mon. Mairret her for all the wrong reasons."

"How can there be wrong reasons for loving someone? You did love her, didn't you?"

Lachlan stared deeply into Beth's eyes. "I thought so a' the time. But . . . things happened. For a long time, I was bitter." He adjusted the blanket about her shoulders and inched closer. "I had this notion all women were like her. Heartless. Greedy. Wantin' mair than a mon cad e'er give them.

"A lot o' couples have come an' gone from this house. Then David an' Carlene came along. They're a guid match. He's the quiet, deep sort; she's fire an' air all awhirl."

Beth laughed at his description. "I guess she hasn't changed. She was a hell-raiser in school."

"She loves you, girl," he said softly, the fingers

of one of his hands playing with a curl at her temple. "She talked a' great length abou' you."

"That must have been boring," she murmured, a flush staining her cheeks. "I never understood why she hung around with me. We were so different. She was always the doer; me, the observer."

"Perhaps we see you differently than you see yerself." He grinned. "We know the fire exists."

"What fire?"

"The fire in yer soul."

He was doing it again, Beth realized. Analyzing her. What puzzled her was his ability to reach into her heart of hearts and surface the woman she could be if she let go of her inhibitions.

"Maybe a small flame," she said to fill the silence between them.

"Na." Releasing the blanket, he gestured widely with his hands. "A *blazin'* fire. I've felt i' scorch me. Whan we're kissin'."

Suddenly ill-at-ease, Beth attempted to get to her feet. But Lachlan gripped the corners of the blanket and tugged her forward, onto his lap. His cool lips targeted her mouth. His arms cradling her, he kissed her deeply, but not with the same intensity as when he'd kissed her in the gazebo. Nonetheless, she melted in his arms and wrapped hers about his neck. Her fingers entwined through his thick hair.

"Yer're makin' me crazy, womon," he rasped, looking down into her glazed eyes. "Do you believe in love a' first sight?"

Beth gave a low laugh. "I don't know what I believe anymore."

"You've a lot ta learn."

"Are you volunteering as my teacher?"

With a groan, he moved her off his lap and rose to his feet. Taking her hand, he helped her up, his clasp remaining as she peered up at him expectantly.

"There's an auld sayin' . . ."

He frowned and shifted his weight. "Stop lookin' a' me wi' those dreamy eyes. Fegs! They mak all thought flee ma mind!"

Beth's smile showed her deep dimples to advantage.

"Yer're acquaintin' yerself wi' yer power o'er me, you minx."

"You mean, exercising my female wiles?"

He nodded.

"Is that what I'm doing?" she mused aloud, a mischievous gleam in her eyes. "I'd forgotten what it was like."

"Torture on the target," Lachlan drawled.

Tilting her head to one side, she seductively arched a brow. "A little suffering never hurt anyone."

"Hmmm." His eyes became hooded. A muscle ticked along his powerful jawline as he inhaled through his nostrils. "I think abou' you all the time, Beth," he said seriously, lifting a hand and caressing the underpart of her chin. "But whan we mak love, I want e'erythin' ta be perfect. Na shortcuts. Na doubts lingerin' in the eftermath."

Amid a rush of thrills at his words, Beth anchored

herself to the earth. "Hey. You offered to make supper."

"Aye."

"I'm starving," she laughed, and lit into a run toward the house.

Lachlan watched after her with a bemused expression. "Women," he muttered, then grinned.

His Yank was a delightful ball of fire, but he had to be careful not to extinguish the flame. Although she was not aware of it, the chemistry between them had already constructed the foundation of their bond, built upon the psychic link she had not as yet consciously accepted.

Two steps remained.

He had to win her love completely, which he was confident wouldn't be all that difficult. She was not the kind of woman to allow a man to kiss and pet her unless her heart was guiding her.

However, the last step troubled him.

Unless she learned to open up and trust him, there would always be a wall between them.

And Lachlan Baird had a thing about walls of any kind obstructing him. . . .

Four

The peacocks shrilled the advent of a new dawn. Beth cracked open her eyes and grimaced. The ache in the back of her head was ever-present. It had been gnawing on her nerves for the past twenty-four hours. She'd needed too many aspirin at bedtime to ease the headache enough to allow her to fall to sleep.

Another succession of caterwauls caused a stabbing pain in her temples, and she mutely wished the peacocks skewered above an open fire.

She lay quietly for an indeterminate time, staring sleepily up at the ceiling, waiting for her body to gather up the energy to rise from the bed. Memory of the supper Lachlan had concocted the previous night brought a whimsical smile to her mouth. Eggs Benedict, wedges of cheese, and fried dough slathered in butter and honey. Anything beyond eggs, he'd told her, was out of his league.

A soft laugh caressed her throat. She'd never known anyone like him— probably never would again. He could be the most entertaining companion, or a royal pain in the—

Carlene and David.

Giving in to a wide yawn, Beth groggily sat up. Surely they would return today, or Beth would give serious thought to returning to the States and getting on with her life.

After a long, leisurely bath, she went through the motions of preparing herself for the day. Dressed in a pair of jeans and a baggy sweat shirt to ward off the morning chill of the house, she left her room. The bedroom door across the hall was shut. A smile on her lips, she headed down the hall.

Never had she imagined a house could be so absolutely quiet, so full of silence, and yet the air seem to possess a tangible presence. Trying not to dwell on it, she headed out through the double set of front doors.

Three of the peacocks called out upon seeing her. Leaning against the stone front of the house, Beth watched the birds.

"Early risers, aren't you, fellas?"

The birds leisurely strutted about, pecking at the ground and fluffing up their feathers. Proud and arrogant. Secure in their surroundings. Going about their business, but keeping an eye on her.

One came close to her and boldly looked her over. Its train of feathers rose up and spread into a magnificent fan of colors. Then, as if to put her in her place, it brushed up against her leg and strutted off in the direction of the house.

Placing a hand over her heart, she laughed.

What had Lachlan called one of the birds the other day?

Brau . . . Braussaw.

An admirable name for such a haughty creature. In many ways, the birds reminded her of Lachlan.

A mist lay over the land. Looking to the west, she thought about the tower and wondered what the view of the loch would be like from that vantage point.

"No time like the present to find out," she murmured.

Returning to the house, she went inside and to the second floor. When she arrived at the drapes that concealed the newel staircase, something else caught her attention. The door perpendicular to the drapes was open. Beyond it was a narrow, descending staircase of stone.

A wonderful aroma filled the passageway and titillated Beth's mounting hunger. She inhaled deeply, moaned longingly, then descended until she reached the bottom and passed through an open, narrow arch. Surprise stopped her in her tracks. A few feet across from her, an elderly woman stood bent over the large, black stove. She looked up at Beth with a curiously nonchalant look, then went about placing the rest of the food she'd cooked on a silver tray.

"Good morning."

Beth's soft voice brought the woman's head around in her direction again. The heavily lined face showed impatience, and her pale watery-blue eyes ran a slow, measuring look over Beth's form.

"Abou' time you came doon. You dinna exspect me ta climb the stairs, do you?"

The old woman was about to lift the tray with

her gnarled fingers when Beth rushed forward and took it into her own hands.

"Is this for me?"

The old woman, barely five foot in height, placed her hands upon her hips and scowled up into Beth's face. "Weel, I'm no' here cookin' for ma health now, am I, Missy?"

Beth's expression sobered. She had the strangest compulsion to apologize to the cook— but for what, she didn't know.

"Did Carlene ask you to cook this for me?"

"His Nibs."

Assuming 'His Nibs' was David, Beth glanced over the contents of the tray. Two boiled eggs on toast. Thick slices of fried ham. Two portly sausages. Orange slices. A small bowl of porridge with a dab of butter in its center, and a tiny crystal container holding blackcurrant jam. A silver pot of coffee.

"Meals in the dinin' room, Missy. I'm tae auld ta be fancier'n tha'. Na bedroom service."

Beth managed a smile, although, for the life of her, she couldn't understand the woman's blatant animosity toward her. "Where is the dining room?"

An ancient arm rose up and the woman pointed across the kitchen.

"Thank you. Are you going to join me, Mrs.— "

"Agnes's guid enough."

"I wouldn't mind the company, Agnes."

The old woman's hard eyes bored into Beth's, but then, a sign of compassion softened them and the old woman scrunched up her face.

"Wadna you, now?"

A musical laugh escaped Beth. "Please? I promise not to talk your ears off."

Agnes gave an airy shrug of one shoulder. "Aye. I guess you wad be gettin' a wee jaggie abou' now. Gae on an' eat while i's het. Me an' ma tea'll be along shartly."

The dining room took Beth's breath away. Above an elaborately carved table for ten hung a five-tiered gas chandelier, its globes resembling large, rose-tinted pearls. Long crystal pendants dangled from four of the tiers, sparkling in the morning sunlight that filtered through rose-colored organdy undercurtains on the two massive bay windows.

Placing her tray on the table, she slowly drew out a chair and lowered herself onto it. Although hunger gnawed at her stomach, the room demanded her attention. Oriental tapestries and portraits covered the walls. An enormous sideboard displayed china and crystal, Oriental and Grecian vases, and a pewter collection of various animals and birds. Above the sideboard was a huge collection of Imari plates. Several whatnot shelves displayed jade figurines and handpainted porcelain Japanese figures.

Standing between the bay windows was a Japanese scroll on a tri-legged stand. Off to one side, willowy peacock feathers sprouted up out of a tall urn.

Color. It was so abundant in this house.

Finally, Beth looked down at her food. Silver utensils were neatly wrapped in a linen napkin.

"I must have died and gone to heaven," she sighed, positioning the knife and fork in her hands.

A cold movement of air passed close to her right. Startled by it, Beth glanced in that direction. She was in the process of telling herself it wasn't unusual for an old house to be drafty when something icy caressed her cheek. Resisting a compelling notion to bolt from the chair and run from the room, she shuddered and clenched the utensils tighter. The phenomenal flurry of air shifted at her side, then moved off behind her.

Beth took a deep breath and looked down at her breakfast. Once she forced herself to begin to eat, the delicious meal brought her jitters to an end. She ate as if she hadn't eaten in weeks. Although the repast consisted of foods she was familiar with, the flavor of everything was quite different from the food back home. Blander, but very good. The ham slices were salty, but tender and delicious.

"You've a guid appetite," cackled a voice.

Beth looked up sharply to her right. Seeing the old woman poised, a teapot in her hands, she rose to her feet and drew out a chair to her right.

Agnes gave her a look of surprise before seating herself.

"Have you eaten?"

"Aye. I've a son still a' home ta tend." The aged features scrunched up again. "No' tha' he cadna feed hisself, had he a mind."

Beth nibbled on an orange slice while watching the old woman pour herself a cup of tea.

"Yer no' wha' I exspected, Missy."

"Have you worked here long?"

"All ma life, i' seems," she grumbled. Then she

met Beth's earnest eyes and she smiled, revealing stained teeth. "Been a Ingliss in this cursed house tae long, we have."

"Ingliss?" Beth dabbed at her mouth with the napkin, then placed it on the table. "Is your husband a descendant of Tessa and Robert Ingliss?"

The old woman let the question simmer in her mind while she took several sips of her tea. When she looked up, Beth was startled to see something darkly akin to anguish in the faded blue eyes staring at her.

"Ma boy's faither ne'er mairret me."

"Forgive me. I didn't mean to pry."

Agnes shrugged it off.

"Are you a descendant, then?"

"Aye. I'm one o' the cursed clan. An' how wad you know abou' we Inglisses, eh?"

"A cabbie told me the history of this house."

The old woman remained silent for several long seconds, her attention on the contents of her cup. One gnarled finger absently dipped in and out of the hot liquid. When she looked up again, a pang of unease churned in Beth's abdomen.

There was a strange lambency in the ancient eyes watching her. Beth tried to attribute it to the woman's age, but some deep inner sense told her there was something very odd— almost haunting— about the cook.

"Miss Carlene talked mair o' you than much else. I understand, now. You've a guid soul, but tha'll change if you stay here tae long."

A chill curled up along Beth's spine. She tried to

smile, but her facial muscles were too tight. It didn't help matters when a cold, shriveled hand shot out and clamped about her wrist. All of her willpower was necessary to not pull away from the old woman.

"Has Lannie molested you?"

A comical expression seized Beth's features. "The ghost?"

"Aye."

"I think . . . he-umm . . . looked in on me the first night. All I could see was a . . . a green mist."

"He'll come ta you, as pretty as you are. He's vile."

Beth tried not to appear amused by the old woman's strangeness. "The ghost . . . he's going to come and . . . molest me?"

"Listen ta this auld womon, silly girl. Leave while you can. This house is cursed!" Her voice a hoarse whisper, Agnes went on, "Lannie's the deil, hisself. Get ou' an' dinna look back!"

"Aneuch!"

The deep voice boomed from behind Beth, nearly causing her to jump out of her skin. She jerked around to see Lachlan standing in front of a massive fireplace.

Agnes' hand turned to ice before the coarse skin slipped over Beth's wrist and away. Beth watched as the woman awkwardly rose from her chair and stepped away from the table, her watery gaze riveted on Lachlan.

Inexplicably, Beth's stomach knotted.

"Tis rude ta fill the lassie's head wi' nonsense, you auld corbie!" he scolded Agnes as he crossed the room and came to stand at Beth's left elbow. "Tis late morn. Return ta yer family, an' be mindin' yer ain affairs."

Beth couldn't take her eyes off of Agnes's deathly pale face. There was fear there, but also a hatred so fierce, Beth felt it to the core of her being.

"I've the kitch— "

"It'll wait."

Agnes looked down at Beth with a silent plea. But the laird's piercing dark eyes could be felt on her soul. Releasing a raspy sigh, she patted Beth on the shoulder and shuffled off in the direction of the kitchen.

"You must forgive the meddlin' auld fool, Beth."

Fighting down the threat of nausea, Beth weakly rose to her feet. Every nerve in her body seemed to be on fire. Her face flushed, her eyes as bright as sapphires, she forced back her shoulders in a gesture of defiance. "How *dare* you talk to her like that," she managed, glaring at Lachlan.

A scolding look darkened his countenance. "The bletherin' womon was abou' ta fill yer head wi'— "

"Who are you to interfere with what is said around here?"

A mocking smile touched the man's chiseled mouth. Beth became immediately disoriented. It was as if something had vacuumed her anger and replaced it with an intoxicating consciousness of his virility. Standing so close to him now, she couldn't help but notice how handsome he was— not movie-star handsome, but that rugged, weathered sort of countenance that invades the fantasies of lonely women.

With all the casualness she could muster, she walked away from him, stopped, and turned to look at him again.

A dark green silk shirt, of the same style he'd worn yesterday, hung loosely on his shoulders, the full, poufy sleeves only partially hiding the muscular contours of his arms. The shirt remained unbuttoned nearly where it was tucked into the waistband of his dark, snug pants, and he was again wearing the black knee-high boots. Her gaze lingered on his exposed chest, on the patch of dark, curly hair revealed in the gap exposed by the shirt Lachlan wore so well.

An uncomfortable warmth began in the soles of her feet and rapidly spread upward.

No man had ever affected her like this. But then, she'd never encountered anyone like Lachlan; bold, proud, arrogant as hell. It was as if he possessed the ability to reach into her mind and challenge her to resist him.

"Are you through lookin' me o'er?" He laughed low at her chagrin and took a step in her direction. "Aye, there are the wee, stockish Scotsmen—" He leaned to and flashed bright white teeth in a grin. "—then there's me, eh? If I say sa maself, I'm a strappin' mon. Yer're no' the first womon ta get a flush in her cheeks a' the sight o' me, darlin'."

His boastfulness delivered Beth from her stupor. "You conceited, arrogant pup."

"Pup, am I?" Laughing, he folded his arms

against his chest. "Am I ta believe you dinna find me pleasin' ta the eye? Ah, Beth darlin', yer eyes tell far mair than yer tongue. Yer're as smitten wi' me, as I be wi' you. Difference is, I'm no' afraid ta admit I'm attracted ta you."

Beth inwardly cursed the tell-tale blush in her cheeks. It was bad enough she did find him attractive, but she was damned chagrined to know that he was aware of her thoughts, almost as if he were a mind reader. But if he was truly that, he would have known the fantasy playing through her mind before she'd fallen asleep last night, and *he* would be the one blushing.

On second thought, she was sure the insufferable man had never blushed once in his life!

The door to the kitchen opened and Agnes waddled in on her thin, bowed legs. Without looking at Beth and Lachlan, she walked directly to the table and began to gather up the tray.

"I tauld you 'ta leave i', womon," Lachlan said in a threatening tone.

Rage, a feeling vile and foreign to Beth, swamped her. "You're *not* her employer!"

"It's all right, Missy," Agnes said submissively, heading toward the kitchen with the tray clutched in trembling hands.

"No, it *isn't* all right!" Beth cried.

Agnes stopped and looked at the couple. "She'll no' tak yer guff," she huffed, a look of satisfaction directed at the laird.

Lachlan's brooding eyes swerved to deal Agnes a

warning look, and before she could stop it, the old
woman released a snort.

"I'll be goin' home as soon as the dishes be done.
I dinna want a clarty kitchen greetin' me tomorrow."

Beth watched Lachlan with deepening resentment. If she didn't know better, she would swear *he*
was the master of Kist House. The animosity between the cook and groundskeeper almost held substance, and it disturbed her, especially since she
seemed so receptive to its presence.

"I dinna give a hang for yer kitchen, clarty or
no'! I'll no' be wastin' ma valuable energy arguin'
wi' you!"

"Damn yer energy, and *damn* you ta hell, you
deil!"

Lachlan stiffened. His expression hardened with
lethal anger even as he silkily responded, "Deil, am
I?" He pointed to Agnes. "An' where be tha' lazy,
greetin' teenie son o' yers, eh? Yer years have been
mair'n fulfilled here, womon. Tell Borgie his time
has come. I'll see him the morn's morn, lest he be
wantin' a visit by none ither than maself!"

"I'll tell him!" Agnes hissed. She started again
for the kitchen. "No' tha' it'll do me a shillin' o'
guid!"

As the kitchen door closed behind the old
woman, Beth released a pent breath. She narrowed
her eyes on Lachlan, her mind working on how to
deliver him a sound scolding, when a sharp pain
knifed the base of her skull. A feeble whimper
spilled past her lips. Cupping her hands over the

back of her neck, she sank her teeth into her lower lip and tried to ride the pain past a point of tolerance. But it only intensified, and as she closed her eyes against it, the room began to spin. Her legs were weakening, threatening to buckle. Numbness was spreading swiftly through her left arm.

Panic clutched her heart. She began to sway. Then, just as she was about to give in to the encroaching blackness, something solid scooped her up. A low, deeply concerned voice whispered above her, "Steady, lass. I've got you."

Through slitted eyes, Beth watched Lachlan carry her into the parlor and deposited her on one of the sofas, then seat himself alongside her. She wanted to tell him to go away, but the crushing pain on the fragile bones in her neck made it impossible. She'd been having these headaches for nearly five months now, but never had they been so severe, or come on so quickly without warning.

"Sit quiet. I'll be back wi' a cauld claeth for yer brow."

The instant he left the room, fear solidified within her chest and spread throughout her system. The pain completely encompassed her head. Her eyes were open, but she couldn't see anything beyond a glare of brilliant light in front of her. Her ears were full to bursting with the sound of her racing heartbeat and the gravelly sound of her lungs straining to breathe. Tears streamed from the corners of her eyes.

"Here you go," Lachlan said, sitting beside her. His soothing words were accompanied by the blessed relief of a cold wet cloth being gently pressed across her eyes and brow. She tried to un-clench her hands, but could not get beyond the fear the pain conjured up in her imagination.

Slipping his cool fingers to the back of her neck, he began to tenderly massage the tension knotting it. "Try to relax."

Beth's attempt to speak came out as a hoarse croak.

"I know i' hurts like hell, love."

Pulling the cloth away, she managed, "Piece of cake." She blinked hard in an attempt to dispel the haze in front of her. She wanted to see his face. He sounded genuinely concerned for her, but with Lachlan Beth found it hard to separate his true feel-ings from his teasing.

Lachlan sighed deeply before angling his head to kiss her lips. He meant it to be a tentative kiss, but at the instant he would have drawn away, he experienced an urgency to taste her more com-pletely than he had the previous night. One hand framing the side of her face, he ignored her slight shiver and fully captured her mouth. She didn't resist his playful plundering of the contours of her lips, his nipping her lower lip with his teeth, his mouth forcing her lips to part. But he did notice a certain hesitancy on her part to let him fondle her tongue with his own, so he withdrew and satisfied himself with the chaste kisses with which she seemed more comfortable.

Then, threading through the desire he felt, came the realization of Beth's lessening pain. He smiled, his thumbs massaging her temples while he kissed her slowly and languorously. It was a mental struggle, but he managed to retain his psychic bond with her to monitor her condition. That had to be his first priority, although he desperately wanted to lose himself within her.

Beth felt warm and secure— surprisingly secure, in spite of the fact that a man who was still a stranger to her was kissing her in the most incredible way. She didn't feel threatened. She wasn't afraid of him at all. The migraine had evaporated to little more than a memory. All that remained was an aftermath of languidness, a familiar numbness now in the back of her head and neck.

She wanted to protest when he stopped kissing her, but she didn't. Before she could respond to the undeniable earnestness his dark eyes betrayed, the sound of a vehicle rolling away over the gravel in the front yard brought back the ugly scene which had transpired in the dining room.

Agnes had gone home. Disappointment with Lachlan's darker side lodged in Beth's heart.

"Forgive me," he murmured. Sitting back, he lifted a troubled gaze to the portrait across the room. "I sud no' have caused a scene like tha'."

"It's a side of you I don't particularly like."

Although her words were not spoken unkindly, Lachlan looked at her as though she had struck him. "I get crazy whan an Ingliss is around."

"She's an old woman— "

"An auld *fool.*"

Lachlan regretted his words the instant Beth

winced. She had a good heart, this woman. "There's so much you dinna understand," he murmured, absently rubbing the back of his neck. He looked again at the painting of Beth, and a wistful smile played along his mouth. "There are some who believe an artist can capture a bit o' his subject's soul on canvas. Carlene certainly did, dinna you think?"

When Lachlan's questioning gaze swung to her, Beth cast the painting a cursory look. "Carlene's very talented, but the woman depicted there isn't me."

Lachlan released a low laugh. Bracing his lower back against the curved, cherry wood arm, he casually rested a booted ankle atop the opposite knee, and laid his left arm along the back of the sofa. "Tis e'ery bit you— a' least the womon you try ta hide from strangers. Carlene's keen eye saw through yer shyness. She freed yer spirit on tha' canvas. Tha' part o' you, I know as weel as I know maself."

Unease returned to Beth. She looked away, feeling as though Lachlan's eyes were boring into her soul. "That's ridiculous."

"Is i', love?" he asked softly. "You've a heart as gentle as a spring's morn, a heart as givin' as none ither I've e'er encountered. Tis wha' I first perceived whan I saw the portrait."

Wide-eyed, she looked at him as though he had lost his mind.

"Have you asked yerself why you fear me no' as a mon?"

Beth made a move to leave the sofa, but Lachlan reached out and took a restraining hold on her wrist. She looked down at his hand. His touch was cool— almost cold.

Unsettling.

"My stomach's queasy."

Releasing her, Lachlan grimaced. "Ah, fegs, wad you really toss oop yer insides on such a fine sofa?"

In spite of herself, Beth chuckled. Her stomach *was* queasy, but she was feeling much better. "I'll do my best not to." Unintentionally, her gaze locked with his own. "You're a strange man."

"Aye, tha' I am. Do you believe in the soul, Beth?"

"Yes." She shot the painting a disparaging look. "But not that any part of it was captured on that canvas."

"How wad you explain then, ma knowin' wha' lies wi'in yer heart o' hearts?"

"You're a mindreader," she quipped with a nervous laugh.

"Are *you?*"

"Certainly not," she laughed again.

"Then how is i' you knew me 'fore you e'er set foot in this house?"

Beth shot up from the sofa and, before Lachlan could make a move to stop her, went to stand beneath the portrait. She faced him, trembling, pale, but with a flash of denial in her bright eyes. "I don't appreciate you trying to rattle me with this hocus-pocus nonsense."

Rising to his feet, he hooked his thumbs into the waistband of his trousers. "I dinna have all the answers, but we have been connected since I first laid eyes on yer portrait."

"Stop it! You're obsessed with the damn thing!"

"You've been aware o' the connection," he solemnly charged, his eyes more penetrating than usual. "I sensed i' the moment you entered the house."

Terrified, Beth lunged for the door to her left. Her hands gripped the knob, twisted and jerked, but the door would not budge. With a cry of frustration, she slapped an open palm against the wood, then gave a desperate turn on the knob once again.

A gasp of alarm burst from her when she became aware of Lachlan coming up behind her. She spun around and pressed her back to the door as his palms flattened to the recessed panels on each side of her shoulders, blocking any chance of her escaping him. Her hands braced at his chest, she looked up at him through a mist of tears.

"Yer're no' threatened by *me*," he rasped. "Only yer ignorance o' wha' is true between us."

"Leave me alone!"

Despite her effort to push him away, he lowered his head and captured her lips. Beth wanted to scream out her anger at him for having the physical strength to overpower her. Her clenched fists were trapped between their bodies as his arms masterfully embraced her. His kiss deepened, threatening to overpower her will, as well. Liquid warmth unexpectedly coursed through her. At once, the fight went out of her. In place of her fears was an ache within her, but one of absolute bliss. The rightness of being in his arms, of his fingers in her hair, of the slow, seductive movements of his mouth against hers, was incontestable.

Lachlan ended the kiss, but brushed a cheek against Beth's before lifting his head and staring into her glazed eyes. "You an' I share the ability ta experience one anither's emotions. Tis wha' you reacted ta in the dinin' room."

"No— "

"I permitted ma rage wi' the Ingliss ta spill o'er on you. You know tis true, Beth. Since yer arrival, twas no' the first time you felt an emotion no' yer ain."

Bewildered, Beth peered into the enigmatic depths of his eyes. "Lachlan, please— "

He gave an adamant shake of his head. "Listen, girl." Resting his hands on her shoulders, he absently caressed her earlobes with his thumbs. "The night o' yer mither's funeral, you were sittin' a' the window, starin' ou' inta the darkness o' yer back yard. Remember? Remember weepin', Beth? Remember the pain squeezin' yer heart as you thought abou' the bed o' flowers you'd planted, tha' yer mither wad no' see?"

The color drained from Beth's face. "How could you know about that?" she gasped, making a futile attempt to move away from him. But Lachlan's hands moved to her upper arms, keeping her rooted in place.

"In a way I canna explain, I was there wi' you. Yer despair was so great, darlin', i' damn near broke ma heart. I made some inane remark abou' life bein' na bed o' roses. It made you smile. Remember?"

Beth did remember, and it frightened her more than she could ever admit. "You're saying you're some kind of psychic?"

"I'm somethin', all right. I'll grant you tha'."

Planting a brief kiss on her lips, he straightened back with a pained expression. "I know wha's been eatin' you oop. Aye, I've known all along, but tis *you* who needs ta say i' aloud."

Beth rapidly shook her head. "I don't know what you're talking about."

"Yer mither— "

"Shut up! Let her rest in peace!"

"She is. Tis *you* I'm worried abou', girl."

Tears streamed down Beth's face as she struck his chest with an open palm. "I *hate* it when you do this to me!"

"Tis past time ta set yer spirit free! Dammit, Beth, yer're sufferin' needlessly!"

"You're a cruel man," she accused, weeping hard. "Leave me alone, damn you!"

Lachlan's features twisted with inner pain. "Ma heart was stone till i' touched yers. Damn me, Beth? You haud e'ery fiber o' ma bein' in yer wee palm."

Numb, thoughts swirling around inside her head, Beth stepped away from Lachlan, not even aware that he had finally released her.

"I need time to' think," she choked, turning toward the door.

"Abou' us?" he asked sadly. "In tha', I have na doubts. As for yer conscience . . . I know the con-

sequences o' harborin' somethin' dark an' fes-
terin'."

Silence stretched between them for a time. Beth
stared at the door, while Lachlan's despondent gaze
remained fixed on the back of her head.

"You push too hard," she said, her voice breaking
with emotion. "I don't know you well enough to
bare my soul to you. I don't know if I want to know
you at all."

Lachlan looked upward, a mist of tears in his
eyes. "If yer're tha' determined ta guard yer privity,
there's nocht I can do ta help you."

"I never asked for your help."

"Tak solace in this, darlin': if i' was yer intention
ta knock me doon a few pegs, you've succeeded. I'll
no' intrude again unless I'm asked."

His promise should have awarded Beth a modicum of satisfaction, but regret seared her heart. She
looked up, expecting to see him standing behind
her. Cold shivers moved along the skin of her arms
when her darting gaze could find no sight of him
in the parlor.

Looking about the room once again, she tried not
to dwell on the weighty, oppressive stillness closing
in around her. But again it struck her how utterly
alone she was, how vulnerable her position was in
this strange land.

Tension curled its fibers across the back of her
neck and skull. Without thought, she reached out
for the brass knob and gave it a turn. The door
opened easily. For a moment, she stood frozen. The
front hall stretched out before her, its silent emp-

tiness bringing an almost unbearable tightness into her throat.

Then she noticed that the sliding wooden doors nearest the front exit were open.

The room beyond proved to be a library, its walls lined with dark-stained bookshelves. The furnishings were sparse in comparison to the other rooms in the house: An overstuffed sofa and two matching chairs with red plaid upholstery. A coffee table of cherry wood. Two round end tables. An enormous braided rug on the floor, extending to a red-brick fireplace with a red-and-black-veined marble mantelpiece.

Entering the room, Beth glanced halfheartedly over the numerous titles on the bookshelves. Several minutes later, bold red lettering on a large volume caught her interest. Plucking the book from the shelf, she glanced at its colorful jacket.

" 'The Lore of Scotland.' Ghosts and folklore. Way to go, Beth. As if you're not spooked enough."

But at least it would take her mind off Lachlan.

Curling up on the sofa with the book, she drew across her legs a colorful afghan that was draped on the back of the sofa. Then she began to scan through the pages of print and black-and-white sketches in the book.

As the morning waned, her headache worsened. The pain was not like the recurring migraines she'd usually had, but it was enough to make her want to sleep it away. Plumping one of the elaborately embroidered pillows beneath where her head would lie, she curled up on her side. She placed the heavy book on the floor by the sofa, then folded her arms against her chest. Within seconds, she was fast asleep.

She dreamed of Carlene, standing within a greenish fog, her arms held out to Beth. "Hurry," she implored, urging Beth to run toward her, but no matter how hard she tried to breach the distance, Beth could not reach her. "Beth, I'm running out of time. You must . . . *hurry!* Lachlan's watching. *Watching. . . .*"

When Beth woke up nearly four hours later, she was exhausted. Her bent legs were cramped. Ignoring her lightheadedness, she sat up and ran her hands down her face. A dull ache thrummed at the back of her neck.

"Some vacation," she grumbled, then worked her mouth to relieve its dryness.

She stared groggily into a well-stoked fire across from her. It was several seconds before it dawned on her that the hearth had been cold prior to her nap. The wrought iron stand next to it was missing several logs.

A ragged breath spilled past her lips when she looked down and saw that the book was not where she had left it. Her movements slow and shaky, she rose to her feet and went to the shelf where she'd obtained the volume. There it sat, snugly in place, making her question whether she had actually taken it down at all. She reached out, but stopped herself from touching the book.

"Get a grip on yourself," she said, striving to cast off the gloom of her thoughts.

Beth left the room and closed the doors. A staccato sound of heavy rainfall could be heard upon the glass roof panes of the greenhouse beyond the front door. Massaging the back of her neck, she headed in the direction of the staircase. She was about to ascend when an unfamiliar, grating bell detonated, echoing discordantly in the hall. Wincing with the pain the sound magnified in her head, she looked bewilderedly about her.

Again the bell called for her attention.

"The door," she muttered, rapidly walking to the end of the hall. She opened the door on the right to find a man standing on the top step of the greenhouse.

"Good afternoon," he greeted, running a hand over his dripping dark hair. He eyed Beth through rain-speckled, horn-rimmed glasses. "I wasn't expecting anyone to be here," he added in his cultured English accent.

To Beth's chagrin, he squeezed past her and entered the hall, where he delighted in having a look at the decor.

"Marvelous," he beamed, inspecting the tiles on the fireplace.

Beth gave herself a mental shake and finally released the doorknob. For a moment there, she'd thought he might be David, but it soon became obvious that this man had never seen the inside of Baird House.

"I must say, I wasn't expecting anything quite so elegant." He reached for the door to the parlor. "I'll just show myself around— "

"Wait a minute," Beth said breathlessly, walking up to him. Of average build and height, a tan raincoat belted about his middle, he turned a smile on her, which didn't waver when she peevishly asked, "Who are you?"

"I do beg your pardon." With a low laugh, he briefly shook Beth's limp hand. "Stephan Miles. I've been checking into this property. I was led to believe the house was vacant. Pleasant surprise finding you here."

"Really," she said dryly. "Despite what you were led to believe, Mr. Miles— "

"Stephan."

"—this house is definitely occupied."

"Are you the owner?"

"No. I'm visiting."

Stephan Miles stepped past Beth and stood at the bottom of the staircase, looking up. "I would love to see the rest of the house." He flashed Beth a toothy smile over his shoulder. "Have you time— "

"I must ask you to leave."

Turning to face her, he slipped his hands into the pockets of his raincoat. "I would like a word with the owners, if it's not inconvenient." He reached into the front of the raincoat and produced a small, white card. After passing it to Beth, the hand went back into the pocket.

"I'm prepared to make a sizable offer for this estate."

Beth looked up from the palmed card and leveled an irritated look at the man. "The owners are out of town."

"I've come a long way . . ." His words drifted off. A crooked grin twitched at one corner of his mouth. "Are you alone?"

Beth stiffened as a red warning light went off in her brain. "No, I'm not. There's a burly ground-skeeper about. I've been led to believe he fertilizes the gardens with the body parts of trespassers."

A short burst of laughter, incongruent of the man's tailored appearance, knotted Beth's stomach. "Dear lady, I'm *interested* in the estate."

"Then I suggest you come back at another time," she said coolly.

A moment passed in silence. Then he turned, stepped up onto the first step of the staircase, and gripped the ornate banister. "When do you expect them to return?" he asked, not looking at her.

"Any time. I want you to leave, Mr. Miles."

Facing her, he absently smoothed a hand along the mahogany rail. "You're American."

Beth heatedly headed for the front door. The sound of a gasp gave her pause. Looking at the intrusive stranger, she saw that he was frozen on the step, his eyes wide with something akin to consternation. She returned to her former position, a frown questioning his odd behavior. His face went deathly pale. His jaw slackened. Beth was about to ask him what was wrong when she noticed his wet hair was moving, as if he were standing in a strong draft. But the coat remained still, and she could not detect anything, although she was standing reasonably close to him.

"Mr. Miles?"

Woodenly, almost in slow motion, his hands went to the front of his raincoat. It took Beth a moment to realize he was cupping his testicles through the layers of clothing. Agony contorted his features. His mouth opened wider in an unfulfilled attempt to cry out.

Beth took a step back as she thought she glimpsed a faint green mist escape the man's ears. The mist swirled about his head, then faded from sight, leaving Beth to wonder if she'd seen it at all.

Stephan Miles jerkily left the step and headed down the hall. Beth watched him close the door behind him, and waited several seconds longer before releasing a pent breath.

Thunder roared ominously above the house. The rain came down harder, the sound filling the hall almost deafeningly. Beth happened to glance down at her leveled palm. A stab of shock impaled her, for the man's card was no longer in her grasp. After a fleeting inspection of the floor around her feet, she wearily started up the stairs.

Two doors standing ajar in the secondary hall caught her attention.

Although her headache steadily worsened, something compelled her to investigate.

The first room proved to be a sitting room, its plain furnishings suggesting it was once the servants' area to relax. The second, larger room was a well-stocked bar, with a counter, stools, and three tables with four chairs each. A high-backed settee was against the right wall, above which hung a painting depicting an open room with men gathered by a blazing hearth, mugs of ale in their hands, and a similar settee several feet away.

She turned her attention back to the bar counter. Beside an opened bottle of Scotch was a short, thick tumbler. Lifting it, she dipped an isolated finger to the bottom.

It was moist.

A droll grin twisted her mouth. "So, Lachlan, you *are* playing mind games." A low laugh rattled in her throat. "Unless you expect me to believe old Lannie enjoys a swig of Scotch, now and then."

Placing the tumbler down, she left the room. A stroll around the grounds would shake the rest of the cobwebs from her head, if only the rain would stop. At least she was a little wiser. Her jitters had played her right into Lachlan's hands.

The next time she came across him, she would know better than to let his teasing manner get to her.

Five

Echoing midnight chimes from somewhere in the house told Beth her birthday was upon her. In four hours and twenty-two minutes, she would officially be thirty years old. As the last mournful dong of the clock sounded, she continued to brush her hair in front of the vanity mirror. The low gas lighting in the room lent soft shadows to the contours of her features, appreciably camouflaging the signs of fatigue she'd noticed earlier in the day.

More than twenty-four hours had passed since her discovery of the library, a time during which her sense of humor had been sorely tested. To while away time, she had rearranged the cupboards in the kitchen, and reorganized two of the linen closets on the third floor. It wasn't until later in the day, when she'd gone to the kitchen to make herself a cup of tea, that she'd realized someone had put everything back in the old order. To her further disbelief, the linen closets were exactly as they had been.

To the best of her knowledge, she'd been alone in the house since Agnes' quick departure after serving breakfast.

All in all, Beth was getting pretty fed up with the isolation. She had expected— and hoped— to see Lachlan. She knew he had to be around. *Someone* was undoing her deeds.

Placing her hairbrush down, she rose from the bench and padded across the floor to the gas lamp. A twist of the key cut off the flame, plunging the room into total darkness.

In Kennewick, Washington, there were always street and yard lights to take the edge off the night.

Not here.

Such darkness.

Such encompassing, dark . . . *darkness.*

She was walking toward the bed when two things stopped her; an unexpected, almost overwhelming sense of despair, and notice of a thin strip of light beneath her door.

Lachlan.

Beth was positive she had turned off the hall lights before she'd come into her room an hour earlier.

Last night, she had lain awake for hours, hoping to hear him go to his room. Although she was sure he was the one playing the pranks on her, she would have liked to have known another living creature was in the house besides herself. If he had returned and left again last night, she wasn't aware of it.

With a hand over her thumping heart, she opened her bedroom door. Two of the lights had been turned on in the hall. And there was a light beneath Lachlan's door. Forgetting the fact she was wearing a thigh-length nightgown, she tiptoed across the hall and placed an ear to his door. The only sound she could discern was that of a crackling fire.

Sinking her teeth lightly into her lower lip, Beth turned the knob and eased the door open. She boldly pushed it open a little more— then again a little more until she was able to squeeze into the room.

A thousand objects vied for her immediate attention. The huge, four-poster master bed carved from walnut. The masculine furniture and heavy, royal blue drapes on the far windows. The sword arrangements on the walls. The paintings. The photographs.

Her gaze swept over the polished, high wainscoting, then the canvas ceiling divided by wood moldings.

Stepping further into the room, she finally focused her attention on the man standing in front of a white-marble fireplace. His hands gripped the mantelpiece. His brow was pressed to its cool surface. He still wore dark trousers, but his feet and broad back and arms were bare. His hair was tied back at the nape of his neck with a dark piece of leather.

Beth's hand remained between her breasts as she watched Lachlan. The despair within her heart swelled, and for a moment, she couldn't help but wonder if in fact she *was* somehow 'connected' to him. The slump of his shoulders suggested he was distraught. How could she continue to scoff at the concept when she was reasonably sure that what she was feeling at the moment did not spring from within herself?

And it struck her that her own loneliness the past years in no way equalled this man's. Despite his merry airs, she was vitally aware of his desperate need for companionship.

Her feet soundless upon the thick, Persian rug, Beth took several steps in his direction, stopping only when she inadvertently looked up at a portrait hanging above the fireplace. She stared in wonderment at the face in the painting. Larger than life, it could have been Lachlan who had sat for the artist. The likeness was so startling, there was no question in her mind that Lachlan had to be related to the Baird clan. Perhaps a direct descendant of that unfortunate man whose dreams were cut short by a knife thrust into his heart. It was little wonder Lachlan loved the house. It was a part of his history.

But how had he come to be a mere employee within the grand walls?

Her heart skipped a beat when she saw Lachlan's head lift. Although she couldn't see his face, she could well imagine his expression as he searched the face of the man in the portrait.

Taking care of her mother had made Beth empathize with anyone suffering. She didn't know a thing about the man across from her— except that he could be an infuriating tease at times, could certainly kiss, and had shown her kindness whenever her need for comforting had arisen.

Rude, crude, and charming. All wrapped up neatly in this man she'd met only three days ago.

And yet, in her heart, she felt as if she had known him all her life.

"Lachlan?

He straightened sharply. Beth couldn't help but notice how taut his back and shoulders became, and she wondered if she hadn't made a grave mistake in intruding where she wasn't wanted.

The light, awarded by two gas fixtures on each side of the portrait, flickered.

Wresting her concentration free of the mesmerizing globed flames, she said by way of apology, "I'm sorry I disturbed you."

But she didn't move to leave. Lachlan turned slowly to face her, his chest heaving with every breath he took. His arms, held slightly out from his powerful build, supported clenched fists.

His gaze fixed on the hand Beth held over her heart. Reflexively, she lowered her arm. Then she looked up at the portrait again.

"You bear a striking resemblance to him," she said nervously.

"You dinna belong in here."

"Is something wrong?"

A moment passed in tense silence. A fey fluctuating sensation played around Beth's heart. Although part of her mind tried to reject the notion, gut instinct told her what she was experiencing was Lachlan's attempt to lighten his mood.

"You sud no' be here," he said finally, a quaver in his tone slipping past his control.

"I'm sorry."

Lachlan forced his stiff fingers to uncurl. What

had she to be sorry about? he wondered. *He* was the reason she had been brought to Baird House. *He* was the one who planned to keep her everlasting.

Never would she live the life of her dreams.

He'd waited too long for a fitting bride to bless his house.

Beth couldn't imagine what was going through Lachlan's mind, not when his features went through a gamut of expressions within a matter of seconds. She was a little afraid of the intensity in his dark eyes until it slowly began to register in her mind that he was looking her over in a way she hadn't experienced since her college days.

"You're still upset with me."

After a moment, he gave a forlorn shake of his head.

"I-I know you were only trying to help me."

"You must help yerself, lass."

Unbidden, tears sprang to her eyes. "I loved my mother."

He nodded.

"She-umm . . . changed during her illness."

"Aye. Tis normal."

Beth struggled with indecision. Deep in her heart, she knew she had to let go of the guilt. But it was so hard. As if to say the words aloud was to destroy the image of the woman she needed to cling to.

"Gae ta yer bed, Beth. Tis late."

Breathing heavily, she moistened her dry lips with the tip of her tongue. "You said you knew."

"Do *you*? Or have you buried i' tae deep?"

"Her suffering was constant. There was nothing

the doctors could do. Nothing . . . nothing offered her the slightest relief."

The tears came faster. "I never doubted her love for me. You have to understand that."

"I do."

"She would never have—" Her voiced cracked, but she forced herself to go on. "—begged me . . . unless she were desperate. Desperate to . . . end the suffering. It . . . it affected her mind— *Oh God!* I can't do this!"

Lachlan's chest filled with pain in sympathy for her, but he could not let it show. "Then stop."

Trembling, Beth struggled to end the war within herself. "Three times she suffered massive coronaries, and three times they brought her back. She w-wanted to d-die. Day after day . . ."

"Wha' happened day efter day?"

"Day . . . after . . . day . . . every time I went near her . . ."

"Gae on, darlin'."

A fey calm befell her. Staring off into space blinking in a mechanical manner, she continued evenly, "She begged me to help her to die. To hold a pillow over her face. End her suffering."

"You cadna bring yerself ta do i'."

Beth slowly shook her head. "I wanted to. There were times when her weeping nearly drove me insane. It invaded my dreams . . . everything. So consuming. I should have loved her enough to do as she asked."

Coming to stand a short distance from her, Lachlan clasped his hands behind his back. "The eve 'fore she passed on, she said some hurtful things ta you."

Beth's eyes looked up into his handsome face. "How could you know?" Not expecting him to reply, she went on, "She said she hated my weakness. Accused me of being heartless. Her fingers . . . so cold, and surprisingly strong, gripped my wrist. She knew she was hurting me. The look in her eyes . . . She hated me, Lachlan. When I woke up the next morning and found her . . . dead . . . I was so relieved, so *grateful* it was over! Not for *her!* For *me!*"

Her gaze searched his face for a sign of his disgust, but his expression was guarded, even his eyes not betraying his thoughts.

"Say something," she choked.

Something awakened in his eyes. Smoldering. Boring into her brain. Beth gulped and backed away two paces. He'd said he'd known her secret, but of course he couldn't have. Now he was repulsed by the woman she'd exposed. That side of herself *she* had trouble accepting.

"I love you, girl."

His words stunned her. Straining to look deeper into his eyes, she brought up a hand to the base of her throat.

"Put yer mither ta rest in yer heart, an' give yerself ta me."

Beth hesitated. Now she knew the intensity was in fact simmering passion. He wanted her, and that frightened and thrilled her. She hardly knew the man, yet her body tingled at the mere thought of his hands caressing her, of his mouth mastering her, taking her to those endless horizons written of in books.

But he was a stranger—

Her heart raced wildly.

The trepidation in her mind did not offset the strangling longing and desire she felt at that moment.

Her fingers kneaded the cotton skirt of her short nightgown. She wished she were wearing silk. Something soft and clingy and sensuous. She wished she was beautiful, not merely benefited by a chemistry that seemed to attract the man.

She'd never considered a love affair. Nor a fling. She'd always been too shy, too insecure to see herself as anything more than slightly attractive, a woman with good skin and a fair build, a woman not unlike the hordes that searched endlessly for the man of their dreams.

If she gave into her feelings tonight, allowed the raw desire within her to surface, what would the morning bring?

How could she face Carlene and David?

What would they think of her, throwing caution to the wind to satisfy a long-overdue itch to know womanhood?

No man had ever made her squirm with a mere look, nor made her skin feel afire at a mere touch.

And he'd freed her. It was as if an enormous weight had been lifted off her shoulders. The guilt no longer hovered at the periphery of her mind. She was free. Free to love. To live . . .

If she abandoned this chance—

Lachlan's impatience broke her spell of indecision. To Beth, he appeared to be but a blur as he rushed toward her. Before she could utter a single word, she was within his arms, her mouth plundered by his own. The kiss was frightening, but so torrid as to seize her sexuality and wash ashore her fears. His hands moved over her back and buttocks, slipped beneath her nightgown, and kneaded the rounded firmness of her backside.

Wrenching his lips away, he moaned by her ear, "Tis so long since these hands have touched such hurdies." To explain his meaning, his hands smoothed over the contours of her buttocks and hips. "I've waited so long for you. I canna wait na mair, Beth. I've got ta feel maself inside you! Can the wooin' come later whan ma brain is no' sa afire wi' need o' you?"

Breathless, her head swimming, Beth looked up into his wild eyes and nodded. With a moan of joy, Lachlan swept her up into his arms and carried her to the bed, where he gently laid her down. But his hands were not so gentle as he parted her legs and knelt between them, then sat back on his heels. His fiery gaze moved over every part of her while the back of his fingers caressed her inner thighs, maddeningly sensitizing her skin.

"I have a serious question ta ask you, girl."

His chest rapidly rising and falling, he let a few seconds pass before asking, "Will you respect me in the morn?"

Beth's rapturous expression cracked with a smile.

She was nervous and shy, but she had never wanted anything as much as she wanted this man.

Lachlan sobered as his gaze settled on Beth's concealed breasts. His hands trembling, he began to lift the gown up and up, over her full breasts, and with her help, over her head. Tossing the gown aside, he leaned to, his weight supported on his forearms to each side of her shoulders. He kissed her, at first tenderly, then more demandingly until he could feel her arch and squirm beneath him. He cupped one of her breasts in a hand, trailed kisses down her face and neck, and made his way to the erect nipple within his hold.

His lips encompassed the rigid nub and gently sucked. She moaned. When the coarse texture of his tongue circled and lapped at the peak, she moaned again.

His kisses moved down her ribs and across the flat planes of her abdomen. With little effort, Lachlan ripped the sides of her panties and tossed the material away. He straightened up on his knees and, staring heatedly into Beth's passion-filled eyes, began to strip out of his pants. His movements were deliberately slow, controlled, to build her anticipation. It was upon him to initiate her into the wonders of lovemaking, although it had been the key that had forsaken his hopes and dreams many years ago. He was determined her first experience would further bond her to him. Patience and gentleness. He had counseled himself on these qualities during the agonizingly long months he'd waited for her.

Beth watched him, marveling in the majesty of

his perfect body. At first glimpse of his arousal, she started to look away, but some inner instinct prompted her to stare at the instrument that was about to play the chords of her yet unfulfilled needs. She wanted to hear angels and birds, to feel the soaring upon penetration described in romance books, to know a climax under the mastery of a man like Lachlan.

His pants flung aside, she expected him to drive his rigid implement to its hilt. But he didn't. Scooting down on the bed, he lowered himself and brushed his lips and tongue along her abdomen, then languorously along her inner thighs. Spasms of tingling delight washed through her. Gripping the pillow above her head, she arched up and released a low, raspy moan.

"Lachlan, what are you doing to me?"

A devilish smile was his only response before he pressed his lips to the valley between her thighs.

"Oh . . . my . . . God," Beth gasped, under assault by so many alien sensations that she couldn't concentrate on any one in particular. Two of Lachlan's fingers glided in and out of her body. Beth arched up and clenched her teeth. The sensations were maddening and frightening and powerfully wonderful, and she thought she was going to burst. Pleasure after pleasure rolled over her in endless waves—

Her climax took her unawares, and a cry escaped her. Lachlan continued his ministrations, causing her to writhe and squirm in an attempt to stop the bursts of sensations before they consumed her.

"Please, stop!" She laughed tearfully. "Lachlan! *Please!!*"

"Tis ta lessen the pain o' first entry, ma Beth," Lachlan explained as he positioned himself atop her.

"How could you—"

"Know you?" he whispered, searching her flushed face in the sensuous gaslight. "Wha' dinna I know abou' you?" he asked cryptically. He ran the fingertips of his right hand down her moist cheek, then brought the taste of her perspiration to his lips.

A sigh escaped from Beth. Everything the man said or did was sensual.

Lachlan lightly brushed his lips over Beth's before gliding himself into her body. The pain startled her, sharp and searing, but Lachlan was quick to kiss her deeply, drawing her attention away from the discomfort and bestowing on her anticipation of another horizon of pleasure. She clung to him, wanting all that he could give, and refusing to let a single doubt enter her mind.

She began to move in the rhythm he set. Closing her eyes, she basked in the sheer delight of his fingers entwining with hers and anchoring her hands above her head. He kissed her again and again, intermittently nuzzling her neck, nipping one of her sensitive earlobes. The cadence of his body movements never wavered until she felt his hands squeeze her own. She became aware of tension building within his magnificent body. And when he lifted his head to stare deeply into her eyes, she read the strain he was under to prolong their love-making.

About to whisper to him not to wait on her, she became aware of a subtle sensation blossoming low in her abdomen. Lachlan brushed his lips across hers, smiling in his secretive way. But she concentrated on what he was doing to her body, on the twinges that rapidly began to vibrate within her, building, almost searing, almost chilling her, building and sweeping throughout her body.

Lachlan released her hands. At the instant they both began to crest the summit of physical rapture, Beth's arms wound about him, drawing him tightly against her as they shuddered in unison. Lachlan's arms snaked beneath and around her, blanketing her within the embrace of his hot, perspiring skin.

Spent, content to lay entwined for some time, they reveled in the blissful aftermath of their experience.

Then Lachlan languidly stretched out alongside Beth and drew her again into his arms. His chest serving as a pillow, she closed her eyes and snuggled closer. She sighed contentedly when he pressed his lips to her brow and murmured a 'thank you' for what she had done for him.

For him?

She wanted to tell him that if love on second sight were possible, then she had fallen victim to its spell. That kiss in the moonlight . . . She had known then, deep down in her heart of hearts, they would become lovers.

"Happy birthday, Beth," Lachlan said huskily.

"What *don't* you know about me?"

Several seconds passed in silence. When Lachlan spoke, there was an edge of sadness to his tone. "How long i' wad tak a mon ta win yer heart."

Beth peered up at his jawline. She didn't know what to say. They had become lovers, but it would end in less than two weeks.

However, a little voice in her head whispered that she would never leave Scotland. Beth naturally assumed it was because she was already falling in love with the mysterious man beside her.

Cold nipping at her nose stirred Beth from her sleep. Reluctant to leave the embrace of her dream, she turned onto her other side and snuggled deeper beneath the warmth of her bedcovers. But the dream was already becoming lost to her. It faded into the recesses of memory, the green hills and romantic picnic she and Lachlan had been sharing moments before, dimming within a haze of dawning reality.

Moaning, Beth reached out to locate Lachlan. A sleepy smile danced across her full mouth as she stretched the arm and slid her palm over the smoothness and warmth of the emptiness beside her. Then it occurred to her that she alone was in the bed. Cracking open her eyelids, she peered about the gray-lit room.

The heavy drapes were closed but for a slash of light where they met. It was morning. Her smile deepening, she luxuriously stretched her arms and legs, then ran her fingers through her unruly hair.

The night had ended too quickly, but she would remember all it entailed for the rest of her life. Sighing contentedly, she rolled onto her back. Every muscle in her body ached.

She was about to fold her arms beneath her head when she realized that she was in her room, not the majestic bed across the hall. The smile and light in her eyes faded to a frown. The last thing she remembered was laying her head upon the hollow of Lachlan's shoulder and feeling his arms hold her close.

So why was she *here . . . alone?*

The empty ache in her stomach made Beth decide to get up. She tossed aside the top sheet and heavy quilt—and received another small start of surprise. She was wearing her nightgown, which, if she remembered correctly, she hadn't been wearing when she'd fallen asleep in Lachlan's arms.

Or had it all been a dream, some cruel wile of her imagination to placate her unease at being left alone in the mansion?

No.

Last night had not been just a vivid fantasy. She *had* made love with Lachlan. All the telltale aches in her body were no figment of her imagination.

But that would mean Lachlan had put her nightgown and panties on her without her being aware of it. And that he had carried her into this room and put her to bed.

A delicate pink stain rose to her cheeks.

Had Lachlan gone through her things and found a fresh pair of panties to put on her?

Swinging her feet to the floor, she released a low, unsteady laugh. After last night, she couldn't believe anything could embarrass her, certainly nothing in connection with Lachlan—

A long-fingered hand flew up to her cheek. "God! I don't even know his last name!"

She slipped her feet into a pair of slippers and rushed to the cedar chest at the foot of the bed. The dampness in the room nipped at her skin. Plucking up a red and dark green plaid blanket from the several within the chest, she shook it open and swung it about her frame in one fluid motion.

And then the awareness crept up on her again.

The house was fraught with silence, stillness.

Leaving her room, Beth tried the handle to the door across the hall. Finding it locked, she walked down the long hallway to the staircase and descended to the second floor, where she knocked then looked in to see if Carlene and David had returned. The bed was empty and fully made as it had been the previous day. Beth closed the door and headed for the staircase.

The smell of coffee greeted her before she reached the ground floor. From the main hall, she went down a narrow hallway, past two closed doors, to the kitchen at the end. Opening the door, she immediately spied the bent, old woman at the stove.

"Good morning, Agnes."

A chilling silence followed Beth's greeting. Then

Agnes looked her way and gave a terse nod of her head.

"Mornin', Missy. Just startin' yer breakfast."

The warmth and delicious odors in the room quickly enveloped Beth. Crossing the kitchen, she brought herself to stand beside the cook. "I'm starving. It must be the air here. I eat like a bird at home."

Pointedly refusing to look again at Beth, Agnes released a snort. "Yer appetite's no' all tha's changed since you arrived."

Beth tried to tell herself that Agnes was probably still worked-up from her confrontation with Lachlan, but she was uncomfortable receiving the brunt of the woman's churlish mood. "Is there, ah, anything I can do to help?"

Silence followed but for the scraping and clacking of metal utensils on the pans. Beth could sense a definite air of hostility in the room. Perhaps Agnes had had another run-in with Lachlan, this morning.

"Agnes, is there anything I can do to help?" Beth repeated, feeling a twinge of annoyance.

"It's ma job, Missy— whan I'm allowed ta do i' in peace. Winna be long. Coffee's— "

"Excuse me, but is something wrong?"

"Leave me ta ma wark, Missy."

Beth backed up several paces, a frown drawing down her shapely eyebrows. There was no mistaking it now. Agnes was upset with *her.*

"Have you heard anything from Carlene?"

Silence.

Beth's shoulders squared back, and her tone took on an edge. "Agnes, please."

"No' a word. But dinna worry yerself abou' her an' the mister."

"Then what is bothering you this morning?"

A breath lodged in Beth's throat when the old woman turned sharply and leveled a look of disapproval at her. "He got you ta his room, dinna he?"

Through Beth's deadpan expression, crimson stole up across her face. "Beg your pardon?"

"Shame on you, Missy!"

"Now wait just a—"

Shaking an isolated finger up at Beth, Agnes forged on, "Soon as I came in this morn, I felt his smugness."

"— damn minute!"

"The house reeks o' the wicked play o' last night! I wad have thought you'd have better sense than ta tak oop wi' the likes o' him!"

Beth was at first stunned by the woman's tirade, then anger began to percolate deep within her. "What happens between two consenting adults is none of your business!"

"You fool womon! Curse his clarty soul! I warned you ta leave. Dinna I? *Dinna I!*"

"That's enough!"

Agnes released another snort and turned again to the stove. "It's no' ma business if you choose ta sleep wi' the deil, but I dinna have ta like i'. Now . . . get ou' o' ma kitchen an' leave me ta ma wark."

"My pleasure," Beth murmured.

"An' since you've got sa much free time on yer hands, I'll no' waste ma time wi' the clean-oopin'."

"Fine."

"Fine," Agnes mimicked haughtily. "Lyin' wi' the deil is no' fine a' all."

Chilled to the marrow of her bones, Beth tried to loosen her white-knuckled grip on the blanket to re-adjust it about her, but it was as if her fingers were locked. With as much dignity as she could muster, and in a tone bespeaking of a hint of authority, she asked, "Have you seen Lachlan this morning?"

"Na, an' I dinna expect he has the nerve ta show his wicked face ta me. I'll put yer breakfast in the dinin' room whan i's ready, then I'll be off."

"Fine. Thank you," Beth murmured as she headed for the door.

Too numb to feel anything at the moment, Beth shuffled down the hall and headed for the front doors. Beyond them, she passed through the greenhouse to the large, black-stained double doors. The instant she stepped out into the morning air, she filled her lungs.

Was she losing her mind, or had everything truly been topsy-turvy since the instant she'd set foot in Scotland?

Hoping fervently Carlene and David would return before nightfall, Beth walked away from the front door and strolled about the graveled yard. Off to her left, at a distance shielded from her view by trees and shrubs, she could hear the bleat of sheep and the occasional lowing of cattle. The sound had to be coming from the field where Lachlan had taken her two nights ago, where he had kissed her in the moonlight. . . .

Expelling him from her thoughts, she stepped up onto a grassy area and turned to view the house in its early-morning splendor.

Bright sunlight slashed across the rooftops of the otherwise shadowed structure. Perched on these peaks, alongside the variously-sized chimneys, the peacocks huddled in the warm rays. Looking down at her from their lofty positions, several released caustic cries, as if telling her they were as much aware of her.

"My sentiments, exactly," she whispered to the birds, then looked about her. Patches of fog hovered serenely over sections of the land, mostly in the darker, shadowy areas.

Peacefulness embraced her once again, the balm of nature soothing her troubled spirit. She couldn't help but wonder what it would be like to wake up in this land every morning for the rest of her life, to stand exactly where she was now, and feel the satisfaction of knowing this piece of the world belonged to her. She already knew it was going to be hard to say goodbye to Kist House when the time came for her to return to the States.

Ten days left. She had to make enough memories of Scotland to last her a lifetime.

A droll smile lifted the corners of her full mouth as she realized she had already made a hellacious start on those memories.

Unbidden, Lachlan crept into her thoughts and she looked up again at the peacocks.

Carlene and David owned the house, but it was Lachlan who gave the impression he was its master. After what they had shared last night, perhaps he wouldn't take offense to her questioning him on the animosity between he and Agnes. From what Beth could gather, it seemed to stem from what had happened to Lannie Baird.

That's ridiculous, she mused. *Lannie Baird died one hundred and fifty years ago.*

Lachlan had to be a descendant, but could a grudge remain between two families for over a century? If so, why would Agnes continue to work at Kist— Baird House? Out of loyalty to Carlene and David?

"So, Lachlan, if Agnes didn't see you this morning, how does she know we slept together?" Beth murmured, shivering as the morning's dampness seeped through to her skin.

"Maybe I misinterpreted what she said. Her accent is so thick. I can't imagine why you would tell her about last night, unless . . ."

Beth frowned. Had last night been a game, a conquest for Lachlan?

Where was he?

Did he usually abandon his lovers in the cold light of dawn?

Her temper surfaced as she ran the possibilities through her mind. She didn't like the fact she'd awakened alone, in her own bed, her nightgown on, as if last night had been nothing more than a dream.

She still couldn't fathom why she had given herself to him with such abandon. He was attractive— no, incredibly handsome in a way she couldn't quite analyze to her satisfaction. She had wanted him to kiss her in the moonlight the first night, and he had. And it had been a kiss unlike anything she'd imagined in her wildest fantasies. She had wanted him to make love to her, and he had.

When she'd gone to his room last night, and he'd turned to stare at her, impulses had swooped down on her and she had surrendered to them. Her physical needs, she had discovered, possessed such utter energy and fire that she found it hard to believe they were an actual part of her.

A feeling of being watched slapped her awareness and she turned abruptly.

"Guid mornin'. Didn't mean ta startle you."

The sight of a man standing a few feet away spilled a gasp past her lips. Closing the blanket even tighter about her, Beth shriveled within the wool fibers.

The man smiled in a lazy, self-assured manner, then dipped his head to one side. "A bit nippy ta be ou'."

Beth offered a strained smile, her gaze flitting to a pair of hedge clippers held in the man's hands. Tall and lanky, thirtyish, with light brown hair and blue eyes, he was a pleasant-looking man, but a man who watched her as if expecting her to run back to the house.

"Good morning. Are you here to work in the gardens?"

He grinned, closing the distance between them. "His Nibs summoned me. You must be Beth Staples. I'm Borgie Ingliss, Aggie's boy. Pleasure ta meet you. Ma mum said you were a fine lookin' womon, itherwise I'd been tempted ta tell auld Lachlan ta stick his demands in his ear. I say a mon has ta draw his lines."

Beth was beginning to wonder if she wasn't still asleep.

"Arrived recently, did you?"

"Umm, yes. A few days ago."

"An' the missus went off an' left you, eh?"

"Carlene? Yes. She went to pick up her husband in Edinburgh. They should be back today." She kept, *I hope*, to herself.

To her unease, the man laughed. "So tha's wha' she tauld you. You'll know soon enough, I guess."

"Know what?"

"It's no' for me ta explain." He started to turn away. "If you start gettin' stir crazy, let me know. I wadna mind rescuin' you an' takin' you ou' ta Shortby's. It's the finest pub aroond."

In stunned disbelief, Beth watched the man disappear beyond the high bushes across from her. If this morning was any indication of what her day was going to be like . . .

Ruefully, she considered climbing back into bed and waiting for Carlene to return, but the ever-growing list of innuendoes was beginning to wear on her nerves.

Deciding to have a long talk with Agnes, she went back into the house.

One straight answer was all she needed to put her nerves at ease. One simple, understandable, *straight* answer.

Were the employees simply having fun with her, or was there something darkly amiss going on right under her nose?

Beth didn't like mysteries, and she had a difficult time understanding the depth of hostility that existed between the two Inglisses and Lachlan.

"Damn," she grumbled upon seeing the kitchen empty of the cook's presence. Turning on a heel, she walked into the dining room and found her breakfast primly arranged on the table.

"Agnes! Agnes, I would like to talk to you, please!"

Silence.

Muttering under her breath, she drew out a chair and lowered herself onto it in front of the aromatic dishes of eggs, sausages, a small chicken pie, strawberries in thick cream, and a freshly baked loaf of bread.

Beth's stomach unexpectedly churned.

She wasn't hungry for food. Just straight answers!

Placing her elbows on the table, she lowered her face into her hands and scowled down at the repast.

She was tired of eating alone, tired of trying to entertain herself.

Fed up with the daily disappearing acts Lachlan and Agnes had perfected to a fine art.

Kist House was rapidly losing its glamor.

Six

The light was again lessening within the house when Beth arrived on the third floor and saw Lachlan's bedroom door open. Walking up to the threshold, she noted first the stoked fire, then the lambskin throw rugs in front of the hearth. To the far side of the rugs, a bottle of champagne sat within a silver ice bucket atop a silver, monogrammed bed tray. Alongside two crystal glasses was bread and cheese, a bowl of luscious strawberries, and a silver container of cream. She stepped farther into the room, to the edge of the rugs, and looked over the blatant seduction scene with contempt blazing in her eyes.

"I've been waitin' for you, love."

Beth looked over her shoulder to see Lachlan standing at the threshhold, a lace gown draped over his left arm.

Slowly turning her body to align with her head, she gawked at the man through a crimson face. "You're . . . naked."

In response, Lachlan grinned broadly and gave the gown over his arm a shake. "For you. A belated birthday present."

After taking a moment to analyze Beth's deadpan expression, he advanced into the room. "It was purchased for Tessa, but she impaled auld Lannie 'fore he cad give i' ta her. You've a better figure than her, anyway, an' I know how much you like auld things. Put i' on, sweets. I've been achin' ta behaud you in i'."

A slow transformation befell Beth. Anger heightened her color, and her posture stiffened. "Of all the nerve . . . You arrogant, smug . . . *jerk!*"

"Me, you say?" He looked genuinely surprised. "Wha' have I done *this* time ta bring abou' tha' beautiful flush ta yer face?"

"Done? *Done?*"

Fuming mad now, she plucked up a black poker from a stand at the hearth, and wielded it shoulder high. "Just for the record, my birthday is over! Where the *hell* have you been?"

Lachlan recovered his wits with the aplomb of a master. "Busy."

"That explains everything."

The bitterness in her tone caused him to flinch. "I saw you talkin' ta Borgie," he said with feigned lightness. He stepped closer to Beth. "A word ta the wise, darlin'; stay clear o' him. He's a foul mon."

"And *you're* not?"

Beth sucked in a breath and partially lowered the poker. She couldn't help but let her gaze roam over his magnificent body. Muscular and perfectly proportioned, his arousal beckoning and taunting her to try to deny the powerful chemistry between them.

"I'm not a whore! And I refuse to be treated like one!"

Genuinely flabbergasted, he gushed, "Yer're the grandest womon I've e'er known, Beth! I've waited a long time for you. I wadna do aught ta hurt you."

Growing more furious by the moment, Beth dropped the poker before her anger prompted her to swing it at him. "I'm getting damned tired of your blarney."

"Tis the Irish who lay claim ta blarney. Ah, Beth darlin'." He came toward her, his arms opened, his eyes gleaming with an unsettling combination of mischief and passion. "Na fightin' between us. Tis a terrible waste o' ma energy, an' I want i' all— *need* i' all— ta pleasure you."

Beth stood her ground with steely determination. When he was within arm's reach of her, she twisted around, bent over, and lifted the container of cream.

"Until Carlene and David return— " Straightening up, she glared at him. "— I want you to stay away from me!"

"Haud yer wheesht!" he boomed.

"If you're going to swear at me, I would appreciate understanding what you're saying!"

Lachlan rolled his eyes and squelched his own mounting anger. "I said, haud yer noise."

"Make up your mind, Lachlan," she said in a saccharine tone. "One minute you're pushing me to open up, the next, to shut up."

A dubious expression crossed his face. "Tis no' exactly wha' I meant, love."

"No?" Beth positioned herself close to him, her upturned mouth mere inches from his chin. "I'm not going to lay all the blame on your shoulders. I made myself an easy mark."

"Haud i'—"

"What really galls me," she went on heatedly, "is that you *believe* I'm so gullible as to fall into your arms again after you disappear like that! *Busy*, Lachlan?" She whacked his chest with such force, her palm stung. "Whatever it was that kept you *so* occupied had better be capable of keeping you warm at night, because I'm through with you. Understand?"

She attempted to shove past him, but he caught her arm and drew her against his primed body. "Look inta ma eyes. How can you think I'd e'er be wi' anither womon? Canna you see how much I love *you?*"

His words caused a terrible ache within the pit of Beth's stomach. Love? Oh, God! She'd never known the love of a man, but a man like Lachlan was incapable of really understanding the word. She wanted to put as much distance between them as possible. Already, her knees were weakening, and the touch of his skin against her own was making her headier by the moment.

"Let go of me."

"Wi'ou' a kiss guid night? Be sensible. You know you need me as much as I need you. Ma poor, wee monhood here is abou' ta snap tis so rigid. Give us a kiss—"

Beth lifted the container and poured the cream

over his head. She stepped back, expecting a burst
of anger from him. But as his fingers threaded
through his dripping hair, he looked up with eyes
filled with laughter.

Rankled by his mood, she hurried to the bowl of
strawberries and dumped these, too, over his head.
He laughed outright. Having caught two of the
plump berries in a hand, he popped them into his
mouth.

"Cad I possibly consider this a bit o' foreplay,
Beth, ma girl?" he chuckled, red juice trickling
down his chin.

"Drop dead."

With another chuckle, he swiped the back of a
hand across his mouth. Then swiftly, he reached
out and captured Beth's upper arms and pulled her
against his hard body. Stunned at how fast the man
could move, she stiffened in his hold. She was determined to retain her anger. She needed it to find
salvation from the treacherous longing igniting
fierce and merciless fires within her loins. But when
Lachlan's mouth swooped down and took possession of her lips, she felt herself weakening.

Damn him!

She didn't want to give in. He possessed an uncanny ability to awaken her every pore to his presence, to vanquish inhibitions that had tagged her a
shy girl throughout her high school and college
years.

She wasn't easy, and it infuriated her that she
found him so difficult to resist.

What happened to her willpower when she was

around the man? Even just the deep quality of his voice weakened her.

Not this time, she vowed, steeling herself to go limp in his hold.

But then his arms enveloped her, and his arousal flattened to her midriff, sandwiched between their quivering, aching bodies. A moan reverberated within her skull as his tongue urged her to open her mouth. Fleeting fantasies of biting him— and worse— flipped through her mind as she unclenched her teeth and parted her lips. If she didn't stop him soon— didn't stop *herself*— she would soon be forever lost to the hold he had on her.

Then she tasted the strawberry sweetness on his tongue and she melted against him. A ritual of dancing, stroking tongues began. Her sensibilities became solely focused on the pulses racing through her body, pumping wildly like thousands of heartbeats beneath every part of her skin.

Drawing his mouth a hairbreadth from her slightly swollen lips, he rasped, "Admit how suited we are for one anither. Oor hearts beat as one. We're linked, you an' I, in mind an' spirit."

Mind *and* spirit?

Wrenching herself from his embrace, Beth glowered at him, her chest rising and falling with her every panting breath.

So, linked were they?

Lust wasn't enough. He wanted her mind and spirit as well! And at this particular moment, she wasn't sure he wouldn't take it all and leave her an empty shell once the thrills dimmed between them.

"No," she breathed, her hands held up to ward him off. "It's not going to work this time!"

Lachlan calmly watched her storm across to her bedroom and slam the door behind her. A quirky smile played on his lips.

God, she had a fine temper!

"Drop dead, she says ta me." He released a low, throaty laugh. "Ah, Beth, you didna drive the poker through ma heart. Tis love, this time."

He made a rueful face as he inspected the scene he'd so carefully arranged for his planned night of lovemaking with the woman. His woman. He'd known that the instant he'd laid eyes on her portrait.

Tessa be damned. His first marriage be damned. This time he'd do it right.

He'd only been more than a hundred years off track. He would never have children to fill his grand house, but he had found a woman to share eternity with him.

What more could any man want?

At a glance from him, the fire in the fireplace dwindled and extinguished.

Lachlan stood in the darkness, staring at the closed door in front of him, aching for that which she had denied him this night.

"I can wait a while longer. I do love you, lass. Soon, you'll know how verra much."

He was a man accustomed to waiting, this Lachlan Baird. It woed him that she'd thought he was merely playing games. He hadn't wanted to leave her for even a second, but his energies were precious little since their passionate love-making.

How he would explain it all to her, he didn't know. But it would have to be soon. If Agnes— or that useless twit Borgie— were to tell Beth his secret . . .

Perhaps she'd question their sanity, but in time she would know the truth, and resent his keeping it from her.

He had to breach his fear of her initial reaction. He already sensed her suspicions. They lay innocently in her mind, but her unwillingness to accept the reality of what her senses told her prevented her from seeing through his facade.

So much lay ahead of them.

Unburdening her guilt had been a step in the right direction. She was a stronger-willed woman than he'd expected, but in the end, it could be to their advantage.

If only he could breach the boundaries of time and see into the future, know for certain how to prepare himself for the events destined to unfold.

She was going to fight him for her life.

He began to fade into the night-cloaked room.

"'Tis a terrible gray limbo I'll wait in ta peak the energy ta return ta you, girl."

His misty form began to move through the room.

"Ghosthood has its drawbacks, but I'll be back on the morn's morn. Until then, Beth, dream o' me kindly."

* * *

Dressed again in the cotton, calf-length skirt and a sleeveless matching top of pale blue, Beth made her way to the far end of the second floor hall. She refused to think about Lachlan. Whatever his excuse, she would never forgive him for leaving her as he had. For that matter, she was at a point of never forgiving Carlene, either.

Days had now passed since her arrival, nearly a week of the most perplexing days of her life. Between the headaches and her restlessness, she'd hardly slept. And when she did sleep, Carlene or Lachlan invaded her dreams.

Sliding aside the heavy drape to the entrance to the tower, she crossed the threshhold to a narrow, steep, stone staircase that hugged the wall. She climbed to the second level. On the narrow floorspace stood a single, unmade bed, a small white dresser, and a clothes rack. Two old prints in handmade frames hung on the stone walls. There was a small, curtainless window that could be cranked open.

On the third level was another unmade single bed, the mattress in perfect condition. A dark-stained dresser was set in the corner. An open closet had been built into one wall. Beneath a cubbyhole under the stairs was an old black trunk. She opened it. Empty. A cross made of straw hung on the wall over the bed. Another curtainless window.

The fourth level had only a single bed, a wooden vanity, and a tiny window with a yellowed valance. Beth sat on the edge of the bed. Sighing deeply, she placed her elbows on her thighs and her chin in her upturned palms.

These rooms in the tower, she reasoned, must have been for servants. But what a lonely, cold place it was for them to sleep. She wondered how the people kept warm back then, as there were no fireplaces on any of the levels.

A movement was caught in Beth's peripheral vision. She stared at a section of low wall, her brow furrowed in deep thought. After a moment, the facing of the mortared rock appeared to shift, as if curtained by a shimmering illusion of heat waves.

Then she recalled Calum's account of where Lannie Baird had been found.

Recoiling, she glanced up and saw a brass bell hanging high on the wall above the base of the ascending staircase.

Clang.

Although she was certain the bell hadn't moved, the sound reverberated in her ears.

Rising from the bed, she went to the window and looked out. At least the view was beautiful. The loch stretched out beneath a gently rolling morning haze. On the fore side of the loch were several homes clustered together. Beyond, rolling green hills covered with trees and low stone walls, demarcated the land boundaries.

Beth ran a finger along the tiny window embrasure, then upturned the finger to inspect it for dust. Amazingly, there wasn't any. Now that she thought about it, she hadn't encountered anything in the house that showed the slightest sign of neglect.

As if compelled, she looked again at the wall behind her. She crossed to it and knelt, then hesitantly laid her palm against the rock. The surface was like ice and, for one frightening second, she believed her hand almost capable of passing through the wall.

Nursing the hand to her breast, she released a long breath.

Poor Lannie Baird.

"Did you suffer?"

Maybe his spirit did still reside in the house. She hadn't had another encounter with him— if it had been him at all.

"I love your house, Lannie. You managed to create something that long succeeded you. Not many people could— " Beth sighed and murmured, "You're losing it, kiddo."

Standing, she turned to what remained of the ascending staircase, steep and narrow. Massaging a nagging stiffness in her neck, she walked to the bottom step and looked up. The steps led up to a dark door in the ceiling.

Beth wrinkled her nose disdainfully. She wasn't fond of heights, but after a few moments of considering how little else there was for her to do to occupy her time, she decided she might as well see all of the tower.

The door opened outward and fell to her right onto the roof. She hurried up the last few steps, drew herself up onto a floor of aged, tarred planks, and clung tightly to a broad flagpole conveniently placed by the portal. Surrounding the perimeter of the tower was a waist-high crenelated wall that gave her a reasonable sense of security. Releasing her deathgrip on the pole, she crossed to the wall and peered down at the side yard over one of the notches.

The ground seemed a very long way down—

A peacock cry startled her.

Turning her head sharply, she tried to locate the noisy bird, but from her position, the wall blocked her view of the house's rooftops. She took a deep breath to steady her nerves, then drank in her first panoramic view from the tower's peak.

A butterfly sensation flitted in her stomach as she slowly digested the incredible landscape. The morning air was crisp and clean, the sunlight bright and promising to warm up the day. A silver mist lay over the shadowed areas near the road to the house, and along the west side of the property. The mist was beginning to dissolve above the loch, revealing water of the truest azure.

Then the blue quiet registered in her mind. Amazingly quiet. There was such serenity surrounding Baird House that her worries began to fade. She felt as if she were the only person left on the planet. A princess in her tower.

Sighing, she closed her eyes and lifted her face to the sun.

And this was how Lachlan first saw her when he materialized behind her. His mouth opened to speak, but no words came out. Elation lit his dark eyes and, feeling breathlessly buoyant, he stepped off to one side to have a better view of her profile.

She was more beautiful than anything he'd ever seen.

The sunlight's kiss on her face, the shine of her curly hair, the contours of her long, slender neck, all aroused his desire to hold her. But he waited. As long as he didn't use excessive physical energy, he could remain with her for most of the day.

Perhaps a picnic in the rose garden behind the house—

No. The last meal he'd had at that particular site was two days before his adoring bride became a widow. The memory certainly dampened his fondness for *that* spot.

A stroll along the south pastures or horseback riding to the border of the Lauder's farm. Or a leisurely boat ride down the loch.

And what would he say to his future bride if his energies ran short and he simply . . . *poofed* away?

Ah, lassie, I've been meanin' ta tell you somethin' for a time now. You see, I've been dead . . . oooh, abou' a hundred an' forty-nine years now. But dinna let i' worry you. Even dead, love puts me in ma cups.

Aye, Beth ma darlin', I'm a ghost. A wee lonely spirit, but one wi' a mon's dreams an' . . .

Lachlan's dark eyebrows drew expressively down above his straight nose. *Say tha', you fool,* he chided himself, *an' she'll whap you oopside the head, an' you'll use oop those precious energies o' yers just tryin' ta haud yer temper!*

He irritably flexed his shoulders beneath a beige shirt which was left open to the waistband of his dark pants.

Weel, tis a fine mess you've got yerself in now, Lannie auld boy. Na, you canna gae spillin' yer woeful stary now— an' tis no' a guid time ta confess you pleasured her wi' a dead thin', either.

Beth opened her eyes and was smiling with sheer bliss when she caught sight of something in her peripheral vision. She released a squeal of surprise, and Lachlan nearly died for the second time. A hand over his phantom heart, his breaths coming in hoarse spurts from lungs the precious energy simulated from his memory, he stared at the woman as if she had lost her mind.

"Dammit, Lachlan, you nearly scared me to death!" Beth made a gallant attempt to compose herself.

"You!" he wheezed. "Guid morn ta you, tae!"

"It *was* until you— " Her eyes narrowed with accusation as she drew her gaze back to Lachlan from the open portal on the floor. "I didn't hear you come up."

"I figured tha' ou' the instant yer voice shattered ma eardrums." Offering his most charming smile, he stepped up beside her until their shoulders were touching, then gestured to the loch.

"Loch Ken, darlin'. Ma personal favorite in all the Lowlands."

"You wouldn't be a little prejudiced, would you?"

The husky timbre of Beth's voice brought Lachlan's gaze to her face. But the light in his eyes dimmed quickly when he realized the depth of her pique with him.

"Abou' last night— "

"I'm fed up with the games and lies!"

"*Lies*, you say!"

"I knew there was something peculiar about this whole business."

"*Peculiar*, now! I'd be watchin' ma words, girl. Tis a sad day whan a fine-lookin' womon like yerself wakes oop lookin' for a fight, rather than—"

Beth's opened hand flew out and caught Lachlan on the side of his face. Stunned that her temper had again prompted her to strike out at him, she curled her fingers over the edge of the stone wall and stared unseeingly at the scenery below.

Sighing deeply, Lachlan gingerly touched his finger tips to his smarting cheek. "I tak i' tis no' a guid time ta ask for a morn's kiss."

Beth turned to him, her face taut from her struggle to hold back the tears pressing at the back of her eyes.

"Sometimes, your humor irks the hell out of me."

"Only sometimes, eh?" He shifted uncomfortably beneath the intense inner pain her eyes betrayed. "You'd have mair heart wi' me if you knew how long I've had ta amuse maself."

"Was making love to me a joke as well?"

Lachlan jerked in surprise. "You know better, girl."

"Do I? I woke up *alone*, in *my* room, then I don't see or hear a word from you for much too long. Then you show up last night, expecting me to jump into your arms! Where were you?"

"Gatherin' oop ma strength."

"On the cot in the carriage house? Because you sure as *hell* haven't been in the house! Save it, Lachlan!" she added bitterly, a hand raised to ward off his attempt to speak as she went on to accuse, *"You* own this estate, don't you!"

Crossing his arms over his chest, Lachlan turned to the wall. A long moment passed in silence. His teeth were clenched, causing a muscle to tick along his strong jawline. He didn't want to look at the damn landscape. He'd seen it a thousand times from this very place.

Morning, noon, and night. He'd seen countless sunrises and sunsets from this tower. In the past, he'd hung around the tower at night, waiting for some fool trespasser to scare the wits out of. But that hadn't been a necessary diversion for his boredom since the Cambridges had moved in.

"Lachlan!"

"Aye, a Baird built i'. A Baird will always ain i'."

An' tha's the truth, he thought smugly. *The fact tha' tis one an' the same Baird is no' relevant right now.*

"Carlene was playing matchmaker when she invited me here."

Lachlan cast Beth an impatient scowl. "Aye!"

"And you were a part of that little scheme."

With a feigned shudder, he crooned, "Ooh, darlin', yer makin' me wish I'd had a wee shot o' Scotch 'fore seein' you."

"You're not going to charm your way out of this!"

Lachlan winced in earnest. "Shudderin' pines, lass, ma ego is badly bruised as i' is from yer sharp tongue!"

"Better your ego than your body."

"I'm no' tryin' ta hide aught from you." *But if I tell you all right now, you'll throw yerself from the tower here, an' winna tha' mak a helluva mess.* "Aye, I pleaded wi' Carlene ta bring you o'er. Wha's the harm, eh? Are you no' happy wi' me?"

"Happy?" Beth's face darkened, her eyes flashed, and her voice dropped two decibels. "Happy? You miserable womanizer! Did you run out of women here in Scotland to seduce?"

Lachlan flinched, but there was a glint of laughter in his eyes. "Ooch. If you wad just calm doon— "

"I've been worried sick about Carlene and her husband! How could you— Oh, why am I wasting my breath! As of tomorrow, I'm out of here! I'm going home!"

Instantly, Lachlan's face grew dark with savagery. *"This* is yer home."

With a guttural sound of disgust, Beth whirled away from him. She was blinded by her anger, and didn't realize where she was walking. A cry escaped her when he took a painful hold on her shoulder and spun her around to face him. She kicked him in the shin, and was trying to twist away when she happened to look downward.

Her blood plummeted. Her face paled.

Two inches away from her foot was the opened stairwell. Another step and she would have fallen.

Determined to make her listen to reason, Lachlan framed her face with his large hands, his thumbs planted firmly beneath her chin to force her to look at him. "Can you really be so silly as ta believe I wad want you here only for sex?"

Beth couldn't answer him. She closed her eyes tightly to shut him out. There was a pulse pounding at her temples, and a sharp pain stabbing at the back of her neck. She was on the verge of tears, but she wasn't sure why.

"Ach! Have the decency ta look a' me when I'm talkin' ta you!"

Her eyelids lifted and her gaze met his. But at the despondency in her eyes, Lachlan released a low moan and laid his brow to hers. "Ah, dammit. Forgive me." He kissed her lightly on the lips, then lowering his hands to the curves of her shoulders, drew back to study her face for several long moments.

"I love a guid sparrin' o' words now an' then, but girl, this is hurtin' like hell. I'm no' perfect. But I do love you mair than life itself."

Again he kissed her, a little longer. When he felt her response— although he was vitally aware of her trying to resist him— he embraced her in his arms and deepened the kiss. His insides heated. It was a blissful, welcomed feeling after the countless times he'd known only the grayness and its companioning cold. The warmth of the woman, the warmth of the sun's rays beating down on his back, were priceless to him.

Reluctantly, he ended the kiss. As he straightened away, he expected to see a glow of passion on Beth's face. Instead, her eyes were unnaturally bright with indignation. He slid his palms down his face before dropping his hands to his sides and leveling a frazzled look at her. "Leave, Beth, an' you'll hurt me mair than you cad e'er imagine."

"There's nothing here for me," she said coldly, her pride refusing to give in to the anguish she read in him.

Lachlan placed a palm to his chest. He could feel the coldness returning, beginning to seep into the very core of him. His high emotions were wasting his energies. He was running out of time.

"I've got ta leave."

Tears rose into Beth's throat. "Then I'll say goodbye now."

"Guidbye . . . ? Na. Whan I return—"

"I plan to be out of this house *today*."

Despair radiated from every part of Lachlan. "Dinna gae, lass. Dinna leave me."

The painful coldness was spreading rapidly through him now. Panic seized him as his gaze dropped to the opening above the stairwell. If he didn't hurry, he would fade before her eyes . . .

"Promise me, Beth! Wait till ma return!"

Pale, trembling, Beth gave a stilted shake of her head.

Indecision ripped through him. If he left, he risked her getting too far away from the house. But if he didn't, and he vanished before her eyes, the horror of her premature realization would scar her deeply.

"Lachlan, are you ill?" Beth stepped toward him, concern further blanching her face. "You're terribly pale."

She caught her breath as he swung her aside,

causing her to cling to the flagpole. Tears welling up in her eyes, she watched him hurry down the steps and disappear into the dark grayness below.

"Oh, damn," she choked, and started after him.

She called out his name repeatedly as she descended one flight of steps after another. It amazed her how fast the man could move— amazed and irked her. Never in her life had she met anyone as elusive as he . . . or as charming, and infuriating, and so absolutely head-spinning. At the moment, she didn't want to dwell on why Carlene would go along with such a subterfuge. She only wanted to sit and talk to Lachlan without their tempers getting in the way.

Running out into the second floor hall, she came to an abrupt halt. Pain capped and squeezed her skull, staggering her. "Oh, God, not another one!"

Tears spilling down her face, she backed up and leaned against the wall for support. She wanted to go on, but it hurt to move. It also hurt to think, and she couldn't slow down the maddening pace of her heartbeat.

She squeezed her eyes shut as the pain became unbearable. The aspirins were in her bedroom on the third floor. If she could only see her way to her room—

With her second step, she fell onto her knees. The pain in her head magnified as unconsciousness began to lower its curtain on her. "Lachlan!" she gasped. Fighting with what little strength she had left, she began to crawl toward the staircase. "My head . . . Lachlan, please, my aspir—"

She collapsed in a heap. Rolling onto her back, her arms angled out from her body, she stared dully into the darkness trying to rescue her from the pain. It was senseless to fight unconsciousness, but instinctively, she resisted it with all her willpower. The pain had magnified to such a degree that she was becoming less conscious of it.

But the fear was ever present.

Migraines.

She'd procrastinated about seeing a doctor to see if the headaches were caused by the fall she'd taken down the stairs, or an allergy to something she was ingesting. But the headaches had never been this severe.

Not until her arrival in Scotland.

They had worsened because of stress.

The long flight.

The time difference.

Carlene going away the same day Beth had arrived.

Lachlan.

Everything was a possible factor.

"Lachlan," she whimpered drowsily, her fingers kneading the rug beneath her.

Tiny lights appeared above her face. It hurt to focus on them, but she couldn't bring herself to close her eyes and shut them out. Tiny, dancing lights. They began to move in a circle above her, gyrating faster and faster, making her dizzier as seconds passed. Her arms and legs were weighted. She couldn't move. She wanted to cry, but no tears came.

Then she became aware of a breath-robbing coldness hovering near her. Something within it moved close by her, then she felt an icy kiss pressed to her brow.

Now she was hallucinating, a new facet to these terrible headaches.

I'm here, whispered a voice inside her head. *Sleep, Beth. You'll feel better in na time a' all.*

Beth's heavy lids closed, but her mind was vitally alert. "I c-can't m-move."

I know. Tis a frightenin' thin' yer're goin' through. But it'll pass. Trust me.

"Trust you?" she croaked, her voice growing weaker. "I want to . . . to . . ."

Kick me a guid one in the bahookie. His laugh was like a caressing whisper within her skull. *Tomorrow, love, an' e'ery morn efter. For now, put yerself in ma care. Sleep, darlin'. Sleep deep an' peaceful.*

Beth gave into unconsciousness. She was not aware of invisible arms lifting her, or of them carrying her to her bedroom and gently laying her atop the bed. Her sandals were removed and placed on the floor. The quilt was drawn up over her and lovingly tucked beneath her chin.

Then a long, shuddering sigh filled the room.

Sleep deeper, darlin'. I'll no' leave yer side till I know dreams o' me are keepin' you safe.

Two logs rose into the air from a wrought iron stand alongside the fireplace. The screen moved aside. The logs glided into place on the firedog. Within seconds, a fire roared within the sole heating unit, and the screen slid back into place.

When the chill was out of the room, and Lachlan

knew Beth was fast asleep, he permitted the void, the limbo of total grayness, to call him back.

She awakened in the middle of the night to a low fire in the fireplace. Disoriented, she stared at it until she finally got her bearings.

"The migraine," she murmured.

With the unsteady fingers of her right hand, she brushed aside the curly strands of hair clinging to her moist brow. The back of her head and neck were numb. Oddly, there was a little numbness in her left arm and leg.

"That was a doosy."

Lachlan.

The thought of him brought her slowly up into a sitting position. She had dreamed they were having the picnic again, in that same place among the hills, beneath a tree. She could still hear his voice and laughter in her ears, and recalled almost too vividly the touch of his hand, the gentleness in his gaze—

The smell of food.

She looked down at her grumbling stomach and made a wry face.

Lighting one of the candles on the mantel, she made her way down to the kitchen, favoring the weakness remaining in her left leg. The uncanny quiet of the house always seemed more so at night, but she refused to give in to her fears. To do so would only invite another headache.

A tomato, lettuce, and ham sandwich, and a large

glass of milk quelled the ache in her stomach. All the while she ate, she peered about the kitchen, halfheartedly studying the shadowy recesses that lay beyond the perimeter of the candlelight's soft, flickering glow. She wasn't sure how she knew it, but Lachlan wasn't in the house. That was all right, she told herself. She was getting used to being alone. Sometimes it was less intimidating than being in his presence.

She needed to get away and try to put everything in perspective. Lachlan would have to understand it was important to her that she know without a doubt that his love was not mere infatuation. And she needed to sit back and analyze her feelings toward him. The atmosphere within the house, her vulnerability, the strong attraction she felt toward Lachlan, didn't necessarily add up to love.

Maybe she was expecting too much.

Feeling drained, she tidied up the kitchen. She was at the far end of the secondary hall when she heard a sound from within the parlor. Opening the door, she was first aware of a roaring fire in the hearth. The room was warm and cozy, with none of the damp chill she'd felt in the kitchen.

"Lachlan?" she called, placing the candle in an empty holder on the mantel.

Her gaze lit on the portrait above the fireplace, and her nose wrinkled expressively. There was no disputing Carlene's talent as an artist, but the painting unnerved Beth. It was definitely her face on the canvas, but Carlene had added elements of color and refinement that Beth didn't see in herself when she looked in the mirror. The face and bearing of the woman above her was that of someone in love with life and nature, a woman who had never known pain or suffering or sacrifice.

"I'm not you," she whispered, an ache in her heart because she was not that person Carlene had portrayed.

A sharp pain, like a snapping at the back of her neck, set off an explosion within Beth's head. Her eyes widened in fear. She swayed on her feet. Bursts of colors flashed before her fading vision.

"Oh, God," she whimpered. *Not another attack so soon!*

She could feel the blood in her veins slowing down with every loud, strained thud of her heart, its beat lessening, winding down, warning her that the mechanics within her body had reached a crucial point.

Pain radiated through her chest and down her left arm. Her left leg went dead beneath her, then the arm became leaden and impossible to move from her side. She struggled to catch her breath, her lungs afire with the strain.

Then something cold and feathery passed through her. Her heart was given a jolt, a surge of energy. She could hear the organ's beat strengthening, the sound crescendoing in her ears.

Stifling a cry, she gripped the mantel with her right hand and closed her eyes for a moment. A fey coldness swept around and through her, again and again. A draft, she reasoned, but every nerve in her body was throbbing from the experience. She was dimly aware of pain trying to make itself known to her consciousness, but her concentration was on the tides of coldness lapping against her, swelling over and crashing down on her.

Something brushed against her ankles, her calves. Startled, she gaped down at the hemline of her skirt, which was swaying to and fro against her legs.

Her breathing quickened, wheezing through her constricted throat. She wanted to run and climb beneath the quilt on her bed and pull it over her head to shut out the madness. But her legs felt too heavy to move.

The house was drafty, yes, but this—

Another explosion of pain ensued, this time at the back of her head. Her legs began to give out from beneath her as a curtain of darkness descended over her mind. But then the coldness slipped within the entire length of her body, filling her completely and reawakening her senses. Revived once again, she homed in on what seemed like a chilling, invisible hand moving up along her inner thigh.

Gasping, she clenched the mantel's edge so tightly her knuckles turned white. The unearthly cold set off the beginning of a sensation that was igniting something fierce and hot within her loins. The caresslike phenomenon climbed higher, so gentle, so enchanting, so . . . *purposeful*. Her body quivered, and she gasped again as her skirt began to lift to her hips—

Tears sprang to her eyes, but it was a near-hysterical

laugh that gurgled from her throat as she bit into her lower lip and dipped her head back. Although a frosty mist enveloped her, she was beyond feeling the bite of its coldness.

Pulses were detonating within every part of her body, maddening, awakening sensations that held her captive. Stroking hands and kisses could be felt on every part of her body. She groaned, the chords in her neck distending as her head dipped back even lower. Her hair whipped about her face. Breaths of air moved across her throat, lingered at her lips, then shifted and ran down her spine, her buttocks, and the backs of her thighs.

Phantom teeth playfully nipped at one ankle, then the other. Hands, like smooth ice, moved over her calves.

Panting, she locked her teeth. Kisses moved in circles up one inner thigh.

"Oh, God," she sobbed.

She experienced a probing movement along the crotch of her panties. For a fleeting moment, her mind revolted, but then the fey stimulus swept her into a fiery responsiveness that shunned her instinctual inhibitions. Nothingness touched and caressed her, kissed and pampered her, awakened and demanded her gratification.

Nothingness?

She'd never felt so alive!

So aroused!

A searing, quivering sensation of liquid fire burst within her loins and spread to the very ends of her fingers and toes. She cried out at its startling swiftness. Her legs began to tremble, threatening to give out beneath her.

The climax was more powerful than anything she'd ever experienced. Even its aftermath sensations were robbing her of strength.

Her brow beaded with perspiration, Beth slowly turned her head and looked through glazed eyes at the candle on the table. It seemed a very long way off in her state of mind.

Breathing heavily, she momentarily laid her brow between her hands on the mantel. The coldness had vanished as unexpectedly as it had arrived.

Summoning up a reserve of strength, she snatched up the candle. Cupping her hand in front of the flame, she hurried from the room. When she arrived at her bedroom, she stopped fleetingly to notice that there was no light beneath Lachlan's door, then hurried into her room. Placing the candle back on the mantel, she sprinted across the floor and flung herself atop the bed.

She was beneath the covers, about to lie down, when she noticed that the fire within the hearth was well-stoked.

Not again!

A whimper rattled in her throat as she laid a cheek upon her pillow. This was surely madness, and it frightened her.

A single tear escaped the corner of her eye and puddled on the side of her nose. She swiped it across her cheek with the back of a hand, then pulled the top covers up over her head.

She was cold, colder than she ever believed was

possible in a human being. Her blood was like ice within her veins; her heart was racing as if was about to explode within her chest. She was conscious of pain, but it was a surrealistic rendition of what her logic told her it should be.

One way or the other, she was going to find a telephone in the morning, and she was going to have her return tickets changed.

She had to get away from Kist House before she lost herself within it.

If it wasn't already too late.

Seven

Beth's eyelids opened fractionally. From the window across the room, a bright shaft of sunlight filtered through the panes to fall across her bed.

It was morning.

Yawning, she ran her fingers through her hair, lazily scratched her scalp, then opened her eyes fully. She felt more rested than she had in years. Sitting up, she peered about the room through an expression of utter contentment. The usual growling of her stomach wasn't there to nudge her to seek breakfast. She didn't feel hungry at all.

The top covers were flipped aside and she swung her legs over the side of the bed. She was about to slide off the mattress when she noticed she was still wearing yesterday's clothing. A little chuckle at herself died in her throat as memory of what had happened in the parlor last night came home with shocking clarity.

"It was a dream," she murmured, her expression growing stormier by the moment. "A very real—" *creepy* "— dream."

A far off sound distracted her. Looking at the window, she concentrated on what the low, intermittent buzzing implied. Then it struck her. The groundskeeper!

What was his name . . . ?

Borgie!

Beth's heart began to race. The sound could only mean he was working on the grounds. It also meant she had a means to get into town and find a telephone!

Fueled by a sense of desperation, she hurriedly splashed water on her face, brushed her teeth, and ran a brush haphazardly through her hair. Then, lacing up her sneakers and tucking her purse beneath an arm, she lit out of the room as if the devil were at her heels. The stairs passed swiftly under her feet. Hugging her purse to her breast now, she turned left on the first floor landing and beelined for the door.

Lachlan stepped into the hall from the kitchen in time to see a figure wrench open the doors to the front of the house and run into the morning mist beyond. It took several moments before the scene registered in his mind, then a look of consternation ravaged his features.

The tea towel in his hand fluttered to the floor. "Beth! Na, Beth! Come back!"

Muttering a string of Gaelic invectives, he ran after her, but the instant he tried to pass the threshold to the greenhouse, he felt himself slammed by an invisible force. He staggered back several paces, incredulity deeply carved on his handsome face. He couldn't begin to imagine what he'd walked into until he looked down at himself and realized he was fading. At that moment, he didn't possess the energy to break through the sepulchral boundaries of his nether world existence.

Fury mottled his features. His fiercely brooding dark eyes looked in the direction Beth had gone, and desperation quaked through the remaining fibers of his being.

"Come back!" he wailed. "You . . ."

The last word eerily reverberated in the hall as he completely vaporized. But an aftermath of his emotional turbulence lingered. Touched upon by the rage of his momentary helplessness, brass urns and knick-knacks, wooden figurines and display tiles braced up on the mantelpiece, began to whip through the hall and bang one wall after another.

Beth was only dimly aware of the commotion behind her. Locked onto the sounds of the hedge trimmer, she ran through wet grass and brush with all the force she possessed.

No one was going to stop her from getting on the next flight to the States— not Agnes, not Borgie, not Carlene or David, and especially not Lachlan!

If she had to get down on her knees and beg Borgie to take her into town, she was determined to do just that. And if he refused, she would walk until she found a telephone!

The sound of the hedge trimmer cut abruptly.

She staggered, slowing her breakneck run as the stillness of her surroundings filled her once again with a terrible sense of isolation. Panic formed a

fist within her throat. Tears sprang to her eyes.
Stopping amidst the fog-mantled row of rhododendrons along the private access road, she anxiously
searched for a sign of the groundskeeper.

Not again! she lamented mutely.

People couldn't just vanish! She'd been closing
in on the sound just a moment ago . . .

"Mr. Ingliss?"

A cry from a peacock perched atop the highest
rooftop of the house caused Beth to flinch. She
glared in the bird's direction, a pulse drumming
wildly beneath her skin. "Mr. Ingliss! Are you here?"

Heaving a sigh of frustration, she walked along
the row of flowering hedges. "Mr. Ingliss! It's Beth
Staples. I need to talk to you, please!"

She clutched her purse more tightly as she peered
forlornly down the narrow decline of the private
road stretched out before her.

How far was it to town?

Surely she could walk there without getting herself lost. And she was wearing her best walking
shoes— her sneakers.

Unexpectedly, Borgie Ingliss stepped out in front
of her from between two of the rhododendron
bushes. Beth squealed in surprise, then, chagrined
by her reaction, she clamped a hand over her
mouth. The man across from her grinned in an
unpleasant, crooked manner as he tipped his head
in greeting. Amusement danced in his eyes. The
idea that he was inwardly laughing at her nervousness caused her to bristle, and it was all she could
do to compose herself.

"Good morning," she greeted somewhat stiffly. "I was hoping to catch you before you left."

He chuckled and removed a red plaid cap from his head. "I just got here."

Beth managed a quirky smile. "I-I was hoping I could trouble you for a ride into town."

"Na trouble a' all. It'll be a few hoors— "

"No!"

Beth laughed at the edge of desperation in her voice. "I'm sorry. It's just that I have to make a very important phone call. Please, Mr.— "

"Borgie."

"Y-yes, Borgie. I'm willing to pay you for your time and trouble."

A shiver passed through her. Borgie Ingliss was smiling pleasantly enough now, but there was something in the depths of his eyes that unnerved her.

You're being paranoid, she scolded herself, straining to maintain what little composure she possessed.

"I'll be glad ta drive you ta toon, Miss. Let me put oop this trimmer. Ma caur's in front o' the house."

The immense relief that washed through Beth left her feeling lightheaded and weak-kneed.

"Thank you. Should I tell your mother you'll be gone?"

Borgie leveled a questioning look at Beth. "She's away. Went on vacation nearly a week ago. Barely said a word ta me." He scratched his head before donning the cap again. "She's a wee senile a' times." His smile broadened. "I winna be long."

Beth watched the man turn down a pathway through the hedges, then released a thready breath.

Agnes went on vacation a week ago?

Rolling her eyes in exasperation, she turned in the direction of the house.

Perhaps Borgie wasn't quite right in the head, but the fact that he drove a car and was willing to take her into town endeared him to her.

If she could only get to a telephone, she could put this whole nightmare behind her.

She walked directly to a small red Volvo parked in the graveled area to the right of the house. Opening the door on the passenger side, she was about to climb onto the seat when a cold draft passed completely through her body. A long gasp ejected from her throat. Straightening up, her left arm braced atop the open door to hold her up, she turned her head and looked at the towering structure of the house.

A pulse began to drum through her, to hum in her veins. Her eyes widened with fear. As if seen through a zoom lens, the house appeared to slide up to her, then fall back at a far distance. Her light-headedness intensified. A sickening sensation began to churn in her stomach, its waves slapping the walls of her stamina.

Beth lowered her head and shut her eyes. Her legs threatened to buckle beneath her as a frightening rush of weakness washed over her. She placed her right arm on the roof of the car, using all of her willpower to resist the spinning in her head that was making the world go round and round, faster and faster. Panic lanced her heart, rooted her feet to the ground.

She looked up at the bright blue sky above the carriage house and released a whimper. The world began to pass her swiftly on all sides, as if *she* was moving with blinding speed. It grew more difficult to breathe as the optical illusion moved faster and faster, until there was but a gray blur whizzing past her.

Then she experienced a sensation of falling—

"No!" she cried.

With startling abruptness, the phenomenon stopped.

Quaking violently, Beth blinked until she could focus on the carriage house. When nothing else occurred for several seconds, she looked over her shoulder to the main house again. And there it stood, looming behind her, every window seeming to be an eye of something watching her, of some unknown, unspeakable thing waiting for her to return within its clutches.

Heavy footfalls upon gravel brought her head around.

Borgie Ingliss approached her from the direction of a storage shed at the far end of the carriage house. Still trying to bring her lassitude under control, she remained by the open door, waiting for the man to look at her—really look at her—and realize that something was wrong. But Borgie went directly to the opposite side of the car, opened the door, and flashed her a smile before climbing in behind the steering wheel.

She waited a few moments longer, closing her eyes and taking several gulps of air in an attempt to steady her nerves.

Had the entire world gone mad and deserted her on the plains of sanity?

Or would she wake up from the strangest dream of her life and discover that she hadn't even left for Scotland yet?

The purr of the Volvo's engine cut through her reverie. Willing her taut muscles to loosen, she lowered her numbed body onto the seat and pulled the door closed. Then, adjusting her seatbelt, she looked at the driver.

"I really appreciate this."

Borgie grinned broadly as he backed up the car. Now that the vehicle was in motion, she released an emphatic sigh of relief.

"Wha' was tha', Miss?"

"Oh . . . nothing."

Forcing herself to relax in the seat, Beth raked the fingers of one hand through her hair. Then a thought occurred to her.

"Is there somewhere I can exchange American money for British?"

Borgie glanced at his watch. "It's only seven-thirty. Won't be a bank open till ten."

"I'll just wait around until one opens."

"For the call, Miss?"

Beth looked at the man's profile. "Yes. I need to contact the airport and change my departure time. Would you happen to know the name of the taxi service that picked me up at Prestwick? The driver said his name was Calum. I'm afraid I didn't notice the name of the company."

Borgie took several seconds to think on her query. "Afraid I can't help you."

There was a stretch of silence while the driver pulled out onto the main road. Then he looked at Beth, and again she saw something in his eyes that troubled her.

No, she chided herself. She was letting her nerves get the better of her.

"I have a phone a' ma cottage. Yer're mair'n welcome ta use i'."

The drumming pulse returned to invade Beth's body. "Thank you, but I don't mind waiting for the bank to open."

"As you wish."

Beth shriveled within. It was obvious from his taut features that she had insulted him by refusing his generosity. And was she really up to hanging around the small town until the bank opened? Although she didn't know the man beside her, he'd certainly been the least complicated person she'd met since her arrival. And the most friendly.

Not that Lachlan hadn't been friendly in his oblique way.

Lachlan.

Why did her heart ache at the thought of leaving him?

Remembrances of her previous night's experience in the parlor blared in her mind with such force that she unknowingly flattened herself against the back of the seat.

Logic dictated that what she thought had happened, *couldn't* have happened. And yet it had been as real as anything she had experienced in her life.

Was she going mad?

Were the headaches in fact a symptom of something that was affecting her mental perception?

"Borgie, I'd like to accept your offer," she said on a rushed breath. It was imperative she return home and find out what was wrong with her. "That is, if it's still good."

The man at the wheel turned his head and smiled kindly. "O' course, Miss. I just thought i' made mair sense than you hangin' around toon for mair'n two hours."

Sighing, Beth thoughtlessly remarked, "I hope your mother isn't upset that I ran out on breakfast."

Borgie gave a snort. "I tauld you, ma mum's been gone for a week." He turned his attention to the road ahead of them and frowned. "First holiday she's taken in many a year. It's tha' house an' i's curse on us."

"Why do you work at the place if you hate it so much?"

Borgie waited until he had completed a turn onto the main avenue in town. "He threatens us, Miss."

"Lachlan? Threatens you how?"

"Hard ta put ta words," Borgie sighed. "He's got a long airm. The last folks ta try ta rent tha' place, died in a motor wreck no' a mile from the house. They're buried in a field a' the back o' the house. I say *he* did i' ta them. He dinna like anyone ta leave unless he's the one ta run them off."

Beth's heart constricted. Lachlan might be a lot of things, but she was sure he was not a murderer.

"Carlene and David trust him," she said defensively.

"Do they now?" Borgie asked with an eerie undertone. "Might be they've changed their minds."

Suddenly, Beth was sure going to the man's cottage was not a good idea. She knew Agnes had not been away on holiday for a week, and she was as sure as she'd ever been about anything that Lachlan wouldn't deliberately take someone's life. For whatever reason, the Ingliss clan were determined to blacken Lachlan's name. She might be confused and unnerved by Lachlan's mysteriousness, but she refused to accept that he possessed this darker, heinous side.

"I think I'll wait for the bank to open," Beth said, trying to keep her tone as light as possible. "I need to pick up a few things in town, anyway."

"Tae late," Borgie said matter-of-factly as he steered the Volvo into a driveway. "We're here."

The engine was turned off, and Borgie was climbing out of the car even as his last words were only beginning to penetrate Beth's mental haze. Then her door opened, and Borgie was reaching in to help her out of the car.

"Come along. I don't bite," he laughed.

I do, Beth fumed as she straightened up in front of him.

"Home sweet home," he intoned, gesturing toward a white, thatched-roof cottage with brown shutters. "The place is a wee messy. Pay i' na mind."

Beth inwardly revolted at the firm hold Borgie had on her elbow. She couldn't help but feel like a lamb being led to slaughter, and when he opened the unlocked door to his home, a spasm of fear sparked off her nerves. At the instant she was to wrench herself free, turn, and flee, the man released her and went on inside ahead of her.

She lingered at the threshhold. Her mind told her to go on in and make the call to the airport before her emotions dissuaded her from leaving. But her *heart* told her to run and not look back.

Forcing herself through the doorway, she entered a cozy parlor and closed the door behind her. A sweeping glance revealed Borgie was not in the room, and she stepped farther inside and scanned her surroundings.

The room was by no means messy. Simple furniture. Country-print curtains on the two windows. The wainscoting was a deep, dark color and highly polished. Magazines were neatly piled on a pine coffee table.

It was a nice, rustic room with a definite homey ambiance.

"Have an ale?"

Borgie's appearance startled Beth and she stared wide-eyed at the bottle being proffered to her. "No . . . no thank you. Your phone?"

"In the bedroom." He casually pointed to a hall to the left of the parlor. "Tha' way. There's a directory in the drawer o' the night table. Help yerself."

Beth glanced in the direction he'd pointed and managed a wan smile. The bedroom, huh? The hairs on her arms seemed to be squirming against her sensitive skin.

"Thank you. I won't be long."

"Na rush," Borgie said as he sat on the couch. Popping the cap off his bottle, he saluted his guest, then took a long swig of the tepid brew as he stretched out his long, thin legs atop the coffee table.

Beth walked to the closed door of the bedroom and opened it. Her nervousness prevented her from noticing the dark pine interior, or the masculine decor. She went directly to the night table and opened the drawer. Sitting on the edge of the bed, she opened the directory and began to scan the yellow pages for a listing of the airport.

Pain squeezed the back of her neck, robbing her of breath and blinding her. Fighting down the threat of panic trying to overwhelm her, she leaned slightly to and cupped a hand over the throbbing area.

Pursing her lips, she forced herself to take slow, easy breaths. Bursts of tiny lights went off in front of her eyes.

"A problem, Miss?"

Again, Borgie startled her with his sudden appearance. Inexplicably, the pain in her head vanished. Not even the usual residual aftermath remained.

She looked over at Borgie. The sight of him hanging in the doorway, gulping down the last dregs of his beer, filled her with sudden apprehension. There was something in his demeanor that triggered her awareness. The man across from her was no longer the gardener who had offered to help her out. The feelings toward him that had surfaced when he had been making those accusations about Lachlan returned with more force.

"No. No problem," she said finally.

She slid the directory back into the drawer and closed it. As much as she wanted to return to the States, her first priority was to get away from Borgie Ingliss before her fears came to life.

Swiping an arm across his mouth, he swaggered farther into the room. "Mak yer call?"

"No. I've changed my mind."

"Guid. Guid. I didn't think you were the hasty sort, Beth."

Shifting his weight to one leg, he cooed, "Oh . . . you don't mind me callin' you by yer given name now, do you?"

"No. No, I don't mind," she said warily.

"Guid. Guid. We Scots are friendly folk. Like ta be on a first name basis wi' those we tak a fancy ta. If you get ma meanin'."

Her body tense with disgust, Beth stiffly rose to her feet. "No, I don't get your . . . *meaning*, Mr. Ingliss."

"I'm just a friendly mon, darlin'."

"I'm sorry I've wasted your time. I'll be returning to Baird House now."

"No' a waste, darlin'." With a swing of his arm, he slammed the bedroom door shut, then slid the emptied beer bottle onto a nearby dresser. "Ma mum tauld me some scary things abou' you, Beth. She said you were sleepin' wi' the deil, hisself. Tha's a fearsome notion. But I keep thinkin' ta maself— "

He haughtily, slowly, approached Beth. "— why wad a womon as fine as you be het for the likes o' him? Can you explain tha' ta me, Beth darlin'?"

"I think you've gotten the wrong idea about me," Beth said heatedly. She tried to brush past the offensive man, but he took a steely grasp on her arm and forced her against him.

"You promised ta pay me for ma trouble, didn't you?"

Beth winced at the fetid, bitter breath spilling past the man's lips. "I meant cash!"

"Cash won't warm ma bones," he crooned, then made a clumsy attempt to kiss her, which she stopped by sinking her teeth into his lower lip. With a howl, he harshly lifted her, swung her around, and tossed her onto the bed.

Before the initial shock wore off, he ripped the telephone from the wall and began to lower himself atop her.

Beth fought back. She slapped his face, hard. Then the slaps became punches when he merely laughed at her efforts and buried his face into the side of her neck.

"Yer're a looker," he chortled, as his free hand worked to undo the front of his pants.

Beth's punches escalated into a frantic fight. She used the heels of her sneakers to pound the back of his thighs and calves, and her teeth to bite into his shoulder. This elicited a guttural sound from him, and for a fleeting moment, she thought he was rising up to release her. But then a hand sailed through the air and caught her on the side of her face.

Through the haze of pain exploding in her head, she saw his lips curl back from his teeth.

"Beddin' him will see you buried behind the house wi' the rest o' them!" he snarled, his fingers curling about her throat to anchor her. "It's a real mon you need, you crazy bitch!"

"Get off me!" she gasped, more terrified than she'd ever been in her life.

Unholy fever gleamed in his eyes as he drew his rigid, curved penis into his hand.

"Scream," he laughed. "Na one will hear you."

The fingers of his other hand tightened about her neck. "I like a fight. It maks me hard. See how hard? An' I'm goin' ta drive i' inta you— "

Beth screamed, but not at his threat. As his words became strangled within his throat, a bolt of lightning streaked across the ceiling. Thunder filled the room. With another outcry, she wormed her legs up under Borgie Ingliss' ribs and gave a fierce thrust. In her panic, she didn't realize he fell back out of fear, but she used the moment to her advantage and scrambled from the bed to the door.

A sound whirled her about, and she gaped in horror at a phenomenon materializing across the room. A ball of bright green mist was hovering above the bed. Multiple appendages of lightning darted from it, licking and jabbing at the man upon the rumpled covers. Mingled with the ever-intensifying thunder were Borgie's cries of fear, shrill cries that beckoned Beth's compassion.

She took a step toward the bed—

The lightning crackled anew. Borgie's wails wrenched a cry from her. As loathsome as the man was, she couldn't let him die at the hands of—

What the hell *was* it?

Temper and fear her avenging shield, she grabbed up the beer bottle and flung it. By the time it had sailed through the mist and shattered against the far wall, she was throwing a small wooden chest from the dresser with all her might. This, too, passed through the phenomenon and dropped to the floor on the far side of the bed, but she noticed the lightning had lessened in brightness and ferocity.

Panting, a man's hairbrush clenched in her right hand, she watched with gnawing trepidation.

"Go away!" she demanded, the strength in her voice surprising her.

"See him for wha' he is!" Borgie wailed, cowering and drawing the bed quilt about him as he lay quaking beneath the manifestation.

To Beth's horror, the lightning became arms of mist and light which gripped every part of Borgie Ingliss and began to shake him insensible.

"Mak him go away!" Borgie screamed. "I didn't mean anythin' wrong by you, Miss!"

The shaking continued for a few seconds longer, then Beth received an impression that the anomaly was waiting for her to say or do something. A pounding began in the back of her head. Tears spilled down her ashen cheeks. She could feel herself rapidly weakening, as if the blood in her body were being unmercifully drained.

With a low cry, she turned on her heel and fled through the doorway. Her legs pumped with all the steam she could muster. Blindly she ran on and on . . . and on until she became aware of running through a gray, endless fog. She staggered and ran. Stumbled and ran. There were no sounds around her but her own sobs. No impressions or colors or life of any kind.

The headaches.

The only explanation was that she was in some kind of a coma. Something had gone wrong inside her head— something, even if it were explained to her, that she wouldn't be able to fathom.

But not madness!

Oh God, not madness, please!

Let it be a coma that she could fight from within.

Something she could eventually emerge from to the promise of life.

Not madness!

Was Scotland, Carlene, David, *Lachlan* real?

How much of her life had been mere dream, fantasy?

She stumbled again, but this time she found herself falling through an endless void. The momentum went on and on, the plunge more terrifying than anything she'd ever experienced. Her arms and legs flailed wildly. If only she could touch something solid— stop the flight— the falling— the . . . *nightmare* . . .

With inertia came a soft, sweet-smelling bed beneath her. Prone, her fingers kneading something dewy and cool, Beth kept her face to the ground and wept from the depths of her soul. When she dared to look up at her surroundings, it was to find that she was lying atop a manicured lawn, a short distance from a bubbling, cement fountain.

The north gardens. She'd noticed the fountain from one of the windows on the second floor.

She was somehow back at Baird House. Safe, but badly shaken. She must have suffered another blackout before locating Borgie that morning, and all that had happened was indeed just a very real nightmare.

A peacock strutted by, its foot a hairbreadth from one of her arms. The indignant angle of its head struck her as funny and she released a raspy laugh. A green and blue-eyed feather swept under her nose before the bird strolled off.

Amazed by the vividness of her imagination, she stiffly drew up into a sitting position.

Her brain felt terribly cramped within her skull, a strong indication that she had in fact suffered one of the crippling migraines. That was all right by her. Any sane, reasonable explanation was appreciated.

Getting unsteadily to her feet, she looked about her. Except for the rustle of the birds ambling about the gardens, and the soothing sound of water bubbling within the fountain, it was peaceful. The morning was warm, the sunlight bright and reviving.

Brushing off her skirt and top, Beth started toward the front of the house. Her body was tired, but her mind was electrified at the prospect of being here at this place, and not in the cottage of that queer dream.

Poor Borgie.

How would she ever look him in the face again if he learned she had dreamed he tried to force himself on her?

Well, it wasn't as if she was about to tell him, was it!

"Coffee," she said, stepping onto a cobblestone path that circled the fountain. She stopped and dipped her cupped hands into the icy water, then splashed the refreshing liquid on her face. Wiping a cool hand across the back of her neck, she turned toward the pathway leading to the front of the house.

It was then that something in her peripheral vision drew her attention to a field beyond the low hedges and trees behind the house.

She was certainly too exhausted to go off exploring, but instinct urged her forward for a closer look.

Muttering at her own stupidity, she trampled through ground vines and low brush until she came to the edge of the field. There was nothing extraordinary to see here. The field was richly green, and there was one huge, ancient tree centered on it.

Still, something beckoned her.

She took her time crossing the field, plucking a blade of grass to nibble on along the way. The closer she came to the tree, the more convinced she was that she was wasting her time. But twenty yards away from her destination, she discerned something standing within the shadows beneath the limbs.

The something turned out to be several head-stones.

Shuddering, Beth began to turn away, until one of two large stones caught her attention before she could ignore it.

HERE THE DEVIL LIES
LACHLAN IAIN BAIRD
13/2/1811-?/1844

Beth sank to her knees in front of the headstone, her gaze riveted on the name.

Lachlan. So, Lannie was a nickname.

Lifting a hand, she gingerly pressed her finger tips to the dates. She couldn't fathom why, but her heart was twisting with pain and sorrow.

Thirty-three years old. Not a long life, and not a fitting way for him to die.

Tears welled in her eyes. She gave herself a shake to ward off the melancholy enveloping her, only then happening to notice another headstone off to the right and set back. Questioning her eyesight, she hesitantly crawled a little closer to it.

A cry lodged in her throat. Her hands flew up to cover her mouth. She was quaking fiercely as her gaze repeatedly ran over the letters on the newer stone.

It wasn't possible.

Someone was playing a very cruel joke on her!

A sensation of scalding fluid shot up into her throat and she tried to scramble to her feet, but her legs were like rubber.

Despite her desperation to tear her gaze from the heinous sight, the chiseled words in front of her seemed to close in.

FATE BROUGHT THEM TO ME
FATE CRUELLY TOOK THEM AWAY
REST IN PEACE, MY FRIENDS
CARLENE AND DAVID CAMBRIDGE
3/9/1962-20/4/1994   11/10/1956-20/4/1994

A blood-curdling wail escaped Beth.

This was insanity!

What kind of a mind would perpetrate this sort of prank?

Carlene and David dead? No, that was impossible! She'd spoken to them on the telephone. Carlene had greeted her upon her arrival from the airport! They had talked over tea! Talked about the portrait!

And Carlene had even shown her to her room on the third floor!

Angry denial entwining with fear, Beth slammed a fist on the ground, and cried, "It's a lie! Carlene! *Carlene!*"

On her knees, her buttocks braced atop her heels, she clenched her fists in front of her and repeatedly called out her friend's name until her raw throat began to protest.

Weeping, she whimpered, "I can't take much more of this."

Anguish, disgust, and fear threatened to overwhelm her.

Fighting with all her willpower to pull herself

together, she began to scoot back away from the headstones. When she had only gone a few feet, her vision zoomed in on the last headstone, standing to the left and alongside that of Lachlan Baird.

The pulse returned and drummed forcefully through her.

The world swayed, while Beth, herself, remained frozen in horror.

MY DEAREST LOVE
BETH MARIE STAPLES
24/7/63-26/7/94

As her state of shock waned, Beth released an hysterical laugh.

She wasn't dead!

TODAY was the twenty-sixth of July!

But that moment of dark humor evaporated to the fires of doubt. It could all only be a fiendish prank, but . . .

Throwing back her head, Beth released a long, guttural wail.

A wind came up around her, as if from the bowels of the earth. Her fists clenched, her arms held tightly folded against her abdomen, she stared at the headstone bearing her name. She was angrier than she'd ever been. Angry, and feeling helpless and betrayed.

How could Carlene help perpetrate a stunt like this? It was cruel, hideous—

"I tried ta stop you, girl."

Jumping to her feet, Beth whirled, then stood as

We've got your authors!

If you seek out the latest historical romances by today
bestselling authors, our new reader's service, KENSINGTON
CHOICE, is the club for you.

KENSINGTON CHOICE is the only club where you can fin
authors like Janelle Taylor, Shannon Drake, Rosanne Bittner, Sylvi
Sommerfield, Penelope Neri and Phoebe Conn all in one place...

...and the only service that will deliver their romances direct t
your home as soon as they are published—even before they reach th
bookstores.

KENSINGTON CHOICE is also the only service that wi
give you a substantial guaranteed discount off the publisher's pric
on every one of those romances.

That's right: Every month, the Editors at Zebra and Pinnac'
select four of the newest novels by our bestselling authors and rus
them straight to you, usually *before they reach the bookstores.* Th
publisher's prices for these romances range from $4.99 to $5.99—b
they are always yours for the guaranteed low price of just *$4.20!*

That means you'll always save over 20%...often as much
30%...off the publisher's prices on every shipment you get fro
KENSINGTON CHOICE!

All books are sent on a 10-day free examination basis, and the
is no minimum number of books to buy. (A postage and handlir
charge of $1.50 is added to each shipment.)

As your introduction to the convenience and value of this ne
service, we invite you to accept

4 BOOKS FREE

The 4 books, worth up to
$23.96, are our welcoming gift.
You pay only $1 to help cover
postage and handling.

To start your subscription
to KENSINGTON CHOICE
and receive your introductory
package of 4 FREE romances,
detach and mail the postpaid
card at right *today.*

We have 4 FREE BOOKS for you
as your introduction to
KENSINGTON CHOICE
To get your FREE BOOKS, worth
up to $23.96, mail the card below.

FREE BOOK CERTIFICATE

As my introduction to your new KENSINGTON CHOICE reader's service, please send me 4 FREE historical romances (worth up to $23.96), billing me just $1 to help cover postage and handling. As a KENSINGTON CHOICE subscriber, I will then receive 4 brand-new romances to preview each month for 10 days FREE. I can return any shipment within 10 days and owe nothing. The publisher's prices for the KENSINGTON CHOICE romances range from $4.99 to $5.99, but as a subscriber I will be entitled to get them for just $4.20 per book or $16.80 for all four titles. There is no minimum number of books to buy, and I can cancel my subscription at any time. A $1.50 postage and handling charge is added to each shipment.

Name _____

Address _____ Apt. _____

City _____ State _____ Zip _____

Telephone (____) _____

Signature _____

(If under 18, parent or guardian must sign)

Subscription subject to acceptance. Terms and prices subject to change.

KC0295

We have
4
FREE
Historical
Romances
for you!

(worth up
to $23.96!)

Details inside!

KENSINGTON CHOICE
Reader's Service
120 Brighton Road
P.O. Box 5214
Clifton, NJ 07015-5214

rigid as stone at the sight of Lachlan standing a few feet away.

"Tis a hard thin' ta accept a' first," he said kindly, compassion softening his features, his hand held out to her. "Tis why I had you come here ta Scotland, ta ma home, Beth. I cadna let you die alone, no' whan I knew I cad— "

"Shut up!" Panting, Beth glared at the man across from her. "This," she charged, jabbing an isolated finger at the headstones, "isn't funny! It's sick!"

"Love— "

"Shut up!"

Inwardly struggling to bring the violent trembling of her body under control, she glared unflinchingly at the man she felt was responsible for the terrible hoax. "I'm leaving here, Lachlan, and I pray to God I never lay eyes on you or this damn place again!"

"If I hadna had ta teach tha' Ingliss swine a lesson a' his place, I wad have been here sooner," he said, his tone heavily laced with sorrow.

"You're insane!" Beth cried, her tone throbbing with hysteria. She backed up two paces, a hand held up to ward him off. "I'm going home— "

"You *are* home."

Beth clamped her hands over her ears.

"You *are* home!" Lachlan averred. "Deep inside, you know you died— "

"No!"

"— a week ago."

"Shut up! *Shut up!*"

"In yer sleep."

"Damn you, Lachlan!"

A tear spilled down Lachlan's face. "I truly thought you'd have mair time than you did. I wanted ta tell you— "

Beth screamed to shut out his words, but Lachlan persevered, "— but I was a coward. You were dyin' in the parlor, Beth. I cadna stop wha' was happenin' ta you. Ma pleasurin' you was the only way I cad help you through the pain."

Garbled denials rattled in Beth's throat as she unsteadily sank to her knees. Lachlan rushed to her. Placing an arm about her waist, he eased her up onto her feet. When she buried her face against his chest and bitterly wept, he hesitantly enfolded her within the security of his arms. Then he raised his face to the heavens and squeezed his eyes shut to free the renewed salty liquid testimony of his own anguish.

"Sweet darlin'," he choked, smoothing the hair at the back of her neck. "I'm sa sarry I cadna heal you, but i' was tae far beyond ma power.

"But death is no' an end for us. You must trust me, girl. This is only oor beginnin'."

With the vehemence of a gale, Beth wrenched from his hold and began to pummel him with her fists.

"Why are you doing this to me!" she cried, its sound producing a rush of tears in Lachlan's eyes. "I hate it! I *hate* it! I'm not— "

As if in slow motion, she felt herself falling forward, falling and falling, and passing through Lachlan as if he were nothing more than an image comprised of air. She hit the ground, twisting and staring up at him in horror.

He appeared solid. A look at herself revealed that she was the image, fading before her own eyes.

A cry of such torment issued from her lungs, Lachlan cried out as well. Rushing to her, he swept her up into his arms, observing her disorientation as she watched herself becoming solid again.

"Haud onta me."

Without thought, she hastily wrapped her arms about his neck, then buried her face against his shoulder and wept. Lachlan cradled her against him, softly weeping himself.

"It's not true," she sobbed. "It's not true."

"Wha' I wad give ta spare you this."

"I'm dreaming."

Lowering his head, Lachlan squeezed his eyes shut and kissed her on one of her throbbing temples.

"I'll tak care o' you, Beth."

A wheezing sound could be heard from her concealed mouth, then a hoarse, "What have you done to me?"

"Sweet Jesus," Lachlan choked. "I've only tried ta—"

"Keep me here," she interjected, looking up at him through lifeless eyes. "You brought me here to die."

Eight

"Have a cup o tea, darlin'."

Beth was only dimly aware of a cup and saucer being placed on a marble-topped coffee table in front of her. Somehow she had come to be in the parlor, perched atop a Queen Anne-style settee with richly embroidered, pink-toned upholstery. She could smell the enticing aroma of the tea.

She could hear a fire crackling in the hearth. She was aware of Lachlan's presence close by, but her state of mind left her with a distorted impression of everything around her.

Numbness cloaked her. It was a blessed relief not to feel anything at the moment. How could she begin to sort through what she'd earlier seen, and what had been said since her arrival in Scotland? To dwell on anything as outrageous as—

Jet lag was no longer a viable possibility.

Either she had lost her mind during the flight, or insanity had run rampant through all those whom she had met since her arrival.

A shiver coursed through her, an icy finger fondling every nerve in her body. Her blood felt like chilly mountain streams within her veins.

"I know exactly wha' yer're goin' through," said a soft voice nearby. "Let me help you through this."

Beth's eyes rolled to target the face of the man who had spoken. Lachlan. He was crouched to her right, concern radiating from his face. One of his hands was resting on her leg, just above her knee. The other forearm was braced on the coffee table.

"Tak a sip o' tea. It'll tak the chill ou' o' yer bones—" Lachlan had the good grace to blush. Lifting the china cup by its delicate handle, he proffered it to her. "Just one little sip. Come on, darlin'—"

To his astonishment, she *poofed* away. He gaped at the emptiness where she'd been a moment before. His hand holding up the cup began to tremble, sloshing its contents. Jerkily placing the cup back on the table, he slowly rose to a standing position and momentarily closed his eyes with a mute prayer for patience.

"It didna tak you long ta learn tha' now, did i'?" he muttered, looking about the room with a shadow of desperation in his expression.

Beth could hear his voice, but it sounded far away and possessed an eerie, vibrating quality. There was endless grayness surrounding her, a universe of nothingness, and such absolute stillness that panic swelled within her.

Turning in place, she wailed, "Lachlan! Where am I? Don't leave me here!"

"Step back through. Tis easy, Beth."

"There're no doors or windows. I can't—"

The abruptness with which she found herself

standing again in the parlor left her lightheaded. The room began to spin slowly, then faster and faster. She grabbed onto the back of the settee to steady herself, but the waves of dizziness continued to pound unmercifully down on her.

"Steady," Lachlan said softly, drawing her into his arms and holding her head to the hollow of one shoulder. "Tis frightenin', I know, but i' will pass. The grayness is oor restin' place, you might say. Tis there we gather the energy ta spend brief intervals in this warld. You'll come ta know i' all, darlin'. Just be patient."

Beth clung to him out of a need to feel the security of solidity. She was too full of fear to hold onto anger at the moment. She wept bitterly against his shoulder, her tears dampening the front of his shirt.

"You cry. You do wha'e'er i' taks ta get you through this adjustment period. I'm here for you." He caressed a cheek atop her crown, and peered upward. "You an' I have all the time in the warld now."

Snuggling her tighter in his arms, he soothingly stroked the back of her hair. He wished he could protect her tender emotions from this new reality. He had often mulled over what her initial reaction might be, and he had believed he had counseled himself to be strong when this very moment came about. But her weeping lanced him, pierced him with such poignant depth that he felt his phantom heart constrict, and a sting of tears form in his eyes.

Then it struck him that he would be able to hold

her like this forever. The promise of an everlasting companion, a mate for eternity, melted his anguish beneath the heat of his rapture.

"We're thegither e'erlastin', Beth," he said a bit giddily. Unraveling his arms from about her trembling torso, he lovingly framed her face with his hands and looked into the turbulent depths of her eyes. "Na one can e'er separate us. We can mak love through countless sunrises an' sunsets. Dwell on the positive o' oor existence, darlin'. It will lessen the ache in yer heart for wha' has passed."

He kissed her mouth, at first gently, then more hungrily as his arms wound about her and molded her to his body. Although the kisses were salty and wet from her tears, he dined on her sweetness and the utter tenderness of her shapely mouth. He wanted to make love with her, to fill her so completely with pleasure she would temporarily forget that she had passed on to a different plane of existence.

Actions, not words, would convince her of her existing abilities to experience life. He had found the gray plane at most times difficult, but then, he'd been alone. She would never be alone, he vowed. She would never suffer the terrible isolation of the grayness.

As long as they were together.

Through the fibers of his reverie came a realization. She was struggling within his arms, grunting against his deep, penetrating kiss. Rattled by the abrupt change in her, he lifted his head. The angry flush in her cheeks prompted him to drop his arms to his sides. He could only watch as she backed away from him, her eyes blazing as she contemptuously swiped an arm across her mouth.

"I've finally figured it out. You've been drugging me, haven't you?" she flung at him with asperity, her body quaking with anger.

"Druggin' you? Beth darlin'— "

"Stop using endearments on me, you . . . you . . . *lunatic!* I want the truth!"

"The truth, you say?" Lachlan wasn't trying to be funny. He was genuinely astonished by her accusation. "Ach, darlin', you sud know me better than tha'!"

"Stop lying to me, Lachlan! Admit it! You've been *drugging* me!" she accused, jabbing a finger at him to punctuate her words. "It's all beginning to make sense. You somehow convinced Carlene to lure me here— "

"Patience, laddie, patience," he groaned, his eyes rolled upward.

"—and sent her away. During that brief time we were talking, I kept getting the feeling she wanted to tell me something. She didn't really want any part of this, did she?"

"She had some doubts."

Breathing heavily, Beth stared at him as if truly seeing him for the first time. "You've made no secret of your obsession with that damned portrait!"

"If no' for the fact I know yer're distraught an' dinna mean wha' yer're sayin', I'd have you across ma knee!"

"You went to a lot of trouble for nothing, mister.

I won't let you try to convince me I'm insane to keep me in this house!"

"Yer're goin' through a denial phase—"

He ducked in time to avoid being hit by an urn Beth hurled. The sound of shattering glass exploded on the fireplace mantel. Straightening up, he stared at the remnants of his precious, thirteenth century Chinese urn, and a whimper caught in his throat.

"Have you an inklin' o' wha' tha' was worth?" he asked shrilly, his gaze upon her questioning her sanity. "Five generations o' ma family—"

He released a squeal and quickly lifted his hands in a pleading gesture when Beth wielded a porcelain Venus figurine above her head. "No' *tha'!*" he gasped, his knees weakening, threatening to give out beneath him.

The precious artifact struck Lachlan's shoulder. His hands made a wild bid to grasp the piece, but like a juggler out of sync, his frantic antics only flipped the figurine this way and that until it slipped through his fingers and crashed on the edge of the marble-topped coffee table.

Lachlan stared down at the countless pieces, horror further whitening his face, then he swung a harried look Beth's way.

To his disbelief, she was tossing a large Austrian crystal paperweight in her hands, glaring at him with an undeniable glint of animosity brightening her eyes.

"I want answers." Beth heaved a ragged breath.

"You've been putting something in my tea, haven't you?"

Color returned to Lachlan's face. Angry color. "I canna believe you wad accuse me o' such a foul thin'! An' you have no' touched yer damn tea," he said through locked teeth.

He took a cautious step in her direction, his gaze riveted on the crystal she held threateningly higher. "I'm willin' ta answer yer questions, but I'll no' stand for you threatenin' me wi' ma ain treasures. Now . . . put . . . tha' . . . *doon.*"

"When I'm damn good and ready. Start talking."

Lachlan's nostrils flared. He arched one eyebrow censoriously and flexed his hands by his sides. "Where do you want me ta start?"

"Anywhere that begins to make sense of all this."

"Efter you put doon ma grandmither's crystal."

A showdown ensued. Lachlan held his ground, confident Beth's anger would lessen and her compassion would resurface. He knew this woman better than anyone—

Or so he thought.

As if seeing it happen in slow motion, he watched the paperweight sail through the air. His phantom heart drummed in his chest. A deafening roar filled his ears. The crystal piece whizzed past his ear. Reflexively, he shot out a hand to capture it. The crystal skimmed past the tips of his fingers. He pushed off on the balls of his feet, but the crystal shattered on impact with the fireplace tiles. He released a string of Gaelic curses as he slapped the floor with the entire length of his body.

"Aneuch!" he bellowed, scrambling back onto his feet. "Tis— " He exhaled sharply at the sight of Beth holding up a jade figurine. "Oh, sweet Jesus," he sobbed, raising his hands pleadingly in the air. "If yer're lookin' ta see a grown mon cry, go ahead an' toss i'. But if there's an ounce o' compassion left in you, you'll put i' doon."

"I want answers!"

A squeaky breath spilled from him as he gestured helplessly with his arms. "I said I'd answer yer questions!" he exclaimed in something akin to hysteria. "Tis no' simple ta explain!"

"Oh?" Beth said. "How hard can it be, Lachlan?" she asked sarcastically. "You *supposedly* died over a hundred years ago. Carlene and David have *supposedly* been dead for three months. And let's not forget, I've *supposedly* been dead for a week. This is all a sick hoax, or I'm hallucinating. Right?"

With a sigh of defeat, he shook his head. "Neither."

Beth glared at him for several long seconds before lowering the jade piece to her side. He gestured at the settee and, after a brief hesitation, she sat and laid the figurine on her lap.

"All right. I'm listening."

Lachlan's throat felt suddenly tight, and he turned away to try to compose himself. But his gaze fell upon Beth's portrait, her features as strong a beacon as ever for his heart. Turning his head, he looked at the three-dimensional vision of the same woman. She was waiting for him to begin, her eyes downcast, her fingers nervously fidgeting with the figurine.

Sighing deeply, he ran his fingers through his hair. He'd wanted to tell her everything since that moment when he first saw her standing on the staircase, but he was still apprehensive. How could he prepare anyone, much less the woman he loved, for something like this? Then she looked at him with tortured eyes. Lachlan gulped past the tightness in his throat and forced himself to begin.

"I guess tis better ta start a' the beginnin'," he said, his gaze flitting over the painting of his long-awaited love. "Ma faither was a successful shipbuilder. Efter his death, me an' ma three aulder brithers teuk o'er the business. By the time I was thirty, I had mair money than maist men see in a lifetime. An' i' was then I decided i' was time ta settle doon an' start a family o' ma ain.

"I'd come ta Crossmichael ta visit a friend a few years previously, an' I fell in love wi' i' here. An' i' was here I found ma land— in 1841— an' started ta wark on this house.

"It teuk two years ta finish, an' anither year ta fill i' wi' all the treasures here now. Then i' was time ta find me a hearty womon ta mairry, a womon ta fill these walls wi' the laughter o' children."

Lachlan swallowed hard, then tried to smile through the tightness in his face. "I went clear ta Aberdeen ta find me a bride, an efter a few weeks, I was introduced ta Tessa by a third cousin o' mine. It teuk me a week ta convince her ta mairry me. Aye, I thought she was the perfect lass for this house. She had a face as soft an' fair as moonlight, an' hair the color o' golden wine. Her eyes sparkled when she laughed. She made me feel young an' giddy, an' I fell sa hard in love tha' I didna think beyond whiskin' her ta her new home an' startin' oor lives thegither. She was sa shy an' undemandin', I cadna refuse whan she asked if her aulder brither cad come ta stay wi' us. This house was big aneuch.

"But ma bride began ta act strangely once we arrived here. She complained o' a feelin' o' bein' watched an' touched by somethin' evil. Oor weddin' night was fraught wi' her weepin' an' complainin' an' usin' e'ery excuse she cad think o' ta douse ma passion, an' I left oor mairriage bed angrier than I'd e'er been.

"She needed time, she said. An' as long as I left her alone, she was attentive an sweet, but each night, she went ta her ain bed, an' me . . . ta mine.

"I got along weel aneuch wi' her brither. He seemed a sympathetic lad. Aye, you cad say I thought verra weel o' Robert.

"Abou' a month efter oor mairriage, I tauld Tessa i' was time she fulfilled her wifely duties. She teuk i' bloody guid, I thought, an' she promised ta come ta ma bed tha' night. There I lay, waitin' for her, all bathed an' perfumed like some poor, love-sick sop abou' ta lose his virginity. But the hoors went by. She ne'er appeared. Come morn, I went lookin' for her.

"An' I found her. In her room. Sleepin' in Robert's airms."

Releasing a scornful laugh, Lachlan turned and finally looked at Beth. It didn't matter to him that she was watching him with a look of complete apathy. His only concern at the moment was to go on with the details of the past, in the hope that talk of their future together would follow.

"I cadna say aught ta either o' them. Just went back ta ma room an' tried ta mak sense o' i' all. Then Tessa came in, wearin' the clingy nightgown I'd bought her for oor weddin' night, tears in her eyes, an' all contrite an' pleadin' wi' me ta understand. Robert, she claimed, was no' her brither, but her lover. They were tae poor ta mairry, she said, an' tae in love ta bear separation.

"I was tae numb ta be angry, an' I was calm whan I tauld her ta leave wi' him. I tauld her she cadna tak aught from the house, though. It was all bought for a carin' mistress o' the place, an' I felt she had na right ta any o' i'. She looked a' me wi' those cursed blue eyes o' hers, tears on her cheeks, an' she tauld me she was sarry she'd hurt me. An' whan she came toward me, words o' regret spillin' like honey from her tongue, I was expectin' a wee kiss on the cheek for ma troubles."

Lachlan sighed deeply, trying to camouflage the pain the remembrance evoked.

"Wha' I got was a dirk in ma heart— ma ain great-grandfaither's jewel-handled dirk, na less. No' a flicker o' emotion was in her eyes whan she done the deed.

"Her an' her Robert thought I'd died right away. I cad hear them discussin' wha' ta do wi' me, an' there I lay, ma life's blood runnin' ou' o' me, an' they thinkin' I'd long since taken ma last breath.

"It was Robert's idea ta wall me oop in the tower.

I remember hopin' ta hear a bit o' sadness in Tessa's tone, but she was cauld, an' anxious ta be done wi' the whole mess.

"Waitin' while Robert tore ou' the wall ta mak ma grave, I kept thinkin' I sud be dead by now. The pain had stopped, but I cad feel ma blood tricklin' ou' o' ma body . . . sa slow . . . sa steady, an' ma blood felt sa het while ma body was growin' e'er sa cauld as the time crept by.

"Robert dragged me inta the openin' he'd made, an' kept crammin' me in tighter an' tighter. I didna find the strength ta speak till he began ta mortar the rocks back in place.

"Robert, I said, *dinna do this.*

"A terrible look o' fear came inta his eyes. For the longest time, he crouched there starin' a' me, an' I found maself thinkin' he didna have the heart ta go on.

"But he did. Rock efter rock was replaced. 'Fore he cad seal me in completely, I warned him, *Robert, I'll ne'er leave ma house. You'll ne'er ain ma treasures."*

Lachlan looked at Beth. Her head was lowered and she was again fingering the jade piece.

"It seemed ta tak fore'er for me ta die, Beth. I dinna know how long for sure, but I stayed in tha' horrible darkness, tryin' ta understand how i' all cad have gone sa wrong. I think I went ta sleep, but i' was no' a sleep I awaked from in the usual sense.

"I was frightened by the absence o' life a' first. The grayness was sa overpowerin'. In tha' new beginnin', Beth, I cadna mak maself seen. Ooh, I cad scare the wits ou' o' ma murderers, an' efter a while,

I discovered I cad keep them from takin' ma treasures, although the bulk o' ma money was ou' o' ma power ta protect.

"Beth, never trust a bank.

"The real anger didna come till efter their first child was born," Lachlan went on, his tone low and raspy. "It was then I realized ma dreams were as lost as ma life. E'ery whimper an' laugh an' cry I heard from the babe, dirked me again an' again."

Beth gave a stifled sob. Lachlan looked down at her bent head, and drew in a breath. He didn't want to cause her further sorrow, or use her compassion to his advantage. But he needed her to understand all the factors that had brought them both to this point in time.

Going to the coffee table, he sat on it across from her. He waited for her to look up. When she didn't, he gently took the figurine from her and placed it on the table alongside him. Then he leaned, rested his forearms on his legs above his knees. Angling his head to have a look at her face, he found he could only discern her tightly compressed lips, and the quivering of her chin.

"Dinna feel sad abou' ma past. If I hadna sa desperately wanted children, I might have seen wha' was comin'."

"Go on," she choked, bending her head further to avoid his prying eyes.

"All right, I will.

"Tessa an' her Robert had nine children thegither, but their mairriage was fraught wi' tears an' anger maist o' the time. Robert wanted ta leave this place. They had ma money an' cad live any-where they wanted. But Tessa was a spiteful womon. She cad sense ma presence, an' she delighted in torturin' me wi' each child she bore in ma ain bed.

"Robert died before the turn o' the century." Lachlan released a dry, low laugh. "Tessa brought in gypsies an' the like ta banish me. But funny thin' abou' the powers tha' be, Beth, we have mair control than we're led ta believe in life. Sa I stayed on.

"In 1904, Tessa died. Her spirit passed on swiftly ou' o' ma reach. Her eldest son, Robbie, teuk o'er the house. His plan was ta mak some minor im-provements, then sell ma home for wha'e'er he cad get for i'.

"They amazed me, these Inglisses. Na matter wha' I did—the howlin', the tossin' things, the threatenin'—maist o' tha' idiot clan refused ta be-lieve I still existed. O' course, Tessa's stary had been I'd deserted her. Cool an' calculatin', tha' one. The family was ne'er sure wha' was hauntin' this place—no' till Robbie uncovered me."

Lachlan linked his fingers. "Two things altered ma existence then, Beth. Whan Robbie opened the wall, I felt maself expel a breath—a great, roarin' breath tha' gave me a sense o' truly bein' alive again. Some kind o' energy moved abou' me. Its power pulled me through the grayness I'd known since ma death. A' first I thought I was comin' back ta life . . . i' felt—*feels*—tha' real. Like we are now, darlin'."

Beth's head lifted slowly. Her tear-filmed eyes re-luctantly looked into Lachlan's. He wanted to pull her into his arms and soothe her, but he knew he had to go on. It all had to be explained before she could begin to accept her own death.

"This energy gives us the ability ta materialize an' spend portions o' time livin' in this world . . . dimension . . . wha'e'er you wish ta call i'. I canna explain how i' comes ta be, but I know i' comes from wi'in this house. I've no' been able ta tap inta i' anywhere else. An' as long as I'm full o' maself— you might say— this energy allows me ta move beyond this property."

"Leave. Like at Borgie's place." Beth accused with quiet disgust.

"Aye. I wanted ta kill him— didna, though. He was alive whan I left, an' tha' was for Agnes' sake. She attended yer funeral— "

Lachlan sucked in a breath as Beth shot to her feet and walked to the far end of the room. After several moments of silence, he went on, "I guess Borgie didna realize you were . . . gone, girl. No' tha' a little matter like *that* wad sway him. But I'm gettin' ahead o' maself.

"I'm no' sure wha' I expected o' the Inglisses once the truth was exposed. Perhaps a wee show o' pity for ma untimely end. But no' one o' them shed a tear, an' i' hurt like hell, i' did.

"Ta further frustrate me, they decided I was no' fit ta be buried in a churchyard. Hypocritical swines!"

He rose to his feet and, with a hand clamped on the back of his neck, walked to the fireplace and looked longingly up at Beth's portrait. "They interred me ou' by tha' tree, wi'ou' benefit o' a kist or words o' remorse. No' a prayer for me, Beth, an' i' made me furious. I'd done nocht ta them but mairry tha' greedy wench. No' a conscience among the bloody lot. Ta this day, they exist on *ma* money— their homes an' businesses acquired from *ma* ain sweat an' blood. An' buried me, they did, in tha' cauld, lonely place, like some craiture wha' died on a roadside.

"Tha' verra day I swore, for as long as this Ingliss clan's blood runs warm, they will serve me an' this house."

Lachlan's voice became husky and deeper, and laced with bitterness. "Lest I visit them in their cozy homes an' remind them o' their debt ta me. Might sound cruel, Beth, but I've come ta realize tis ma hatred for this clan tha's kept me here— tha' alone givin' me the strength ta co-exist wi'in the grayness an' this warld.

"Till *you* came inta me life."

Amid the tension in the room, Beth's voice, cold as the Arctic, said, "I don't want to hear anymore."

"Have you listened ta a word I've said?"

She looked at him for the first time since the tale began. Absolute loathing contorted her features. "You're a master at deception, but I'm not buying any of it."

To Lachlan's disbelief, Beth ran for the door. His energies began to plummet. "Beth!" he called as she flung wide the door to the hall and dashed toward the front doors.

Electricity crackled about him, causing a breeze

to lift his hair back from his face. His features lined
with anguish, he bellowed, "Ach, Beth!"

His corporeal appearance broke down into a
greenish mist, which moved in the same direction
Beth had gone. He had to stop her. He had long
ago learned that unstable emotions in this form of
existence could evoke strange meteorological occurrences. Poor Beth was so desperately clinging to the
hope of life. Her emotions were indeed unstable,
her sanity teetering in the face of what had happened to her.

Lachlan had to force her to accept the truth.

Silver-blue beams of moonlight bathed Beth's
blind flight. She was determined to escape this
nightmare, even if it meant running indefinitely.

Several peacocks called out, shattering the stifling quietude of the night. Beth ran on faster and
faster, her heart a fragmented thing within her
chest. A deep-rooted fear that maybe Lachlan was
right, that it wasn't all lies, fueled her desperation
to escape. She couldn't let her heart go out to him.

To believe any of what he'd said would mean that
she had to accept his claim of her own death.

And she was definitely alive!

Her heart was thundering behind her breasts.
Her lungs were aching with the strain to breathe.
The cool night air had raised goose flesh on her
arms.

She *was* alive!

She'd either been drugged, or she'd gone insane.
It really didn't matter which. She had two terrible
choices. She was lost to the world she'd thought

she'd belonged to, or lost to the only love of a man she'd ever known.

A sound stirred in her awareness. A sound both familiar and prosaic— the hiss of tires on asphalt, and the hum of an engine.

The tarred private roadway passed beneath her feet, and when she came to its end, she forged into the street beyond. The high beams of a car came swiftly around a bend in the road. Beth laughed with elation as she flagged her arms wildly above her head to attract the driver's attention.

The headlights rushed on toward her, the bright beams smarting her eyes, impairing her vision. But more afraid of losing this chance to escape Kist House than of being struck by the vehicle, she jumped up and down and began shouting for the driver to stop.

The lights came at her, bearing down on her with a swiftness that was startling. The driver *had* to see her. She was directly in front of the vehicle's path—

She felt her body jerk in a spasm of shock as an image of herself catapulting on impact blared before her mind's eye. Air was sucked sharply into her lungs, then galed back out when she felt the car pass through her.

Not over her.

Not around her.

Not touching her in any usual sense of the word.

It passed right through her as though she were nothing more than thin air. She could feel an icy rush go through her at the precise moment it happened— a rush and a turbulent several seconds of her atoms dispersing in every direction, then regrouping.

Terror swelled within her stomach and rocketed upward, lodged within her throat. Her head bent back, she frantically clawed at her neck to release the agony within her. When the sound finally erupted from her, it was in the form of a blood-curdling wail.

The peacocks in the distance raised their voices in a cacophony of shrill calls.

Unbeknown to her, Beth's newly acquired telekinetic properties were released from her. A wind materialized, increasing in strength until its howl became a fierce, piping sound through the branches of the trees. High in the night sky above her, an enormous vortex yawned to life. Beth felt herself slipping upward and away, beyond the reach of the raging elements she had unknowingly evoked. She didn't try to stop her flight. She was too frightened, too confused, too exhausted to care what awaited her.

"Haud on!" The voice was omnipresent. "I've got you!"

Beth was only conscious of moving with great speed. Her body and mind were buoyant. It was a horrible place, this endless nothingness. There was nothing to see or feel. Utter obscurity in its most horrifying form.

The fall went on and on, but she was dimly conscious of an element of control in her momentum.

Lachlan.

He was guiding them through the gray void.

Their semi-transparent figures, wrapped tightly about each other, passed through the roof, the attic, and came to fall upon the bed in the master suite. Beth lay beneath him, her glazed eyes staring into space. Lachlan, panting from his exertions, propped himself up on his elbows and peered down into her face.

It had been too close a call, and this frightened him.

What had she done to cause that opening between the dimensions?

What would have happened to them if he had not had the willpower to whisk them free and return them home?

Not to mention the faculty to stop their plummeting at the right moment!

A storm played across his features when Beth closed her eyes. She had scared the wits out of him— put him through the worst hell he'd known, and hoped never to experience again! He had worried about the spontaneous *poofing* she would endure in the beginning, but he was beginning to discover that was the least of his troubles. She seemed to have a readier access to the energies than he. And that could lead to some dire complications.

"Beth?"

Her only response was a strong shudder.

Lowering himself, Lachlan buried his face within the soft curls at the side of her neck. "If you wad only listen, I cad have spared you this."

Worming an arm and a leg beneath her, he drew

her onto her side and cradled her against him, his cheek pressed to the crown of her head.

"You've go' ta give i' some time. Poor, darlin', yer're shiverin'."

"I want to go home," she choked.

Pain racked Lachlan's face as he fought back a threat of tears. "*This* is yer home, now. Guid lawd, Beth, come ta terms wi' wha' I'm offerin'."

He kissed the top of her head and snuggled her closer. "This is oors, fore'er. Whan the shock o' yer death wears off, you'll start ta understand how verra much we have thegither."

He released a cry of pain at something pinching a section of his midriff. His arms slackened. To his disbelief, Beth wrenched free and sat up on her bent legs with a swiftness that stunned him.

"How much *we* have?" she cried, yanking his exposed earlobe. "*You* did this to me!"

With a grunt, Lachlan scrambled to a sitting position, cupping his throbbing ear with a hand. "Have you gone daft, womon? I may be dead, but tha' hurt like hell!"

"You're not dead, because I haven't killed you . . . *yet!*"

She took a swing at his face, caught him on the jaw, and sent him tumbling over the opposite side of the bed. Her eyes wild with anger, she watched as his head came up over the edge of the mattress. She lifted a pillow and whipped it down on his head. He made a feeble attempt to grab it from her as he jumped to his feet, but she was quicker and hit him in the mid-section with it.

"Aneuch!"

But Beth was too fired-up to stop.

Standing on the bed, she repeatedly swung and pummeled him with the pillow until its feathers began to spill into the air. Swearing a stream of Gaelic, Lachlan made every attempt to anchor her arms. He was getting very close when she jumped down from the bed and slammed her foot into his groin. Feathers sailing on his expelled breath, he slowly sank to his knees and bent over with a groan.

Beth stepped back within the flurry of feathers. Her anger was winding down. Logic vied with fury to take over her labored emotions.

"I haven't figured it all out yet," she panted, absently brushing aside the annoying feathers hovering in front of her face, "but I *will!*"

When Lachlan lifted his head and cocked an expressive eyebrow at her, she added, "In the meantime, stay away from me!"

With a guttural, unintelligible oath, Lachlan cranked himself up onto his feet. The fury in his face matched that of Beth's. He exhaled theatrically and made a grand gesture with his arms. "Perhaps you'd like me ta stay in the carriage house? Or wad you prefer the top o' a tree?"

"I would prefer you crawled into a doghouse!"

"Doghouse, you say!" Crimson flooded his face. "This is the thanks I get for carin' abou' you, you ungrateful—"

"You never cared for anything in your miserable life, you scheming . . . womanizing . . . *twerp!*"

"Twerp," he muttered. He closed one eye and

glared at Beth with the other. "Yer're tae fond o' tha' word."

Beth gave a toss of her head and backed up toward the door. "Everything's a joke to you, isn't it? Stay away from me, understand?"

"Aye, but I'm a wee confused as ta why you think I'm deaf all o' a sudden. Correct me if I'm wrong, sweet . . . lovely . . . thin' . . . tha' . . . you . . . are, but tha' is the reason you've been shoutin' a' me, is i' no'?"

"You're a sick man."

"I'm beginnin' ta think sa, maself. Why else wad I love such an unreasonable— "

"*Love?* You haven't an inkling what love is! You're an obsessive sociopath, and I'm going to do whatever it takes to get far away from you!"

When the door slammed behind her, Lachlan threw his hands up in sheer frustration. He addressed the heavens above him.

"Ah, sweet Jesus, you cadna have blessed me wi' a bonnie *mute* lass, cad you now! Is this ma payment for ma troubles, I ask you?"

He glowered at the door across from him. "Obsessive. *Bah!* An' wha' be the meanin' o' 'sociopath', eh?

"Twerp. Sociopath. *Jerk?* Nice language . . . if her tone is any indication as ta their meanin'."

Placing his hands on his hips, he rapped the ball of a foot on the floor. "This has got ta stop, Beth." He stalked across the room. "I'm a reasonable mon." He flung the door wide and stepped into the hall. "Tis time you learned ta respect me!"

Her bedroom door was open. He knew without checking that she was not within.

"This is na way ta treat yer husband ta be, womon!"

Every door in the house began to slam open and shut.

Lachlan stood frozen, his nerves jumping at every sound.

When the house became as still as death a few seconds later, he pressed his brow to the wall adjacent to his bedroom door.

"Now I've a bloody megrim," he rasped.

A last door slammed and scared the wits out of him. He glared down the hall. In his mind's eye, he could see Beth descending the staircase. She was still itching for a fight, but now, so was he.

In his time, women knew their place. The man was lord and master of his home; the provider.

Women of good breeding were basically gentle. Soft. Needful of masculine authority. Reared to respect and please the men in their lives. A thought jarred him as he considered this.

So Tessa was an exception.

Or was she?

Lachlan's brow furrowed thoughtfully.

How much did he actually remember about his era?

Fegs, what did it matter!? Of one thing he was certain.

Proudly squaring his shoulders, he called out, "Beth, I know you love me!"

Silence greeted his proclamation, and it chinked his confidence.

Longingly peering down the hall, he made a wry face and shuffled his broad shoulders.

"Reasonably sure. I only hope you come ta yer senses some time in *this* century," he went on in a low tone. "The waitin' is makin' me a wee . . ."

He sighed with exaggerated self-pity. ". . . testy."

Nine

Time had lost all sense of boundary for Beth. Minutes, hours, days, possibly weeks passed by while she flitted in and out of consciousness, between the gray world and the walls of Baird House. To hold on to what little sanity she had left, she told herself she would eventually come around from the aftereffects of whatever drug Lachlan had used on her. She had to be patient. Nothing could last forever.

Most of the time, she felt oddly at peace. Her headaches had not recurred. Physically, she had never felt better.

Carlene and David would return and apologize for leaving her in Lachlan's unscrupulous care. And Beth would forgive them for their part in this most bizarre matchmaking attempt. Her parents' house was waiting for her. The plants would have to be watered and moved about. Dusting and vacuuming. Laundry. There were a lot of details she had to take care of before she began college in the fall.

On one of her more lucid days, she found herself in the attic. It was as if she had *poofed* there without the slightest understanding as to how she'd arrived. Not that she attempted to understand. She refused to allow herself to dwell on the unexplainable. It was much safer to simply accept each occurrence as it happened. Pretend everything was as it should be.

Humming, she whiled away the better part of the day rummaging through a host of trunks and boxes. The discarded treasures of the past fascinated her, a proliferating means by which to preoccupy her mind. Nineteenth-century clothing and accessories, old books, newspapers, toys and knick-knacks, uncannily preserved, as if time and its ravages had never trespassed within the walls of this house.

She tried on several long dresses and pairs of high-button shoes. Corsets and loops and pantaloons. Various men's dress and smoking jackets.

Then, in a trunk hidden away against the wall beneath the slanting roof, she found something of immense interest. Her heart fluttered wildly behind her breasts until she finally brazened to lay a hand on the object. Electrical pulses tickled her palm, then raced up her arm, eliciting a musical laugh to caress her throat. Her eyes brightened within her flushed face.

Carefully unfolding the garment from its musty bed, she carried it to the sole port window in the attic and wistfully inspected it. The long, empire-style gown was made with layers of delicate white, rosette lace. Someone long ago had favored wearing it, for the satin belt was yellowed and frayed along the edges in sections.

Beth closed her eyes and took a moment to draw the gown across the bare skin of her left forearm.

The soft lace whispered against her flesh, beckoning to envelop her.

Stripping down to nothing, she slipped the gown on. To her delight it fit her perfectly in length and through the bustline, but the bell-shaped sleeves hung to the knuckles of her hands. With the satin belt tied in a neat bow beneath her breasts, she lifted the skirt and began to pirouette on an unlittered strip of floor, the full skirt belling out with each turn.

Then a fey sense of air shifting wound down her lighthearted mood. Standing starkly immobile, she tried to analyze the deeply-rooted impression that something had changed in her surroundings.

Her fingers kneaded the skirt of the gown as her gaze repeatedly scanned every inch of the attic. Crawly sensations moved along the back of her neck and arms.

Again the shifting occurred.

A haze of movement.

Almost imperceptible.

A tingling feeling moved along Beth's hands. Looking down, she released a gasp. The lace gown was fading, becoming invisible with each passing second. Then her eyes rolled up, as if drawn by a magnetic force, and her gaze lit upon the second anomaly.

The trunk from which she'd removed the gown was no longer there.

Heat rushed through her as she numbly backed toward the door. Naked, trembling, she mutely noted other discrepancies in the room. Boxes and traveling trunks, mirrors of all sizes, a large rocking horse, two bins of toys, were gone . . .

And what remained in the attic was coated with a thin layer of dust.

Something she had not seen since her arrival in the house.

Swallowing down a scream, she dashed down the narrow, steep stairs, and didn't slow her pace as she made her way to the main floor. Mindless of her nudity, she was about to turn in the direction of the front doors when a woman's laugh, rich and vibrant, brought her to an abrupt halt.

Blood pounding at her temples, Beth gaped at the closed parlor door.

The same woman laughed again.

Beth was hesitantly opening the door when a male voice said, "She seldom tires, as you can see. Most women wad be nursin' a case o' the vapors efter such a long journey."

Even before Beth fully opened the door, she knew the voice had not belonged to Lachlan. The instant she spied the laird standing beside a short, well-built man, and a stunning blonde woman sitting on one of the sofas, Lachlan spoke.

"No' *ma* darlin' bride," Lachlan boasted, bending and planting a kiss on the woman's fair-skinned brow. He lingered bent over for a moment longer to look deeply into her eyes, then straightened up with a grin splitting his face.

Beth experienced a painful stab of jealousy, and her temper flared at the idea of Lachlan going through this performance to punish her for avoid-

ing him. But if such were the case, why were his
eyes soft with undeniable love as he stared down at
the woman like a love-sick adolescent?

"Lannie," she cooed, her low tone seductive.
"Might I trouble you for a brandy?"

Lannie?

Breathing heavily, Beth stepped into the room
and slammed the door behind her.

"Merra!"

Not only had everyone ignored Beth's presence,
but the slamming of the door as well. A moment
after Lachlan's call, a young woman dressed in a
long, somber dress, a white apron, and a cap entered the opposite side of the room from the dining
room door.

"Aye, Master Baird?"

"Fetch yer mistress a brandy, please."

"Peach, if you have i'," the blonde said to the
second woman.

"Aye, ma'am." She looked at the men standing
shoulder to shoulder at the blonde's side. "Anythin'
for you, sirs?"

Lachlan flagged a hand of refusal. The other
man flashed his teeth in a grin before replying,
"Scotch."

With a bow of her head, the dark-haired woman
hurried off through the door.

"Lannie?"

Lachlan smiled down at the blonde.

"I wad dearly love a bath."

"I'll have— " He stopped and puffed up his chest.
"I'll tend ta i' maself, darlin'. Robert, keep an eye

on her, eh?'' Lachlan winked at the man. "I canna have ma bride gettin' lost, can I?''

Robert gave a shake of his head. "I'll guard her wi' ma life.''

Lachlan began to walk toward Beth, who stood frozen in disbelief. She stared at him through widened eyes. Although she had no doubts that this was Lachlan, he looked very different. Younger, somehow. His skin was no longer pale, but deeply tanned.

He was nearly upon her when she remembered her state of undress. Folding her arms against her breasts, she stammered, "I'm s-sorry. I didn't know—"

He stopped, reached through her, and swung open the door in the space she was occupying. Before she could gather her wits, he walked through her and closed the door behind him.

A mist of tears filled Beth's eyes as she gazed bewilderedly at the couple several yards away. They were staring at her, or at least she believed so until the man said with unmistakable animosity, "He'll no' be easy ta put off.'' Coming around to stand in front of the blonde, he scowled. "I canna bear the thought o' him touchin' you.''

A slow, evil smile spread across the woman's mouth as she reached out with a gloved hand and boldly cupped the man's crotch. She gave a tug, urging him closer. Then she leaned to and pressed her lips to his lower abdomen.

Beth gave a shake of her head as it dawned on her what was happening. She was caught within another hallucination. Why else would the man and woman be dressed like something out of the mid-nineteenth century?

"Tessa," the man groaned, dipping back his head, his features deeply carved with need.

"The poor sod will ne'er have me, Robert." Running a hand over the rigid erection concealed beneath his fawn-colored trousers, she peered up through thick, pale lashes. "Tis you I love. *His* paughty hands will ne'er touch ma skin, I promise."

Robert Ingliss sank to his knees and hungrily pulled the blonde into his arms.

For several long seconds, Beth watched them passionately kiss, then stormed across the room.

"You slut!" Beth wailed, stopping alongside the couple. "Stop it! *Stop it!*"

Tessa straightened back, her head turning in each direction, her eyes wide with suspicion.

"Wha' is i'?" Robert asked, vainly trying to kiss her.

"I thought I heard somethin'," she whispered.

Robert released a nasty chuckle, and pinched her chin between a thumb and forefinger to force her to look at him. "It'll tak his lordship a while ta run yer bath. Dinna tease me, Tessie. I winna stand for i'."

Tessa leaned forward to kiss him. But before their lips touched, Beth reached out to give the woman a shake. Her hand passed through Tessa's shoulder. The blonde sprang up onto her feet, her face deathly pale, her azure eyes seeming too large for her face. Robert stood, his dark look questioning his lover's strange behavior.

"Canna you feel i'?" Tessa asked in a low, husky

voice. "Cauld as death, i' was." She looked beseechingly into Robert's eyes. "We're bein' watched, Robert."

"Na, darlin'— "

The aproned young woman entered the room, carrying a tray. Barely glancing at the couple, she placed the tray on the coffee table, then gave a curtsy. "Anythin' else?"

"Na," Robert said, with a curt, dismissive gesture.

Merra spared Tessa a long glance, then hurried from the room. Before the maid had disappeared into the room beyond the door, Tessa tipped the snifter to her lips and downed the peach brandy.

"Tak i' easy," Robert scowled, as Tessa discarded the emptied glass upon the sofa.

"Dinna tell me wha' ta do." With a haughty toss of her head, she eyed the young man with unmistakable superiority. "Tis thanks ta *ma* cunnin' we're in this fine house, laddie. Dinna e'er forget tha'."

Robert's eyes flashed a warning before he turned and walked to the fireplace. Staring up at a portrait of the laird, he said, "He is no' a mon ta be trifled wi', love."

A smug smile hardened the blonde's delicate features. "I can handle him."

Disgust brought on a weightiness in Beth's chest. Hallucination or not, she couldn't suppress a deep-rooted desire to protect Lachlan from his bride. Her mind scrambling to recall all that he'd told her about Tessa, she walked to the front of the woman and ran a measuring glance over her.

The mistress of Baird House was undeniably

beautiful, but for the life of her, Beth could not understand how Lachlan could not see the emptiness in the woman's blue eyes. They were devoid of compassion. Certainly devoid of love, even for Robert. Her outer perfection was but a thin cloak. And yet Lachlan had fallen in love with her.

"We cad have i' all," Tessa purred, daintily tugging on each finger of her gloves until she held the lace set in one hand. "His grand house. His lovely wealth."

Robert slowly turned until he was facing Tessa, his features cast in gloom. "I think you underestimate him, an' o'erestimate yerself, darlin'."

"Ye o' little faith," she laughed, then gasped when Beth's phantom hand passed through her breast. The feeling of ice hardening around her heart elicited a cry from her.

"Darlin'?"

The door opened. Lachlan walked in.

"Yer bath's— "

Tessa dashed for him and flung herself into his arms. Beth's furies loosed. The snifter shot through the air. Robert ducked aside in time to avoid being struck by it, but the snifter shattered upon impact with the mantel, and slivers of glass rained on him.

"Wha' the hell!" he wailed, jumping to Lachlan's side and staring at the mantel in stark terror.

Baffled, Lachlan demanded, "Wha's goin' on?"

Beth clenched her fists. The sofa Tessa had been sitting on abruptly moved several feet away.

Releasing Tessa, Lachlan hesitantly moved to the

center of the room, his dark gaze probing his surroundings.

Beth's fists trembled, and she closed her eyes against the fury coursing through her. The two doors in the room began to repeatedly open and slam shut. Amid the blonde's shrieks, Lachlan boomed, "Stop!"

All became very quiet and still within the room. Beth glared at the blonde, her mind groping for a means by which to warn Lachlan of the woman's treachery.

"Tis spirits," Tessa accused.

"No' in *ma* home," Lachlan said assuredly. Placing his hands on his hips, he made a complete turn. "There has ta be a reasonable explanation."

"Such as?" Robert flung sarcastically, his pallor the color of chalk. "Ta wha' kind o' place have you brought ma sister, eh?"

Lachlan scowled at the younger man. "Are you suggestin' ma home be haunted, Robert?" He gave a low laugh. "Might be, the long journey's playin' tricks on oor minds. A guid night's rest— "

"I sense an evil presence," Tessa huffed, her posture rigid, her eyes flashing with defiance.

Again Lachlan laughed low, and crossed the room to his bride. Placing his hands upon her shoulders, he kissed her on the brow. "Some gentle lovin' an' ma chest beneath yer fair head, darlin', will ease yer fears."

"I'm tae oopset," she mewled.

Standing at Lachlan's side, Beth carefully watched his pained expression as he searched his bride's face.

"'Tis oor weddin' night."

"Ma sister is weary," Robert put in, his defensive tone causing one of Lachlan's eyebrows to arch. "Have a heart, mon. You have the rest o' yer lives."

"'Tis true, darlin'," Tessa said gently, placing a hand to Lachlan's cheek. "Wad i' hurt you terribly ta allow me ta gather ma wits for a time?"

Lachlan's gaze moved from Tessa to Robert, then back to Tessa. "As you wish." He dropped his hands to his sides and forced an understanding smile. "I'll stay in one o' the guest rooms tonight."

"I refuse to deny you yer bed, love," Tessa said, her soft tone convincing, her eyes as innocently winning as those of a doe. "Let me bathe."

"May I a' least wash yer back?"

Rising on tiptoe, Tessa briefly kissed Lachlan on the mouth. "Anither time. I'm exhausted. I pray you understand, love."

Beth locked her teeth as Lachlan gave a nod of his head.

"I'll see her ta yer room," Robert said, placing a palm at Tessa's elbow and turning her toward the door. "Which room is i'?"

"Third floor. Fourth room on the right."

The dullness of Lachlan's tone wrenched on Beth's heartstrings. Helpessly, she watched Robert escort Tessa from the room and close the door after them. Lachlan stood very still for a time, staring absently at the door. Then he went to one of the wing chairs and lowered himself onto it.

Beth stood in front of him, her eyes soft with compassion. This Lachlan possessed different qualities than the man she knew. He appeared younger. Vulnerable. Lost, at the moment.

"Can I get you somethin', sir?"

Both Beth and Lachlan looked up at the maid, who stood poised by the dining room door.

"Come here a moment, Merra," he said wearily.

Without hesitation, she came to stand in front of him, unaware that Beth had moved aside, so as not to touch her.

"Aye, sir?"

Lachlan's mouth twisted in a halfhearted grin. "How long have you been here, Merra?"

"Near eight months, sir."

"Have you. . . ." He frowned and looked off to one side. "Have you e'er sensed somethin' . . . unnatural in this house?"

He looked up in time to see a flicker of surprise move across her face.

"Unnatural, sir?" Her small hands kneaded the front of her apron. "I dinna understand."

With a fortifying intake of breath, Lachlan said seriously, "A ghost, girl."

"Ghost, sir?" She giggled. "Are you pullin' ma leg, sir?"

Lachlan chuckled. "Aye, Merra, I am. Tis guid ta be home."

"Tis guid ta have you back, sir. The house felt quite empty wi'ou' you."

"Tis kind o' you ta say so," he said distractedly, gazing off to one side.

"Can I get you somethin', sir? Somethin' ta eat, or a Scotch, maybe?"

Lachlan smiled tiredly up at her. "Na, thank you. Wha' I need is a guid, long sleep. Merra, I'm countin' on you ta mak yer mistress feel welcome here."

"Aye, I'll do ma best, sir. But . . ."

Lachlan arched a questioning brow. "But?"

"She's no' wha' I expected, sir."

"In wha' way?"

Merra smiled shyly. "I'm no' sure. But she *is* verra lovely, sir."

"Aye, she is. Tha's all for tonight. An' Merra? The mistress prefers coffee ta tea in the morn."

With a nod, the young woman left the room.

For what seemed a long time, Beth stared down at Lachlan, who was lost in thought. She went down on her knees in front of him, studying the striking contours of his features, the expressive movements of his eyebrows. She couldn't begin to guess his thoughts, but he was troubled. He was a groom without his bride on their wedding night. If only he knew what was to come. . . .

Without thought, she placed her hands atop his knees. He gave a violent start, his horrified gaze riveted where Beth had quasi-touched him.

Anguish swelled in her throat as she rose to her feet.

"Lachlan, can you hear me?"

He continued to stare at his knees, his hands gripping the arms of the chair so fiercely, his knuckles were white.

"She's going to murder you!" Beth cried, frustrated that he couldn't seem to hear her. "Your beautiful young bride is going to drive a knife into your heart!"

Lachlan rose from the chair. Casually walking about the room, he ran a hand through his thick, shoulder-length hair.

"Lachlan, dammit!"

He stopped and appeared to keen an ear.

Walking up to him, Beth went on, "She's going to murder you. Lachlan, Robert is not her brother. He's her lover!"

He gave himself a visible shake, as if to dispel his weariness.

"Damn you, Lachlan, you must hear me! She's— "

Beth stiffened.

What was she doing?

She'd been reacting to an hallucination as though it were real!

How convenient for Lachlan, she fumed, taking two paces back. How *bloody* convenient for him that this occurred, filling her with sympathy, and reinforcing her love for him!

"You bastard!" she hissed, trembling with anger. "What is this, s-some kind of hypnosis you're using on me? It won't work. Do you hear me? *It won't convince me to remain with you!*"

Lachlan sighed as he again raked his fingers through his hair. "Wha' are you sulkin' abou', mon? You've waited thirty-three years ta have a womon. Wha's one mair night, eh?"

Sitting on the sofa which had inexplicably moved minutes before, he ran his hands up and down his face, then slapped his palms on the upholstery to each side of his slim hips. "Yer're jaggie, mon. Desire's cloudin' yer mind; playin' the deil wi' you."

Beth headed for the door to the hall. So Lachlan had been a virgin— at least in this most bizarre daymare. She found it disturbing, especially in light of the fact he'd told her he'd been murdered before his marriage was ever consummated.

Going up the first flight of stairs, she reminded herself, *Or another ploy to win your sympathy.*

By the time she reached the third landing of Baird House, she was numbed by her warring thoughts. It had been her intention to return to the attic, but she unexpectedly found herself in the master bedroom.

Her eyes widened in disbelief. Naked, Robert and Tessa were in each other's arms, within a metal tub set before a roaring fire in the hearth. Steam rose from the scented bath water sloshing over the rim of the tub as Tessa pumped her groin atop Robert's lap. Her head was tipped back, her features betraying her mounting ecstasy.

Beth wanted to look away, but couldn't.

How daring of the couple to make love in Lachlan's room. How daring and . . . utterly vulgar to betray him in such a manner.

Had the woman no shame?

Beth stepped back, ignoring the fact that she passed through the closed door as if it were mere air.

"I won't be tricked like this," she vowed, storming in the direction of the attic door. When she arrived back at the topmost room of the house, she stood fuming for several seconds.

"Lachlan, I'm not even sure if my love for you is real anymore. Is this what you've been hoping for, a state of mind you could easily sway to your will?

"I'm not that weak. I hate to disappoint you, but I'm going to survive this brainwashing. I'm going to go home and put all this behind me. I'm going to forget you, Lachlan."

She released a jagged breath. "Whatever it takes, I will get over you."

"Beth."

The zephyrous voice gave Beth a start. Her darting gaze searched every corner of the attic.

"Beth, it's time."

Coldness invaded every part of Beth's body. At the same moment she mutely admitted to recognizing her adoptive mother's voice, she glanced down to find the lace gown had materialized on her slim form. A sob caught in her throat as denials reared.

"Leave me alone!"

"Daddy's here, Beth. We're waiting—"

"No more!"

Beth covered her ears with her hands.

A bright light appeared in front of her, an infinite light so bright that she looked away.

"We're all waiting," crooned Rita. "Waiting for you to join us."

Beth forced herself to peer into the radiance. Images began to move toward her.

"Ma? No. No! Leave me alone!"

One of the countless shadowy figures continued in her direction as the others stopped. A moment later, Rita Staples stood before Beth, as real as any-

thing Beth had ever seen. Her arms were held out.
A beguiling smile was on her lips. The lines of pain
which had rapidly aged her during her illnesses
were not present.

"Don't be afraid, Beth. We're all going to be together again."

Beth stepped back, shaking her head repeatedly.
"You're an illusion."

"Take my hand— "

"No! I did everything I could for you, Ma. It may
sound selfish of me, but I want my life back!"

"It's too late, darling."

"I know you're hiding behind a mask of her,
Lachlan! Stop this!"

"Beth— "

"Go away!"

The light, images, and Rita Staples, vanished.

Struggling with each breath, Beth quaked. She
desperately needed to feel anger, but she couldn't
summon it. She was beyond fearing madness, too.
Her instinct to survive, to cling to life, was the sole
driving force keeping her mind and spirit united.

As seconds ticked by, she calmed until she felt
she was in control again. She could only bide her
time until the drug wore off. Once she escaped its
influence, she would be free. Free of Lachlan. Free
of the lies. Free to experience a life she'd as yet only
dreamed about.

Faraway voices caught her attention.

Keening an ear, she waited breathlessly for a time
before fleeing the attic.

Without thought to her state of dress, she dashed

through the greenhouse and threw open one of the outer doors. She ran out into the late afternoon air—

And gasped at the chill that embraced her.

Her eyes wide with disbelief, she looked about the landscape. Everywhere lay coatings of sleek ice and glittering frost. The change in season so perplexed her, she almost didn't notice a bent figure walking toward a red van parked at the corner of the house. A crunch of ice penetrated her stupor.

Recognition slammed home.

Running toward the figure, she cried, "Agnes! Agnes, wait!"

Beth came to an abrupt halt and stood rigid in disbelief when the cook turned and stared at her with a look of utter horror.

Her reasoning beginning to spin in her head, Beth tried to force herself to concentrate.

She looked halfheartedly aside.

Was Agnes part of the winter wonderland illusion?

Her gaze shifted back to the cook, whose frail body was covered in an oversized blue coat. A dark blue knitted cap was pulled low on her brow, concealing most of her white hair.

No illusion, Beth realized, her flared nostrils breathing in deeply the crisp scent of winter. Gathering her wits about her, she breached the distance and managed a light laugh. "Agnes, I'm so glad to see you!"

It didn't pass Beth's notice that Agnes seemed to have aged drastically. The shrewd eyes were sunken and underscored with shadows, and seemed far too large. The lines around her mouth were deeper, the skin covering her distinct cheekbones, taut and owning of a grayish pallor.

"I'm sorry if I startled you," Beth went on, desperation etched in every fiber of her being. "I was beginning to think no one would ever show up here again!"

Agnes' arm flew up in front of her face to ward off the sight of Beth.

"What's wrong? Agnes, please, say something!"

The arm lowered. Watery blue eyes swept down the length of Beth, then Agnes quickly blessed herself and started to turn.

"Agnes, please!" Beth gasped, placing a restraining hold on the woman's arm. "I have to talk to you!"

Fear emanated from the woman's eyes as she swung her head around to look up at Beth. The wrinkled mouth drew down at the corners. The sagging chin quivered. She turned to face Beth completely, a film of tears misting her eyes.

"Wha' are you doin' *here*, lass?"

"Well, uh, I haven't been able to leave. I know this sounds crazy, but I, ah, haven't been well. Yes, I've been ill. The last I remember, it was . . ." Beth made a helpless gesture with her shoulders, and completed with a shaky laugh, "summer."

"Sa sarry, sa sarry," Agnes murmured.

"Help me," Beth pleaded, then was distracted when someone in the van turned on the engine. She could see a man sitting behind the wheel, but she was anxious to persuade Agnes to help her escape Baird House.

"Agnes, I need a ride to the airport. Please, I know I'm imposing, but I have no one else to turn to . . ."

Her voice trailed off as the old woman began to weep. A handkerchief was withdrawn from one of the coat pockets. Agnes dabbed at her eyes with a trembling, gloved hand, her gaze trained off to one side to avoid looking at Beth.

"Agnes, I wouldn't ask— "

The van door opened.

Frustrated with the intrusion, Beth watched a man climb out and amble across the gravel. He was a large man, nearly as tall as Lachlan, but built larger through the chest and shoulders. Coming to stand at Agnes' side, he scowled at Beth as if her presence were some kind of threat to the elderly woman.

Instinctively, Beth stiffened. But her defensiveness was betrayed by the haunting desperation in her beautiful eyes.

"Is there a problem here, Aunt Aggie?" he asked gruffly, looking suspiciously from Agnes' sickly pallor to Beth.

Beth looked the stranger straight in the eye. "I was only trying to ask Agnes for a favor."

"Tak me home, Roan," Agnes whimpered, clinging to her nephew's arm as she turned her back to Beth. "I'm no' feelin' tae weel."

The man's thick, sandy-colored eyebrows arched above soft-brown eyes. "Do you know this womon, Aggie?" he asked, his gaze unsettlingly searching Beth's features.

"Aye," Agnes whispered, then closed her

gnarled, gloved hand over the handkerchief and held it to her breast. Taking a steadying breath, she forced herself to look at Beth. After a tense moment, she vainly attempted a smile.

"Aye, I know her. You teuk me by surprise, Missy."

"I'm sorry," Beth said irritably, although she was trying not to succumb to a strong urge to flare up at the man's continued perusal. "Agnes, I really need to get to the airport. David and Carlene haven't returned, and Lachlan . . . he's, ah, he hasn't been himself. I just want to return to the States."

Again, Agnes' reaction took Beth aback. The old woman released a wretched wail and turned away. Before Beth could think to stop her, Agnes was shuffling awkwardly over the slick ground. The passenger door slammed shut before Beth took a step in the vehicle's direction.

"Haud i'," the man warned, gripping Beth's upper arm. "Yer're an American, aren't you?"

Beth glared at the large hand, then looked up. "Yes, I am. Now if you would kindly take your oversized mitt off me!"

The man's grip lessened, but remained firm enough to keep her in place. Although she didn't feel threatened by him, her temper began to warm her insides. "Mister— "

"Ingliss. Roan Ingliss."

With an inward groan, Beth irritably brushed her unruly hair from her face with the back of a hand. "Then perhaps, Mr. Ingliss, *you* can help me."

A look of wariness crept into the man's eyes. "Depends on wha' you need, lady."

"A ride to Preswick Airport."

"The airport, eh?"

"I can pay you in American money for your trouble."

A smile tugged at the corner of Roan's mouth. He couldn't for the life of him figure out what an American was doing at this place. His aunt had told him the last resident— also an American woman— had died some months ago.

Releasing Beth, he called over his shoulder, "Aunt Aggie, come here." He waited for several long seconds before protesting, "Aunt Aggie, i's tae damn cauld ta be tryin' ma patience. Come along now."

The van door opened.

Roan looked at the stranger and found her anxiousness to be a curious thing. Then it dawned on him that the perplexing Yank was wearing nothing more than a lace gown.

"Are you tryin' ta put yerself doon wi' pneumonia?" he asked harshly. Yanking off each glove and tucking them beneath an arm, he began to unbutton his lamb's wool coat. "You must be frozen near ta death— "

Then something extraordinary materialized beside the woman.

Ten

A man appeared alongside the young woman with such unexpectedness, Roan was momentarily frozen in shock. There was little else he could do but stare incredulously into the riveting dark eyes across from him.

"She needs nocht from you," the new arrival said, his tone as acid as his fierce look.

Struck speechless, Roan continued to gawk at the man. His heart thundered almost painfully. If he didn't know better, he'd swear the stranger's gaze was condemning him. Never had he witnessed such tangible hatred in another man's face. If the newcomer's eyes could strike him down, Roan was sure he would be lying on the ground, his blood spilling from his body.

"Get off ma property, you Ingliss swine!"

Roan gave a shake of his head. He glanced over his shoulder to see his aunt frozen in place, the look on her face bringing home a reality Roan wasn't sure he was ready to accept.

He'd heard tales of the ghost of Kist House all his life, but to be confronted with him was mind-boggling— certainly something he never really expected to personally experience. But the man's sudden appearance from out of thin air was not something a living being could accomplish, unless he were a magician.

"Return ta the house," Lachlan ordered Beth, his gaze continuing its slow drill into Roan's face.

Beth's eyes flashed up at his profile. "I'm going home!"

Lachlan clenched his teeth so hard, a muscle bunched up along his jawline. "You *are* home! Now, get in the house! I'll join you whan my business wi' this Ingliss swine is finished."

"Wait just a damn minute," Roan sputtered.

Quaking with anger, Beth stiffened and looked at the stranger. The man's face was racked with uncertainty and awe, but she sensed a strength in him that offered her hope of escaping the insanity she'd been trapped within since her arrival. "Will you give me a ride to the airport, Mr. Ingliss?"

Roan swallowed hard as Lachlan Baird's scornful eyes delivered him a mute warning. But he wasn't a man who easily gave in to intimidation. He was also concerned for the woman.

What on earth was a *ghost*— although he was still having trouble accepting the man as such— doing with a flesh-and-blood beauty like the American?

"Aye, Miss, I'll give you a ride, but first I need ta have a word wi' His Nibs."

"I'll no' let you leave, Beth," Lachlan growled, his glower riveted on Roan.

"Get yer things thegither," Roan told Beth. "I'll be waitin' here whan yer're ready."

"The hell— Beth!" Lachlan barked when she whirled away in the direction of the house. "You cad a' least give me the courtesy o' hearin' me ou', first!"

"Drop dead!" Beth hissed over her shoulder.

"I am dead!"

Lachlan sucked in a breath as Beth ran to the house. When he looked again at the Ingliss man, fury masked his face. "You've a lot ta learn, laddie. This once I'll forgive yer arrogance, but the next time you interfere . . ."

His face flushed with anger, Roan released a mocking laugh. "Don't waste yer threats on me, auld mon. If no' for you makin' a bletherin' fool ou' o' ma cousin, an' Aggie pleadin' wi' me ta tak over the wark here, I'd no' be dirtyin' ma boots on yer damned soil."

A sardonic grin sprang to Lachlan's mouth. So, at long last, one of the Ingliss clan showed some spine. He sensed a strength in this one that, were it displayed by anyone else, he would have admired. But this was an Ingliss, and the presence of Ingliss blood, warm and flowing through a living body, clouded Lachlan's thinking.

"So, yer're ta tak Borgie's place, are you?"

Roan flexed his broad shoulders beneath his lamb's wool coat. "Wi' a few revisions ta the arrangement."

"Wha' be they, eh?" Lachlan asked in a low, sinister tone.

"We Inglisses have been little mair than slaves ta you in the past, Baird."

"The term 'slaves' applies ta human bondage. We

both know there's no' a worthwhile human trait in one o' yer clan. Tis a debt ta me an' this house you owe— "

"Long paid," Roan bit out, his livid expression matching that of his adversary. "I'm here ta mak you an offer, if you've the sense ta listen."

"Watch yerself, laddie boy."

One of Roan's eyebrows rose expressively. "It's a fair enough deal I'm offerin'. It'll be na skin off ma nose if you turn i' doon."

"Fair, you say?" The air about Lachlan began to crackle with energy. "Tis me who'll determine wha's fair or no', you blastie!"

Roan drew in a long breath and gave a solemn shake of his head. "I'm glad i's beneath yer dignity ta resort ta name-callin'. Now, do we talk like civilized men, or do I leave you ta yer tantrums, *Mister* Baird?"

Beth hurriedly packed the remains of her belongings. Her features were lit with excitement, her movements almost spastic. She refused to think about Lachlan, or what Carlene and David would say when they returned to find her gone. Once she was far away from Baird House— preferably in the quiet security of her home in Washington State— then, and only then, could she begin to make sense out of the twisted bouts of delirium plaguing her.

Snapping the suitcase shut, she looked over the slacks and top she'd laid out. This was it. All she had to do was change into her own clothing and walk out the front door. She would not look back, and certainly would not meet Lachlan's mesmerizing eyes.

Then her hands smoothed out the front of the gown as a queasy feeling stirred within her stomach.

Was it excitement unsettling her, or was she actually experiencing pangs of remorse at the thought of putting Lachlan and the house behind her?

Fool!

She squeezed her eyes shut against the tears trying to build up within her.

She'd never known an indecisive moment in her life until she came to Scotland, and that seemed an eternity ago. Her previous life seemed more like a dream now.

How could she love a man like Lachlan after all he'd done?

Love.

The thought was utterly agonizing.

She did love him. God help her, she couldn't deny it. But entwined with the love was mistrust and anger. The two should overwhelm the former, but they didn't. He possessed her heart so utterly, she couldn't trust herself to be alone with him for even a few seconds.

Damn you, she cursed him, a tremor coursing through her body. *Your obsession with me is what caused this mess!*

"Beth."

The soft voice caused Beth a violent start. Snapping her head around, she gaped at two figures standing by the window nearest the bathroom.

A shroud of incredulity descended over her brain.

The man was dressed in a dark dress suit and shiny black shoes.

The woman—

Carlene was dressed in the same outfit as when Beth had last seen her.

"We've come to take you back with us," Carlene said with a tenuous smile.

A long minute passed in silence.

Carlene's hands came up, and she exposed her palms to Beth in a gesture of sorrow. "We wanted to appear before now, but we were afraid Lachlan would— "

"Carlene," Beth said dully, her body as numb as her mind.

"Yes, Beth." Carlene released a broken laugh. "I-I'm sure you believe I betrayed our friendship, but Lachlan— "

"Yes . . . Lachlan." Beth felt a quick rush of dizziness sweep through her before she could bring herself to draw upon an inner reserve of stamina.

So, Carlene and David had decided to come home.

Too bad it was too late, for Beth was determined to leave Scotland before the day was over.

"Beth, you've got to listen to me."

"Why?" Beth gave an airy shrug of her shoulders. "You decided to play matchmaker, didn't you?"

"Beth— "

Anger flashed in Beth's eyes. "It nearly cost me my sanity, damn you!"

"You have to let me explain my side of this."

"I'm leaving. Sorry we don't have time for a nice little chat, but my ride's waiting."

"Lachlan won't let you leave!" Carlene cried, taking a step in Beth's direction.

Beth calmly raked a measuring look over her friend, then took an added moment to study David. As lifeless as the curtain hanging behind his right shoulder, he continued to stare at her as if unseeing, his hazel eyes set within a pale, well-boned face. Although his countenance was devoid of expression, Beth sensed his unease.

"No one can stop me from leaving. I'm really disappointed in you, Carlene. I thought we had the kind of friendship that could withstand anything."

"There isn't time to explain everything right now!" Carlene exclaimed with mounting irritability.

"Right. Because *I'm* leaving!"

"Beth, if Lachlan discovers we've come for you . . . Dammit, he wants you to stay in this house with him!"

"Tell me something I don't know," Beth sneered. "Do you know he believes he's dead?" She laughed humorlessly. "But what's even more outrageous, he believes *I'm* dead, too. Oh, and you and David as well. There are headstones bearing our names in the back field."

"Beth—"

"Swell character you tried to fix me up with, old buddy," Beth went on, bitterness lacing her tone as she took two steps in her friend's direction. "Personally, I can't ever recall saying or doing anything to give you the impression I was *that* hard-up for male companionship."

"Beth, *shut up!* Just come with us. David and I will take care of you."

Beth's mouth gaped open in disbelief, then shut. "I don't need anyone to take care of me."

"We haven't much time— "

"I'm going home. Sorry if this sounds a . . . *wee* . . . ungrateful, but go to hell! Carlene, I don't want to ever see or hear from you again. Am I making myself clear?"

Snatching up her slacks, panties, and top from the bed, Beth stalked toward the bathroom. But Carlene was quick to stand in the doorway, refusing to move as she stared heatedly into Beth's fiery eyes.

"You still refuse to accept it, don't you?" she flung unkindly.

Beth made a move to shove past her friend, but Carlene pushed her back a step.

"I knew you were dying several months before David and I were killed in the accident."

Beth flinched. "You're insane."

"The fall you took down the stairs had nothing to do with— "

"What did he offer you to go along with this . . . this sick hoax, huh? What did it *take* for you to sell out our friendship!"

"In the beginning, I-I approved of Lachlan's plan to bring you here, but I began to regret the decision before you left the States. But Lachlan wouldn't let me warn you, Beth! You have to believe me!"

"Believe you?" Beth parroted sarcastically.

"You're not listening to what I'm saying!"

"I *am* listening, but the words are coming from the mouth of a madwoman! I would know if I was really dead. Wouldn't I? *Wouldn't I?*"

Carlene's demeanor wilted and tears brimmed her eyes. "I couldn't stand the thought of you dying alone. That was the only reason I went along with Lachlan's plan. You've got to believe me."

"I'm not de—"

A swell of anguish moved up through Beth, but she locked her teeth and clenched her fists to abort it from escaping her in the form of a wail. Her slender body quaked. Despite her resistance, the mental wall she had so carefully constructed against the truth began to crumble.

"David and I have been hiding just out of Lachlan's reach. We don't know what is waiting beyond for us, but we'll be together, Beth. Don't be afraid to pass on to the next plane of existence with us. We love you. There is only Lachlan keeping you *here.*"

Unexpectedly, Beth experienced an electrifying wash of sensation sweeping down through her body. A curtain of absolute calm descended on her. Her anger waned. The deep-rooted threads of self-grief shredded as the workings of her thoughts fell quietly into place, at long last ending her torment of denial.

The oddly rapt expression on Beth's face set off an alarm in Carlene's brain. "Beth, what's wrong?"

"Nothing. Nothing's wrong."

"Something's happening—"

Beth's wistful smile took Carlene aback. "Yes,

Lachlan is keeping me here," she said quietly, "but not in the sense you mean, Carlene. He loves me. And I love him enough not to want to be separated from him."

"You don't know what you're saying. You don't understand the power—"

"His power over me?" Beth gave a low chuckle, then sobered. "What caused my death?"

"We don't have time—"

"Never mind," Beth said, already turning toward the door. "I'll ask Lachlan."

"Beth, *please!*"

With calm and dignity, Beth tossed her clothing back atop the bed and headed for the hall. At the threshhold, she stopped and looked over her shoulder, her eyes warm with compassion. "I'm sorry I lashed out at you. I understand your motives now, really I do. You and David go on. I'll find my own way."

"Lachlan won't ever let you leave this house. He's obsessed with you!"

"I'm a lot stronger than you think."

When Beth disappeared into the hall, Carlene buried her face in her hands and began to weep. David watched his wife for several seconds before going to her and resting his hands upon her trembling shoulders.

"There isn't any more we can do."

Like lightning, Carlene slapped David's chest. "Thanks for the backup!" she charged, tears streaming down her sallow face. "You just stood there like a zombie!"

"I'm beginning to feel like one." With a wry grin, he entwined his fingers through her hair. "We've done all we can. She's awakened to the truth. Let her make up her own mind as to what she wants."

"She's confused."

"Not anymore."

To keep his wife from staying behind, David Cambridge wrapped his arms about her and anchored her to him. They faded together as one, then began their long journey to what lay beyond the grayness where they'd hidden for what seemed an eternity.

"Yer're daft!" Lachlan hissed. "*Pay* an Ingliss? O'er ma dead, rottin' corpse!"

Roan stubbornly folded his arms across his broad chest. "You'll be gettin' yer money's worth."

Lachlan sucked in a great breath through his nostrils. The Ingliss' request had stunned, then amused, him, but when he realized the brazen man was quite serious about the arrangement he'd suggested, Lachlan's temper was quick to surface.

"I'll be havin' yer head on a silver tray, you useless corbie. You've got nerve. Na brains, but nerve."

"I'm an honest, *fair* mon," Roan corrected, his tone deep, controlled.

"An Ingliss knows only takin'."

Roan locked his teeth so hard, pain shot up along his jawline. "Seems ta me, auld mon, you've been doin' the takin' for o'er a century now."

"I'm warnin' you, Ingliss—"

A tunnel of mist appeared behind the baird's left shoulder. Beth quickly walked from within it. "Lachlan!"

The master of Baird House turned his head sharply at the command in Beth's tone. He waited in simmering silence until she was at his side, then with as much calm as he could muster, he said quietly, "I ask you kindly, now, Beth, gae back ta the house an' wait for me."

"It still sounds like a command, and it'll be a cold day in hell when I start taking orders from you," she huffed, unconsciously responding to the negative emotions vibrating from him. "We're going to talk. *Now.*"

"Whan I'm through wi' this Ingliss— "

"I've said all I came ta say," Roan interjected. He cast his aunt a look that told her to stay where she was by the van. "The rest is oop ta you, Baird."

He was turning away when Lachlan's hand shot out and cinched his broad neck. Taken aback by the strength in the specter's hold, he looked helplessly into the brooding dark eyes before him.

At that moment, something swept into and filled Beth completely, choking off her senses. Panic swelled within her. For several seconds, she could not understand what was happening to her. Then it dawned on her that the terrible feeling trying to overcome her was rage— and it was coming from within Lachlan.

"Let him go!" Beth warned. "Lachlan! Do it *now*, or I swear I'll follow Carlene and David!"

Releasing Roan, Lachlan dropped his arm swiftly

to his side. Ignoring the man, who now stood bent over, his hands gingerly massaging his neck, the laird turned an incredulous, wounded look on Beth. "Carlene an' David?"

Beth forced her revulsion down and managed to appear reasonably calm. "I just had a talk with Carlene." She swung a sympathetic look at Roan, who was straightening up with a furious glint in his eyes. "Mr. Ingliss, I think you should go."

"Are *you* ready ta leave?" he asked Beth, casting Lachlan a defiant look askance.

"Stay ou' o' this!" Lachlan hissed. "Her place is here wi' me!"

Chagrin shadowed Beth's face. "Lachlan, you don't own me."

"Roan," Agnes croaked as she closed the distance on unsteady legs. She met Beth's unreadable gaze, then shrugged deeper into her oversized coat. "Roan, come away wi' me *now.*"

"Agnes, is it true you attended my burial?"

The answer was clearly written on Agnes' weathered face.

Beth swallowed hard past the tightness in her throat. "Thank you. That was very kind."

"Yer're the dead womon?" Roan whispered, looking at Beth with raw astonishment. "The American womon who died a few months back?"

A few months back?

Beth cast a furtive glance at the landscape. Yes. It was definitely winter. Death apparently played havoc on her sense of time.

"I've regretted ma words ta you, Missy," Agnes

sniffled. "I've regretted them a hundred times an' mair. I'm sa sarry. Sa sarry this happened ta you."

There was no longer any doubt in Beth's mind that she had actually passed on. What puzzled her was the serenity she felt at having finally accepted the truth.

"*She's* the dead one, Aggie?" Roan rasped, his gaze volleying between his aunt and the American, his face ashen and taut. But then he blinked numbly at Lachlan's features, and it occurred to him that if the old master of the place could appear so real, why wouldn't the woman?

"Aye, we'll talk," Lachlan said gruffly, taking Beth by the arm and turning toward the house. "Ingliss, I'll no' consider yer ou'rageous offer. Be here in the morn ta start wark, or I'll be payin' you a visit you winna soon forget."

"Hold it, Lachlan." Beth wrenched free of his hold and fixed her attention on Roan. "Why did you come here, Mr. Ingliss?"

"Tis business done!" Lachlan snapped.

Beth shot him a warning look, then settled her gaze on the other man's face. "Well?"

"I offered him a proposition."

"You insulted me!"

"You auld bag o' wind!" Roan roared, jabbing an isolated finger at Lachlan. "Yer threats don't frighten me, Lannie. Visit me, eh? I'll laugh in yer face!"

"Stop it!" Beth demanded, placing her hands on each of the men's chests to keep them separated. "Mr. Ingliss, exactly what *was* your proposition?"

"Ach— "

"Shut up, Lachlan. I'm talking to *him*."

Roan drew in a deep breath and released it slowly. "I've been laid off ma job. I wark construction. Aggie tauld me abou' Borgie's trouble, an' asked me ta tak o'er until some ither arrangement cad be made."

With a pause, Roan raked a dark look over Lachlan's stormy face. "I need ta wark this winter. Wi' the masonry needin' repairs on two o' the chimneys, an' the rotted boards ta be replaced in the carriage house, I offered ta wark here till spring."

"For board an *pay!*" Lachlan hissed.

"For use o' the cot in the carriage house, an' a fair wage. Nothin' in this warld wad get me ta set foot in yer damned house."

"I'd tear ou' yer heart if you tried!"

"Enough!" Beth bellowed. "The two of you are carrying on like children!"

"An Ingliss issuin' *me* ultimatums!" Lachlan ranted. "Beth, darlin', you know I'm a patient mon— "

Beth impatiently flagged a hand to silence him. "You have a blind spot where the Inglisses are concerned."

"Wi' reason!"

"I think a one-hundred and forty-nine year grudge is carrying things too far," she countered impatiently.

Lachlan began to spout off in Gaelic. Beth allowed him several long seconds to spend his outrage, then lifted a hand in a demand for silence.

To her immense relief, the man beside her quieted, although he impaled Roan Ingliss with his dirtiest look, one resembling that of a hovering vulture waiting for its impending meal to draw its last breath.

"What's unfair about hiring the man?" Beth asked Lachlan calmly. His gaze shot to her own, questioning her sanity.

"Is there masonry work that needs to be done?"

"Aye, but— "

"Is there rotted wood in the carriage house?"

"Aye, but— "

"Then it seems to me you would want someone you could trust to do the work."

Lachlan's spilled breath frosted about Beth's face. "Trust an Ingliss?" he asked shrilly. "Are you daft, womon! Dinna you listen ta a word I said— "

"Tessa drove the knife into your heart," Beth interposed, "and it was *Robert* who walled you up in the tower. *These* people haven't done anything to you!"

"Tis in their blood ta— "

"Oh, give it a rest," Beth sighed with exasperation. "You keep telling me this is my home, too. Well personally, I'd like to know the repairs were in the hands of a man *I* trust."

"You trust, you say?" Lachlan said in a barely audible voice, slapping a palm to his brow. "Weel, why sud you no' trust the mon, eh? I' was no' *yer* blood the Inglisses spilled, was i'?"

"When could you begin the work, Mr. Ingliss?"

Roan couldn't help the laugh that shot from his

throat. The woman might be a ghost, but her spirit was mightier than any living person's he'd ever met. "Monday."

"Monday, then," Beth said resolutely.

"A dirk in ma eye!" Lachlan exploded. "I'll no' have *this* Ingliss warkin' ma home!"

"You're not. I am." Beth looked at Agnes. "I'm sorry all of this has been so upsetting to you. I give you my word, nothing will happen to your nephew."

"I hope no', Missy," Agnes said nervously, her gaze trained on Lachlan's stormy countenance.

"Assure her, Lachlan," Beth said, giving Lachlan's arm a jab with an elbow. Then, leaning to, she whispered in his ear in warning, "Darling, must we get ugly about this?"

Lachlan frowned as he looked deeply into Beth's eyes.

Ugly?

He could hear her thoughts as clearly as his own. She was threatening his treasures again. "Yer're an unscrupulous womon," he grumbled.

Beth offered a smug half-grin to Roan and Agnes. "He'll behave, I promise. Agnes, it was good to see you again."

Agnes allowed a smile to soften the tautness of her face, then linked her arm with her nephew's. "Come now, Roan. The cauld is settlin' in ma bones."

Beth turned her attention to Lachlan. "We have a few matters to discuss, don't we?"

Before Lachlan could respond, Beth slipped an arm through his and gave him a pull in the direction of the house. Roan remained as still as a statue until the couple was beyond the front doors, then he turned and looked down at his aunt with wry amusement dancing in his eyes.

"You cad have warned me the lady was a ghost."

"She teuk me by surprise," Agnes murmured, staring forlornly at the front of the house. "Do you think she'll stay wi' him?"

Roan glanced at the house. "Hard ta say. She sure keeps him on his toes."

A frown doubled the wrinkles on Agnes' brow. "Why wad she stay, though?"

Placing a hand on her back, Roan directed his aunt toward the van. "Just keep in mind, auntie, oor purpose in comin' here."

"But she's a kind lass, Roan. It's sa unfair she's stuck wi' the likes o' Lannie Baird."

"Careful gettin' in," Roan chided as he helped his aunt onto the passenger seat.

"I'm no' sa auld I canna buckle maself in!"

With a low chuckle, Roan kissed Agnes on the cheek. "Sarry, love."

"Sarry enough you'll forget yer silly plan?"

"Oh, na. I've sworn ta banish tha' mon from oor lives, an' I intend ta see i' through."

A look of despair dulled and clouded Agnes' blue eyes. "You've seen how human he can appear a' times, Roan. No' an exorcist in all o' Great Britain cad banish him. His hate for us runs tae deep."

Roan's eyes hardened as he looked again upon the house. "He has a weakness, Aggie. Tha' womon. If she decides ta leave here, he'll follow her."

Closing the door, Roan walked around to the driver's side and climbed in behind the wheel. He started the van before Agnes spoke again.

"You have three days ta change yer mind."

Roan gave a determined shake of his head as he started the van forward. "Five generations o' sufferin' is enough, Aggie. I'll no' fail. Have a little faith."

"Faith, ha! Lannie's got poor Miss Staples trapped here, *torturin'* her for all we know."

Releasing a groan, Roan pulled out onto the main road. "She doesn't strike me as the kind o' womon ta be strayed from her ain mind. If anything, she gave me the impression she's runnin' the show."

"Maybe," Aggie murmured thoughtfully.

A soft thud outside prompted Roan to roll the van to a stop. He hastened out the door, Agnes anxiously watching for his return. When he appeared at the open door, she stared in openmouthed horror at what he held dangling upside-down in his hand.

"Guid lawd!" she squealed, a hand placed over her racing heart. "You've killed one o' his birds!"

Climbing back onto the driver's seat, Roan nonchalantly tossed the dead peacock on the back seat.

"The damned things have the run o' the place," he said, turning the ignition. "He won't miss one."

"Oh lawd, oh lawd, you dinna know him! His precious bird, Roan! He's names for e'ery one o' the flock!"

Roan grinned wanly as he steered the van off the access road. "Sa we have Roger stuff the damn thing, an' we'll put i' in plain sight. Baird will ne'er know the difference."

Agnes hurriedly blessed herself. "Now yer're thinkin' he's a fool, eh? We're doomed."

Casting his aunt a sideward glance, Roan scowled. "Na we're no', Aggie. We're soon ta be emancipated."

She would be sixty-eight in a few weeks. She had worked at Kist House, on-and-off, for thirty years. Most of her life had been spent fearing and trying to outsmart the devil whose presence cast such a terrible pall over her family.

Yes, she had thought Roan's plan a viable one at first, his convictions and strength of character rekindling the hope she'd thought was lost long ago.

Her clan was still sizable. There were others who would work at the Baird House with a little nudging from her. They all feared the threat of visits from the ghost, the intrusions into their personal sanctuaries— their homes and workplaces. But Roan . . .

Now out of work, with too much time to think, her nephew had somehow developed the crazy notion that he could alter their lives for the better.

Dear Roan, who had lost his wife and young son to a terrible fire. Roan, who, whatever his personal feelings toward a family member, could always be counted on in a pinch.

And now she was going to lose him to Lannie Baird's wrath.

She was so positive of that, she wept.

Eleven

Although her mind was elsewhere, Beth handled a number of the brass collection pieces on the shelves by the fireplace in the parlor. Several hours ago, after leaving Roan and Agnes, Lachlan had beelined for the bar, telling Beth he wouldn't be long. Overly conscious of his dark mood, she'd decided it was best she gave him a little time to collect himself.

She'd made the decision to hire Roan Ingliss out of pure spite, although she hadn't a clue how she was going to actually pay the man. There was still a modicum of anger in her toward Lachlan for his unorthodox method of procuring himself a lover and companion. He should have told her the truth right away, given *her* the option to decide what to do with what life she had left, and where she would die.

Oddly, she felt no animosity toward Carlene. She had felt her friend's anguish, and heard the fear clear enough in her tone when she'd spoken of Lachlan.

"I didna think you'd deny me a guid-willie-waucht," Lachlan slurred, lifting a half-emptied glass of Scotch in a shaky salute as he weaved into the room.

After a moment of offering up a prayer for patience, Beth slowly turned to face him. There was no doubt in her mind that he was very near to falling flat on his face.

Resting an elbow on the mantelpiece, he noisily chugged down the rest of his drink. He grimaced as the fiery liquid made its way to his stomach, then he gave a theatrical shudder and tossed the glass into the blazing hearth.

"I've come to a decision. I'll no' stand for the arrangement wi' the Ingliss," he said, choosing to stare up at the portrait rather than meet Beth's gaze. "Tis no' yer place ta dictate ma feelin's toward tha' pack o' wolves."

"Let's discuss your feelings toward me."

Lachlan cast her a worried look, frowned, then peered up at the portrait again. "I've tried a hundred times ta explain— "

"So, try again."

With a sound of woe rattling in his throat, he turned to face her completely. But the movement was too quick, making him sway, and he braced a hand on the ledge of the mantel to steady himself.

"Try again, eh?" He ran his free hand down his face and tried to shake the proverbial cobwebs from his mind. "Might be I'm no' in the mood. Yer paughty interaction wi' the Ingliss cut me deep— as well you knew i' wad."

"Yes, I would have defied your decision no matter what it had been," Beth admitted calmly. "But I do

believe your grudge against that family has gone
on long enough."

"Tis *ma* grudge."

"Tis *your* grudge, *your* house, and *your* treasures.
You're a self-centered, spiteful little man, Lachlan— "

"Haud i'!"

"— and I'm fed up with the world—'and beyond—
revolving around what *you* want."

His face shockingly pale, Lachlan clapped an
open hand over his pseudo heart. "You wad choke
on a kind word ta me, wadna you?"

"No. You do have your moments."

A cracked cry burst from his throat. Looking up
at the portrait, he languidly wagged a forefinger at
the depiction of his love. "There's no' a cruel line
in yer face, darlin'. How was I ta know you wadna
be as sweet in the flesh as you are on the canvas,
eh?"

"Talk to *me.*"

Lachlan's head bobbed as it turned toward Beth.
"Talk ta *you?*" He jabbed an isolated thumb up at
the portrait. "She's far kinder. I can tak ma lickin's,
girl, but yer tongue has a fierce sting ta i'."

Beth sighed with a hint of annoyance. "You're
drunk."

"Nearly on ma lips," he grinned crookedly. "For-
tification, darlin'."

"Lachlan, why am I here?"

The soft sound of Beth's tone caused a shiver to
pass through Lachlan's numbing body. Turning
away, he braced his elbows on the mantel's edge.

He buried his face in his palms and tried to will away the disorienting effects of the alcohol he'd consumed.

"When Carlene an' David first came here as prospective renters, I was excited," he began dully, straightening, but keeping his profile to Beth. It was easier to stare up at her portrait than anticipate anger or disgust flashing in her real eyes. "It had been a while since a young couple had considered the place. Oh, many had come wi' the notion ta reside wi'in these grand walls, but I ran them off for one reason or anither. Carlene an' David were different from the rest. They talked abou' havin' children wi'in these verra walls tha' first day. I cad sense they felt a strong love for this place.

"It was abou' a week later 'fore I made maself known ta them. David teuk ma presence calm aneuch. Carlene . . ." He smiled wistfully. "Weel, efter a time o' hysterics, she decided I was a bonus. It was the first time since ma death I felt comfortable aroond the livin'. It was nice, Beth. Real nice. David cad play a sportin' game o' chess.

"A month efter they moved in, Carlene asked if she cad hang oop yer portrait here. The first time I laid eyes on i', I felt this . . . punch in ma gut. As days slipped inta weeks, Beth, I found maself comin' here all the time ta talk ta you. There were times, I swear, you talked back ta me— but wi' a kinder tongue than I've heard since you arrived, I can tell you!"

Delivering Beth a petulant look, he went on, "I'm no' sure whan I began ta link wi' you. Suddenly, I was receivin' yer thoughts, an' feelin' the warkin's o' yer body as though they were ma ain. I endured the headaches wi' you, an' terrible they were. I kept tryin' ta will you ta have the problem checked wi' a doctor, but you ne'er seemed ta pick up *ma* thoughts."

Lachlan fell sullenly quiet for several long moments. He was tired and feeling out of sorts. And drunk. The Scotch was doing crazy things to his system, but he went on nonetheless.

"I tauld Carlene I was sure you were dyin', an' I feared you had na inklin' o' wha' was happenin' ta you. We agreed you should be brought here. David wanted nocht ta do wi' any o' i'. We'd planned ta tell you e'erythin' right away, but then Carlene an' David were killed in their motor carriage."

A wounded look softened Lachlan's face as he looked at Beth. "For the record, Carlene wanted ta stop you from comin'. I wadna let her. David was tired o' the whole business an' went on. I forced Carlene ta remain till efter you'd arrived. I'm no' proud o' tha', but she left me na choice. The day she brought you here, she returned ta David, an' left you in ma inestimable care."

"You betrayed their friendship."

"Fegs, Beth! I was desperate ta haud you!"

"Why didn't you tell me I was dying?"

Lachlan gestured his frustration. "I cadna brin' the words ou', love. I tried. I knew the hemorrhagin' was worsenin'— "

"Hemorrhaging?"

"The coroner tauld Agnes there were indications

o' cerebral em-bo-lisms— wha'e'er tha' means— but the cause o' yer death was a cerebral hemorrhage."

"The embolisms were the cause of my head-aches?"

"I believe sa. Agnes remarked the doctor said i' was a miracle you didna suffer a stroke."

"Right . . . a stroke," Beth huffed. "I guess I was just damn lucky that it killed me, instead."

Lachlan took three long strides to bring himself directly in front of Beth. Hesitantly, he rested his hands on her shoulders, then gave them a tender squeeze. But Beth continued to stare dully at his chest, awarding him a moment to try to steady his legs beneath him. "The Scotch is buzzin' in ma head."

Her gaze lifted and searched his face through an unreadable expression. "Do you want to sit?"

Lachlan hesitated, then gave a single nod. Beth guided him to one of the sofas and helped him to lower himself onto it. Choosing to remain on her feet, she went to stand behind him.

"Something happened to me this morning."

Cradling his head with his hands, he looked up at her over his shoulder.

"I was in the attic," she began in an absent tone. "I found this dress in one of the trunks, and put it on. Not long after, I felt something change— the air. Or something. I came downstairs and found you in this room."

A pain-filled scowl masked his face. "I wasna doon here this morn."

"You weren't alone." Beth looked down and

locked eyes with him. "Robert and Tessa were with you."

Lachlan laughed, then grimaced as its sound lanced his aching head. "You have gone daft, womon."

"It was your wedding night, Lachlan. Tessa was wearing a purple and red gown, and purple lace gloves. A little hat with feathers was cocked to one side on her head. Cocked on the right side, if memory serves me. All I really remember about Robert is that he had longish, fine brown hair, and narrow eyes. Oh, and a pointy chin.

"A maid came in. Tessa asked for peach brandy."

Despite his pounding headache, Lachlan bolted to his feet and faced Beth. Her unreadable expression chilled him, made him wary of further disclosure. "What witchery be this?"

"You drew her a bath, remember?" Beth went on quietly. "You left them alone in this room and, when you returned, Tessa was hysterical. Her brandy glass mysteriously flew through the air and smashed on the mantel. I was aiming at Robert, but missed."

"It canna be," he murmured, trembling with shock.

"Robert escorted her to your room. They made love, in the tub, in front of the hearth."

"Stop!"

"You once told me that Tessa felt this place was haunted. It was. Briefly. By me. Somehow, I went back."

"Tis no' possible!"

"At first I thought you were somehow responsible for the phenomenon, but I know now you had no hand in it. I tried to warn you about her, Lachlan. You sat in that— " She pointed with an isolated finger. "— chair, and I touched your knees. You, too, were aware of my presence, but you chose to ignore me."

Shaking his head in confused denial, Lachlan stared off into space.

"If I managed to go back, then you must be able to as well. Go back, Lachlan. Change the past."

"Na!

"Live your life!"

"Wi'ou' you?" he asked harshly.

"We'll go back together."

He adamantly shook his head. "Truth be, I've been happier in this existence than the ither. An' truth be, Beth, there's na guarantee you'll be able ta remain in ma century. Let i' be."

"You could find someone else. Have children!"

"I want nocht but *you!* Why is i' sa bloody hard for you ta accept tha' I love you mair than anythin'— especially a flesh an' blood existence, eh?"

"You thought you were in love with Tessa."

"I was a fool," he grumbled.

"A virgin, you mean."

Her words shocked him, and he gaped at her.

"I'm sorry. I guess men don't care to be tagged virgins, do they?" she sighed.

"Bestill yer tongue, girl," he said darkly, obviously ill-at-ease with her knowledge.

"You have the infuriating habit of talking to me as though I were a subservient nineteenth-century woman. I don't like it, Lachlan. I have as much right to speak my mind as you do."

"Aye." Wearily, he seated himself again on the sofa. "You've thrown yer independence in ma face often aneuch."

"I don't like decisions being made for me."

Lachlan grunted in agreement. "Tis yer decision ta stay or pass on," he said, the words stilted, as if saying them took great willpower. "You've accused me o' keepin' you here against yer will. Truth be, lass, I havna the power ta stop you. Yer conscience an' yer heart have kept you here."

He was right, she knew now— perhaps had known all along. "If I do stay, Lachlan, then we must agree to a companionship of equal status; not what Lachlan wants, Lachlan gets."

"I've heard o' women's lib," he grumbled, and cranked himself around to look up at her. "But I've a suspicion yer're talkin' specifically abou' the Inglisses."

"I am."

"Na. Na way." Lachlan forced himself up on his feet and faced her, the sofa between them. "Some thin's remain a mon's business, Beth. The Inglisses— "

"Tell me something," she interrupted blithely, her lofty mood setting off a warning signal in Lachlan's mind. "How do you manage to keep this place in repairs? Who pays for the gas, and the food? Do you have a water bill?"

Lachlan looked about him, wondering where this line of questioning was going to land him. "Aye, there are bills an' repairs."

"Don't tell me the Inglisses pay them."

Impatience stormed across Lachlan's face. "Yer pity for them wounds me deeply."

"Just answer me, please."

"I give Viola Cooke money ta tak care o' the bills."

"Who is she?"

"A dear, auld soul wi' a love for the supernatural. Her grandmither, Violet, was the founder o' the 'Call Way' in Castle Douglas many years ago. She was a staunch believer in the efterlife, an' funded the preservation o' estates blessed wi' the spirits o' the long dead. She came here durin' the last decade o' her life, an' we had a hearty talk, we did. I was quite surprised whan she tauld me I was the maist vibrant spirit she'd come ta meet.

"Fancy tha', Beth. Many o' oor kind dinna have the energy ta pop in an' ou' between the two warlds as you an' I do. She tauld me willpower had a lo' ta do wi' ma abilities."

"Wonderful," Beth muttered.

Ignoring her, Lachlan went on, "Whan Violet passed on, her daughter, Rose, teuk o'er. Now, Viola, a third generation, is helpin' us."

"Do you materialize to her, too?"

"Aye. Viola's a sweet auld lady. E'ery All Hallow's Eve, she has a seance here wi' her group. A few groans an' the like keep her happy for anither year."

"That's degrading."

Lachlan grinned and gave a lift of his shoulders. "She taks care o' the legal wark ta keep this place ou' o' the Crown's hands. She also teuk care o' the arrangements ta inter you, Carlene, an' David. There are some thin's we spirits canna do."

"How did you get this woman to pay for my taxi ride here?"

Hiding a grimace at the accusation in Beth's tone, Lachlan gave an airy shrug of his shoulders. "I asked. She's a kind womon."

"Does she know I'm . . ." Beth rolled her eyes as she mentally fumbled for the right words. "One of the 'vibrant inhabitants' now?"

"Weel, no' exactly. I dinna want you exposed ta the public, sa ta say."

"Meaning what?"

"Ah, darlin', I hear yer temper simmerin' beneath the calm o' yer stance. The meanin' be, I'm Scotland's maist notorious ghost. Ma name's in books all aroond the warld."

"You're saying that if I do decide to stay, I'm to be your *secret* lover?"

Lachlan frowned. He didn't like Beth's breathy tone, or the vibes she was sending out. "'Tis for yer ain guid. Wad you really care ta have strangers gawkin' a' you?"

He saw the rigidity in her body slacken, and he smiled with satisfaction. It was seldom he won a point with her—

A tingling sensation began in his toes and swiftly coursed through his body as all his beloved treasures in the room soundlessly rose into the air. Beth's eyes were calm, but the floating objects told another story. The air about her was crackling with something akin to hostility.

"Darlin' . . ." He laughed unsteadily. "No' ma treasures again."

"Oh? And why not?"

He laughed again, low and choked with emotion. "You have a cruel streak in you, womon."

"I'm just thinking of what's best for you."

"For me, you say?"

Phantom perspiration broke out on his brow. "Darlin', I prefer yer temper on the fore. This . . . calm o' yers is scarin' the hell ou' o' me. Now please, lass, carefully return ma treasures ta their places an' stop tormentin' me wi' the threat o' their demise."

"Tormenting is a mighty strong word," Beth sighed in mock sorrow.

Lachlan's features grew sicklier. "Wha' have I done? A' least tell me *tha'* much!"

"I'm not a child, Lachlan. I'm a woman with a mind of my own. I understand your chauvinism stems from your upbringing in the wrong century—"

"Is tha' an insult ta *me* or ma century?"

"If I were to smash all your treasures to free you from your material obsession, would you be upset?"

A deadpan look came down over Lachlan's features. "I'd blow me a rooftop."

"Then stop making decisions for me."

To Lachlan's relief, the artifacts settled back in their places. A long sigh escaped him. He'd certainly gotten that message, although he would have been happier had she simply stated her feelings.

"Weel . . ." He gave Beth a wink. "Now tha' we've the hardships behind us, there's a nice warm bed waitin' for us, an' a fire in the hearth ta warm oor bones."

He held out his hand to Beth, but lowered it as she stood silently watching him.

"Beth . . . *darlin'*. I've been patient, have I no'?"

"You'll have to be patient a while longer."

"Give me one bloody guid reason—"

"I'm not in the mood."

"A little gentle persuasion—"

"I have a lot of thinking to do."

"You've had months!"

"I need more time," she said quietly, and started toward the door to the main hall.

"Beth!" He waited until she had stopped and looked at him. "I do love you."

"I know you do. And I love you."

"Then wha's the problem?"

Beth looked longingly in the direction of the door to the hall. It would be so simple to walk— or *poof*— away and leave this discussion for another day. But when she looked again at Lachlan, she realized the extent of his despair over not understanding her continued emotional distance from him.

For him it was a simple matter.

He loved her. She loved him.

The bed was upstairs.

But before she could commit herself to eternity with him, they had one last hurdle to surpass.

"Your bitterness toward the Inglisses— "

"Darlin', tis no' a subject we'll e'er agree on. Let i' be. You canna change how I feel abou' those people."

Despite her determination not to break down in front of him, tears swiftly brimmed her eyes. "And there lies the problem."

"Tis none o' yer business— "

"It most certainly is! I feel your hate and bitterness as if it were a part of me, Lachlan. It's like having a cancer eat away at me. Our . . . link . . . does not permit me to shut out *your* emotions."

"Beth— "

"No! No platitudes, please. Until you can resolve your anger with the Ingliss clan, I'm going to put as much distance between us as possible. It's the only way I can dim the emotional transmissions I'm getting from you. It's the only way I can bear this quasi-existence."

Lachlan stood as still as a statue, misery lending him an air of stark vulnerability.

"I'm sorry," Beth said in an aching whisper. "I don't like hurting you."

"But you do i' sa weel," he rasped. His attempt to come across as flippant fell short, and he quickly turned away to hide his mounting pain from her inspection. "Gae away, Beth. Do wha'e'er maks you happy. I'll ne'er kiss oop ta an Ingliss, but I will be here waitin' for you when you come ta yer senses."

A flicker of anger glistened in Beth's tear-filled eyes. She tried to speak, but the words would not leave her throat for several seconds.

"You love me, but it's a conditional love, Lachlan."

"Conditional?" he volleyed bitterly, casting her a disparaging look. "Ask an' I'd move heaven an' earth for you!"

"All I ask is that you free your hatred of the Inglisses."

"Ne'er."

A hand pressed over the thudding remembrance of her heart, Beth choked, "I refuse to experience it through you again," and she ran from the room.

As soon as she was gone, Lachlan furiously sliced the air with a hand. Unbeknown to him until it was too late, a minute portion of his energy slipped from his control. Two porcelain figurines to his left flew off their shelves and crashed to the floor behind him. He solemnly stared at the damaged pieces.

"Wait, she says. Wait, an' swallow ma hatred for tha' murderin' clan!"

Lifting a crystal dove in his hand, he laconically tossed it behind him. He was walking toward the same door Beth had used when the valuable piece shattered on the coffee table. Muttering, "Obsessed wi' ma treasures, ma bahookie," he shuffled out of the parlor and into the hall.

"An' as for those Inglisses . . ."

Roan was sleeping fitfully on his cousin's bed. Borgie was in St. Ives, England, visiting a friend—hiding from the ghost was more accurate, but Roan

couldn't think his cousin such a terrible coward anymore, not after having finally met the family's
nemesis himself.

A window was open, letting the chill of the night
embrace his breathing passages. Two wool blankets
were pulled up to his ears, and his thermal-clad
body beneath was almost curled in a fetal position.
He was dreaming of an ugly confrontation with
Lachlan in the tower. But he had the upper hand.
The razor-sharp tip of his sword was edging the
laird back toward the wall where he'd been interred.

A little more—

It felt as though liquid ice had washed over him.

Bolting upright in the bed, Roan made a scramble of throwing the covers aside. Gasping, bluster-
ing, he shot from the bed and closed the window
then, hugging himself, danced from foot to foot on
the cold, planked floor while he tried to figure out
what had happened to him.

He was dry, but his skin felt an icy sluice of water
washing over him still, repeatedly, until the terrible
coldness began to coil about his bones.

A nasty, omnipresent laugh filled the room.

With the realization that the ghost was nearby,
Roan felt the coldness lose its integrity.

"Baird!" he whispered through clenched teeth.

The laugh grew louder.

"You uncarin' bastard! Aggie needs her rest!
Show a little respect for her age!"

The laughter cut to a smothering silence. Fur-
tively glancing about him, his hands rubbing his

arms for warmth, Roan took several hesitant steps toward the center of the room. When Lachlan abruptly appeared, Roan nearly fell back.

"Steady, now, laddie," Lachlan taunted. His large hands gave a firm squeeze to Roan's shoulders.

Shucking off Lachlan's touch, Roan padded to the foot of the bed and turned to glare at his unwelcome visitor. "Wha' do you want?"

"Ta leave you wi' a word o' warnin'," Lachlan said ominously. "Dinna ever try ta pit ma womon against me again."

"You managed tha' yerself."

Lachlan calmly walked up to the dresser mirror and lightly touched his fist to the cold surface. Soundless, countless cracks spread throughout the glass.

"Dinna try ma patience, little mon. Watch yer ain whan Beth's around, an' be careful o' wha' you say ta her."

"Or wha', auld mon?"

Lachlan's smile was sardonic. "Ma guess is, you'll know soon aneuch."

"Tell me somethin', Baird," Roan began all too nonchalantly. "Are you haudin' a grudge against yer kin? I hear, Baird, yer brithers ne'er teuk their noses ou' o' their business journals long enough ta search for you."

Roan studied the ghost's eerie frozen state. The dark eyes that had been slicing through him moments before were now devoid of expression. But Roan knew that if he looked long and deeply into those eyes, he would see the pain his words had inflicted. "An' those still alive," he pressed on, shutting out the compassion trying to surface in him, "consider you a thin' ta be shunned, an embarrassment ta the Baird name."

To Roan's disappointment, Lachlan grinned. "Did you feel guid stickin' me ta the quick wi' yer words abou' ma livin' clan, Roan-you-slime? Aye, you did." Lachlan tapped his right temple with two isolated fingers of his right hand. "Tis a guid feelin', eh? Tis how I feel e'ery time I mak an Ingliss squirm."

Lachlan slowly began to fade. "An' I'll be feelin' tha' kind o' guid for a verra long time."

When Lachlan was no longer visible, Roan released a long breath. He sank on the edge of the bed and lowered his head, then linked the fingers of his hands and draped them over the back of his neck. His insides were queasy, his nerves strung taut.

"I'll send you ta hell, Baird."

At yer heels, laughed a voice within his head.

The color drained completely from his face when Roan realized it had been the ghost's voice he'd heard within the supposed privacy of his mind.

Angrier than he'd ever been, Roan buried himself beneath the covers on the bed and tried to push all thought of Lachlan Baird from his mind.

Beth breached the haze of the between-world's passageway and stepped into Lachlan's bedroom. She took but a moment to metabolize the energies at her disposal into a semblance of the woman she had been. There was no way for her to judge how long she'd retired to the grayness. The surcease had awarded her the tranquillity she'd needed to sort through her turbulent emotions. A calmer woman stared at the man who was sitting cross-legged on the foot of the bed, staring dully into the fire glowing within the hearth.

Her retreat had awarded her more than just a chance to come to terms with her feelings. There in the infinite grayness, alone, without anything to distract her, she'd come to touch upon the *knowledge*— atoms of information, revelations, floating in the otherworld, waiting to be absorbed by an intelligence and utilized. It was as if every person who had ever traveled through the passageway— the between place of the real world and the grayness— had left behind some part of their being, some portion of the experiences they'd had in life. And it had struck her that high emotions were attached to every molecule, as if the passageway was a repository where journeying souls purged the psychological ties of their past existence.

She had found her own fear of death among those fragments, along with the stark grief she'd known after the deaths of her adoptive parents. There wasn't a whole lot of Beth among those atoms, which told her she was still holding dear to a life that was forever lost to her. She had yet to release the anger, the joy, the other sorrows she'd known. But these she could not relinquish as yet. She would hold them dear for as long as she could, for she had learned that she had a purpose in this quasi-existence, one vital as the role she'd played in making her mother's last years as comfortable as possible.

Now she was here for Lachlan, to challenge the anguish and rage that kept him bound to his present existence. Somehow, she had to abolish his vista of his past, or at least prompt him to concentrate on the positive events prior to Tessa's betrayal.

Lachlan sighed and lowered his face into his hands. Painful heart sensations gripped Beth. She didn't like to see him so despondent, so lonely. But she had to be careful how much she gave in to him. Lachlan was a charmer, a man confident in his prowess. Beth wanted nothing more than to lie in his arms for countless hours, but lovemaking with him had a tendency to reinforce his beliefs that a surrender to her needs meant waiving her will as well.

A tingling sensation began in her abdomen and slowly spread through her body with an accompanying warmth. Releasing a thready breath, she closed her eyes momentarily in a vain attempt to still the desire simmering within her. She had come to talk to Lachlan, to try to reason with his obstinate side—

As if her hands had a mind of their own, her trembling fingers untied the satin belt beneath her breasts. She shucked the gown downward until it was but a lacy pool about her ankles, then stepped out of it. The fireplace's glow tinged her nudity in golden and orange hues, shadowing and accentuating the seductive curves of her body. Steeling herself against the shyness trying to beach her compelling awareness of what her appearance would incite in Lachlan, she gracefully approached the bed. He remained unaware of her. When she stopped within an arm's reach of him, and still he did not look up, her confidence began to succumb to a feeling of ridiculousness. She was about to turn and retrieve the gown when something warm and firm clamped about her right wrist. Startled, she found herself staring down into the dark, turbulent depths of his eyes.

Her taut facial muscles would not permit anything more than a nervous tic at one corner of her mouth. She waited anxiously for Lachlan to say something as his eyes made a slow appraisal of that part of her body visible above the mattress. When his gaze lazily lifted to meet hers, she could not determine his thoughts or his mood.

And when he finally spoke, it was not what Beth had hoped to hear.

"Wha' do I have ta sacrifice for this wee mercy?"

A slow burn ignited within Beth's core. Here she was, as naked as the day she was born, and Lachlan was being flippant and snide.

Jerking her wrist free of his hold, she whirled away. She kept her teeth clenched against a retort as she snatched up the gown and fumbled to find the hemline to slip over her head. Her skin was scorched with humiliation, especially the back of her, which was exposed to his scrutiny.

He didn't want a companion, she fumed, he

wanted a mindless lover! A woman without a voice or a will of her own!

She was about to pull the gown over her head when the material was yanked from her hands. Sharply turning her head, she saw the gown land on the floor several feet away. Then strong, large hands were at her waist, and she was spun around to face an imposing body as naked as her own.

"I'm not in the mood now!" she hissed, pushing against his broad chest.

"Darlin', yer're wearin' me thin," he sighed, his eyes gleaming with frustration. "Come ta bed—"

"Forget it, you louse!"

Muttering in Gaelic, Lachlan swept Beth up into his arms and unceremoniously tossed her onto the bed. She squealed in surprise, but as soon as she hit the mattress, she was working up to slip into the grayness. But Lachlan moved swiftly, throwing his body atop hers and pinning her wrists to the bed as he positioned himself to straddle her squirming hips and abdomen.

Beth became livid with impotent anger. As long as he was touching her, she couldn't slip away to the grayness.

His focused energies had her grounded—

Working one of her wrists free, she rammed a fist into his jawline. Lachlan released a cry of surprise and pain combined, then, to her disbelief, he laughed.

"You love ta bust ma chops, dinna you?" he chortled, anchoring the assaulting hand back to the bed.

"Get off me."

Lachlan gave Beth the impression that he was seriously considering it, then he grinned broadly down at her.

"Give me one guid reason, sweetness."

"Because if you don't . . ." Beth deliberately let her words trail off, her warning lingering ominously in the air. But she should have known how Lachlan would respond to that.

"I knew you'd miss me," he laughed, sensuously leaning to and nestling his arousal against the softness of her belly. "Yer spittin' words come from a mouth achin' for ma kisses. Na. Na. Dinna deny i', lass. Yer're pantin' for me. Admit i'."

"You *worm!*"

Lachlan released a guttural sound. Beth wasn't certain whether it indicated exasperation or amusement. He lowered himself to capture her lips, but she stubbornly turned her head aside and released a grunt of disgust. However, Lachlan was not to be put off so easily. His lips, feeling shockingly warm against her skin, moved against the side of her neck. His teeth nipped, heightening the sensitivity of her flesh. Then his tongue began to stroke, to call upon the fires deep within her to quell her anger with him.

Almost against her will, she moved her head, her lips seeking the texture and firmness of his jawline. She slid a kiss along that ridge, her eyes closing to the exquisite sensations frolicking in every part of her body. His lips continued to move along her neck, over her collarbones, leaving a burning trail of after-sensations.

"Lachlan," she moaned, breathless with desire.

She gave a halfhearted tug to free her hands, wanting to thread her fingers through the thickness of his hair and guide his tormenting mouth to other yearning parts of her body. But Lachlan wasn't prepared to release her yet. Lifting his head, he stared deeply into her eyes, his own betraying the fierce desire within him to possess her body. His grip light but firm, he stretched her arms high above her head, then lowered his own and targeted one of her earlobes with his teeth.

A spear of delight pierced her. Shock waves of pleasure, searing and wondrous, crashed down on her, banishing any residual resistance that might have been lingering deep within her subconscious.

"I love you," he rasped by her ear. Lifting up, he ran his hands with seductive slowness down her arms, his gaze heatedly locked with hers. "We belong thegither."

"Don't talk."

Lachlan kissed her then, hungrily, deeply, his tongue exploring the warm, moist recesses of her mouth before their tongues began to stroke in rhythm to the movements of their bodies. Instinctively, he slid between her thighs, nesting himself against the enticing valley that had been unmercifully dogging his thoughts for what seemed an eternity.

The kiss went on, Beth's arms locking about his neck, Lachlan's brawny hands petting and kneading her shoulders, her back, her hips. She was blissfully lost to all but the incredible sensations filling her.

Lachlan had a way of making her feel more than any living soul could. His mouth made an ardent trail to her left breast, where he surrounded the dark, erect peak and began to suckle.

Her groan came from the depths of her.

His teeth nipped with maddening gentleness, then his tongue swirled and lapped and teased, bringing her to a point of desperation to quench the fires building within her loins.

"I love you," she gasped, and closed her eyes when, muttering Gaelic endearments, he moved his hands to her shoulders and drew her up. She reveled in the kisses he planted all over her face. His hands, smooth and strong, slid over her spine and hips, drawing her further onto his lap, inching her toward the rigid male member throbbing to enter her body.

Impatient with his slowness, Beth wrapped trembling fingers about his manhood and guided it into her. A stilted groan emanated deep from within Lachlan, while she released an airy, slow breath of satisfaction. She was about to thrust herself completely onto him when he gasped. His hands flew to her shoulders and, to her utter disbelief, he held her away with a look of shock tightening his features.

Her first notion was that he thought her too bold, but the more she studied his face, his expression crumbling to something akin to horror, the more confused she became.

Unwilling to dwell on what was wrong with him, she moved her hips forward, taking him in deeper, and using those muscles to entice him back into his previous mood. But Lachlan groaned piteously.

"I forgot! Damn the stars, womon, I canna waste ma energies now!"

Beth's mouth dropped open as she stared at him in sheer incredulity. She remained in numbed shock when he quickly lowered her to the mattress and sprang from the bed.

"Tis a night o' business, Beth," he explained breathlessly, scrambling into his clothes while casting her body several looks of raw yearning. "Yer timin' is lousy."

Blinking, her lips still parted, Beth drew herself up into a sitting position. "What?"

"Yer timin', womon!" He expelled a breath of exasperation and brushed the back of a hand across his brow. "This will have ta wait. Sweet Jesus," he added with a groan, hungrily staring at her breasts. "The one night a year . . . Weel, tis business. You understand?"

"No, I don't understand." With a shaky laugh, Beth made an airy gesture with a hand. "Was it my imagination, or were we just in the midst of making love?"

"Aye." Lachlan leveled a vulturous look at her. "An' I'll be in a warld o' hurt for the rest o' the day," he grumbled, tugging on the crotch of his black pants. "Was tha' yer plan? Ta mak me forget ma responsibilities?"

"Now wait one . . . damn . . . minute," she fumed, slipping from the bed. "What the hell are you talking about?"

Lachlan didn't answer right away. His expression was that of a tortured man as his gaze moved up and down her body.

"Lachlan!"

Reluctantly, he looked into her fiery eyes. "Aye, love?"

"Have you been drinking?"

"No' a drop. I tauld you, I've business. You know we canna stretch oor energies tae thin."

Brushing past him with an unmistakable air of hostility, Beth retrieved her gown. But as she was about to put it on over her head, Lachlan again snatched it from her grasp.

"Give me that!"

Lachlan flipped the gown behind him and placed his hands on his hips. "It maks you look like a bloody spook."

His words had the effect of a slap in the face, and she went rigid with anger. "I happen to like that dress. And, I *am* a spook! Or aren't you that same pain-in-the-ass who was so determined to make me accept my death?"

"Pain-in-the-*ass*, you say?" Lachlan puffed himself up, his eyes furious and snapping. "A lady wad choke sayin' *bahookie*, let alone . . . *ass!*"

"Maybe in *your* century," she spat, and made a move to get her gown, which Lachlan blocked with a swift side step.

"I'll burn the damn thin'!"

"Try it." Beth straightened back her shoulders and flashed him a lancing look. "You have far more to lose in this house than I do."

"Yer're just bein' stubborn! I hate tha' gown!"

"I *love* it!"

A visual showdown ensued for several long moments.

"Tis the gown Tessa wore whan she done me in," he rasped finally, his shoulders quaking with anger.

"You're full of it."

Lachlan thought about this for a moment, then groaned. "Sa i' was no' the damn gown, but i' rattles me ta see you wearin' somethin' as . . . as dolorous as tha' rag.

"Dolorous?" Beth laughed. "You just want to dictate what I wear! Well, I won't stand for it. I like the dress. I like the way it feels on me, and I intend to wear it."

"An' if I said I loved the damn thin', *you'd* toss i' in the fire!" With a sound of disgust, he swooped the gown up into a hand and tossed it to Beth. "Fine. Have i' yer way! But I'm warnin' you." He leveled an isolated finger and wagged it at her. "A mon only has so much patience, an' yer're tryin' mine ta the quick! You know how I feel abou' tha' dress, so dinna come ta me in i' again."

Beth quickly slipped into the gown and, while Lachlan watched her with a scornful eye, she tied the belt into a neat bow, then flamboyantly twirled the end of the ribbon to annoy him.

"Yer're an incorrigible tease," he scowled.

"Poor baby." Smiling sweetly, she added, "I hope your 'business' proves satisfying, Lannie, because it's going to be a *very* long time before— "

"I've a mind as ta the rest o' the taunt," he interjected irritably, and arched a censorious brow. "You've yet ta come ta know wha' maks a guid relationship wark."

"Oh, really?"

"Be snide ta yer heart's content, but *I* . . . ma fine lass . . . tak *ma* responsibilities verra seriously. Tis the difference between a mon an a womon, an' why tis the mon who's always worn the trousers in the real warld."

Beth was too stunned to speak right away. Then, casting off her stupor, she calmly gripped the front of Lachlan's shirt and jerked him forward, placing their faces inches apart. "I'm beginning to understand why Tessa dirked you. I'm feeling the urge myself."

Shaking himself free, Lachlan took two paces back. "Now dinna you be attackin' ma monhood!"

With a pointed glance down, Beth quipped, "It's your one asset."

"Ach! You've a mouth tha' needs a guid washin'— "

Beth *poofed* away.

With an exasperated roll of his eyes, Lachlan muttered, "Wha' a mon does for love."

Twelve

Giving in to his restlessness, Roan left his cozy quarters in the carriage house. His gloved hands lifted the lamb's wool collar of his coat as he leisurely strolled toward the west grounds. The air was crispy cold, but clean and invigorating. The downy snow that had fallen the previous evening was only ankle deep, but it covered slick, frozen older snow. Frost and ice glistened like diamond dust on the naked branches of trees and shrubs.

Stopping at the fenceline to the Lauders' property, he gazed wistfully across the pristine fields. The house to the far side of the field was lit up. He wondered if the family was gathered around a wood stove, sipping tea or hot cider as he wished he was at this moment. He hated being on the Baird estate, hated it more every morning when he awakened and looked out at the house.

Wrapped in melancholy, he pushed away from the fence and, mindful of his steps, headed back along the same path. But instead of returning to the carriage house, he took a snow-covered footpath by the main house that led to the north pasture.

He still wasn't sure what had brought him out on this night, but *something* was beckoning him.

Lights came on in the library, the unexpectedness of the occurrence causing him to nearly jump out of his skin. He glowered at the windows covered within by sheer amber curtains, then carried on with his walk. He came to the edge of the wooded area that bordered the uncluttered north field, and was about to turn back when he spied movement by the solitary tree in its center.

Roan crouched low and squinted hard to better discern the figure in white. In the past weeks, he'd seen Beth Staples wandering about the place, most times striking him as being the loneliest soul he'd ever known. He had never felt the slightest animosity toward the woman— ghost. The few times she'd spoken to him while he was going about the work in the first fireplace, he'd found her pleasant and easy to talk to, as long as the master of the house was not mentioned.

And yet it was because of the master of Baird House that he was there, subjecting himself to the intervals of visits from Lachlan, and the baiting remarks issued to provoke him into walking off the job, or perhaps into inciting a showdown. If Roan'd the slightest idea how to fight a spirit, he would certainly provoke such a match, but as it was, he was as helpless as a child on that score. He wasn't even sure how much damage Lachlan could actually do to a living being. From Borgie's accounts of what had happened to him— in his own house, no less—

Roan knew that Lachlan did possess some kind of power.

Beth Staples was his only hope.

Rising and stretching his stiff legs, he watched the figure for several seconds longer. The field between him and her was bathed in blue moonglow, making the distance appear eerie and starkly remote. His courage wavering, he glanced back at the house. Only a glimpse of window light could be seen through the ice-laden tree branches and the evergreen shrubs. But that glimpse was enough to fuel his determination to sway the woman— the female ghost— to his side.

A thin layer of ice on the field gave a crunch to his footfalls as he made his way to the solitary tree. Beth was waiting for him when he came to a stop several feet away from the headstone she was standing behind, her fingers absently smoothing the top of the stone's rounded edge.

"Guid e'enin'," he said lamely, a nervous twitch of a smile playing on his lips.

"How long were you watching me?"

Roan dipped his bare hands deep into his coat pockets. "I wasn't sure if I sud intrude."

"How's the work going?"

"Verra weel. I'm waitin' for a shipment o' mortar ta come in. Two or three days."

"Are you comfortable enough in the carriage house?"

"Surprisingly, I am, thank you."

Roan appeared startled by something, and began to unbutton his coat. But as he was about to shuck

ut of it, he stopped and shook his head as if to
clear his thoughts. "Aren't you cauld?"

Beth smiled. "Actually, I'm between the two
worlds right now."

"Between?"

To explain, she calmly moved one of her hands
through the headstone. When Roan's expression
became sickly, she stopped.

"I don't feel anything at the moment."

Roan slowly fumbled to rebutton his coat, his
gaze glued on her face. "Whan yer're . . ."

"Solid?"

"I guess tha's a guid way ta put i'."

"Yes, when I'm 'solid', I feel everything as I did
before I died. I can even enjoy food, and soaking
in a hot bath."

Roan was impressed, if not befuddled. But he
was losing sight of his objective.

Casually stepping closer, he looked at Lachlan's
headstone. His gaze darted to the one beside it and
he felt his insides tighten. When he looked into
Beth's eyes, he was unsettled to find her watching
him with uncanny calm.

"Are you angry abou' losin' yer life sa young?"

"Not anymore. It was hard, at first."

Pulling a hand from a pocket, he rubbed an earlobe nipped by the cold air. "I guess i' wad be—
Weel, I guess i's no' a subject you care ta discuss."

Beth came around the headstone and stood directly in front of Roan. He couldn't stop his gaze
from sweeping over her figure, lingering on the
feminine shoulders left nearly bare. When he real-

ized he was treading on dangerous ground, he quickly looked away and pretended to reread the words and dates on the laird's headstone.

"What do you think of this dress?"

Roan's head snapped around and he glanced over the gown briefly before looking into the alluring eyes studying him.

"The dress?" He swallowed and managed a strained smile. "It's fine lookin'. Why do you ask?"

"I'm not trying to seduce you," Beth chuckled.

Crimson stole into Roan's cheeks.

"I only asked because Lachlan hates it."

"Mmmm."

"Which means, you probably love it, right?"

"I do like i'," aye."

"Does it make me look like a . . . bloody spook?"

Roan smiled at the accent she affected. "Weel, Beth, i's got a flow abou' i'. An' the sleeves. I guess you cad say i' adds ta yer mystique."

With a lopsided grin, she admitted wryly, "Maybe he does have a legitimate reason for disliking it."

"The auld mon? I wadn't let him talk you ou' o' i'— "

Roan nearly choked on his words when he realized what he'd implied. Although Beth laughed softly, he felt as if his humiliation would melt him into the ground.

"I didn't mean tha' like i' sounded."

"I know. Roan, did you come here to talk about something specific?"

"It was just somethin' I've been wonderin'." Resisting a notion to moisten his dry lips with the tip of his tongue, he shuffled himself more comfortably within his heavy coat. "You know, I see you sometimes, wanderin' aroond. I get the impression yer're no' happy."

"You're wondering why I stay."

Roan nodded. "Is i' *him* keepin' you from goin' on?"

Unbeknown to Roan, annoyance began to simmer within Beth. "You make it sound like I'm his prisoner."

"Seems ta me, you are."

Beth moved swiftly, catching Roan off guard. He gasped as something passed through him, something so cold it could not be of his world. Every nerve in his body seemed under assault by ice-hot sensations, and turning one hundred and eighty degrees, he gaped at the woman in something akin to horror. He realized she had passed through him, but the reason for her action befuddled him.

"I'm not a prisoner here," she said in a chiding tone, her body held rigid. "Let me ask you something, Mr. Ingliss." She stepped up to him and directed his attention to Lachlan's headstone. "Does it bother you that *he* died young?"

As hard as it was for him to look upon the fury in her eyes, Roan did. And with the moon's blue glow on her face, her features were all the more eerie, rivetingly haunting.

"I can't say I feel anythin' for him, no' efter wha' he's put ma family through all these years."

"But you see, that's the whole problem. Lachlan

isn't the only one holding a grudge. Do you know what's really holding him here?''

"Spite."

Beth whirled away in exasperation. When she faced Roan again, he was stunned to see tears welling in her eyes.

"Try to imagine what it was like for him that night! Roan, for one minute, try to imagine the woman you love stabbing you in the heart, then coldly telling her real lover to dispose of the body.

"Lachlan was still alive when Robert was walling him up."

Feeling his stomach churn, Roan tried to turn away, but Beth solidified and her icy fingers clamped onto his chin and forced him to face her. "Robert *knew* he was entombing a *live* man! Think about what must have been going through Lachlan's mind while he was waiting for death. Imagine being in that cold, dark place in the tower, knowing you're bleeding to death, and wondering if you'll suffocate first!"

"Stop!"

Roan wrenched free and staggered back. He leaned against Beth's headstone, struggling inwardly to keep his legs from buckling beneath him. Fearfully staring at the woman, he swallowed what felt like his heart rising in his throat.

"Actually," Beth went on in an airier tone, determined one way or the other to penetrate the hatred bred into this man's heart, "Lachlan's got quite a sense of humor in regard to that whole business. The part he's having trouble coming to terms with is the fact that after your family found his remains in the tower, he was buried out here like some evil thing to be forgotten. Not a tear was shed for him.

"Lachlan has all his faculties and emotions. He can be hurt, and his emotional scars are greater than you could ever imagine."

"I can't change wha' happened in the past!" Roan cried, straightening up. "My cousin's hair turned snow-white efter Lannie nearly scared him ta death!"

"Borgie?"

"Aye, Borgie. He's younger than maself!"

"Your cousin," Beth began stiffly, her tone as chilling as the night air, "kindly offered to let me use the phone at his cottage. We ended up in a wrestling match, Roan. Lachlan showed up in time to save me from a degrading act."

"Borgie tried ta force himself on you?"

Beth gave a stilted nod of her head.

After several moments of trying to digest this information, Roan stated huskily, "But you were already dead when i' happened."

"I wasn't aware of it. Obviously, neither was your cousin."

"Damn," Roan breathed, his expression racked with guilt. "I'm sarry, Beth. Truly, I am. I sud have guessed there was mair ta the stary than Borgie let on."

"You're hoping I'll go on, and Lachlan will follow me."

The dully spoken words knocked the breath from Roan.

"Don't bother to deny it."

"I'll no' insult yer intelligence by tryin'."

"Good, because I won't leave him. I love him."

She released a laugh that was choked with tears. "It's impossible not to love him, but your family won't even try to know him!"

"He's been dead for— "

"Can you explain to me why you always refer to him as a man?"

Roan looked helplessly in the direction of the house, then despondently into Beth's eyes. "This warld is for the livin'. You an' I both know tha'."

"It's the *living* keeping him here. Roan, for as long as you and your family resent his presence, Lachlan will remain. It isn't the house keeping him here. The house . . . what he calls his 'treasures', they're all he's had, but they're not the chains keeping him earthbound."

"He has you, now."

"I'm not enough." Beth lowered her head and tried to still the threat of tears. "I don't have the power to heal his wounds."

"Or the will?"

Roan's sarcastic tone brought Beth's head up sharply. "You really don't understand, do you?"

"I guess no'."

"Has he offered you pay for your work?"

Taken aback by the left-field question, Roan took a moment before replying, "Aye." Fishing into his right pants pocket, he withdrew something and held it up for her to see. "A ruby equal ta a month's wark."

"He's paying you in precious stones?"

Nodding, Roan rolled the stone around in his palm. "He tells me he has a wee chest hidden away in the attic." His dryness remained when he looked up at Beth. "I believe he's hopin' I'll prove ta be a thief."

Beth sighed deeply. "That explains his generosity in paying you."

"Aye. Look, Beth, I'm sarry yer're in the middle o' this. But there's nothin' you can say or do ta change wha's between ma family an' Baird."

"Except to pass on? Well, you can forget that idea."

"It's the only way. . . ." His words trailed off when her attention was drawn to the sound of vehicles pulling up at the house.

"Are you expecting company?"

Roan replaced the precious stone in his pants pocket. "It's All Hallow's Eve. I daresay the auld mon is entertainin' the loony troop."

"The what— oh, never mind. It's Halloween already?"

"Aye."

"Does Lachlan do this every year?"

"As far as I know, he does. It maks for comical readin' in the papers for a time efterward." Roan poised his hands to accentuate his next words. "LAIRD OF KIST HOUSE RETURNS TA LAMENT HIS HEINOUS MURDER. All the locals know he's here all the time, but still the papers write oop their crazy staries."

"Holding these seances is Lachlan's way of re-paying Viola Cooke for her help over the years."

"Aye, I know abou' her, but trust me, lass, Baird's main objective is ta poke jabs a' ma ancestors o'er the wrongs they done him."

"I hardly think Lachlan would stoop that low."

"Ask him," Roan challenged airily. "He'll tell you right quick he looks forward ta this night. Gives him a chance to reopen the wounds o' the past. A friend o' oor family sat in on one o' these seances once. He claimed auld Lannie put on quite a show, no' leavin' ou' a single, bloody detail o' the whole affair. Sa, you see, Beth, it's hard ta leave the past be whan there's so much still breathin' life inta i'."

"How far are *you* willing to bend to end this feud?" Beth asked softly.

"I'll no' shed a tear o'er him, if tha's wha' yer're askin'."

Beth began to dissolve. "Wrong answer."

When Roan could no longer see her, he shouted, "Then wha' is i' you want me ta say? Yer're the only one who can end this!"

"Wrong again," came a zephyrous voice. "It's between you and Lachlan."

A long, singsong moan filled the dining room, augmenting the chilling ambiance of the flickering candlelight that cast long, squirming shadows on the walls. The moaner, sitting regally at the head of the table, lifted her aged, finely-boned hands in a gesture of supplication.

"Come to us, spirit," she warbled, her eyes closed to the enraptured audience who filled the rest of the twelve chairs about the table. "Hear us and obey. *Appear!*"

This was Lachlan's cue.

Positioning himself between the two worlds, he began to expose a translucent self to the anxious group. He intended to play his part to the hilt this year, right down to the smallest detail. He'd taken particular care in his choice of dress this evening. Although he'd died in a nightshirt, he refused to be caught dead in one again. In lieu of this, he wore a ragged, full-sleeved white shirt, and black, tight-fitting pants with slashes about the thighs.

He was barefoot. Burdensome-looking chains were draped from his shoulders and arms. And to further compliment his efforts to appear the unfortunate victim of a love triangle, he manifested a delightful greenish aura about him.

The seance group was too intent watching Viola Cooke's antics to notice Lachlan's wavering presence by the cold fireplace. This piqued him, but he didn't lose heart. He couldn't risk doing anything too suddenly. The old tickers about the table had to be taken into consideration.

The head of Call Way moaned as she rolled her silver, curly-locked head from side to side. How she knew she wasn't sure, but Viola *was* aware that Lachlan had materialized behind her. The drama she was lending to the sham invocation was for the benefit of those watching her. It simply wouldn't do for Lachlan to nonchalantly appear and have a nice tête-à-tête with them. No, that wouldn't do at all. The credibility of her grandmother's organization was at stake and, like her grandmother and mother before her, she preferred her one-on-one relationship with the charming laird to remain just that.

"Come to us, Lannie Baird. Breach the barrier separating you from your former life and connect with us once again."

More groaning.

"I beseech you, spirit, *appear.*"

Straining not to grin, Lachlan raised his arms and rattled the chains. As expected, the elderly visitors riveted their attention on him. Three new members, the youngest of whom was eighty-one, nearly bolted from their chairs, their eyes wide with fear. Lachlan felt a strong compulsion to laugh. To camouflage this, he raised his hands to his face. The loud clanging of the chains covered the sounds of his mirth until he was able to bring himself under control. Then he lowered his arms, in a deliberately slow manner that always pleased the onlookers, and through a scowl, he demanded, "Who . . . has . . . summoned . . . me?"

Viola Cooke settled her rounded body more comfortably on the chair. Although she dearly wished she could watch Lachlan perform, she was careful to stare ahead, trancelike.

"There are a few among us who doubt the existence of the afterworld. Enlighten the disbelievers, spirit."

Lachlan released a groan to abort a gurgle of laughter.

"The efterwarld is for those freed o' their earthly bonds. I . . . canna . . . leave . . . here . . . e' er."

"Tell us why, spirit."

"Betrayal an' greed shackle me ta this purgatory."

Lachlan moaned piteously, thrilling the rapt audience. He swayed. The chains jangled. "The livin' continue ta dirk me." He sank to his knees, his hands held out. "I . . . can . . . find . . . naaa . . . peace!"

"Oh, give it a rest."

The omnipresent voice even stunned Lachlan, whose darting glances swept the room. He had a terrible suspicion as to whom the voice belonged. There was something very familiar about the snide tone.

Viola searched the mixed expressions of her companions. She hadn't a clue who had spoken. "Spirit?"

Refusing to dwell on Beth's reasons for interrupting 'business', Lachlan forced himself back into his expected role. "I . . . am . . . here."

"Is there another spirit trying to contact us?"

The laird slowly rose to his feet. "I . . . have . . . sent . . . the . . . *disrupter* . . . away."

"Do you have any idea how ridiculous you look?" chided the omnipresent voice.

Chagrined, Lachlan tried to ignore the questioning looks trained on him. Even Viola turned in her chair to cock a pale eyebrow in his direction.

"I . . . am . . . a lost soul!" he cried theatrically, throwing his arms wide in the hope his lady love would abandon her scheme to mortify him. "I come . . . ta—Ooh, sweet Jesus," he groaned as a beautiful apparition began to form on the center of the dining room table. "No' *now*, darlin'!"

Beth fully materialized, her stance regal with anger, her arms folded against her chest. She didn't spare the visitors a glance. Her stormy gaze was riveted on Lachlan, much to his distress.

"You had ta come, eh?" he scolded, his hand gestures making the chains ring discordantly. "Why, I ask? Are you *tha'* determined ta spoil wha' little happiness I get in this life?"

Beth lowered her arms to her sides, clenching and unclenching her hands. "You're dead, remember? Besides, *darlin'*, I thought *I* was your happiness. More blarney?"

Twelve gazes volleyed to Lachlan's corner, but he was too livid to pay them any heed. "Aneuch, womon! Get doon from tha' table, lest I haul you doon maself an' lay you cross ma knee!"

In response, Beth knelt in front of a startled woman. "You're Viola Cooke, aren't you?"

The woman's pale eyes widened as she bobbed her head.

"I'm Beth."

"Hel . . . lo."

Beth smiled. "Do you like my dress?" Standing, she gracefully lifted the skirt, turned in place, and asked the group collectively, "Does it make me look like a . . . *bloody spook*?"

While two men smiled up at her—one without a tooth in his mouth—most of the others at the table shook their heads. One elderly woman gave a shrug and squinted to have a better look at the gown.

"He doesn't like this gown," Beth sighed, gazing with mock despair at Lachlan. "And he doesn't believe women should have a mind of their own."

To Lachlan's stark dismay, the group fixed deadpan looks on him. Someone in the room clucked in disapproval.

Viola was obviously dumbstruck by the whole turn of events. And to make matters worse, Lachlan had fully materialized without realizing it.

"Tha' Ingliss swine put you oop ta this!" he fumed. He attempted to approach the table, but his legs got caught up in the chains and he slapped the floor the length of his body. He was up on his feet like a shot, his furious scowl savaging his features. "Come doon here!" he demanded, clumsily shucking out of the chains until he was free of them all. "I want ta have a word wi' you . . . in *private.*"

"You're upsetting our guests, darling," Beth drawled laconically, poised like the belle of a ball atop the table. "Now stop acting like an ass—"

"Ass!" he squealed in sheer exasperation. He offered a simpering look of apology to those about the table. "The transition has affected her mind," he rushed to say. "Ma poor love—"

"Lachlan, stick it in your ear."

The frustrated laird's eyes rolled up to issue her a warning, but Beth went on, "Ladies and gentlemen, I'm sorry, but I'm going to have to ask you to end your meeting. His lordship—"

"Dammit ta hell, Beth!"

Lachlan's roar sent the group scrambling from their chairs. Viola remained behind while the others hastened to the hall door. When she looked up, it was to see the new mistress of the house looking kindly down at her.

"I am sorry, Miss Cooke. Perhaps another time."

After a single nod of her head, Viola Cooke left the room and discreetly closed the door behind her. Now that they were alone, Lachlan slammed his fist on the table.

"You had ta do i'! You just *had* ta do i'! Why, Beth? I tauld you i' was business!"

"Am I or am I not the mistress of this house?"

"Aye, but shrewishness is no' necessarily a condition o' tha' position!"

Beth sat on the table, then slipped to the floor and stood on her bare feet. Lachlan's anger permeated the air between them, crackling as if owning of life. She faced him, her own turbulent emotions shielded by an outer calm.

"I'm leaving."

"Leavin' *again*, you say? Ta sulk?"

She searched his ruggedly handsome face for a long moment. What she was about to say would hurt him, but she had come to realize that this was the only way to penetrate his stubbornness. "I'm passing on, Lachlan. With or without you."

Painful sensations gripped her. Lachlan looked as if she had just slid a dull batter knife slowly into his heart. "I can't talk to you. I can't reason with you."

"The Ingliss."

His flatly-spoken words brought a tinge of anger to her cheeks. "Why do you always blame everything on *them*? I'm leaving because it sickens me to live with a man motivated by hatred! We don't belong here, Lachlan. Roan was right about one thing: this world belongs to the living!"

"I love you."

The words welled tears up in Beth's eyes. His tone and bearing were lifeless. "No. I don't believe you do, Lachlan. I conveniently died here for you, but I don't think we would have gone beyond testing the chemistry between us under normal circumstances. You've lived without compassion too long. You use something akin to it when you want something."

"Stop," Lachlan murmured, leaning against the table as his legs weakened beneath him. "You dinna mean wha' yer're sayin'."

"I've had plenty of time to think this through," she choked. "It's no good between us."

"'Tis the Inglisses you side wi'! E'er since tha' mon came ta this house, you've been growin' mair an' mair distant wi' me!"

"No." Beth's body began to shimmer, then fade. "It's the darkness in you separating us, Lachlan. You allow it to keep you chained to an existence that goes against the laws of nature. I won't share in this bondage. I'm sorry, but sometimes we have to hurt the one we love, to save them from themselves."

"Beth—"

Lachlan stared with stark anguish at the emptiness where Beth had stood moments before. He refused to accept that she was really gone— had passed beyond the grayness to a plane of existence out of his reach.

They were more than lovers! She had to know she was his *life!*

His despondent eyes searched the shadowy stillness of the room. Loneliness returned ten-fold upon him, suffocating him as it closed in tighter and tighter, as if to squeeze him out of existence.

She was hiding from him again, but she would return. Between now and then, he would have to come to understand what exactly it was she expected of him. But right now, a fire was twisting within his gut, and there was only one way to relieve himself of its tormenting presence.

He appeared in the carriage house on a gust of wind, startling Roan as he was about to stretch out on a cot in the corner of the room. When Roan saw him standing several yards away, hatred a very real mask on Lachlan's livid face, Roan plucked up a blanket from the cot and swung it over his thermals to help ward off the cold of his temporary quarters.

"E'er hear o' knockin'?" Roan asked.

"Wha' did you say ta Beth?"

Roan didn't answer right away. When he did, his words came out on a sigh of irritability. "Whan, auld mon? I've spoken ta the lady a number o' times."

"This eve."

"Aye, we spoke a' the graves."

"Abou' wha'?"

Roan scowled. "It was a private conversation, Baird."

"Private, you say? *I* wadna have been part o' tha' wee talk now, wad I?"

"Some," Roan admitted begrudgingly. His feet were numb from the cold emanating from the cement floor. "Wha' is this abou'? Or are you simply in the mood ta harass someone?"

"She's gone, Ingliss," Lachlan said through clenched teeth. "An' I want ta know wha' stirred her oop this eve!"

"Wha' do you mean, 'gone'?"

"Some place I canna sense her!"

Roan was genuinely perplexed. Beth had sworn earlier she would never leave Lachlan. What had happened since to change her mind?

Roan stiffened defensively when Lachlan closed the distance between them. He read rage in the ghost's eyes, but he was also sure he read desperation, and it touched him.

"Wha' was said!"

"She maistly defended you," Roan said, his brow furrowed in thought. "Are you sure she's really . . . *gone*?"

Placing his hands on his hips, Lachlan clipped, "Why wad she have cause ta defend me, I wonder?"

"Ach, mon, she wanted one o' us ta see reason."

"An'?"

"No' a thin'— Wait." Roan drew the blanket

about him more tightly. "She asked if you'd paid me."

It seemed incredible, but Lachlan's face grew more taut.

"You tauld her I let you know abou' the jewels."

"Aye."

Roan swallowed. He was violently shivering, but he realized it was not all from the cold. It was an emotional response to the anguish emanating from his enemy. "Wha' I said was no' in harsh words. I thought yer ploy amusin' an' childish."

"You lyin' snake-in-the-grass!"

"I'm na thief, Baird. An' I've ne'er known a guid enough reason ta lie abou' anythin'. If she *has* gone on, i's *yer* doin', no' mine!"

"Yer're fired, Ingliss."

"Tha' truly breaks ma heart."

The air about Lachlan crackled with electricity. "I've a mind ta cram yer sarcasm doon yer miserable throat. Dinna e'er come back here. You'll no' like wha'll be waitin' for you."

Lachlan turned and lethargically began to walk from the carriage house. Roan watched him, emotions warring within him. He was certain Beth had not been angry when he'd last seen her—disappointed, maybe.

What had happened in the last hour to make her change her mind about Lachlan?

Sinking onto the cot, he scratched his nose with a blanket-covered finger.

"Why do you care?" he muttered. "Baird will follow her."

He looked in the direction the laird had gone.

Roan Ingliss didn't want to believe that something he said had sent the woman on. For some inexplicable reason, Lachlan's anguish touched him— deeply disturbed him. The man had been dead for one-hundred-forty-nine years! But Roan had responded to him as he would have to any *man* in such misery.

Closing his mind off from the turmoil of his thoughts, he stretched out on the cot and waited for sleep to deliver him from his conscience.

Thirteen

Winter thoroughly blanketed the land. From Lachlan's vantage point, a stark white world glistened beneath opulent moonlight. Downy snow swirled about the tower, swept along upon the minute tides of energy he was unknowingly frittering away. Loneliness had driven him to seek visual solace. Since dawn that morning, he had remained atop the tower, watching the day play upon the land he so dearly cherished. But he knew, inexorably, he would be drawn back into the house. In the blink of an eye, he would find himself staring up at Beth's portrait, and the terrible emptiness he'd known the past weeks would again seize every part of him.

The torment of her absence shadowed him, walked abreast with his ever-deepening frustration. If only he had one more chance to talk to her. One more chance to understand what she expected of him.

His grudge was part of the package. He certainly didn't love her less because of her temper. . . .

His attention became drawn to a pair of weaving lights a short distance from his private access road. Although he'd never ridden in a motor carriage, he could well imagine how treacherous were the icy avenues. As the lights drew closer, he leaned over one of the crenelations and tried to focus better on the vehicle. Then, as if in slow motion, he saw the lights come up onto his property. The vehicle slid rightward, and he straightened up. A sickening, echoing crash was followed by the blare of a horn.

He froze in disbelief, but the incessant trumpeting from the vehicle prompted him to react. Vaporizing, he glided through the air, then materialized at the roadside by the accident scene. The vehicle had gone off the drive and plunged down a steep embankment. The front of it was now bent around a massive oak. Although the engine was no longer running, the horn continued to ravage the otherwise stillness of the night. Steam rose from beneath the accordianed hood—

Lachlan sucked in a sharp breath as a small face became visible in the rear window angled up at him. Scrambling down the embankment, he was beside the car when two other visages pressed against the rear side window.

Children.

Fear lanced him when he attempted to open the door and his hand passed through the metal. A cry of outrage rose in his throat, but he quelled it lest he would frighten the children more than they were already. He could hear their little fists pounding on the glass, hear their cries.

The horn shrilled on, adding to his disoriented state.

He forced his attention to the slumped figure at the steering wheel.

An unconscious woman.

Passing his arms through the vehicle door, he made a futile attempt to right her in the seat. Self-recrimination pounded down on him. He had wasted his precious energies feeling sorry for himself!

One of the children began to scream.

Mindless that his transparency was the cause, he leaned into the vehicle. He desperately wanted to console the poor little tykes, but he was in no condition to help whatsoever. Then the largest of the boys shoved open the far door. To Lachlan's further consternation, the children fled out of the vehicle and began to run toward the road beyond the privacy trees.

Moving with the swiftness of lightning, Lachlan tried everything within his power to herd the children away from the road. He called upon the wind through his will, conjured up lightning to crisscross their path, but the headstrong, frightened children, led by the hand by the eldest of the three, defied the warnings.

As if his mounting terror for their safety was not enough, he spied lights coming down the road.

Lachlan hovered, his brain afire, unaware that he appeared to be a greenish, brilliant haze to the driver rapidly approaching. The children were forging on, nearly to the road. Lachlan looked from them to the car . . . back to them. Frustration knifed him unmercifully. If he didn't find a way soon to stop those children—

At first he thought his vision was playing a cruel joke on him. The vehicle with the lights was rolling to a stop a few feet away. Lachlan could do nothing but watch as a man climbed out of the driver's side. The children ran through the laird and into the road—

"Stop them!" Lachlan called, trying in vain to solidify himself.

The man in the road seemed at first stunned, then, to Lachlan's great relief, he corralled the youngsters in his arms. Lachlan was about to move in closer when the man's head turned in his direction. The moonlight lit upon the man's features.

"Wha' the hell is goin' on?" Roan bit out, doing his best to calm the boys even now trying to elude his hold.

"A motor carriage went off ma drive," Lachlan breathlessly explained, moving to within a foot of Roan. "There's an unconscious womon a' the steerin' thin', Ingliss. I canna solidify aneuch ta help her or these poor children."

"Lead me ta—"

"Tak yer carriage," Lachlan advised. "You'll need i' ta get them ta the house. I'll wait for you by the wreck."

Muttering beneath his breath, Roan managed to get the boys into the backseat of his Volvo. He grimaced at their shouts and wails as he drove cautiously to the access road and started up the incline. The vehicle slid on the ice, but he adeptly managed to keep control, even when one of the boys began to pound the back of his neck with a fist.

"Calm *doon*, laddies!" he ordered, bringing the car to a reluctant stop. He focused on Lachlan's dimming haze, then turned to visually locate the oldest boy, who was sitting in the far corner, glaring at him. "Wha's yer name, boy?"

The younger boys slunk in the seat beside their brother, who glared at the driver with undisguised animosity. Roan searched their pale, defiant expressions and sighed.

"C'mon, laddies. We'll need to see how yer mither's doin'."

When Roan got out of the car, the boys refused to join him. And Roan was not about to trust them alone. "Do you see tha' ghost there?" he asked, leaning through the open door. "See the greenish mist, an' how i' looks like a mon? Weel, boys, he's a personal friend o' mine, an' if you don't get yer bottoms ou' here this minute, I'll ask him ta breathe his foul breath o' death on you."

The threat brought the boys scrambling out of the vehicle.

"Wha'e'er warks," Roan muttered.

To insure that the boys would stay with him, he grabbed two by the coat collar with one hand, and the older boy by the arm with his other hand. He followed Lachlan down the embankment, slipping and sliding as the boys made every attempt to worm free. When he reached the car, he forced the boys to sit on the ground, and gestured forcefully with a gloved hand.

"Don't move, laddies!" Then Roan looked at Lachlan. "If they try ta get away, breathe on them." He gave the ghost a conspiratorial look. "Turn them ta stone if necessary."

Although Lachlan was amused by the man's tactics, he glanced down at the boys and made a fierce scowl. The children huddled together in the snow, staring wide-eyed at the terrible apparition hovering between them and the car.

Roan checked the driver's pulse. Weak but steady. Unbuckling her seatbelt, he gingerly lifted her into his arms and withdrew her from the wreckage. "Yer mither's goin' ta be all right," he told the boys.

"She's not our mother!" the oldest boy spat, while the youngest scrambled forward and sank his teeth into the calf of Roan's right leg. Roan released a howl of pain. Lachlan instinctively reached for the boy, who, upon seeing the greenish, glowing hands coming toward him, scooted back to his brothers.

Lachlan straightened up and exchanged a harried look with Roan. Then Roan scowled down at the boys and said huskily, "Whoe'er she is, I need ta get her ta the house. Which means, you little monsters, I need you ta behave an' do as yer're tauld. Now get yerselves oop an' follow me back ta the caur."

"I'm bein' pulled back ta the grayness," Lachlan whispered to Roan.

"Dammit, mon, pull yerself thegither. I'm goin' ta need a hand wi' this lot."

"Canna resist the pull," Lachlan rasped as he

faded into the night, leaving Roan to deal with three frightened, obstinate children and an unconscious woman.

"Just ma bloody luck," Roan grumbled as he cast the children a disparaging look. "The one bloody time I want him around, he vaporizes on me."

It seemed an eternity before Lachlan was able to acquire the energy to solidify again. He had not wasted a moment's time trying to check in on his houseguests; he'd not allowed anything to sway him from focusing on the importance of being fully useful. He had thought a great deal about the Ingliss, which had served as a surprising buffer to the anguish of thinking about Beth. Roan Ingliss had arrived miraculously to compensate for Lachlan's inability to help the living. Whatever had brought the man back to the estate after Lachlan had dismissed him weeks ago, he was grateful. Serious injury could have befallen those children if the situation had been left in his hands.

Coming to terms with the realization of his true limitations had served to strengthen the laird's character. It was a calmer man who materialized on the second floor where his sixth sense told him the woman and children were sleeping.

The hall was dimly lit by two of the gas lamps. Gently opening the door, he walked into the bedroom and spent several long minutes staring at the other occupants. The woman, seeming hardly more than a child herself in the feather bed, was sleeping peacefully on her side with an arm about the shoulders of one of the boys. Behind her, the other two were curled up beneath the double quilts. The drapes on the two windows across the room were open to allow the moonlight to filter in. A low fire burned in the grate, keeping the chill out of the room.

A notion that he was being watched prompted Lachlan to look over his shoulder. Roan was braced in the doorway, a look of surprise adding animation to his haggard appearance. With a last glance over his guests, Lachlan turned and followed Roan into the hall. He closed the door behind him, then gave his full attention to the man who was irritably looking him over.

"Nice o' you ta mak an appearance," Roan grumbled, running a hand through his thick, disheveled hair. His bloodshot, soft brown eyes narrowed. "It wad have been nice ta have had a wee help wi' those little monsters in there," he added in a hushed tone.

"I returned as soon as I cad," Lachlan said calmly. It was obvious that the Ingliss was exhausted. "Suppose you fill me in o'er some Scotch."

Roan's expression went deadpan. "Scotch?"

"Aye."

Roan silently followed Lachlan to the first floor, down the secondary hall, to the first door on the right. Lachlan went on into the dark room beyond. Within seconds, a lamp was lit. Roan was delighted to see a fully equipped bar and two tables and chairs.

From behind the bar, the laird gestured for Roan to sit. Roan chose the nearest chair and wearily lowered himself onto it. The finger tips of one hand moved across the bare expanse of his chest, which was exposed by his unbuttoned shirt. His socked feet shifted beneath the table and, placing his elbow on the top, he rested his chin in an upturned palm. His eyelids were half-closed. Two days' growth of beard shadowed his face.

"Ma grandfaither was considered one o' the great distillers o' whiskey in his time," Lachlan offered as he filled two short glasses with the pale amber liquid. He carried the opened bottle and one glass to the table where Roan was sitting, placed them down, then reached for his own glass. Seating himself across from Roan, he took a healthy swig. "A' sixteen, he started makin' the brew for family an' friends. By the time he was in his early twenties, he ained a distillery. On a guid day, he cad produce better than three thousand gallons o' whiskey."

Roan tipped the glass to his lips and emptied the contents. He grimaced as the liquid burned its way to his stomach, then released a breath through pursed lips. "Guid stuff, Baird."

With a crooked grin, Lachlan downed the remainder of his Scotch. He refilled both glasses, after which he held his glass up to reverently study the contents.

"But as goes maist thin's in life," Lachlan went on, "his dreams were cut short. The English distilleries didna like the saturation o' oor stuff. In 1778, they lobbied the Crown ta raise duty an' tighten oop the regulations. Ma grandfaither— along wi' many o' his competitors— went bankrupt."

Roan, now on his third Scotch, bobbed his head enthusiastically as he aimed the rim of his glass at his lips. "Finest whiskey— " He downed half the contents. "— I've e'er had the pleasure ta sample."

Amusement danced in Lachlan's eyes. "I've a few bottles left. Tell me, are you always so soon in yer cups?"

Placing the drained glass down, Roan woozily regarded his host. "Na. I's been a long two days." He blinked hard several times in an attempt to clear his head, then scratched the nape of his neck. "You purposely left me wi' them, didna you?" He groaned and ran his large hands down his face. "The womon shames a Scotsmon's stubbornness. An' the boys are spawns o' hell, I tell you!"

"I came as soon as I was able." Lachlan refilled their glasses and watched as Roan handled his as if unsure whether he should have another drink. "I tak i' the womon's injuries were superficial."

"Aye. A nasty crack on the head. Scared, mair than anythin' else."

Roan's bloodshot eyes tried to focus more clearly on Lachlan. "I've no' eaten all day. Itherwise, Baird, I'd drink you under the table."

"Wha's the womon's stary? Why was she ou' on such a terrible night wi' three children?"

Roan pushed the glass away and massaged the taut muscles in his thick neck. "She's a Yank. They produce some stubborn females, eh, Baird? Course,

I'd probably be defensive, tae, if I foond maself i
her predicament.''

''Wha' *is* her predicament?''

''She's the boys' aunt. Her brither died o'er a yea
ago. The stepmither called the States an' taul
Laura— ''

''Laura?''

''Laura Bennett. She's a little thin', but stubborn
Stubborn.''

''Right stubborn, I tak i'?''

Roan nodded his head. Exhaustion was weighin
heavily on him, and the fiery whiskey was dullin
his concentration. ''The boys' stepmither . . . sh
tauld Laura she desperately needed her. Laur
flew— in a plane, you understand.''

Several seconds passed in silence before Roa
groggily murmured, ''Where was I? Ah. The emer
gency proved ta be a farce. The stepmither— ;
young thin'— cadna handle the boys. Two days efte
Laura arrived, the girl teuk off.''

''Laura ends oop wi' the nephews, eh?''

''I said tha', didn't I? Weel, no' only does she ge
stuck wi' the little monsters, but the stepmithe
went off wi' the boys passports an' stuff.''

Lachlan drained the contents of his glass. ''An
Laura went ou' in this weather lookin' for an acci
dent ta happen?''

''Na, you fool,'' Roan slurred. ''Her purse wa
stolen, an' she cadna pay for a room. Wi' wha' little
money she had left, she was tryin' ta mak i' ta Ed
inburgh . . . ta the American Consulate. She want
ta bring the boys back ta the States.''

"I tak i' her stay here has no' been a guid one."

"Here?"

"Scotland, you booby."

Roan was too numb to react to the insult. "She's all fired oop ta walk ta Edinburgh, if necessary. I tauld her the roads are no' fit ta travel right now, an' wi' a storm front comin'—"

"She'll have ta stay here wi' the boys for a while."

"Aye. But shit, mon, try ta convince her! She's a stub—"

"Stubborn womon."

"So you *have* me' her!"

Lachlan grinned. "I'm takin' yer word for i'."

"The word of an Ingliss?" Roan's laugh was interrupted by a hiccup. He started to rise to his feet, but the swimming in his head made him sit again. "Scotch on an empty stomach is na guid," he muttered in a slur. He looked up to say something to Lachlan and was startled to find the ghost was not in the room.

"Fine," he sneered. Folding his arms on the table, he lowered his brow atop them. "Leave me ta the little horrors again, you swine."

He closed his eyes and drifted off into sleep. The past two days had been harrowing. Not only were the boys impossible to handle, but they unknowingly triggered Roan's memories of his own son—painful memories, as they only served to reawaken his poignant loss.

He awakened with a grunt. Someone was annoyingly shaking his shoulder. *No' the boys again,* he mutely groaned, but as he was straightening up in the chair, marvelous odors filled his nostrils.

"You'll need yer wits abou' you, Ingliss."

Roan thought he was dreaming and hesitantly inhaled the steam rising off the plate in front of him. No, it wasn't his imagination. Poached eggs on toast. Three thick slices of fried ham. Scones dripping with honey. And a pot of coffee. He looked up as Lachlan seated himself in the same chair he'd occupied earlier.

"Eat, Ingliss. Lest yer growlin' stomach is a figment o' ma imagination?"

Lifting the fork on the plate, Roan hungrily dug into the food. He didn't look up or stop shoveling food into his mouth long enough to utter a word. Lachlan kept the coffee cup filled until the last of the brew was emptied from the pot. When Roan had cleaned his plate, he set down the fork and released a sigh of satisfaction.

"Wha' do I owe for this kindness, eh?"

"Na strings," Lachlan said quietly, but his eyes were unnervingly studying Roan's face.

Roan frowned as he lifted the coffee cup to his lips, his gaze unwaveringly locked with Lachlan's. He took a long sip of the now tepid brew, then cradled the cup in his hands.

"Three weeks ago, you tauld me ta get off yer property an' ne'er come back."

"But you did return," Lachlan said evenly.

"Ah. Listen, Baird, I wad have had ta have been a blind mon no' ta have seen the fear in yer eyes the ither night. You were genuinely concerned for

he womon an' boys. Beth tried ta tell me you had
uman feelin's, but I was tae stubborn ta want ta
elieve i'."

Roan paused. He was painfully aware of the tor-
nent the mention of Beth caused Lachlan. "Look,
uld mon, I'm no' goin' on like this because I'm
issed on yer Scotch. Ma head is clear. I think you
auld me ta leave three weeks ago because you knew
cad see yer pain."

"Tis Laura we should be discussin'," Lachlan said
urtly, his features tight, his eyes dulled with sorrow.

Roan nodded and set down his cup. "Her caur
s totaled. If the roads weren't a sheet o' ice, I'd tak
er ta Edinburgh. But I'm no' willin' ta risk her an'
he lads in ma caur. It's fine for goin' short dis-
ances . . ."

He shrugged. "She's no' ma concern, though, is
he, Baird? I've got a life o' ma ain. An' quite
rankly, if I spend much mair time aroond her, I'm
ikely ta pull her across ma knee an' give her her
icks."

"I'll mak i' worth yer while ta see her through
his."

A mask of incredulity slid down over Roan's face.
'Wha' do you care wha' happens ta her?"

"Tis a loose end."

Leaning back in his chair, Lachlan crossed an ankle over a knee. "I've decided ta gae on."

"Efter Beth?"

The laird gave a single nod of his head.

Here was Roan's dream unfolding before him.

His heart began to race wildly within his ches
"Whan?"

"As soon as I have yer word you'll see the womo
an' boys ta Edinburgh."

"How does this concern you?"

"I want ta gae on, feelin' like I've somewha' mad
ma peace here."

Roan dipped back his head and raked his finger
through his hair before looking at Lachlan again
Since Beth's departure, Roan'd known somethin
vital had died in the ghost. Even when he was com
manding Roan to leave and not return, there ha
been no anger in the tone or bearing. A ringin
began in Roan's ears. He knew he had only to kee
silent about his suspicions regarding Beth, and h
family would be free of Lannie Baird forever. Agre
to whatever the ghost wanted, and go on with h
life.

But it was not in Roan's nature to deceive.

"Tak the jewels an' cash them in," Lachlan sai
dully. "See ta i' the womon an' the boys get back t
the States as soon as possible. Do wha' you want w
the money. I'll have na use for aught where I'r
goin'."

Lachlan rose to his feet and slid his chair int
place beneath the table. "The wee chest is in th
attic. You know where."

Looking up into Lachlan's dismal face, Roa
swallowed past the tightness in his throat to sa
"Aye. You were hopin' I'd thieve from you."

"'Tis unimportant now."

Roan, his face reddening, slowly stood. "Wha'

gotten inta you, mon? For a century an' a half, you've been unmovable from this damned house!"

"Aye," Lachlan said, leaning over the table and bracing a hand atop it. "Yer're a bitter mon, Roan. Tak a guid look a' me an' see wha' *tha'* brin's you! The house, the treasures, mean nocht wi'ou' someone ta share them wi'!"

Straightening up, Lachlan made a feeble gesture with a hand. "Sittin' talkin' ta you here . . . weel, i' made me realize wha' Beth was tryin' ta tell me. Ma bitterness toward yer bloodline sent her away. There is no' a treasure in the warld, Roan, tha' equals the love between a mon an' a womon. But then, laddie, you've ne'er known true love, have you?"

Roan's face drained of color. "Ma private life is none o' yer damn business!"

"I agree," Lachlan said softly. His features took on a surreptitious expression. "But sometimes, Roan, I unintentionally link wi' a livin' soul. Tis how I knew Beth was dyin'. Yer wife an' son were on yer mind when you were pullin' Laura from the motor carriage."

"Enough! I'll tak yer damned insults, but I won't stand here an' listen ta—"

"I understand sorrow an' grief," Lachlan cut in heatedly, a hand raised to ward off Roan from advancing toward the door. "Only anger was always mingled wi' them. Anger toward Tessa an' Robert; anger for all the dreams their betrayal cheated me o'. Wha' did i' gain me, eh? You think you understand the meanin' o' lonely? Let me tell you, laddie, you have no' a clue."

"You want ma word I'll see the womon an' her nephews ta Edinburgh, you got i'! But spare me the lecture!"

Lachlan stared dolefully at the man across from him. "I guess we each must learn in oor ain way."

He was beginning to fade when Roan shouted, "Wait!"

Lachlan hesitated, then fully solidified himself. He watched Roan inwardly struggle with something, and frowned.

"Tak wha'e'er you want from this house. I'll no' be back ta bother you or yer family again."

"Beth didn't pass on," Roan blurted, but as soon as the words passed his lips, he sighed with relief.

A scowl darkened Lachlan's face. "Wha' are you tryin' ta pull, Ingliss?"

"I left the pub an' was headin' ta Aggie's whan I heard a voice in ma head say there was trouble here. Actually, the voice said *you* were in trouble, an' needed me. I thought i' ludicrous you wad need me, or tha' I wad give a hoot, but I found maself drivin' here as fast as I cad."

Lachlan remained as still as stone.

"It was Beth's voice I heard," Roan averred. *"She* was the reason I showed oop whan I did."

Still Lachlan remained motionless, but the furies of hell were dancing in his dark eyes.

"Damn you, mon," Roan gasped, and slapped his palms to the man's chest. "We shared yer grandfaither's Scotch, didn't we? Why won't you believe me?"

"I wad know if she was here, you swine."

"Swine, am I?" Roan drew back his shoulders and scowled at Lachlan. "I wad dearly love ta send you on yer way, but I'm no' willin' ta hide a truth ta do i'. She's here, I tell you. Some . . . where. An' she's probably smilin' doon on us because we managed ta sit across from one anither wi'ou' goin' for the jugular."

Lachlan looked about the room like a man lost. When he began to walk about the table to the far side of the bar, his movements were leaden, stilted. Roan watched him; unsure how he actually felt about losing his one chance to see the ghost gone.

Ghost. Spirit.

Beth had told him at the gravesite, in so many words, that Lachlan was more man than spirit. From that first moment when he had actually met the laird, Roan *had* thought of Lannie as a man. And perhaps that was what had confused Roan all along.

He watched the perplexing laird sit on an antique spooning chair against the wall across from the bar. "Wha's goin' through yer mind, auld mon?"

Lachlan didn't look up at the softly spoken words. "A poem ma grandfaither used ta tell me now an' then. He ne'er got o'er losin' his distillery."

Turning his chair around so that the back faced his host, Roan straddled it. He folded his arms across the back and rested his chin atop them. "Wha' poem was tha'?"

"One by Robert Burns."

"Ah, I believe I know i'."

Lachlan looked up. "Do you now?"

"Aye—

> *Thee Ferintosh! I sadly lost!*
> *Scotland lament frae coast ta coast*
> *Now colic-grips an' harkin' hoast*
> *May kill us a'*
> *For local Forbes charter'd boast*
> *Is taen way!*

"— An' on tha' note . . ." Roan reached for the bottle of Scotch and filled both glasses nearly to the brim. He passed one to Lachlan, then lifted his in a salute. "Ta Robert Burns, *an'* yer grandfaither."

Lachlan chuckled despite the gloom still shrouding him. The rims of the glasses clinked, then the contents were swigged down. Roan gave a shudder and smacked his lips.

"Roan, yer're sure i' was Beth's voice you heard?"

"I'm sure. Lannie . . . ?" Roan squeezed an eye shut. "You suppose Beth caused Laura's accident— ta bring us thegither?"

Lachlan scowled thoughtfully. "Na. She wadna do somethin' like tha'." Sighing, he gave a shake of his head. "But she did use i' ta her advantage."

"Aye, seems so. She's a fine womon. A gentle soul."

"Wi' a fiery temper ta beat all."

A smile twitched at the corner of Roan's mouth. "Aye, she's a temper. Women are funny craitures.

Just whan yer're sure you know one as weel as you know yerself, they oop an' change their stripes."

"Ooh, I think they give us the signs, right aneuch, Roan," Lachlan said, a slight slur to his words. "I think we men fail ta read them in time."

Roan thickly shook his head. "I don't agree."

Refilling his glass, he returned the bottle to the table. "This is queer, you know."

"Queer, how?"

"I'm sittin' here talkin' ta a ghost," he gurgled. "No' any ghost, but *you!* Am I in ma cups or wha'?"

Lachlan flashed a silly grin. "We're both in oor cups. Tell me, Roan, were you e'er a wee in' fear o me?"

"The truth?"

Lachlan nodded.

"No' really. Now, yer womon rattled me, she did. Her words cut deep an' true. Maybe she affected me because I knew she spoke from her heart. I cadna understand wha' a fine womon like her saw in the likes o' you."

"You just insulted me," Lachlan slurred.

"Na. I'm pissed. Did I tell you Kevin bit me?" Roan lifted a leg and braced it on the back of the chair. Tugging on the hem of his pants, he chortled, "Right on the calf of ma leg. He's the youngest. Three, I think. He likes ta bite. As stubborn as his aunt."

A grin split Lachlan's bobbing head. "You repeat yerself a lot."

"Do I now? Did I tell you the lads are real horrors?"

"Aye . . . you . . . did."

"Hmm. Did I tell you Alby, the middle lad, tried ta set fire ta the rug in the room they're in?"

Lachlan grimaced and shook his head.

"Seems the lad has a fondness for settin' fire, accordin' ta Laura. Little wonder the stepmither left."

Now Roan grimaced. "Little wonder Laura is such a sour puss."

"Pretty, is she?"

Roan looked genuinely befuddled. "Hard ta say. She's a little thin'. The top o' her head doesn't reach ma chin. Green eyes. Pretty green eyes, but she frowns an' scowls tae much. Hey, Baird?"

Lachlan squinted at Roan.

Roan tried to stand, swayed, and plopped back onto the seat. "I think we're *really* pissed."

With a throaty chuckle, Lachlan cranked himself up onto his feet. Once standing, he was forced to brace an arm against the wall to stop from keeling over. "I've got ta find ma Beth."

With a grunt, Roan rocked to his feet. He tripped over the legs of the chair and crashed into Lachlan. Spirit and man went down hard, but they were laughing as they wrestled into sitting positions.

"Why wad she put me through so much pain?" Lachlan asked, laughter bubbling within him. "They say they love you, then— " He sliced a hand across his throat.

The gesture prompted a burst of laughter from Roan, and raising his hand, he pretended to dirk himself in the heart with an invisible knife.

"They put i' in an' twist i', Baird. We men have always been a' their mercy."

The laughter escalated.

"For wha', I ask you?"

Roan quickly sobered. "A wee pleasure."

Now Lachlan sobered, and draped an arm about Roan's shoulders. "God, I miss her."

"Beth?"

"Aye. But I'm gettin' mad as hell now."

With the help of the chair and table, Lachlan pulled himself up on his feet. When he looked at Roan, the man was staring dumbfoundedly up at him.

"You know, she cad have calmly explained wha' she considered ta be ma faults. I'm a reasonable mon."

He reached down and clasped Roan's outstretched hand. Hauling the man up, he nearly fell over. Their legs rubbery beneath them, both men sat atop the table.

"Fine Scotch," Roan slurred, smacking his lips.

"Yer're definitely in yer cups."

"No' as pissed as you."

Lachlan turned slightly toward Roan, his eyebrows arched in mock surprise. "Shall we see which o' us maks i' ta oor room wi'ou' fallin' on oor lips?"

A secretive smile played across Roan's mouth. "You have an extra landin' ta climb, you auld fool."

"Why do you always call me *auld* this an' tha', eh?"

"You're a damn sight aulder than me," Roan chuckled. "By a hundred years an' mair."

"Truth be, Ingliss, I was a wee younger than you are whan I died. Ghosts dinna age, you know."

Roan took a long moment to ponder this information. "Whan yer're right, mon, yer're right." He looked Lachlan straight in the eye. "You know, had thin's gone different back then, you wad be ma ancestor."

Sliding off the table, Lachlan grimaced. "Perish the thought."

"But then you wadna have had a reason ta be hauntin', wad you?" Roan murmured.

"Hard ta say. C'mon, the morn's comin' in a few hoors."

Roan's eyes widened. "An' the boys will be oop!"

Lachlan took a hold on Roan's arm and pulled him to his feet. "An' the green-eyed lass will be rested an' full o' fire."

Moaning, Roan clumsily fell in step beside Lachlan.

Leaning on one another, the two men staggered from the room.

"If you had a heart, Baird, you wadna haud me ta ma promise."

Stopping at the foot of the staircase, both men wilted to a sitting position on the bottom step.

"Abou' the womon?"

Roan nodded. "You know, the boys keep talkin' abou' the ghost they saw efter the accident. Laura scoffs, but they're as sure as rain they saw wha' they saw."

"Have you given them an explanation?"

"Abou' you?" Roan laughed, belched, then made

an airy gesture with a hand. "I tauld them you were a horrible figment o' their imagination. Damn, mon, I'm no' sure maself yer're no' a figment o' *mine*."

Frowning, he added, "I prefer ta deal wi' you than Miss Laura Bennett."

"Tak a wee bit o' advice," Lachlan began with a crooked grin, his eyelids growing heavier by the moment. "Whan she starts ta wear on yer nerves, laddie, kiss the fight ou' o' her. It warks e'ery time."

"Kiss her, you say? But wha' if she has tha' bitin' gene in her, eh? I don't fancy losin' a lip—"

"Where's yer spine?" Lachlan grimaced. "You can kiss a womon proper, canna you?"

Roan snorted and scowled into Lachlan's face. "I've ne'er had a complaint."

"Weel practiced, are you?"

Lachlan's questioning was beginning to wear on Roan. "Aye, I've had ma share o' women."

"Then you can handle a wee thin' like Laura."

Roan grinned sardonically. "Probably wi' as much aplomb as you've handled yer Beth."

"Careful, Ingliss."

"Ah! Now i's no' so funny, is i'?"

"You gave me yer word— an' o'er ma grandfaither's Scotch!"

"I know." Roan groaned and lowered his face into his palms for several seconds. When he looked up, he added, "But she's a green-eyed nightmare, Baird. All starch an' vinegar." He feigned a shudder. "It's hard ta help someone whan they harp on you for e'ery . . . wee . . . *wee* suggestion."

"I've ma straits, an' you yers. Agreed?"

"I think I'm gettin' the short end o' the stick, here," Roan grumbled.

"Just remember who wears the trousers."

"Meanin' wha'?"

"Women like ta be dominated, laddie. Ooh, they put oop a fuss abou' i', but they expect i' na less. Tis a matter Beth an' I did come ta terms on."

"Really? She doesn't strike me as the type ta want ta be dominated."

"Aye. An' she— " Lachlan's eyes widened. His jaw went slack, and a pitiful moan rattled in his throat. Roan, too, looked up. A smile readily beamed on his face, but as quickly died at the sight of the woman's austere look.

"Beth!" Lachlan rasped.

"Just in the nick of time," she said, an edge to her tone. She looked directly at Roan and arched a censorious brow. "If you listen to him, you're going to find yourself in a world of hurt. Women are *not* mindless possessions."

"Ah, sweet darlin," Lachlan crooned, shooting to his feet. "I ne'er said you were mind— "

As straight as a board, Lachlan passed out and struck the floor face down. Beth simply stared at him for several long moments, then looked at Roan.

"His grandfaither's Scotch," Roan grinned ludicrously, then passed out himself and sprawled on the floor beside Lachlan.

Beth stared at the men for a moment longer, then rolled her eyes heavenward.

A smile tugged at the corners of her mouth.

"Thank you, Laura," she whispered.

Fourteen

Lachlan was first aware of a grueling headache. It squeezed his temples, crimped the back of his neck, and was making an earnest attempt to seize his shoulders. He cracked open one lid to find that he was lying face down on his bed. Sunlight filled the room— painful light that jabbed unmercifully at his exposed eye. Something had crawled into his mouth and died. Working his tongue to try and alleviate its terrible dryness, he made a feeble attempt to raise himself up on his elbows. He collapsed and released a pitiful groan.

The sound brought Beth's head around, and a smile touched her lips as she regarded Lachlan. He was truly a sad sight, lying there atop the bed as if he hadn't an ounce of strength. And little wonder, she thought ruefully. After he and Roan had polished off the bottle of Scotch, a two-day sleep and hangover was expected. For all his bluster, the master of the manor was not a drinking man.

Beth had come to realize the extent of his vulnerability. Her ruse had been successful, but Lachlan had suffered more than she'd intended.

Flattening her palms to one of the semi-frosted

window panes, she looked below once again. Roan Ingliss was shouting at Laura Bennett, his arms moving wildly through the air, punctuating his frustration. The woman was standing defensively still, her arms folded across her chest. The boys were nowhere to be seen, but Beth sensed they were in the kitchen having a snack.

Lachlan moaned again as he propped himself up on his elbows, his head hanging between his slack shoulders.

"Would you like some coffee?"

It took the laird's muddled brain several seconds to identify the softly-spoken voice. He cranked his head to the right, but the sunlight pouring in forced him to close his eyes.

"Or would you prefer another bottle of Scotch?"

Dropping his face to the pillow, he released a string of muffled Gaelic. The heart sensations were there swelling in his chest, the joy, the relief, the elation of knowing that his love had not gone on. But he was in physical agony. He couldn't recall being subjected to such misery *prior* to his untimely death.

He felt the mattress sink beneath an added weight. Groaning again, he drew the second pillow over his head. He couldn't think without the pseudo-sound knifing him.

With a grim shake of her head, Beth got up from the bed and walked into the bathroom. She placed a wooden stopper over the tub drain before she turned on the marble taps to a desired water temperature. The sound of running water filled the spacious bathroom. Going to a carved-door cabinet over the sink, she removed a bottle of bubble bath she'd brought from the States. Two capfuls were poured into the water, which instantly began to foam with iridescent bubbles. She returned the capped bottle to the cabinet, then sat on the edge of the porcelain clawfoot tub and waited until it was three-quarters full.

She was still wearing the gown that had so piqued Lachlan. Standing, she untied the belt, shimmied the garment past her hips, then stepped out of it when it fell in folds to the floor. First one foot was lowered into the steaming water. Blessed warmth swirled about her ankle and she sighed in sheer satisfaction. Ignoring Lachlan's moaning in the other room, she sank into the embracing bubbles until only her head could be seen above them.

She had always preferred a long hot soak to a shower, but it continued to amaze her how many of the old pleasures she could delight in although she had been dead for five months. There was no longer a need in her to have explanations for her state of existence. Life went on in one form or another, and she was content to end the self-grieving stage that had nearly spoiled her companionship with Lachlan.

Closing her eyes and wallowing in her bath, she pondered the term 'companionship' in regard to what she shared with Lachlan.

They were not husband and wife— likely, they would never know a true connubial state. She would never wear a flowing white gown of shimmering, layered material, a train of lace and tiny white roses that would trail behind her as she paced her steps down the aisle to the man she would vow to love forever **more**, to honor and cherish . . . the obey part would give her pause.

Sighing, Beth brought the sides of her hands together to fill her upturned palms with bubbles. She blew them into the air. Lowering her arms back into the water, she absently admired the iridescent flecks of colors on the tiny air balls as they drifted in descent.

"Yer're a cruel womon, Beth Staples," rasped a voice.

Beth turned her head and ran a slow perusal over Lachlan. The door frame was supporting him upright. His clothing was wrinkled, the unbuttoned shirt hanging off his broad shoulders. Wisps of his mussed hair hung in his face, which was pinched in misery.

"No' a wee comfort from you, you wicked girl."

She turned her face away from him to hide the smile vying to light up her features.

"How cad you leave the mon you love alone . . . sufferin' . . . in his cups wi' misery."

Keeping a tight rein on her amusement, Beth leveled on him a look of wifely censure. "In his cups with a hangover, you mean."

"Hango'er, you say?" he gasped, then grimaced and gingerly capped his pounding skull with his hands. In a softer, whisperlike voice, he added, "I' was no' the Scotch wha' dirked ma tender heart again an' again these past weeks. You disappeared

wi'ou' a care for me, or for wha' I wad suffer wi'ou'
yer company."

One gurgle of laughter escaped Beth before she
could stop it.

"Mock me, womon," he growled low, straightening away from the doorframe. "I deserve— "

A muffled bang startled him.

"Wha' in hell?"

"That was probably Roan."

Squinting at the light from the window, Lachlan
peered below at the ground. A frown drew down
his expressive eyebrows. Laura was standing as still
as a statue, her arms folded against her chest.
Shortly, she kicked at the soft new snow on the
ground, then began to make wild gestures as she
talked to the air.

"Wha's goin' on wi' them?"

"She's determined to get to Edinburgh." Beth
shifted in the tub, then dipped her shoulders below
the water line again. "I can't say I envy her position.
The children are a handful."

"Ah, but they're only little boys," Lachlan murmured.

His guest's obvious frustration bothered him.
Why were women so unreasonable? Roan was only
trying to help the fool woman. What was it about
the fairer sex that drove them to question the in-
herent logic of men?

"It's that kind of chauvinistic thought that keeps
you in the doghouse," Beth said dryly.

Lachlan glanced at her over his shoulder, then
looked below again. "Stop readin' ma mind."

"We're linked, remember? Besides, you've been traipsing through my thoughts long enough."

"Wi' reason."

"Says you."

Lachlan frowned at Beth, but his attention was drawn back to the woman below. "She's in a tizzy, she is. Wha's the rush, I ask you? Today, next year, Edinburgh will no' vanish from the face o' the earth."

"She's anxious to be done with the legal problems."

"Wha' legal problems?"

"She can't return to the States until she can locate the kids' stepmother and obtain their' birth certificates."

Again Lachlan turned his head and frowned at Beth. "So wha's the big deal abou' a birth certificate? They're her nephews. Canna she just— "

"The boys need passports to fly back to the States with her," Beth explained patiently. "And they can't get passports unless they have birth certificates."

Lachlan looked below at Laura, who was still venting her frustration in gestures. "Sounds like the modern warld has tae many precepts."

"Aye," Beth sighed, her gaze roaming lazily over his back and shoulders. "Lachlan?"

"Hmm?"

"Why are you so interested in pushing Roan and Laura together?"

"By the way, love, have you noticed auld Braussaw lately?"

"Lach . . . lan."

"He just sits there by the fountain, starin' off inta space."

"Lachlan, I asked you a question."

He winced, then forced a ghost of a smile on his face before he looked at Beth. "Weel . . ." He squirmed a bit, then looked below again. "Roan an' the womon click."

"Click?"

"Aye, Beth. We . . . clicked, you know." He grinned at her now. "You thought i' was the moonlight, darlin', but a mon knows these thin's." He looked below and released a quick breath. "Finally the damn fool is takin' matters ta hand like a mon."

Something in Lachlan's smug tone set off a warning in Beth. Hastening out of the tub, her body slick with water and patches of bubbles, she went to stand beside him.

Below, Roan and Laura were in a heated exchange of words. Beth didn't need to hear them to know their stubbornness was escalating the awkward situation between them. It was easy for Beth to sympathize with Laura's unease at being stuck in a foreign country with strangers. But she also admired Roan's determination to do what he thought was best for the woman and her nephews. Any other man might have said to hell with the whole mess. But if Roan was about to do what she thought he might—

Beth groaned as she observed the man below yank the woman into his arms and kiss her to silence her onslaught of verbal abuse. Looking askance at

Lachlan, she saw his expression was radiant with pride. It was *his* advice that Roan was acting upon.

However, it was Roan who was about to pay the penalty.

"Tis a smart mon who listens ta his elders," Lachlan crooned, a twinkle in his eyes.

But his expression crumbled to one of disbelief when Laura wormed out of Roan's arms and her knee shot up to slam him in the groin. Lachlan shriveled as if he were the one left kneeling on the ground. Turning, he shuffled to the toilet and lowered himself onto the wooden seat. Beth watched him, a grin twitching on her lips.

"He said she was a stubborn womon," he muttered, running his hands over his face.

"I don't think she retaliated out of *stubbornness,*" Beth said airily, slightly peeved that Lachlan had not as yet noticed her nakedness. "Roan is a big man. She probably reacted out of fear."

"Fear, ma eye," Lachlan growled, scowling up at Beth. "Tis a sad state o' affairs when a mon canna carry on the monly traditions o' his forefaithers!"

Beth released a terse laugh. "Meaning, grabbing a woman and kissing her when she doesn't want to be kissed?"

A retort aborted on Lachlan's lips and a flustered tint of red colored his cheeks.

"What's this affinity you have with Roan all of a sudden?"

"Tis wha' *you* wanted," he scowled. "Twas *you* who sent him here whan the accident happened!"

"Yes, it was me."

Lachlan rose to his feet. "You wanted ta throw us thegither. I admit I cad do nocht ta help the womon wi'ou' him, an' I've tauld him as much. I've offered him ma precious stones, an' he can have this damn house an' e'erythin' in i'—"

Beth's laugh further rattled Lachlan. Closing the distance between them, he curled his strong fingers about her upper arms and drew her against his hard body, his hangover forgotten.

"Yer're the maist fickle craiture I've e'er had the displeasure ta know, Beth Staples! I gave Ingliss guid advice. A womon is ne'er mair flexible than whan she's in love!"

"Laura Bennett and Roan Ingliss are strangers to one another," Beth said calmly, resisting a strong urge to press even closer to Lachlan's body. She was enjoying him being on the receiving end for a change, but she also wanted desperately to lay in his arms.

"So were we."

"But the connection, *ma lad*, hurried things along," she reminded him. "So let nature run its course. The advice of a nineteenth-century ghost will only complicate matters."

"Complicate, you say!"

"Why do you always repeat something I say?"

"Just add i' ta the long list o' faults I have, darlin'," he said heatedly, unconsciously kneading the soft, moist flesh held captive beneath his fingers. "Tell me somethin': is there a damned thin' I do *right* in yer eyes?"

Beth deliberately let him think she was mulling

over a reply. When several seconds passed, she said with deceptive ease, "You make a decent cup of tea. You can be compassionate and generous when the mood strikes you. You're an adequate lover— "

The rest of the sentence became lost in her throat. Lachlan's head lowered and his mouth swooped down to imprison her lips in a masterful, torrid kiss. Beth sighed within herself as his arms circled her, molding her against the hard planes and contours of his body. She knew his initial intention was to punish her for her words, but he kissed her deeply, with the love for her she knew filled him so completely.

Sliding her arms around to his back, she reached up to thread her fingers through his thick hair. She loved the feel and smell of him, the physical strength and mastery of him. She loved everything that comprised the very essence of Lachlan Baird. In her heart of hearts, she regretted having made him suffer for a moment on her account. But she had freed him, opened his compassion toward a member of the clan that had emotionally scarred him so long ago. In time she would explain her reasons to him. But now the fires of passion were raging within her. Gratification was not only for the young or the living.

Love existed on and on, through time.

Lachlan's large hands framed her face. He kissed her hungrily, want and need vying to wash asunder the tenderness he strove to bestow on her. He didn't want to argue about past issues. They were beings of different conditionings, of different cultures, of different minds, but they were as right for each other as two lovers could be. If to pass on to the next plane made her happy, he would join her without regret.

His hand slid down the delicate contours of her back, over the smooth, rounded firmness of her—

"Guid God, womon!" he groaned, only separating their mouths by a hairbreadth. "You've no' a stitch on!"

"Sometimes, Lachlan," Beth sighed with an undertone of amusement. Placing her hands on his powerful jawline, she stared adoringly into his eyes. "I love you."

"Wi' all ma faults?"

She smiled through a blush. "Aye."

"I know I can be headstrong." He kissed her brow, then the tip of her nose. "But I do love you wi' e'ery fiber o' ma bein', Beth."

"I know you do."

A shy smile quirked on Lachlan's mouth, this boyish side of him sending a thrilling sensation through Beth. Lachlan swept her up in his arms. He kissed her briefly, then, to her confusion, he stepped in the direction of the tub— not the bedroom as she had anticipated. Without explanation, he lowered her into the water. He kissed her again, lingeringly, then straightened up and peeled out of his shirt.

Beth watched him, her gaze sweeping over him, cataloging his every movement. When he tossed his pants aside and placed one foot in the tub, she stared up at him in awe. His body never failed to excite her, to leave her in wonderment. She managed to meet his gaze as he lowered himself into her bath, the water rising to the rim of the tub. They were facing each other, his knees peaking the ebbing foam, his back braced to the side of the faucet.

"This is nice," Beth quipped, her eyes lit with mischief.

"Weel, now, darlin'," Lachlan drawled, bringing cupped water to his face and splashing it over him. " 'Fore I drag yer enticin' bones inta the next room an' ravish you— " He paused to flash her a devilish smile. "—there's a few matters we need ta settle."

"Oh? Can't this wait till later?"

Lachlan released a long sigh, its sound telling Beth that he was as impatient as she to retire to the bedroom and make love until their energies were spent.

"I may be o' a . . . primitive mind in this day an' age, but I do wha' I believe is right. Granted, the grudge I held wi' the Ingliss clan was long unreasonable, but I have made ma peace wi' Roan. Now— "

"Lachlan— "

"Dinna be interruptin' a mon whan he's abou' ta choke doon a fat, auld corbie."

"A what?" she laughed, then sobered. "Sorry."

"Yer're forgiven this time." He winked at her. "Now, ma part o' the enmity is gone, an'— "

"You're sure about that?"

"As sure as can be. You dinna share yer best Scotch wi' a mon unless there's bondin' ta be done."

It was all Beth could do to keep a straight face. "Of course. Go on."

"Sa, I've made ma peace wi' the mon, but I want you ta know, Beth, i' was a cruel means you used ta put he an' I thegither."

"It wouldn't have been necessary if you both weren't so damn thickheaded."

"I see." Lachlan folded himself in half and dipped his head beneath the water. As he straightened up, he flipped his wet hair behind his head. Beth and Lachlan's every movement sloshed water over the sides of the tub, but they hardly were in the mood to care.

"Tell me, Beth, did you miss me a' all those long weeks?"

"Terribly."

Lachlan arched a brow. "An' yet you stayed away?"

"I felt I had no choice."

"Sa . . ." Filliping the water, he sent a spray at Beth. "You must be feelin' smug tha' yer scheme warked."

Linking her fingers at the back of her neck, she grinned at him. "Smug is a good word. Yeah, you could say I'm feeling a *wee* smug."

"An' are you o' the opinion you'll always get yer ain way?"

"Only in matters I feel strongly about."

Lachlan bobbed his head, his brows drawn down in thought. "So we're goin' ta disagree now an' then, are we?"

"We'll probably always disagree on some things."

"Does tha' bother you?"

For several long moments, Beth studied the troubled depths of Lachlan's eyes. "No, it doesn't bother me. Most couples have differences of opinion, but it doesn't stop them from loving each other."

"But the Inglisses—"

"That was different. Lachlan, all the qualities I love most in you became lost to that hatred. Even if we hadn't been connected, I couldn't have stood by and allowed it to go on."

Planting her feet to each side of Lachlan's hips, Beth pulled herself closer to him. When she stopped, Lachlan reached beneath the water, flattened his palms to her lower spine, and drew her forward until their groins were touching. Beth cupped her hands behind his neck, leaned to and kissed him briefly on the chin.

"In our own clumsy ways, we've been helping each other to grow. You did everything in your power to make my death as easy as possible for me, and I did what I thought was necessary to help you rid yourself of your emotional shackles."

"Do you understand why I brought you here?"

"I do. Oh, Lachlan, I'm sorry I didn't believe you sooner, but I needed the time alone to come to terms with myself. And now that I have, I promise I will never leave you again."

"I'll pass on wi' you, Beth— through the fires o' hell if necessary." He pulled her into his arms, heedless of the water pooling on the floor. "I'm no' afraid o' losin' you, anymair. I refuse ta believe a merciful God cad separate us. There's the purgin' 'fore we can gae on . . ."

He kissed her deeply, and when he lifted his head and stared into her eyes, his own were filled with apprehension. "Oor love will gae on wi' us, winna i'?"

"It will. I promise," Beth said breathlessly. "We'll always be together, and feeling as we do now." She brushed the backs of her fingers along his cheek, then rested her brow to his chin. "But we don't have to pass on until we're ready." Looking into his eyes again, she smiled. "I agree with tying up loose ends."

The worry fled from Lachlan's face, and his eyes danced with joy. "You do, do you?"

"Yeah. I'd like to spend some time here with you before we trek off into the unknown."

"An' here I thought I loved you for yer button nose," he chuckled.

Together they stood in the tub. Lachlan stepped out first and, turning, he scooped Beth up into his arms. She wrapped her arms about his neck, her cheek pressed to his collarbone as he carried her into the next room. Through his force of will, three logs rose from a black wrought-iron stand beside the fireplace and inserted themselves in the hearth. By the time he lowered her upon the bed, a glowing fire was taking the chill out of the room.

The feather mattress sagged beneath his weight as he lowered himself atop her, into her waiting arms. They kissed long and passionately, deeply, exploringly. Then he shifted to one side to allow a hand the pleasure of roaming over her slick form. For what seemed an eternity, he'd ached to touch her again.

His trembling fingers moved along the contours of her breasts, the flat firmness of her belly, the soft-skinned slopes of her inner thighs. He ended the kiss to seek the hard, erect nipple on one breast. Enclosing it within the soft inner lining of his lips, he brushed his tongue along the peak. The sound of her moan filled him with warmth. His tongue circled the nipple again and again, prompting her to arch up against him. When she could no longer bear the gentleness of his suckling, she threaded her fingers through his wet hair and urged him closer.

Lachlan complied without hesitation. The hand kneading her other breast slid down her belly and moved between her thighs.

But as he was about to explore her readiness, the bedroom door wrenched open. Roan raced by.

Beth and Lachlan bolted up on the bed, Beth scrambling beneath the quilt to hide her nakedness. Both stared wide-eyed at the bathroom door. A stream of invectives— laced with a pronounced burr— came from within. Water could be heard going down the tub's drain. There was a rattling of something, then of something else being dragged across the floor. A cabinet door was opened. Seconds later it was slammed shut.

Several minutes ticked by before Roan emerged from the bathroom carrying a wastebasket heaped

with sopping towels. His face was flushed with anger, his movements stilted.

"I'm losin' ma mind," he muttered. "How did
the little monsters get oop here? I wad swear— "

He looked at the motionless couple on the bed,
but it was several seconds before his mind cleared
enough for him to grasp the meaning of the bathroom flood.

And another several seconds before he realized
what he had interrupted.

His face crimson, he stammered, "Land s-sakes,
mon! You s-scared the w-wits ou' o' me!"

The couple continued to stare at him as if they
were frozen in time.

"There's water leakin' through the ceilin' b-below,"
Roan went on, glancing about the room in a futile
attempt not to stare at the couple. "I thought . . .
weel, I'm no' sure wha' I thought."

He looked at them again and managed a wan
smile of apology. "I'd na idea you were— " His mortification deepened. "I'd better . . . leave."

He was halfway to the door when the wastebasket
slipped from his hands. The towels plopped onto
one of the Persian throw rugs. Falling to his knees,
he scrambled to get them back into the basket, but
his frayed nerves made it impossible for him to grip
the container properly.

As soon as he attempted to stand, the basket and
its contents thumped to the floor again.

"For pity's sake, mon!" Lachlan gasped. Quickly
leaving the bed, he gathered up the towels and
crammed them back into the basket. But instead of

handing the basket to Roan, he purposefully shoved it aside, then gave the other man a helping hand to his feet.

"I canna say much for yer timin', but there's na need ta get yer liver in a squeeze!"

"Lachlan, be nice," Beth chuckled, clutching the quilt to the base of her neck. "We were careless with the tub water, Roan. We'll clean it up."

A nervous tic came into Roan's eyes as he forced himself to look at the mistress of the house. "Ma apologies, Miss— "

"Beth."

"It's guid ta see— " His voice cracked on the latter word. "— you again."

She smiled her warmest for him.

A sound seeped up through the floors below.

Roan looked dazedly at Lachlan. "Someone's a' the door."

"Tha' probably means you sud answer i', eh?" Lachlan said with a devilish grin.

"But who wad— "

"Cad be Miss Cooke."

The sound came again, more insistent.

"Show her ta the library. I'll meet you there in a bit."

"In claithin', I hope," Roan grumbled, critically looking over Lachlan's nudity. Then shock whitened his handsome face. "The boys! We just got those little buggers doon for a nap!"

When Roan ran from the room, Lachlan looked at Beth and laughed.

"Miss Cooke?" Beth sighed. "Don't tell me we're going to be interrupted by *business* again."

"I'm no' sure why she's here," Lachlan said, going to the bed and planting a kiss on the tip of Beth's nose. "But her timin' cadna be better."

"Why?"

"Loose ends, darlin'."

Lachlan went to a wardrobe across the room. Aware that Beth was watching his every move, he took his time donning clean black pants and a red shirt. Socks and his boots were put on last, then he returned to the bed and gave Beth a teasing kiss on the lips.

"Winna be long, I promise."

Beth waited until she heard the door close after him before she tossed the quilt aside. She wasn't peeved that Lachlan was leaving her for his 'business' again, but she was determined to be a part of whatever was going on.

Not wanting to take the time to get something of her own from the room across the hall, she slipped into one of Lachlan's shirts, a blue one, and a pair of his socks. She gingerly combed her fingers through her curly mane as she padded toward the door, a bounce in her steps that bespoke her cheery mood. It didn't occur to her to simply materialize in the library . . . at least not until she was stepping off the staircase on the first floor.

From the direction of the kitchen, a woman came from the secondary hall and stopped in her tracks upon seeing Beth.

The woman's green eyes widened. A delicate

flush colored her cheeks. Then with visible effort to compose herself, she walked up to Beth and extended a hand. The handshake was brief. Beth wasn't sure what to say to the woman.

"Are you the mistress of this house?"

A crooked smile twitched at one corner of Beth's mouth. "I think so."

The woman's expressive eyes showed a moment of uncertainty. "I-umm . . . this is very awkward."

"Are you and your nephews comfortable?"

"Yes, but I really— "

"I'm sorry," Beth interjected, as kindly as she could. "I'm late for a meeting."

"Oh, but— "

"Sorry." Beth practically dashed in the direction of the library. Sliding the door aside, she slipped into the room and closed it after her. She turned to find three pairs of eyes on her. Roan's were full of amusement. Lachlan was scowling in disapproval of her attire. The elderly woman, Viola Cooke, appeared to be shaken by Beth's unexpected arrival, but she was quick to offer the mistress of Baird House a smile.

"How good to see you again, Beth," she said, her warble-of-a-voice higher-pitched than usual.

"I was hoping for a chance to apologize to you for Halloween."

"No need, my dear."

"C'mon here," Lachlan cooed, drawing Beth into his arms. His elation rapidly seeped into her, prompting a glow to heighten her features. "Beth, darlin', I'm sa happy I can hardly stand maself."

"Are you, now?" she laughed, staring into his sparkling eyes. "I know what you're planning."

Lachlan arched a brow. "Does i' please you?"

"Oh, yes. Tell him, Lachlan."

Draping an arm about her shoulders, he planted a kiss on her temple, then looked at Roan. "Laddie, the time's come ta legalize ma promise."

The two men stared into each other's eyes, Roan's expression one of apprehension. "I've a bad feelin' in ma stomach, Baird. I'm really no' in the mood—"

"Och, be still an' listen for once," Lachlan said merrily. He looked at the elderly woman. "Miss Cooke, you've been a guid friend for a number o' years, an' i' has meant a lot 'ta me ta have you ta depend on. You, yer mither, an' yer grandmither have been guid ta me an' ma home."

"It's been our pleasure, Mr. Baird."

"Weel . . ." Lachlan's grin was sheer charm in itself. "I need you again, sweet lady. You see, Beth an' I wad like ta retire from the hauntin' business—"

"Oh, but Mr. Baird—"

"Now, now, Miss Cooke," Lachlan cooed, releasing Beth and taking one of the old woman's hands between his own. "I'm tae happy ta be lamentin' the wrongs o' the past. Ingliss here, weel, he an' I have made oor peace, an' Beth an' I wad like ta gae on wi' oor lives— such as they are."

Viola's eyes misted with tears. Although she was reluctant to let go of her favorite— her only *true*— ghost, she could never deny Lachlan Baird anything.

"I see," she sniffled. "What can I do for you?"

Lachlan bent over and planted a kiss on her wrinkled cheek. "Yer're the salt o' the earth, Miss Cooke," he said, straightening up. "I want this Ingliss ta have ma home an' e'erythin' in i'."

"Haud i'!" Roan gasped. He came around from the back of the sofa to face Lachlan. "Wha' are you oop ta, Baird?"

"Keepin' ma word," Lachlan said matter-of-factly, and clapped a hand on the man's shoulder. A bewildered frown flitted across Roan's face, deepening Lachlan's grin. "Tis all yers, laddie. All ma treasures I'm passin' doon ta you— exceptin' Beth." He looked at her and winked. "She's the only one I intend ta keep e'erlastin'."

"I'm the only one you can't get rid of," Beth said happily.

"Thank God." Lowering his arm, Lachlan searched Roan's bemused face. "I only ask tha' you pu' aside the grievances o' the past an' mak this yer home."

Pain throbbed at Roan's temples, adding to his befuddled state of mind. "I-umm, I canna afford the oopkeep—"

"I've already given you the precious stones. I've also some money stashed away in one o' the rooms. Yer're set for life."

"I don't want yer damn money!" Roan drew in a deep breath to compose himself. "I'm a builder. I wark wi' ma hands. I'm no' the kind o' mon ta live in a grand house!"

"Tis grand, all right," Lachlan said softly, his tone touching upon something deep within Roan.

"But tis an empty house, eh? Yer're a young mon wi' prospects for the future. Hopes an' dreams . . . no' unlike how I was 'fore ma death. I've wasted immeasurable energies keepin' away yer family, Ingliss. But had thin's been different, this wad have been yer family's home."

"He's right," Beth said, coming to stand alongside Lachlan. Linking an arm through his, she rested the side of her head against his arm. But her gaze was upon Roan's pallid face. *"Your* history is here, too."

"I don't know wha' ta say," Roan murmured, then raked a hand through his hair. He looked into Lachlan's eyes, his own dulled with bewilderment. "I came here ta banish you."

Lachlan grinned and nodded.

"I came here ta rid ma family o' you!"

"I know. Roan, tis a wonderful gift I'm offerin' you."

Words bubbled up in Roan's throat, but before he could speak, he went through numerous hand gestures and shrugs. "Why, though?" he finally gushed. "Yer're willin' ta give e'erythin' oop, just like tha'?" he asked, snapping his fingers in emphasis.

"Aye." Stepping behind Beth, Lachlan wrapped his arms about her. "Wha' I've gained— " He kissed the top of Beth's head. "— is far mair than wha' I've e'er had. This place was built for the livin', Roan. A mair worthy mon to carry on, I cadna find if I tried."

Roan looked from Lachlan, to Beth, to Miss

Cooke, his astonishment a cloak about him. "There's a catch here," he said with a nervous laugh.

Beth and Lachlan exchanged a look of wry amusement.

"There is a condition," Lachlan admitted.

"I knew i'! Come now, you auld swine, wha' is i'?"

"Weel, Beth an' I wad like to have the use o' the master bedroom for a wee time mair. A few months or sa. Tis the only room I'd be askin' you ta leave alone an' locked. For oor privacy, you understand."

"The master bedroom?" Roan looked at Miss Cooke and frowned. At least *she* was as confused as he by this request. "You want the room kept locked?"

"Tis all I ask. You've already agreed ta see the womon an' the boys ta Edinburgh."

Roan gave a shake of his head. "I'm goin' ta wake oop. I know i'."

"It will make us both very happy to have you here," Beth said softly. "You have it within you, Roan, to bring hope and laughter back into this house."

Lachlan held out a hand. "Do we have a deal, Roan?"

Roan stared at the outstretched hand for a long moment before clasping it. With difficulty, he looked into Lachlan's dark eyes. He was sure there was an ulterior motive, but he was too rattled to try to sort through his fevered thoughts at this time.

He had never wanted the house or Lachlan's treasures. He had never thought about any of it one way or the other. What *would* he do with a place like Baird House?

"Tha's oop ta you," Lachlan chuckled.

Roan numbly gave a shake of his head. "I've go' ta think abou' this. It's a lot o' responsibility."

"You keep in touch wi' Miss Cooke. Whan yer're ready, let her know."

Looking at the old woman, Roan gulped past the tightness in his throat.

"Miss Cooke?"

Viola's features were glowing with awe as she looked up into Lachlan's face. "Yes, Mr. Baird?"

"Do you foresee any problems wi' Ingliss havin' legal possession o' ma property?"

"No." Her sagging bosom heaved with her watery sigh. "I'll have the deed transferred to his name."

"You have ma undyin' gratitude, dear lady." To Roan, Lachlan added, "In the future, how abou' knockin' on ma bedroom door, eh?" He paused a moment. "The little womon an' I have a lot ta mak oop for."

"Right," Roan said, but in a sound that resembled a strangled breath.

Beth opened her eyes. The room was cast in inky darkness. The hearth was cold. She was on her side, a cheek cradled in the hollow of Lachlan's bare shoulder. One of his arms was beneath her. The other was draped over her waist.

Running her finger tips through the curly hair on his chest, she asked, "Are you awake?"

"Hmm."

"I'm so proud of you."

"We're a guid team, lass."

"When we're not arguing."

Lachlan's deep chuckle vibrated beneath her fingers. It made Beth smile until she became conscious of a familiar tingling throughout her body.

"We're fading again."

Lachlan turned his head and kissed her on the brow. "Dinna be sad, love. We'll be back in a few hoors."

"Lachlan?"

"Hmm?"

"I love you."

"An' I love you, darlin'."

"Lachlan?"

He grinned in the darkness. "Hmm?"

"You have something planned for Roan, don't you?"

"Planned, you say?"

"You always wanted children in this house," Beth sighed as she snuggled closer to his diminishing solidity. "I like Roan. He has a good heart."

"Aye. He's a fine mon. An' he'll be a guid husband ta Laura.

Beth groaned. "You're not . . ."

They faded into the night, their essences wrapped about one another.

"I am," came a deep chuckle.

The sound lingered in the empty master bedroom, echoing eerily for some time. But the rest of the household was unaware of it, sleeping soundly.

Fifteen

A scream wrenched Roan from his deep sleep. Groggily stumbling out of bed and to the door in the dark, he muttered choice curses. He was sure one of the boys was at it again. Two days had passed since the laird's declaration that the house was to be turned over to him. Two of the longest days of his life.

Laura was a bundle of nerves. Roan, himself, was at his wits' end. The house was simply too large to keep track of three willful lads. One way or the other, he had to get the family to Edinburgh before he lost what little sanity he had left.

The instant he opened the door, an acrid smell assailed his nostrils. Then something stung his eyes, making it impossible for him to look into the dimly lit second floor hall.

The scream came again, but this time he realized it was Laura crying out his name.

Then it dawned on him what was happening.

And something in his mind snapped.

Taking three paces into the hall, the heels of his hands pressed against his closed eyelids, he mistakenly attempted to call back to Laura.

Searing smoke filled his lungs. His hands dropped away as a curtain of blackness threatened to descend on him. He staggered blindly. Hitting one of the walls, he keeled over face down on the floor.

"Roan!"

The voice penetrated his daze with the effectiveness of a sharp blade. But it was Adaina's voice he thought he'd heard, as he had when she'd screamed his name moments before he'd helplessly witnessed her being swallowed up in a billowing rush of flames.

"Jamey," he choked, struggling to get up onto his hands and knees. "Haud on, son . . ."

An explosion rocked the house.

One of the paintings on the wall came down, a wooden corner of the frame striking him on the temple. Pain radiated through his head and neck, vertigo nearly overwhelmed him.

Tears streaming down his cheeks, he inched on hands and knees in the direction of the boys' room. At the far end of the hall, flames lapped up the walls and curled across the ceiling.

The shrill cry of a child gave him the stamina to force himself on. When he finally arrived at the bedroom door, coughing violently, trying to expel the smoke in his lungs, he turned the knob and fell across the threshhold. After a moment, small hands gripped his wrist and began to tug, but he could not stir himself beyond the gray haze of near-unconsciousness.

"Scared," three-year-old Alby whimpered, tug-

ging again and again in a futile attempt to revive
Roan. "Want my mama. Please, want my mama!"

With a moan, Roan turned his head in the direction of the voice.

Coughs racking his thin little body, Alby buried
his face in the man's neck. He didn't like the big,
gruff Scotsman, but he desperately needed an adult
to cuddle him. He was afraid, yet knew not why.
His brothers were gone. His aunt hadn't heard his
cries. His eyes burned, and it hurt to breathe.

"Jamey, boy," Roan rasped, struggling to draw a
breath into his aching lungs. "I'll save you, son."
Sitting up, he drew the trembling boy into his arms.
"Don't look back," he murmured, lost to another
time, another similar disaster.

Somehow, Roan managed to get up onto his feet.
He carried Alby into the bathroom. Placing the
child into the tub, he climbed in and turned on the
cold water tap. Alby cried furiously, swinging out
his fists at him as Roan proceeded to thoroughly
soak them both. Then, Alby thrashing and whim-
pering within his weakening arms, Roan blindly
stumbled back into the large bedroom.

He stopped, teetering on his rubbery legs, his
bloodshot eyes widening at the sight of flames filling the doorway.

No' again! he mutely cried, cradling Alby tightly
against him. "No' ma son, again!" he shouted, then
fell to his knees as coughs agonizingly pummeled
his chest.

Where was he?

Adaina and Jamey were dead.

He'd seen them die.

He'd identified their burnt remains.

So where was he?

"Roan!"

The feminine voice seemed omnipresent.

"Adaina."

His head bobbing on his weak neck, he squinted about his surroundings. "Tak Jamey. I'm dyin'."

"I'm caught between the two worlds. Get up, Roan! Dammit, get on your feet!"

Despite the pain in his eyes, Roan managed to glimpse a transparent image in front of him.

"Beth?"

"The lower floor's consumed. Get up, Roan. The best I can do is give you a little help. You must go out one of the windows. It's the only way out."

After several attempts, Roan managed to get onto his feet again. "The window?" he choked.

Swiftly, a dark cloud materialized above Roan's head, then expanded across the room. Thunder roared. Lightning flashed.

Befuddled, Roan folded himself over the child in his arms. Alby's sobs and gasps for breath tried to breach the stranglehold of death's waiting arms, but Roan was declining quickly, weakening with each passing second. The gash at his temple had stopped bleeding, but the side of his face and neck were a dire testament to the blood he'd lost.

Another explosion came from below.

The gas lines, Beth whispered in his head.

"Gas," he croaked, jerkily attempting to straighten up. A flash of lightning pained his eyes. "Gas . . ."

At first, his fevered mind was only aware of coldness. Then it began to dawn on him that he was standing amidst a deluge. Lifting his face to the hovering cloud, he lapped at the blessed relief the rain offered.

Then he felt a blast of air pass through him. The sound of glass exploding turned him in the direction of the windows. One of them was completely missing. Only a gaping entry to the night remained.

"Hurry, Roan. I don't know how long I can keep this up."

Flames tried to cross the threshhold, sizzling and hissing as they became caught beneath the driving force of the rain.

"Beth, I'm tae scared ta chance carryin' the boy— "

Roan looked down at the wan face of the unconscious boy in his arms.

Alby.

Jamey was forever lost. And whatever it took, Roan vowed, he would not let this child be taken by fire as well.

But when he went to the spot where the window had been, he could not see to gauge an escape.

"Jump!" someone shouted from below. "Hurry, mon! We've a catch!"

"Roan, you have no choice. Drop Alby. Roan! Do it now!"

Shouts rose from the east yard. After a moment's struggle with fear, Roan held the boy out as far as he could beyond the portal. Then, with a mute prayer for the boy's safety, he released him. Roan trembled violently for what seemed a very long time, until he heard a man shout that the laddie was safe. Then voices were shouting for him to jump.

A whooshing sound came from behind Roan. The rain had stopped. Unbearable heat pressed against his back.

"Roan, I'm too weak to do any more!" Beth cried. "For God's sake, *jump!*"

"Roan! Don't be afraid! Jump!"

Recognizing the second female voice, Roan murmured a sickly, "Laura."

"Roan, please! The men down here will catch you in the blanket!"

Blanket?

Roan's head seemed to spin faster and faster.

Wood creaked from every part of the house. Fire roared in his ears.

Planting his bare feet on the remains of the window sill, he precariously balanced himself for several more seconds. He couldn't shake the memory of his wife becoming consumed in flames. He couldn't cut off the remembrance of the sounds of her screams.

Then he was sailing through the air. Instinctively, his arms and legs scrambled to halt the flight, to touch upon something solid. But there was nothing but flight. Terrifying flight.

Something caught the length of him, but his momentum didn't stop. He bounced up and, when he came down, struck hard ground.

"Guid lawd!" someone cried. "Gentle, now! Get him away from here! Hurry, now! *Hurry!*"

Barely conscious of being lifted by his arms and legs, of being carried off, he strained to force his lungs to accept air. Then he was laid upon a blanket on the ground, and was covered by numerous coats.

Another explosion. And another, the force of which elicited cries among the growing spectators gathering on the private roadway. Window panes exploded outward from every side of the house.

"Roan! Roan, did you see Kevin? I couldn't find him! Roan!"

Roan opened his eyes. After several moments, he was able to focus somewhat on Laura's features.

"Kevin?" he rasped.

Laura burst into tears and drew the boys in her arms closer against her. "I couldn't find him. And I couldn't reach you."

"Stand clear!" a rough-voiced man ordered.

A large shape went down on a knee to Roan's other side. "Roan, laddie. It's Ben. Yer pub mate. Can you hear me?"

"Aye," Roan wheezed. "I'm no' deaf."

Resisting the hands trying to keep him down, he sat up. Coughs seized him. Ben's hand none-too-gently clapped him on the back several times.

"Tak i' easy, mate. You swallowed doon some smoke, by the looks o' i'."

"Jamey . . . My son— "

Reality cruelly returned home to Roan. He stared into the rounded face of his old friend, and felt a swell of tears lodge in his throat.

"Jamey's gone, mate. But you saved the lad here."

Roan squinted at Laura, then at the back of the boys' heads she kept pressed against the hollows of her shoulders.

"Kevin," he said. He was about to push up to get on his knees when excruciating pain razored through his left arm.

"My airm's broken!" he gasped, then doubled over during a coughing fit.

"Lucky tis no' yer back," Ben said gravely. He looked at Laura, then again at Roan. "She claims one o' the lads didna mak i', mate," he said solemnly. Then he glanced up and scowled, and bellowed to the crowd pressing closer for a look at Roan, "Get back! If you canna lend a hand, gae home, the lot o' you!"

Roan. "Roan."

In front of the curious spectators, Beth materialized and immediately knelt to one knee in front of the new laird of Baird House. "Are you all right?"

Roan nodded. With Beth and Ben's help, he got up onto his feet. Neither he nor Beth noticed the sickly shock on Ben's face, or the awed expressions of the strangers filling the roadway.

"I've got ta get Kevin," Roan insisted, finally beginning to feel like himself again, despite the pain racking his body.

"Lachlan's searching for him."

Blinking hard, Roan looked deeply into Beth's troubled eyes. "Can he help him?"

"If it's within his power, he will," Beth said, her voicing cracking with emotion.

"Kevin," Laura whimpered, rising to her feet with a boy sitting on each of her hips.

With his right arm, Roan reached out and urged Alby to come to him. Surprisingly, the boy clung to Roan's broad neck.

Laura, who had not realized Beth had actually materialized from thin air, turned in the direction of the house and uttered, "Please, God. Give me a second chance to do right by them."

Roan stepped to her side. "Lannie will find him. Have faith, Laura. We must have faith."

Sobbing, Laura laid one side of her face to Roan's chest. "It all happened so fast!"

"Aye, lass. I know," Roan soothed, absently planting a kiss on the crown of her head. "Thank God you two made i' ou' okay. Kahl? Yer're no' hurt, are you?"

"Where's Kevin?" the five-year-old demanded bitterly.

Roan cast a fearful look in the direction of the house. "Comin', laddie. Lannie will save him. I feel i' in ma bones." *Dear God, mak i' true. For us all, mak i' true!*

Tongues of fire lapped at the night through the ravaged portals of what had been the windows. A chimney on the west side of the house began to crumble. Flames reached high into the midnight sky from several of the rooftops.

"Lannie," Roan said in a prayerlike whisper. "I'll

promise you anythin' if you just bring Kevin to us, alive an' unharmed."

Fed by the broken gas lines, the flames grew until the manor's stonework exterior could barely be seen. Not a murmur stirred among the spectators. All eyes were riveted on the destructive element consuming the region's most famous house.

Then, amidst the blaze, an image was spied slowly emerging.

"Lachlan!" Beth cried joyously, her diaphanous form moving toward him as he lumbered toward Roan and Laura. They, as well as everyone else, remained frozen in shock when Lachlan and Beth came to stand in front of the anxious couple. In Lachlan's arms was a wide-eyed Kevin, who, for the first time in his life; was absolutely speechless.

"The saints be wi' us," Ben muttered, hastily blessing himself as he stared wondrously into Lachlan's taut face.

Joy overcoming him, Roan released a sob and sank to his knees. He hugged Alby tightly with his good arm, then with a kiss to the boy's cheek, set him on his feet. Lachlan placed Kevin down, his gaze never wavering from Roan's ravaged features. Kevin endured hugs and kisses from his aunt, then turned to stare for a long moment into Roan's tear-filled eyes.

Although Roan suspected Kevin had started the fire, he reached out with his left arm and drew the boy against him. "Thank God," he repeated, over and over, until Kevin stepped back and pointed up to Lachlan.

The crowd inched closer. No longer was the manor the center of their attention. It was the man who'd walked through the flames, unscathed, carrying a boy in his arms who also appeared untouched by the wrath of the blazing inferno.

Beth stared proudly at Lachlan's profile. She could feel the pull of the grayness tugging on her, but she clung to this world, relishing the rise of emotions emanating from Lachlan.

A portly woman came through the crowd and beelined for the children, gathering them into her arms and holding them to her sagging bosom. "The bairns are cauld. I'll tak them ta ma caur ta warm them oop."

Laura was too rattled to object. She'd seen the master of Baird House walk through the flames with Kevin, but her mind refused to accept it as reality. In an absent gesture, she helped Roan to his feet, and stood close to his side as he and the laird stared intensely into each other's faces.

"Thank you," Roan said in a barely audible voice to Lachlan, and made a helpless gesture with his good arm. In the next second, Lachlan was embracing him.

Another hush fell over the crowd.

Lachlan held Roan out at arm's length and looked deeply into his eyes. The laird was beginning to lose his physical integrity, fluctuating between the two worlds.

"Dusk before dawn, laddie," he said with a crooked smile. Then stepping back, he drew Beth's fading form into his arms, and together they vanished into the night.

Laura fainted.

It was a week later before Roan returned to the remains of the manor. The seven days which had passed were but a blur to him. His casted arm rested in a sling about his neck. He'd lost weight. His rugged features bespoke the trials he'd endured that terrible night of the fire. He'd grown quiet and remote, a man existing under a cloud of hopelessness, especially since Laura and the boys had left for Edinburgh three days prior.

He stood at the front of the cottage, staring at the blackened exterior of the main house. Very little life was visible in his usually expressive eyes.

"Lannie? Beth?"

He didn't expect them to answer. Since that night seven days ago, he hadn't seen or heard from them. The manor was destroyed, and its lord and mistress had completely vanished. Not too long ago, he'd plotted to rid his clan of the laird. And yet, the idea now of never seeing Lachlan or Beth again left him a void that was almost unbearable.

"Laura an' the boys have returned ta the States." He sighed, ignoring the ache that remained in his lungs. "Tha' promise has been carried through, you auld corbie."

Emotional pain became deeply etched in his features. "It sudna have ended like this. Yer home, mon." Tears brimmed his eyes. "Aggie says guid riddance. She doesn't understand. You an' yer damn grandfaither's Scotch, eh? We bonded, all right. You teuk a piece o' me wi' you, you bloody pain-in-the-arse."

Jabbing at the air with his left index finger, he went on bitterly, "It was simpler whan I hated you, Lannie. Damn you, mon, you filled ma head wi' dreams na mon like me has a right ta haud dear ta his heart!"

Picking up a rock, he walked to within five yards of the front of the house. Angrily, he flung it at the wall, desperate to release his anguish. His feet slid out from under him. He slammed onto the icy, graveled yard, and released a stream of Scottish invectives.

"Breakin' yer arse winna accomplish a thin'," said a grave voice, as hands hooked beneath Roan's coated armpits and hauled him up onto his feet.

Astonished, Roan turned to find himself staring into Lachlan's brooding eyes. Just beyond the laird's shoulder, Beth tipped her head and smiled at Roan.

"Where the hell have you two been?" Roan said in an inordinately high-pitched tone.

"Gatherin' oop oor energy," the laird said matter-of-factly.

Beth stepped to Lachlan's side. "How's your arm?"

"Fine," Roan grumbled.

"Laura an' the laddies have left, eh?"

"Aye." Roan gave a negligent shrug. "She cadn't get away fast enough."

"I'm sorry," Beth said gently.

"For me?" Roan released a scoffing laugh. "She was an impossible womon. I'll miss the boys."

Lachlan and Beth exchanged a dubious glance.

"You'll miss her, tae," the laird said gruffly. "Yer're a fool ta have let her gae."

"Don't stick yer nose inta ma lovelife, Baird."

"Wad if you had one," Lachlan grinned, then his gaze shifted and he soberly scanned what remained of his house. "Tis sa bleak."

Roan couldn't bring himself to look upon it again. "Aye. I'm sarry. I know how much this damn place meant ta you."

"Aye," Lachlan sighed.

Beth silently observed the two men, a slim eyebrow arched. Lachlan had surprisingly accepted the destruction of his treasures, his home, although Beth had been aware of a void within him that he did his best to camouflage. And Roan. He was so easy to read. He was lost and bewildered. For too short a time, Laura and the boys, and the responsibility of becoming laird to the manor, had given him renewed purpose. He believed it all lost to him now, as it had been when he'd lost his wife, son, and home to a fire.

These two men, who Beth loved so very dearly in different ways, seemed incapable at the moment of realizing just what the future held for them. So it was upon her, she felt, to enlighten them. But to succeed, she knew she was going to have to resort to something stronger than a mere suggestion.

"You promised Lachlan anything if he saved

Kevin, didn't you?" she presented to Roan, who arched a questioning brow at her.

"Aye, but— "

"You're a man who keeps his promises," she added in an airy, cheerful manner, ignoring Lachlan's frown at her.

"Aye, but— "

"Roan, you're wasting valuable time wallowing in self-pity," she sighed.

"Wha's gaein' through yer mind, darlin'?" Lachlan asked suspiciously.

Beth's sparkling eyes scanned Roan's features. "You're a carpenter. Right?"

Aghast, Roan shot a look at the house behind him. "I'm no' a miracle worker!"

Dawning lit upon Lachlan's face. "Ah." He smiled broadly, then kissed Beth briefly on the lips. "Wha' a deilish mind you have, lass."

"You can't be serious," Roan said shakily. "Restore Baird House? I'd need lifetimes— "

Sounds drew their gazes to the private road. Shortly, four cars and two large trucks parked on the graveled area in front of the carriage house. As people began to emerge from the vehicles, Roan recognized Ben and several other men from the pub. Then, to his amazement, Agnes stepped from one of the cars and led the small group to the waiting trio.

To Roan's further astonishment, his aunt beamed a smile at the laird, and gave a bob of her head in greeting to Beth.

"Sa, you didna high-tail off," she cackled to

Lachlan, her high spirits taking years off her age. "Ma worst luck, eh?"

Lachlan smiled, then bowed graciously to her. "Guid ta see you tae, you auld corbie."

"Nice way ta talk ta the lady plannin' ta see yer grand house restored," she huffed humorously.

"Aunt Aggie, wha's gaein' on?"

Ben, his gaze remaining riveted on Lachlan, spoke up. "Aggie's come oop wi' a plan. Crossmichael an' Castle Douglas are joinin' thegither ta rebuild this place."

Color returned to Roan's face, and he laughed unsteadily. "Yer're serious?"

"Ne'er mair serious," Agnes chided.

"The power of the people," Beth murmured, her eyes misting with tears. When Lachlan's arm went about her shoulders, she pressed closer to him. "Thank you, Agnes."

The old woman proudly thrust back her shoulders. "Merchants are willin' ta supply e'erythin' we need. Baird House is a landmark. An' we Scots are no' 'fraid o' hard wark, are we, Roan?"

"Aye," Roan grinned. "We're strong o' back an' spirit."

"'Tis a debt I'll ne'er forget," Lachlan said to Agnes, his tone thick with emotion.

"'Tis one I winna let you forget!" she exclaimed.

Roan unexpectedly walked away. When he stopped, his back was to the group. With a gesture for the others to remain where they were, Beth went to him and placed a hand on his shoulder.

"Tha' dress *does* mak you look like a spook," he said unsteadily, avoiding looking at her directly.

"She'll be back."

"Who?"

Beth slapped him on his uninjured arm, then stepped directly in front of him. This time he looked into her eyes, although it took all of his willpower to do so.

"You may be able to fool everyone else, but Lachlan and I know you're in love with Laura Bennett. She will return, Roan. And with the boys."

"Yer're sure o' tha', are you?"

"As sure as I know I was always meant to be here," she replied softly. "Don't ever forsake love, Roan."

"She ne'er said guid-bye."

"Maybe because she knows she's going to return."

Roan digested her words, then looked up at the charred ruins with an enigmatic light in his eyes. Drawing in a fortifying breath through his nostrils, he searched Beth's lovely face.

"I owe you ma life."

"Then live it to its fullest." Placing an arm about his middle, she urged him to walk alongside her toward those waiting patiently for their return. She retained her hold when they stopped, and smiled at Lachlan when he stepped to Roan's other side and draped an arm over the man's shoulders. The scene depicted the trio's strong bond of friendship, and a single tear escaped down Agnes' weathered cheek.

Suddenly it occurred to Roan what Lachlan had meant the night of the fire when he'd said, "Dusk before dawn, laddie."

One phase of life had to end before another began anew.

Roan wasn't sure if Laura and the boys would return, but if they did, Baird House, restored in all its glory, would be waiting for them.

In the meantime, he once again had a dream, and family and friends to take the edge off his loneliness.

One thing he *was* sure about: Beth and Lachlan would remain for a very long time. For as long as he needed them.

Which, in his heart, would be until the dusk of his corporeal life.